BETRAYED

BETRAYED

An Alec Caldwell Novel

George Feild

To order additional copies of this book, contact:
Xlibris Corporation
1-888-795-4274
www.Xlibris.com
Orders@Xlibris.com
69937

perseverance to get through a difficult task. I'm sure if I had asked anyone other than Margo to read through this manuscript and make whatever corrections to spelling and punctuation were necessary, the whole mess would have been thrown back in my face after the first few pages. Not Margo. She persevered, and even made several marginal notes that reassured me she had not lost her wonderful sense of humor, something most anyone else would have lost before they got through the proofreading task. To emphasize just how daunting the task was, I only found seven pages out of a total of 419 that did not bear Margo's *red marks*. Most pages reminded me of the profusion of corrections I received as I struggled through high school English grammar classes.

And last, but never least, my daughter, **Laura Feild Holland**, whose talents with computers and creative images developed the front cover for this and the first two novels in this series, while balancing the time for her very demanding job as a computer specialist for a major national corporation, delivering her first child, my third granddaughter, and keeping her household together. With all of that, she still has time for her Dad. Bless her heart!

I hope you enjoy reading this novel. If so, and if you haven't read the first two, ***The Irish Conspiracy*** and ***Deadly Agendas***, they are available through my publisher at *www.Xlibris.com* and through *www. amazon.com*. Should you wish to read more about these two novels, check out my website, *www.aleccaldwellsagas.com*.

Thank you,
George Feild

CHAPTER ONE

Somewhere on the Baja Wasteland
Baja California Sur, Mexico
Monday, April 9—Dawn

IT WASN'T SUPPOSED to be like this! She was supposed to be lying on the beach with her friends, soaking up the warm sun of the Mexican Baja, sipping cokes spiked with rum, maybe even smoking a joint, letting the narcotic take her senses to new heights. After all, it was *spring break*. But, something had gone terribly wrong, and she couldn't focus her thoughts. She only knew she hurt all over and couldn't freely move her arms or legs.

When she first came awake, still in the drug-induced state of the previous evening, she was lying on her side on the shack's floor, made of smooth flat stones picked up in the surrounding hills. Her legs were tucked close under her chin in the fetal position, arms wrapped around her legs. As she awoke, she began to cry, whimpers really, helpless, like a dog that had just been hit by a car and couldn't get up and run away.

It was noon and the sun was merciless, beating down on the rusting tin roof of the old woman's shack made of discarded boards and timbers she had collected in the barren hills. The temperature inside had already climbed above the one hundred degree mark and it was only mid-day.

When she heard the girl's cries, the old woman pulled herself out of her rickety chair in front of the door, hobbled back into the two-room shack and stood in the doorway of the room into which the girl had been dragged by the three young men. The old woman's face was tanned and deeply wrinkled, like dried, cracked leather. Her eyes, deep-set in her weathered face, were almost black, without expression. She was bony, short, less than five feet, and her stooped posture accentuated her diminutive stature.

The girl couldn't focus on the old woman's silhouette against the glare of the sunlight filtering through the opening, but she knew someone was there. She had seen the movement.

"Help me," she moaned, trying to focus on the figure in the doorway. She tried to hold out her arms to whomever was there, but couldn't. Her wrists were bound with a heavy plastic tie that cut into her white flesh. "Please," she said, her eyes pleading; "Help me, please."

The old woman looked at the young girl lying on the stone floor, but said nothing. There was no emotion in her dead eyes, no expression of sympathy on her face, no pity.

"Feed her, old woman," they had told her when they brought the girl there. "We'll clean her up when we come back."

The old woman didn't know when that would be. She was afraid of them, afraid to ask. She only did what she was told to do. She turned and went back outside to her chair without saying a word to the girl, and continued her vigil as she had been instructed, looking out over the surrounding hills, little more than a barren moonscape. Beyond, in the distance, she could see the calm turquoise waters of the Sea of Cortez to the east; the mountains towered above her to the west.

The small satellite cellular phone had been placed on a rusting up-ended tin pail beside the old woman's chair. She had not touched it since they left. If anyone came near the shack, she had been told to pick it up, press the number five, wait until someone answered, and report what was happening. That was all. They would take care of everything from there. And, the money was good, at least for someone of such meager means as the old woman. But, they knew no one would come to the shack because there were no defined roads leading through the barren hills to her shack, just an inconspicuous path, fit more for a burro than a small car. No one ever came to this remote, desolate place. There were no beaches to attract the sun bathers, no crashing waves to entice the surfers, no off-shore reef to bring the SCUBA divers, and no land that would grow the marijuana plants for the lucrative American drug trade. It was a desolate place that no one cared about, and no one visited. As a waypoint, it fit perfectly into their plans.

*   *   *

The girl began to focus on her surroundings as the drugs slowly wore off. Her throat was dry, her lips parched. There was a cup of water nearby, but she couldn't reach it. The throbbing in her head felt like someone using a sledgehammer to drive in a railroad spike. She tried to move her legs apart, but her ankles were bound together with a plastic tie, as were her wrists. As she lay on the dirty floor in the sweltering heat, she realized she was naked, except for the tattered blanket covering her body. *The old woman must have covered me*, she thought. She didn't have to touch her groin to know she had been raped. She could feel the dry blood and semen and feel the pain of repeated penetrations. But fortunately, she had no memory of these violations, just the dull pain. She began to cry again, more from despair than from her physical pain. But, the old woman did not look in on her.

"Oh, God, what has happened to me?" she cried, as she dragged her bruised body up to a sitting position against the flimsy wall of the shack. The girl's name was Katherine McKenzie, and there was no one there to answer her question.

*   *   *

Fox Hall Finishing School
Boston, Massachusetts
Thursday, April 5 – Mid Morning

Katherine Buchanan McKenzie glanced at her watch momentarily, closed her eyes and smiled. Another five minutes and the World Economics lecture would be over, her last class before spring break. Tomorrow, she and five of her closest friends, all seniors attending the exclusive Fox Hall Finishing School in Boston's Old Town, would be winging their way to Cabo San Lucas for six glorious days of basking in the warm Mexican sun, drinking Tequila Sunrises, smoking dope, and chasing boys. She had already packed her clothes, including the new bikini that had set her father back a considerable sum. But, she had to have it, and after all, she was her doting father's one and only daughter.

She and her friends had decided they wanted to take a spring break trip on their own, no chaperones, no parents, and definitely no boyfriends; totally free to do what they wanted to do, when they wanted to do it, and with whom they wanted-every teenager's dream.

Kathy had begun working on her parents over the Christmas holidays. Promises of being careful, calling them every day, not wandering into the wrong parts of town, not drinking and all the other parental trappings designed to limit the fun she felt she deserved, were agreed to before her parents finally acquiesced, albeit reluctantly, to her pleading.

*   *   *

Boston, Massachusetts
A Look Back

Kathryn McKenzie was born into money and social status. The McKenzies could trace their lineage to the early settlers of the Massachusetts Bay Colony in the sixteen hundreds. One such ancestor even earned a degree of notoriety as a participant in the

1773 Boston Tea Party that helped spark the American Revolution. Mrs. Nancy Bingham McKenzie, Kathy's mother, kept the spirit alive through her work with the Daughters of the American Revolution as the Massachusetts State Regent, and ultimately the organization's National President. Ancestors of both the Bingham and McKenzie families had stood side by side in the Nation's fight for independence over two centuries earlier.

Kathy's father, Horace Rumsford McKenzie, III, hated his nickname, *Rummy*. Although short for Rumsfield, he had really earned his nickname from his drinking habits during his wild college days at Harvard. But, he tolerated its use. He could have cared less about his or his wife's family lineage, regardless of how elevated their ancestors, or how dedicated his wife was to preserving their heritage. He was a practical man, well educated with a degree in International Business from Harvard; a man who understood world economics and worked tirelessly to enhance his position in the ever-changing and highly challenging world of global finance. He served as Chairman and Chief Executive Officer of McKenzie Bank and Trust, named for his grandfather who founded the institution some ninety-three years ago, but which, under the skillful guidance of his father and then under Horace III's leadership, had spread initially across Massachusetts, and ultimately across the Northeast, before merging with First Trust of Atlanta. The resulting institution, First McKenzie Bank, FMB, as their public relations firm had coined, was now ranked among the top ten largest financial institutions headquartered in the United States, with retail offices in all of the contiguous forty-eight states.

In addition, McKenzie was currently serving his first term as one of three Class A directors on the Board of the First Federal Reserve District Bank in Boston. It was rumored that he was at the top of the short list to be nominated by President Hunt for the slot on the seven-member Federal Reserve Board of Governors, the vacancy resulting from the death of Lawrence Dixon. McKenzie's senate confirmation was all but assured. At forty-six, he would be the youngest member of this prestigious and very powerful board.

As with his father and grandfather, banking had served McKenzie well. A well-known Boston philanthropist and a staunch party supporter, he had always been a loyal and strong supporter of the conservative ideals on which the party had been founded. He and John Hunt, the current U.S. President, had been classmates and fraternity brothers at Harvard and had remained close friends as he assumed his position in his father's bank, although their political philosophies had been at opposite ends of the political spectrum.

* * *

Hunt had gone on to law school at Yale, then returned to his home state of Texas to launch his political career as a promising prosecuting attorney in Dallas, first as a Republican, but later embracing the more liberal political views of the opposition.

Because of their earlier friendship, McKenzie had become a major contributor and fundraiser for Hunt in the several campaigns he had launched as he worked his way up to the highest office in the nation. During Hunt's first term, and in each of the three years of his second term, McKenzie had served on President Hunt's Economic Roundtable, and, within the beltway, he was considered a close and personal friend of the President-a friend with unlimited access to the oval office, a position of envy by many of his associates.

* * *

Katherine Buchanan McKenzie was only seventeen, still a minor, but no longer a virgin. On a dare from her best friend the year before, she had lost her innocence at sixteen behind the locked door of her bedroom. She had sneaked the boy up the back stairs of her parents' mansion so no one would know he was there. Her lover, if you can call him that, was also sixteen, and had no more sexual experienced than she.

It was not what she had fanaticized it would be. There was no foreplay, just painful penetration, full of passion, but lacking in emotion and caring. And, it was over almost before it started. She felt unclean, and ashamed, as she lay on the bed. When her lover was through, he had dressed quickly and left, not bothering to kiss her goodbye. She had thought he would stay beside her, telling her he loved her, kissing her small breasts and caressing her hair. It was supposed to be like that. At least that's the way it was in all the magazines and paperbacks she had read.

She decided to put off further sexual experimentation until the bad memory faded. That was a year ago and she was now ready to try again. spring break would be the perfect time.

Kathy's looks and poise marked her as someone older and wiser than her years. Her blue eyes and fair complexion enhanced her natural good looks. She usually wore her long, naturally blonde hair in a ponytail pushed through the back of her Red Sox cap, giving her a perky air of someone who could easily pass for the girl next door, somewhat of a tomboy image.

Fox Hall Finishing School had done wonders for her self-esteem. She had learned how to walk with grace and with an air of confidence, speak with knowledge and with authority, while not appearing to be condescending. Also, she had a smile that would melt the hearts of just about every man she engaged, young and old alike. Her mother had often told her, *Etiquette and good manners are the products of good genes and good breeding*. Her good looks were a bonus.

*   *   *

McKenzie Residence
Boston, Massachusetts
Monday, April 9 – Early Morning

McKenzie stood at the window in the living room, drinking coffee and looking out at a beautiful spring morning. He was worried, but he tried not to show it. He had been waiting for his driver to bring the car around. He always left for the office at precisely 6:00am. It was important to him to be at the bank before anyone else arrived. *Teach by example* was his motto. He was about to walk out the front door when the phone rang.

Nancy McKenzie snatched the receiver off the hook before the second ring. "Kathy, is that you?" she asked before the person on the other end of the line could speak. She had slept fitfully the previous night. Kathy had called her every night, as promised, at precisely 9:00pm, six in the afternoon in Carbo San Lucas where she and her five girlfriends were spending their spring break. But last night was different. She hadn't called, and her mother was unable to reach her on the cell phone her daughter was supposed to carry with her wherever she went. She had tried numerous times before giving up and retiring to a fitful sleep that had left her irritable when she awoke. It was now 3:00am in Carbo San Lucas, too early for the girls to be up and about.

"What do you mean she didn't come home last night?" Kathy's mother shouted. "You were supposed to stay together. All of you promised!"

McKenzie heard the alarm in his wife's voice and walked back into the hall. His wife was shaking all over when he took the phone from her and helped her into the straight back chair beside the telephone table.

"I knew something was going to happen," she cried. "I knew it." She looked up at her husband, her eyes pleading.

McKenzie held the receiver to his ear and placed his other hand on his wife's shoulder. "Who's speaking, please?" he said, as calmly as possible. "Oh, hi Tricia. Calm down, young lady, and tell me what's going on. Tell me everything." McKenzie listened intently as Kathy's best friend and next-door neighbor, Patricia Heinz, told him everything she knew about what had happened earlier that evening. Unfortunately, she knew very little.

"O.K. Trish, listen to me carefully and do exactly as I tell you. Go to the hotel manager and tell him everything you told me. Don't leave anything out. He'll personally escort you girls to the local police station, and you also must tell them what you told me. They'll ask a lot of questions, but they need to know everything to be able to help find

Kathy; so, don't hold anything back. I know the people who own the hotel you're staying in, and I'm going to call the CEO now. He'll contact his hotel manager and the police, so they'll know you're coming to see them. And Trish, if Kathy hasn't returned by noon, your time, three o'clock here, call me. Understand? I'll fly down immediately. And don't worry, Tricia, Kathy is just fine. Maybe a little hung over, but she's all right."

McKenzie replaced the receiver and looked at his wife. His expression was grave, but he tried to make light of the situation to calm his wife, who was about to go to pieces. "Kathy didn't come back last night, and the other girls haven't heard from her. She'll probably sober up in a couple of hours and come staggering back to the hotel."

"Kathy doesn't drink," she snapped, her voice trembling as though she was about to cry.

McKenzie rolled his eyes. He knew better.

"I told you we shouldn't have let her go without a chaperone. What else did Trish say? They were supposed to always stay together. Kathy promised us they would." Her voice broke and a flood of tears ran down her face.

"Trish says they were all together, just as they promised."

"Then what happened to her?" she whimpered. "Where is she?"

"Nothing has happened to her, Sweetheart. From what Tricia says, they met some boys the day after they arrived. She said they were locals. They weren't staying in the hotel, but were at the hotel pool. One of them runs a SCUBA diving shop just off the beach, sells equipment, gives lessons, and takes tourists on his boat out to snorkel and SCUBA dive on the coral reefs. She says the other two boys work for the young man who owns the shop. They went out snorkeling with them yesterday, and the boys invited them to go to a club that caters to young people: rock music, psychedelic lighting, all the trappings of the new Mexican youth culture. Tricia said they felt since there were five of them, and they would be together, they would be safe."

"Yes, well evidently something did happen."

"That's not necessarily true, dear. Evidently Kathy got sick at the club, almost passed out. The boy who owns the SCUBA shop volunteered to help her to the restroom to freshen up. The other girls were dancing so none of them went with her. She never came back. Tricia said that after about thirty minutes they went looking for her, but she was gone. They assumed she had gone back to the hotel to rest, but they didn't check on her until they went back to the hotel and she wasn't there. So, they went back to the club to get the three boys to help them find Kathy, but they weren't there either. That was around one o'clock this morning. They've been up waiting for her for the past two hours, and finally decided to call us.

"I told Trish to be sure the police question the three boys they were with at the club, first thing, especially the one who helped Kathy to the restroom. He was the last person they know who saw her."

"And what are you going to do?"

"First, I'm going to call Jim Rogers, the CEO of Horizons Group, the people who own the Melia San Lucas hotel where they're staying. He has considerable political clout down there, and he'll see to it that enough pressure is put on the local authorities to find her in short order. He's a personal friend and business associate, and we're mutually involved in several high-stakes real estate deals in Mexico and the Caribbean. He'll do everything he can to cut through the bureaucratic crap you have to put up with in Mexico to get anything done. It shouldn't be too difficult; he's paid enough bribes down there to cover just about any problem."

"I know Jim Rogers. He met us at the club for drinks last year after you closed the deal on the hotel down there. But what if they can't find her? What then?"

"If she's not back at the hotel by noon, I'm going down there and look into it myself. I'll call and have the company plane stand-by at Logan just in case. We should be able to get there without having to make a fuel stop, and at over six hundred miles an hour, I can be there in just over four hours. And, we can land at Los Cabos International. It's about forty-five minutes from the Melia. That gives the police some six hours before we lift off here and another four to five hours flight time before I get there."

"What do you think you can do? You don't speak their language and you don't know anyone down there."

"I may not know anyone in Cabo San Lucas or San Jose, but I know some people who do, and I'm not above calling them if I run into a brick wall."

"Well, I'm going with you."

"I don't think so, dear. It's a long flight and you'll just be in my way. I don't want to have to worry about you while I'm there. I'm going to have my hands full. I promise I'll call you as soon as I know something. In the meantime, you call the boys and tell them their little sister is missing. You can tell them everything I've told you, but it's too early to speculate about what may have happened. And, I don't want them down there either. Tell them to stay at school and we'll let them know what's happening when we know anything. I've told Trish to tell the other girls to stay put until I get there. I'm going to question each one of them individually, once I'm there."

*   *   *

Cabo San Lucas
Baja California, Mexico

There was nothing in writing. No signed contract providing a written record of the consideration to pass between the parties consummating the deal. There was nothing that would leave a paper trail for someone to discover and follow. Just a telephone call made in the dead of night from a distant country on another continent. A call routed through several communications satellites before the connection was made. A call from an untraceable cellular phone purchased by an anonymous person. When the call was concluded, the phone was disassembled and the parts destroyed. The call was untraceable. The instrument no longer existed.

The phone had been purchased for just this purpose, one call, and one call only. The anonymous buyer had traveled to London to purchase the unit, one of more than a hundred pre-paid cellular phones, all untraceable, all purchased on a street just off Trafalgar Square. They had been placed in a diplomatic pouch, away from the prying eyes of the British Customs Service inspectors, and flown directly to Saudi Arabia. They were now safely hidden away in a storage vault in Riyadh, the Saudi capital.

The instructions were simple, but precise. The Package must fall within a specific age range. Height and weight were critical as were body shape and muscle tone. Skin color, complexion and natural hair color were also precise requirements. Most important, a measure of intellect, manner of speaking, diction and the absence of vulgar speech were non-negotiable. These attributes required more than just a casual observation. They required personal contact, and Antonio was good at personal contact. Religion, excluding Judaism, did not matter, but background did. The Package would embrace Islam. If she refused, she would just disappear.

At one time, years ago, virginity was the most sacred requirement in such transactions. But western civilizations had abandoned the strict personal values still embraced by true followers of the Muslim faith, and an unmarried virgin in her late teens or early twenties in the Christian communities in the United States or other western countries was rare, almost impossible to find. For the younger members of the Royal Family, this didn't matter. For the older purchasers of young western women, it remained a cardinal requirement. For those young women who volunteered for this life, some minor surgery was normally required to give the appearance of virginity. However, virginity was not a factor in this transaction.

The purveyor would have to interact with his Package to determine if certain required attributes existed. He had done this before for the same client, and from time to time for other members of the family, and he was well up to the task. He had only to canvas the bars, pools and beaches of the posh hotels that line the Golden Corridor, find several likely candidates, and after casual interviews in the guise of idle conversations, select the most qualified candidate. Then, if the final interview was satisfactory, subdue and deliver the Package to the designated waypoint for final delivery.

Finding a young girl who could meet these requirements would not be difficult in Cabo San Lucas. The Golden Corridor, twenty miles of pristine white sand beaches and craggy coves between Cabo San Lucas and San Jose, had become the high-end holiday destination for the rich and famous. Luxury hotels now dot the landscape overlooking the southern tip of the Baja where luxury yachts now call the up-scaled marinas their homes.

People come here for the beautiful weather, the excellent SCUBA diving and snorkeling, the high-stakes Marlin tournament fishing, high-end shopping, golf and every other pursuit of human pleasure you could name, including the oldest profession in the world.

Equally important, young people come here to be seen, and hopefully discovered. Hollywood had invaded the Golden Corridor in recent years, and star-struck hopefuls parade their scantly covered bodies around the luxury hotel pools and on the adjoining beaches, both fertile hunting grounds for the purveyors of human flesh.

There was a time he had thought about pursuing this part of his lucrative tradecraft in one of the spring break destinations in Florida, possibly Fort Lauderdale, where most of the young women attending the prestigious universities of the northeastern states flocked in April to shed their winter clothes and their inhibitions. But he knew his task would have been more difficult there. On the Golden Corridor most of the young women came from money. He had found that where money was apparently abundant, breeding was more easily recognizable, something on which his clients insisted. Not every young woman in Fort Lauderdale possessed that trait. In fact, most didn't.

*   *   *

Antonio Mendez wasn't his real name. He had used it on his first contract and liked the ring of it. It seemed to fit his personality. He was a beautiful young man, *star quality* his mother used to say. Black wavy hair combed straight back from his forehead with a short ponytail tied with a ribbon, always a red ribbon. Smooth bronze skin and a toned body he worked on daily to stay in shape. Eyes like dark mysterious pools of liquid, and a glib tongue.

His friends teased him about his looks. A young *Antonio Banderas*, they would say. He liked that. Jose Antonio Dominguez Banderas, the Spanish actor, was his idol, and he tried to mimic his walk, his speech and his mannerisms. His idol must have been the idol of many of the young girls who visited the Golden Corridor because he had no problem picking up and bedding any unattached woman he desired. It was a gift he constantly strived to perfect, one that had served him well since long before completing his first contract.

Antonio's real name was Felipe Hernandez Garcia. He was the son of Jose Manuel Garcia, Mexico's Minister of Energy and a close ally and personal friend of President Carlos Montoya. Only Antonio's two friends and business associates knew his real identity, or at least, that's what he thought. And, he wanted to keep it that way.

Felipe's father knew his son's interests extended beyond his legitimate business pursuits, and were possibly illegal. But, that was the way of many people in Mexico, particularly in the tourist areas and especially among the holders of government offices, including his. He just didn't want to know what his son was involved in, so he didn't ask.

His father knew that his son had recently purchased a new 68-foot Evolution luxury yacht, designed by Stefano Righini and manufactured by the premier Italian yacht builder, Azimut, at a cost of several million dollars. He also knew that Felipe couldn't make that kind of money in the SCUBA business. He had thought several times about investigating his son's activities. *You never know when that information could be useful, even if my son is involved,* he reasoned. But his government work was just too demanding to allow the time to conduct any more personal business than he had going already. *Besides, what if someone opened an investigation of my office. With what I've got going, that could be dangerous.*

*   *   *

The McKenzie Residence,
Boston, Massachusetts
Monday, April 9 – 6:32am

As soon as he was seated in the rear of the limousine, McKenzie instructed his driver to take him directly to his office, closed the glass privacy partition, and, using the limousine's satellite phone, dialed a number he knew well.

"Jim, Horace McKenzie here. I know it's early, but I need a favor."

"Hello, Rummy. Long time no see! What can I do for you, my friend."

"My daughter's vacationing in Cabo San Lucas and she's missing."

"Kathy?"

"Yes. She and five of her friends from school flew down for their spring break four days ago. According to one of her friends, they were together at a club last night, actually just a few hours ago. She disappeared after she became sick and went to the ladies' room. They haven't heard from her since. I told them to tell your hotel manager all they know and you would have him take them to the police so they could begin a search for Kathy. None of that *missing for forty-eight hours* crap. They need to get on this now, and I need you to intercede for me as soon as possible. You have some clout with the authorities down there and I don't. I don't know what has happened, Jim, but I'm afraid, from what her friends told me, Kathy might have been drugged and kidnapped. For what purpose I don't know, but if the authorities don't move fast, Nancy and I may lose her forever."

"Have you told Nancy?"

"Yes, she knows, but I didn't tell her my fears. I told her Kathy probably got drunk and is sleeping it off somewhere. I doubt if she believed me, but it was the best I could think of at the time."

"Don't worry, my friend. I'll call the Municipal Police right away. I've had dealings with the captain in charge of that district. He owes me a few favors."

"Jim, you need to go higher than the Municipal Police on this. Go to the FAI."

"Who?"

"The Federal Agency of Investigation, Mexico's special anti-organized crime unit. They're like our FBI. In fact, Mexico used our model to create their own version. I think this may be bigger than the locals, and the FAI would be the agency to investigate this. They're the people who investigate organized crime, and down there an organization of three or more persons involved in some form of illegal activity falls under their purview. One of Kathy's friends told me they were with some local boys at the club when she disappeared and one of them took her to the ladies' room. I suspect they may be involved and there were three of them. That puts this situation into the FAI's court."

"OK, Rummy. Will do. Is there anything else I can do?"

"No, if Kathy doesn't show up by mid-afternoon, I'm going to fly down there and start my own investigation. I'll talk with the police. If I get the run-around, I'll pull out the big guns. But, if you can have a car and driver for me I would appreciate it. Be sure the driver is someone I can use as an interpreter and someone I can trust to tell the authorities what I'm saying if they can't speak English."

"Will do. If you think of anything else I can do, I'm just a phone call away."

"Thanks, Jim. I knew I could count on you. Please give my best to your lovely wife. I'll call you if I need anything else."

*   *   *

Logan International Airport
Boston, Massachusetts
Monday, April 9 – 1:28pm

Kathy had not returned to the hotel as her father had hoped she would. Her friend, Patricia Heinz had called him promptly at nine her time, noon in Boston. In just over an hour, McKenzie was in the air, flying southwest in the fastest corporate jet on the market. Something was terribly wrong, and he was in a hurry.

The Cessna Citation X had lifted off from Logan International at 1:25pm and climbed quickly to its assigned altitude. Aside from the flight crew, the only passenger on board was Horace McKenzie. First McKenzie Bank owned the "top of the line" corporate jet. The flight took just over four hours.

The captain of the Cessna lined up the twin turbofan jet aircraft on the down-wind leg of his landing pattern a mile south of runway 27 at Los Cabos International, dialed in twenty degree flaps and decreased the engines' rpms to bring the aircraft's speed down to 190 knots. They had made the flight from Logan International in four hours and twenty-seven minutes. With the Citation's fuel range of 3,250 miles, they did not have to refuel in-route, making the 2,585-mile journey much quicker than had McKenzie flown commercial.

As instructed by the ATC, the pilot flew the aircraft to a point fifteen miles beyond the end of runway 27 and executed a 90-degree left turn onto his base leg. When the Citation was almost abreast of the runway, he made a second 90-degree left turn onto his final, picked up the outer marker and flew the glide slope to the end of the runway and touched down forty yards from the leading edge of the tarmac. With full reverse thrusters engaged, the aircraft rolled to a smooth stop as it was handed off to Ground Control for directions to the fixed-base operator's executive-jet parking area.

*   *   *

Los Cabos International Airport
Cabo San Lucas, Mexico
Monday, April 9 – Late Afternoon

It was 7:45pm on the East Coast, 4:45pm in Cabo San Lucas. Los Cabos International Airport was exceptionally busy at this time of day with a mix of commercial and private aircraft coming and going. The commercial airlines serving the area tried to schedule their flights during daylight hours for the convenience of the hordes of tourist that flocked to this vacation paradise. Commercial flights were given preferential landing slots during afternoon hours, but the pilot of the Citation X was given a straight-in clearance and landed without delay.

As the aircraft was maneuvered to its assigned tie-down location, a Land Rover rolled onto the tarmac and made its way past the other corporate jets parked on the flight line to the passenger-side door of the aircraft.

"*Senor* McKenzie! I am Jorge Campo. *Senor* Rodgers called and asked me to meet you here. He also told me about your daughter. I am very sorry, *Senor*. Have you received any word from the police?"

"Not yet, Jorge." McKenzie extended his hand in friendship. "I've spent the last few hours in the air, but they had my cellular number, so they could have called if they had anything to report. What can you tell me?"

"I took your daughter's friends to the police station to report her missing as *Senor* Rodgers instructed. They were polite to the young ladies, asked them numerous questions, but really didn't seem very interested in doing anything. They did say they would look into it. I think they knew you would be coming to see them."

"Can you tell me anything else? Do you know if the police questioned the boys who were with my daughter and her friends last night?"

"I don't know, *Senor*. One of your daughter's friends, I think her name is *Senorita* Patricia gave the police their names. I have heard of these boys, *Senor*. What I have heard is not good. They are like gigolos, male prostitutes. And, I hear they are in the business of selling drugs to the tourist. There are rumors of even worse things, but I don't know. I try to keep them out of our hotel, but they bribe my employees and they protect them. I call the police when I see them here, but they don't pay any attention. Maybe they bribe the police also. There is corruption everywhere here, *Senor*."

"And you, Jorge. Are you also corrupt? Mr. Rodgers tells me I can trust you. Can I?"

"*Si, Senor* McKenzie. I'm not from here. I'm from Mexico City. I've been with the Horizon Group for over fifteen years and I've been the general manager of the Melia San Lucas since it opened a year ago. My honor is above reproach, *Senor.*"

"I apologize, Jorge. I had to ask. I need someone down here I can trust, someone who will be my eyes and ears if Kathy doesn't turn up soon."

"I understand, *Senor*. I'll do everything I can to help you. I have asked my kitchen and housekeeping staff to make some discreet inquiries on the streets tonight. They hear things that are not said to me, and they know people to whom I have no access. If there is word on the streets about your daughter, they will hear it and tell me. I have posted a rather substantial reward, so I hope to hear something by tomorrow morning."

"Good thinking, Jorge. I want to talk with the police. But first, let's go to the hotel and talk with Kathy's friends. I want you with me everywhere I go, Jorge."

"*Si, Senor*, I will be happy to help you."

*   *   *

Melia San Lucas Hotel
Cabo San Lucas, Mexico
Monday, April 9 – Late Afternoon

Horace McKenzie arrived at the Melia San Lucas hotel at 6:01pm and spent the next three hours with Kathy's friends going over every detail each could remember about the night of her disappearance and the events leading up to her becoming ill and going to the club's ladies' room. He interviewed each in private. Generally, each story was similar, even though there were minor differences. Every comment made in the interviews was recorded. McKenzie would replay the conversations when he had time to concentrate on every detail.

It was early evening and there had been no word from Kathy in over twenty-four hours. McKenzie would wait until 8:30 am the next morning before visiting the police captain whose name Jim Rodgers had given him. He didn't expect much help from the police, and was more convinced than ever that his daughter had been kidnapped. He had been disappointed that Jim had not wanted to involve the Mexican Federal Agency of Investigation until the municipal police had been brought into the picture, but he had acquiesced, although he felt it was a waste of time dealing with the locals. Corruption and the culture of bribery there were well-documented. Evidently, Jim didn't want to offend the local police by not involving them. McKenzie felt that involving the local police would only serve to alert the kidnappers of his presence and keep them in hiding.

Earlier, during his flight to Cabo San Lucas, McKenzie called a friend in the Sexual Assault Unit of the Boston Police Department who was stationed at their headquarters in Lower Roxbury, and gave him all the information he had, plus his opinion of what may have gone on down in Cabo. Although they had no jurisdiction, they immediately set up a crisis response center in his living room in Boston should a call come in with ransom demands while he was in Mexico. He was trying to cover all the bases.

It was just before dawn when McKenzie was awakened by a soft knock on his hotel room door. The sound brought him awake instantly, and he raced to the door, hoping it was Kathy.

Jorge Campo, the hotel manager, was standing in the hall with a cart and tray of coffee, orange juice, and croissants that he wheeled into the room, closing the door behind him.

"What news, Jorge?"

"I'm sorry, *Senor* McKenzie, I have no good news."

"But you do have something?"

"Si, Senor, but what I've been told isn't good."

"Sit down, Jorge, and tell me everything. Not knowing is worse than knowing the truth. Would you like some coffee?"

"*Ningun gracias, Senor.* As I mentioned when you arrived, I asked my second shift staff when they clocked out at ten o'clock last night to find out what they could on the streets about your daughter, and tell me what they had found this morning when clocking in. I offered a substantial reward for any information that could be substantiated.

"*Senor* McKenzie, there is word on the street that a fair-haired young American girl was taken against her will at a nightclub the night before last. From what I'm told, no one really knows who kidnapped her, or if they know, they aren't saying. My people can't find out where she's been taken, but there is speculation she'll be put in the pipeline to the Middle East soon. I think this may have been your daughter, *Senor.*"

"Pipeline? You're telling me she's going to be sold to someone?"

"*Si, Senor, como esclavo del sexo.* She will be sold to someone with a lot of money in a Middle Eastern country as a sex slave."

"A sex slave? My daughter?"

"*Si, Senor.* I can only tell you what my people tell me. There is an underground market here in Cabo for beautiful, young Caucasian women. Young, attractive women from the United States and the United Kingdom, non-Jewish, to be sold to Muslim Arabs in the Middle East; I presume to be added to their harems. I am told there was a time when being a member of a Sultan's harem commanded much respect. They were revered, but no longer. Many of the old Arabic and Turkish ways have been corrupted, as have many of western society's ways. The respect is gone and women must be taken against their will. It is no longer an honor to be a member of one's harem.

"I am also told the rewards are quite handsome for the purveyors of these women, well worth the risks of being caught. And, if caught, who says the police won't look the other way for the right price? As I told you, *Senor,* corruption is rampart here, in politics as well as in the ranks of our law enforcement officers.

"They say that money does not change hands in these transactions, *Senor* McKenzie. Payment is usually made in drugs, cocaine mostly, which is moved up the Baja through Tijuana and Mexicali into California for distribution in L.A. and San Francisco. I am told the exchange usually takes place off shore, away from the eyes of the authorities and the public.

"Unfortunately, I suspect several members of my staff may be involved. Again, I am telling you only what has been whispered to me. I don't know who is involved, but I have my suspicions. These people are paid to identify possible candidates to be kidnapped. They know what to look for, and since many of my staff have access to our guest records, they are a good source of information. I can only speculate that the bribe is such that some can't resist. These are poor people, *Senor* McKenzie, with limited education and no real opportunity to improve their lot. Money is the most important thing in their lives. They never have enough money, just enough for their necessities. They have nothing to keep them honest except their conscience."

"You're telling me that these people are both kidnappers and drug dealers?"

"Si, that's what I am told."

"Was there any reaction among your staff when you asked about the three boys who were with Kathy and her friends when she disappeared?"

"Si, but not directly. When I mentioned the names of the boys, some of my staff got quiet, as though I had asked something that wasn't supposed to be asked. They wouldn't say anything else, just stopped answering my questions. But later, one of my people told me the three boys were protected. That was all she would say, and she seemed very concerned that word would get out that she had told me this. There is more to this than meets the eye, as you say in the U.S., *Senor.* I think the police protect these boys, the ones with your daughter, but why, I don't know."

"If what you say is true, then there's a good chance Kathy is still alive. That buys us some time and eliminates what I had feared most-that she could already be dead. But, it adds another dimension I never considered, that someone would kidnap my daughter to sell her to some bastard in the Middle East who just wants a sex toy."

McKenzie sat in silence for a moment, drinking coffee and looking at Jorge. "All right, Jorge, change of plans. I'm going to visit the police this morning, but I really don't expect to learn anything. I'll drop the names of the boys we know were the last to see Kathy and judge their reactions to the fact that I know who the prime suspects are, or should be. I want you there with me in case we have a language problem."

* * *

Tuesday, April 10 – 6:15am

McKenzie showered, shaved, and put on fresh clothes, one of the Brooks Brothers suits he always carried on extended trips away from the Boston area. Unlike many of his peers, he had not abandoned his clothier for the less expensive goods produced by Jos. A. Bank. He didn't believe the quality was there, and when Claudio Del Vecchio purchased Brooks Brothers a couple of years ago for $225 million, he knew he had made the right choice.

McKenzie picked up his cell phone and punched in the speed-dial number for his pilot. "Bob, you and Sam get the plane ready. I want to leave here later today. Try to get a departure slot sometime around mid-day, IFR to Washington. If the winds are right we can do this trip without a fuel stop. You'll drop me off in D.C. and take Kathy's friends back to Boston. I may be in Washington for a couple of days, but will get in touch with you when I'm ready to return to Boston. You can come down and pick me up then. I'm going to make a call in a minute and try to get authorization to land at Andrews Air Force Base. Normally that's impossible, but since you will be dropping me off and not staying, I may be able to get the White House to get us clearance. Go ahead and file for National or Dulles. We can make the destination change when we're in the air, if we get the Andrews clearance. What do you think our ETA will be?"

*   *   *

Metropolitan Police Headquarters
Cabo San Lucas, Mexico
Tuesday, April 10 – 8:30am

McKenzie's visit with the Municipal Police of Cabo San Lucas was less than satisfying, and not unlike what he expected, having been forewarned by the manager of the Melia San Lucas resort hotel, Jorge Campo, who accompanied him.

When confronted with the names of the three young men who had been with his daughter and her friends at the club on the night she disappeared, the police captain seemed to become defensive, and stated emphatically that his detectives had thoroughly investigated the three men, and they were beyond suspicion. McKenzie knew he was lying. He knew how to read body language, a process he had picked up in one of his psychology classes at Harvard, which had served him well in negotiating contracts for his bank. The actions of the police captain confirmed his suspicions. The police were protecting the boys, but he didn't know why, and no one seemed to be able to shed any light on the reasons, only that they were being protected.

The captain had said that his people were looking into other possibilities, but they held out little hope that Kathy McKenzie would be found. He tried to float the theory that she ran off with someone, another tourist probably, and was holed up somewhere on a deserted beach on the Sea of Cortez, drinking and screwing. "What every young American girl wanted to do," the police captain had said with a smirk on his face. McKenzie would have decked the man had the circumstances been different.

McKenzie left the police station as angry as he had ever been in his life. He had not lost his temper in the presence of the police captain. He was too smart for that. But, Jorge could see the anger in his face and kept quiet. They drove back to the hotel in silence.

"All right Jorge, since I don't seem to be getting anywhere with the damned police down here, I'm going to do this my way. If those bastards think they can run rough shod over me, they're sadly mistaken. I know they're lying about the guy who runs the SCUBA shop and his two stooges. They're protecting that little prick, and I'm going to find out why, and who he really is.

"I'm leaving today, Jorge, and I'm not sure when I'll be back, but someone will be back, and damned soon. It may even be the U.S. Marines. They think they're playing with someone whose hands are tied. Well, my friend, they haven't seen me pissed off yet. The shit is about to hit the fan down here, and I'm going to be the one feeding the fan.

"I want you to do a couple of things for me, Jorge. Have some of your people, those you can trust, watch the three boys and record everything they do, where they go, who they see, what they say. I need to know everything. See if they can get in close so they can hear what's being said. I would get a private detective to do that, but like you said, whom can you trust down here?

"Second, have your people report to you every day if they hear anything else about Kathy. Somebody might slip and give something away. It could be these boys use the club they took Kathy and her friends to as a place to subdue and kidnap their victims, so have someone become a regular there so their face will be known. And, if the police come around asking questions, tell them I left, bewildered and dejected. As far as they're concerned, I don't have a plan. Tell them you don't know if, or when, I will be coming back. I don't want them to find out you're working on this with me. When I decide what I'm going to do, I'll let you know.

"Jorge, as I told you earlier, I need you to be my eyes and ears down here. And by the way, Jorge, I will reimburse you for any cost you incur on my behalf, and I will reward you handsomely for your efforts. Kathy is my only daughter and she means the world to her mother and me. Money is no object when it comes to getting her back."

"*Si, Senor* McKenzie. I will do my best."

"Thank you, Jorge. You've already been a great help."

CHAPTER TWO

Somewhere on the Baja Wasteland
Baja California Sur, Mexico
Tuesday, April 10—Noon

IT HAD BEEN two days, maybe three. She couldn't remember exactly. Everything was still running together, day and night, not in real time, but in slow motion, frame by frame like an old black and white western movie made in the 1920s. The massive dose of drugs they had given her had left her with some residual effects, inability to concentrate, and short-term memory loss. But, she was slowly regaining her memory of the events that led up to her being in this awful place. Her initial fear had turned to anger.

The old woman had cut the plastic tie binding her wrist so she could eat more comfortably and wash up in the bucket of brown water she had placed beside the makeshift bed where the girl was now permitted to sleep. But, as instructed, she had left the girl's ankles tied to prevent her escape.

It was mid afternoon when Antonio arrived, unexpectedly. His presence seemed to frighten the old woman. He brought food and fresh clothes for the girl.

"You raped me, you bastard," Kathy screamed, throwing the tin water cup at him.

"Shut your stupid mouth, little girl, or I'll do you again, just to hear you scream now that you are awake."

"Screw you, *Antonio*, you and your two friends. You wait until my dad gets hold of you. He'll tear you apart and spit you out in little pieces."

"Listen closely little girl. You aren't going to see your daddy again, so get used to the idea. In a week or so, you'll be taking a long boat ride. You can do this my way and everything will go well for you, or you can give me a lot of attitude and end up a crack head on a street corner in Juarez, turning two-dollar tricks to feed your coke habit. And, little girl, I can put you there in a heartbeat, so behave yourself and listen closely. Your life, for the moment, belongs to me.

"And, you're wrong. We didn't rape you. We just had sex with you. You didn't tell us not to. Hell, you just lay there and took on all three of us. Of course, your being all drugged up didn't hurt either. Not that I need to tell you this, but we used rubbers. You Gringos call them condoms. So, you aren't pregnant, bitch, at least not by any one of us. You wouldn't be any use to me if you were.

"Just so you know what your future holds, you've been sold to a pretty rich dude in Saudi Arabia, an Arab prince, member of the House of Saud. And for a right smart quantity of coke I might add. He and some of his towel-headed cousins like young American girls, and they aren't fussy about them being virgins like the older men are, so my boys and I figured his highness wouldn't mind us tasting a little piece of the pie before you're delivered to him. Of course he won't know we did a little dipping with his new chick, and you aren't going to mention it either, because he might just slit your throat if he finds out."

"What in the hell are you talking about? I thought you kidnapped me for some ransom you wanted my daddy to pay."

"That isn't exactly how this is going to play out, little girl. We're not after your daddy's money. The only place you're going from here is on a boat ride to the Middle East, so start getting used to the idea.

You sure as hell aren't going back home to your comfortable life style in Boston. By the time you get to Saudi Arabia, you'll be over your *I can't believe this is happening to me* crap and you'll resign yourself to the fact that you'll be just another member of this guy's harem, and your sole responsibility will be to please him. And here are a few things you had better learn quickly: you will embrace his Muslim faith and the customs of the Middle East. You will wear their style of clothes and you will keep your opinions to yourself. You won't speak unless spoken to, and you will never make eye contact with any man except your owner. Hell, you'll be making a lot more than eye contact with him," Antonio said, laughing. "And you'll keep your eyes downcast and head and face covered when you're out in public. Your only job will be to give your owner lots of sons. If you do, your life will be one of leisure. If you don't, you can't imagine the hellish nightmare your very short life will be.

"So, get yourself cleaned up, little girl. No makeup, and start wearing these clothes. They're what the Muslim women over there wear. Get used to them. And I would suggest you study these two books." He threw a package on the bed wrapped in brown paper and tied with string. "You will become a Muslim, like it or not, so start learning something about their faith by reading the Koran. Find out why they believe so strongly in their prophet, Mohammed.

"The second book will give you an insider's view of life in a modern-day harem. Understand that I'm not giving you these because I like you. You aren't even good in bed, no experience, until now. It's just a matter of economics for me. The faster you get with the program, the better my services look and the higher the price I can charge for little white girls like you."

"Screw you, you wetback!"

"One more thing, Smartass," Antonio said, as he grabbed her by the throat and pulled her close to his face. "I'm going to cut the tie around your ankles so you can walk around. Get outside and get some sun. You're going to be here a week or so longer, then you're out of here. If you try to escape and the coyotes and rattle snakes don't get you out in this god-forsaken scrub country, the hundred-plus heat or the scorpions will. You won't last more than a day. You'll die of thirst. There's no shade for miles, and no water. Nobody lives out here except this old woman. The nearest village is thirty miles away, and if you, by some chance, make it there, the bandits will take you in for their personal pleasure. They like pretty young gringo girls, so stay put, Smartass, you're safe here. Eat the beans and tortillas the old woman makes for you, and get your head on straight. You're mine for a while, sweetheart, so make the best of it."

Kathy threw her plate at him as he walked out the door, collapsed on the bed and began to cry again. *Where are you, Daddy*, she sobbed.

*   *   *

Melia San Lucas Hotel
Cabo San Lucas, Mexico
Tuesday, April 10 – Mid Morning

Horace McKenzie returned to the hotel from the police station at ten, packed his bags, paid his hotel bill, and was driven to the airport by Jorge Campo.

When he was aboard and the Cessna had crossed into U.S. airspace, he picked up the secure satellite phone he always carried when he needed to talk with associates in total confidence. The number he punched in connected him to the White House switchboard.

"Would you please connect me with the President's secretary. This is Horace McKenzie calling."

"One moment, please."

"Mr. McKenzie, nice to hear from you, Sir. The President is in the Oval Office with the Secretary of Defense. They're having a bite of lunch, and I suspect they're talking about their golf games. I'll tell him you are holding. I'm sure he would like to speak with you."

President Hunt answered the phone as soon as his secretary had told him who was on the other end. "Rummy, you old fart! Are you in town?"

"No, Mr. President. I'm on my way to Washington from Cabo San Lucas. I need an audience with you, tonight if possible."

"You sound serious, my friend. What's up?"

McKenzie told the President everything that had happened beginning with the night his daughter had been kidnapped. "John, if we don't get her back, I've been told she's probably going to be taken to the Middle East and has been contracted as someone's sex slave. The word down there is that the buyer is probably one of the younger members of the House of Saud, maybe not a Royal Prince, but possibly a distant cousin. Our wonderful allies in Saudi Arabia are at it again."

"Christ, Rummy. You mean Kathy?"

"I'm afraid so, John. What do you think I should do now? I'm not going to get any help from the police down in Cabo, and I'm afraid her time may be running out."

"All right, I'll get you clearance to land at Andrews and I'll meet you there. I'll probably bring the director of the CIA and my chief of staff with me. I'm not sure who else. When are you leaving and what's your arrival time?"

"We cleared U.S. air space at Del Rio a few minutes ago on a northeast heading towards Dallas. We won't need to refuel until we reach D.C. Is it possible to refuel at Andrews? I'm sure they're not set up to sell fuel to civilian aircraft, but we will need to refuel there or go over to National. We're flying First McKenzie Bank's new Citation X, so we should be there around nine this evening, maybe earlier if we get a break with the winds aloft. Is that too late for you to see us this evening?"

"No, that's fine, Rummy. I'll be sure you're cleared into Andrews and that they are aware you will need to refuel. I'm sure the Air Force has a few extra gallons of Jet A they can spare. I'll come over by helicopter and see you there around 9:30. No need for you to have to catch a ride to the White House. And Rummy, I'll pray for Kathy's quick return."

"Thanks, Mr. President."

"Cut the bullshit, Rummy. We've always been on a first name basis, even after I got this job. We may not have always shared the same political philosophy, but we've always been friends in spite of our political differences, so save the *Mr. President* crap for when we're in public together."

McKenzie walked up to the flight deck of the Cessna Citation. "Another change of plans, Bob. The President is getting us a clearance into Andrews, so change your primary landing designation and list National and Dulles as your alternates. You can close out your flight plan at Andrews."

"Close it out?"

"Yes. We're going to stay on the ground there for a while, then continue on to Boston. I don't know how long we'll be there, probably only an hour or so, but it could be longer. It depends on how my meeting goes, but the President is going to meet us at Andrews. You and Sam can get a little shut-eye there before we go on to Boston. And, you can file to Logan just before we leave. There won't be any wait time for an IFR flight plan approval if you're filing out of Andrews. It's all priority. Anyway, I'm sure the girls will be asleep. Just be sure they have some food and pillows and blankets for the trip."

It was 11:45am.

*   *   *

Andrews Air Force Base
Prince George's County, Maryland
Tuesday, April 10 – 8:18pm

The Air Traffic Controller in the FAA's Command Center in Herndon, Virginia, monitoring the Citation's flight as it entered the restricted air space well outside the Nation's capital, handed the aircraft off to Andrews Air Force Base Approach Control after verifying that it had been pre-authorized to land there. The WH prefix in their clearance designation indicated the landing had been approved by the White House, and that alone jumped the Cessna ahead of several military aircraft already in the landing pattern.

The Cessna landed at Andrews at 9:02 in the evening of April 10, taxied to a stop at the end of the 11,300-foot western runway, and held there until given the *Follow me* signal by the Humvee, armed with a manned 50-caliber machine gun, that was waiting for them. The pilot followed the vehicle down a long taxiway to a rather non-descript hangar with no lights on its perimeter. When the pilot shut down the Cessna's engines, as instructed by hand-signal from the Humvee, the doors to the hangar slid silently open and the aircraft was towed inside. It was pitch black, but the silhouettes of armed military personnel could be seen both inside and outside the hangar. As the doors were closed, floodlights came on inside and the pilots could see there were no windows to alert the outside world that the building was occupied. Parked outside on the tarmac, surrounded by a contingent of armed military police, was one of two Boeing 747-200B aircraft used by the President as his flying Oval Office. With the President aboard, its designation was always *Air Force One*. When he was not on board, it was not just another 747. The highly sophisticated electronic equipment on board, and the modifications that had been made to the interior and exterior of the aircraft, set it fully apart from other 747s.

The passenger door of the Cessna was opened and an Air Force Captain entered the aircraft. "Mr. McKenzie, I'm Captain Russo. I've been instructed to escort you to your meeting with the President. He's scheduled to arrive at 9:45, Sir." Russo turned to the two pilots still seated in the cockpit. "Gentlemen, you are to remain with the aircraft as well as your other passengers. We have restroom facilities here as well as a small kitchen should anyone need to use the facilities or wish to have something to eat. Our menu is limited, of course. Regulations dictate that an armed guard will remain at the bottom of the steps at all times, as much for your protection as the President's. Should anyone wish to leave the aircraft, a guard will escort you. Otherwise, you are not to leave the aircraft at any time."

The prop wash of a helicopter landing outside the building could be heard. The Air Force captain pressed his ear piece, nodded and said "Yes, Sir. Right away, Sir."

"Mr. McKenzie, the President has arrived. Please follow me, Sir."

CHAPTER THREE

Washington, District of Columbia
A Look Back

I N THE WORDS of the political pundits of the day, *He doesn't stand a snowball's chance in hell*!

That was six years ago, just months before the landslide victory that propelled John Hunt into the White House on the groundswell of public disillusionment over the war. Sentiment was high to effect political change, especially in the White House, even though the electorate knew full well that electing a Democrat would guarantee higher taxes and massive entitlement spending in an economic environment teetering on the edge of a recession. That didn't matter. Change was the watchword, regardless of what it would ultimately cost the voters. Most were caught up in a movement that had no real basis in fact. It didn't hurt Hunt's chances either when his party's two frontrunners, both considered outstanding candidates to effect change in the name of the Democrat party, went down in flames.

First, it was the candidate from Maine around whom the party's movers and shakers had rallied. It wasn't anything he did. It really didn't matter to his supporters that he had no practical political experience and no real foreign policy background. He had charisma, and he was demanding an end of the war, and tax relief for everyone except the very rich, who now were already paying some seventy percent of all personal taxes collected by the IRS. Also, he was a full-blooded Sioux Indian whose family had left the plains generations before and made their fortune in the legal gambling casinos operating openly on lands now considered Indian Reservations. He was riding the high tide of sentiment to have a minority in the White House, and he was capitalizing on that sentiment. It was his wife who destroyed his chances of being handed his party's nomination when she bombed on NBC's Sunday morning *Meet The Press* with the comment, *"Go Figure,"* when Tim Russet asked if she had ever expected to be the nation's First Lady. It wasn't a comment one would have expected to hear from the lady who would be entertaining world leaders in the White House or with her husband representing the nation on the world stage. It was more a comment one would hear in a casual conversation in a neighborhood bar, not something the future First Lady would say on television in front of several million potential voters.

Immediately after her slip of the tongue, cartoons began to appear in several widely circulated newspapers on the East Coast of the candidate and his wife in full Plains Indian regalia, entertaining world leaders while astride two palomino ponies. They became the butt of many mean-spirited jokes that substantially diminished the candidate's chances of receiving the party's nomination.

Public support for her husband evaporated overnight. Of course the black leaders in the party who had rallied around the minority candidate blamed it on the American voting public, most of whom were white, not being ready for a minority president. But then, that was their typical response to most setbacks.

When Senator Hunt heard the comment, which was reported and commented on much more frequently by Fox News commentators than the liberal media outlets, he toasted the television set with his glass of Glenmorangie, his favorite single-malt Highland scotch, as he lounged in his Georgetown mansion. *One down and one to go*, he mused.

The second contender to go down in flames was the lady who had campaigned on her years of political experience. She was confident she would receive her party's nomination and could beat any candidate the opposition party could throw at her. And with *"that Indian fellow"* out of the race, it surely was hers for the taking. Unfortunately, she was a Washington insider, and the electorate was clamoring for change-real change. Not just a game of Washington musical chairs. Her campaign was beginning to fall apart when a rumor surfaced that she had had an affair with another female student while attending Vassar. The rumor smoldered for a while, and probably wouldn't have hurt her candidacy had the lady with whom the candidate supposedly had the affair not come forward with a *tell-all* exposé, with pictures, in a popular rumor-mill tabloid. It was the straw that broke the camel's back.

The *Keep the Dyke out of the White House* bumper stickers that suddenly appeared everywhere across the nation just after the exposé, were the final blow. The source was never discovered, and the lady who did the exposé disappeared. John Hunt was beside himself. The party was in disarray, and there was no one left on stage who could be considered a serious candidate in the race for the presidency. That was, of course, just the environment Hunt was waiting for. It was later debated that Hunt may possibly have orchestrated the downfall of the two leading candidates on which the party had hung its hopes. But no one could prove the accusation, and like most of Washington's dirty tricks rumors about the *party of the people,* it eventually washed down the Potomac with the evening tide.

As members of the press looked around to see who they could find to champion the party's hopes of adding the White House to the House and Senate they had taken two years earlier, they could find no one. Then, as if on cue, John Hunt announced his intention to run for the Presidency. His public relations people, who seemed to be patiently waiting in the wings for the right moment, but who had been working diligently for months, set their political machine into motion. Timing is everything.

Like a fiery phoenix, John Hunt rose from the ashes of his party and took center stage, calling press conferences to outline his platform and expound on his positions on various domestic and international issues, carefully crafted to make him appear to be the one person destined to heal a much divided nation-a nation that had lost its former position of strength and respect on the world stage. Hunt was a little known Democrat senator, a born again Republican, so to speak, who had seen the light. He was for the most part unknown by the Washington press corps. All of a sudden, every talking head in Washington was clamoring to give him on-camera live interviews, and Hunt was only too happy to oblige. His years in the Senate had made him a consummate speaker and a genuine bullshit artist. During the six months remaining before November, he appeared multiple times on every news talk show on the airways. The media had decided it was their destiny to do everything in their power to elect a candidate that represented their views, but the two candidates, behind whom they had thrown their support and considerable free airtime, had lost favor with the voters and were now not considered electable. They now had no champion to give to the American voters other than Hunt.

Hunt rode into the White House on one of the highest voter turnouts in electoral history. He loved it. He had made many promises he knew he would not be able to keep, but he was the President of the United States and that was all that mattered. He didn't feel he had been handed a mandate with his election, so he could do what he damned well pleased.

The press learned to love John Hunt, as his advisers knew they would. The party leaders had no choice. The several minor candidates whose names surface every four years had folded their tents as expected, pocketed their campaign contributions, and faded into the night. The public was enchanted with Hunt, and the party leaders reluctantly accepted his nomination, as the delegates, in a show of enthusiasm, trashed the Atlantic City Convention Center. Hunt had played the game just the way his advisers had told him to. They had scripted everything.

After all, they had been secretly working on his campaign tactics well before any other candidate had announced. Hunt was in residence before he knew that 1600 Pennsylvania Avenue was the address of the White House.

* * *

With his party's control of Congress, and now the White House, Hunt's first four years were smooth sailing. He and Congress had quietly withdrawn U.S. troops from the Middle East conflict. By design, there was very little press coverage of the fall of the democratic regimes in Afghanistan and Iraq as the various terrorists' organizations, formally running those countries, reestablished their power bases, killing thousands of innocent people who had supported freedom for their people. This was the second time the U.S. had betrayed the people of Iraq. With the promises of freedom taken away from them again, many Iraqis willingly joined the terrorist groups. Their hatred for anything American was so strong that many volunteered to sacrifice themselves to bring death and destruction to the Americans. Terrorists' attacks in the United States quadrupled as western interests around the world suffered, but Hunt blamed the increased incidents of terrorism on the former administration's policies, and the American public, as a whole, didn't really care.

Hunt's advisors knew well that the American public responds only to what they are told by the media. If the Middle Eastern situation were underreported, the public would soon forget their country's commitment to support peace and stability around the world, and concentrate on themselves and their insatiable appetite for cheap foreign goods. Nine out of every ten Americans had no idea what the balance of trade meant or what impact it would ultimately have on the nation's economy if left unchecked. They only knew they wanted what they wanted, and they insisted their leaders get it for them. Hunt had been a willing provider, regardless of the price America would ultimately have to pay.

*　　*　　*

Hunt was now well into the third year of his second term as president of the United States. He was coasting, and loving every minute of his last years in office. He had won re-election handily over the opposition party's ultra-conservative candidate almost three years ago. Hunt's tax-and-spend policies had served him well during his first term. He and Congress had targeted the wealthy, substantially increasing their tax burden to support their expansion of the entitlement programs that kept most of his party's faithful in line. *Give them what they want and they'll vote for you* his advisers had often reminded him behind closed doors. *Don't worry about the long-term health of the nation. Let the other party clean up the mess when they regain power.*

*　　*　　*

On a personal note, half-way through the first year of his second term, John Hunt lost his wife to cervical cancer. His marriage had suffered greatly during her long bouts of sickness brought on by the massive doses of radiation and chemicals she had to endure as her cancer spread. Unfortunately, the treatments were not successful.

Still a virile man with normal human desires, Hunt had secretly bedded several very attractive women supplied by one of his wealthy Hollywood supporters, a motion picture mogul who assured him that no one would ever know of his infidelity. His wife's passing was a relief. He could now pursue his sexual fantasies as the nation's most eligible bachelor. *I'll probably be applauded for my conquests*, he thought. Little did he know that the CIA was documenting his acts of indiscretion.

* * *

Maximum Security Area
Andrews Air Force Base
Tuesday, April 10—9:23 pm

President Hunt arrived fifteen minutes before his scheduled meeting in order to have a few minutes to talk with the director of the CIA before his friend, Horace McKenzie, was escorted into the room. He wanted to go over their plan one more time. Armstrong had laid it out for him earlier in the day following McKenzie's call to the President. Hunt had first suggested they do nothing and tell McKenzie they had failed, but Armstrong knew Hunt would blame the failure on the CIA and would use the fabrication to cast doubt on the effectiveness of the agency, ultimately calling for Armstrong's resignation. He wasn't about to let Hunt sabotage his career and told him as much.

Hunt hated Armstrong, who had been CIA director through two administrations before his. Firing him wasn't an option, but the thought of doing so always made him smile.

Hunt was sitting across the table from Don Armstrong in a secure conference room. The small, soundproof room had been built for the President's use when meetings were better held away from the White House and the eyes and ears of his staff.

"Don, I appreciate your coming out this evening to meet with us, and I apologize for the short notice. I know we don't have a very good personal and working relationship, and I truly regret that. You are one of the most honest and trustworthy public servants in my administration, and the CIA is much the better with you at its helm."

"Thank you, Mr. President." Armstrong had heard that bullshit before. He knew the President hated his guts, and would like nothing more than to fire him, publicly if he could, to maximize the embarrassment. But, he knew he wouldn't. Armstrong knew too many secrets, and Hunt knew he knew. It was a standoff, and Armstrong loved it.

"You're most kind, Sir," Armstrong said, as graciously as he could. "I've been giving this situation a great deal of thought and have discussed it with Rob Downing, my deputy director of special operations. Also with the field agent we will use for this mission if you and I agree on the final plan." He knew Hunt would agree with anything he suggested if it looked like the plan might work and the President could take credit for its success. It was also meant as a veiled reminder that the President was not in control when it came to the CIA's involvement.

"Good. My friend, Horace McKenzie, will be joining us momentarily. As I told you over the phone this afternoon, he's quite distressed over the disappearance of his daughter, and rightfully so. I know he's going to want me to send in the Marines to rescue her, and nothing would give me more pleasure than to kick some ass south of the border. But, relationships with Mexico must remain stable. If we didn't need their oil, it would be another matter. But, their goodwill is essential to the survival and growth of our economy. He only knows his daughter is in harm's way, and he wants me to make the harm go away. I can't do that, Don, at least not publicly with a show of force. Even a small contingent of Delta Force types would arouse suspicions. And, right now we don't know who may be involved. But, you and your agent may be able to get her out."

"I understand, Sir."

The President lifted his eyes and looked away from Armstrong towards the door. "Come in," he said, his voice raised in response to a soft knock on the door. It was exactly seven o'clock.

"Rummy, you're a sight for sore eyes," the President said, standing up and grasping his old friend's hand. "I wish I could take away your anguish, Old Friend. I know this isn't a good time for you, so let's sit down and talk this thing out. By the way, this is my National Security Advisor, Dr. Louise Betters, and this is Don Armstrong, my CIA

Director. And of course you know Fred Pendleton, my Chief of Staff."
They shook hands all around.

McKenzie went over every detail he had regarding his missing
daughter, stopping occasionally to answer questions from the
President and his Chief of Staff. Armstrong remained quiet, listening
to everything McKenzie had to say. He noted the genuine anguish
Horace McKenzie was feeling. It was evident in his voice and in his
expressions, although he was trying to appear calm and present the
image that he was in control. He wasn't, and Armstrong felt genuine
sorrow for him in his grief.

"Gentlemen, I'm going to send one of my agents down to Cabo
tomorrow," Armstrong said, interrupting the conversation. He had heard
everything he needed to know. "He'll interview the hotel manager, Mr.
President. Hopefully he'll have more information by then. Our agent will
size up the situation and contact us through his handler, Rob Downing,
and that's about all I can tell you now. Except, Sir," he turned to face
Horace McKenzie, "if your daughter is still in Mexico, my man will find
her. He's the best we have, and I must agree with the President, it's in
everyone's best interest if we do this without public disclosure. The press
calls such operations, *black ops*. No Marines, no publicity, no political
considerations, just in and out quietly, with no fanfare."

Armstrong continued, "We don't know if the Mexican government
is involved. I suspect they aren't. But they could have knowledge and
are just being complacent. My man will find out. We have assets at
our disposal that you couldn't imagine exist, and we know how to use
them, and use them effectively.

"My suggestion to you, Mr. McKenzie, is to go home. Go back
to Boston and comfort your wife. What you've done down in Mexico
will be very helpful, but we want you to stay away now. You've opened
a door for us, but let us handle this from now on. If she's being held
against her will, we don't want the kidnappers to feel any pressure and
try to advance their timetable. We need time to be on our side. When we
strike, it has to be quick and a complete surprise to those we will target.

"We've had some dealings with the police down there, and although they talk a good game, they won't be any help. They don't have the manpower or the willpower to effectively investigate this, and most of them are on the take at one level or another. They won't even know we're down there. If they did, it could jeopardize your daughter's life, so stay away, Mr. McKenzie. Call your contact and the police every day as a distraught father would do. You must maintain that front to keep suspicions from being aroused. When you talk with the police, praise them for the job they are doing in trying to locate your daughter. They will believe you are sincere and not go looking for us. They may have your hotel manager's phones bugged, so let's play the game their way until we know exactly what the game is."

"Thank you, Mr. Armstrong. You've made me feel some better, but I can't stop worrying. Here, take these tapes. I transcribed all my conversations with Kathy's friends, the police and even with the hotel manager and his staff, while there. No one knew I was wearing a wire. They may be beneficial to your man."

"Thank you, Sir. I understand how you must feel. Please know this type of situation is what our agent has been training for all his life. If anyone can get your daughter back, he can."

"Can you tell me his name, Mr. Armstrong? I want to meet him when he returns, hopefully to thank him for bringing my daughter home."

"I'm sorry, Mr. McKenzie, I can't. I can't even tell the President who he is. You may get to meet him later, but right now his identity can't be revealed. He'll be going in under cover so his true identity wouldn't be of any value to you anyway."

CHAPTER FOUR

The Castle Mountains, Montana
November 14th, Early Morning
The Previous Year

ALEC LAY ON his back on the rock outcrop in a pool of blood, moving in and out of consciousness. Beth had removed his coat and placed it under his head as a pillow. The bullet had entered his right pleural cavity, nicked the right lobe of his lungs, and exited his back, creating an exit wound the size of a silver dollar. The *through and through* shot had missed bone and his spinal column, but the trauma had caused his right lung to collapse and he was close to going into shock.

Using Alec's Falcon II Manpack radio given to him for an earlier mission for the CIA, Beth had first reached Rob Downing, his CIA handler, with whom Alec maintained a precise communication schedule. Downing immediately realized the seriousness of the situation and relayed the call to Benefits Healthcare in Great Falls, Montana. They quickly assessed Alec's condition and launched the Mercy Flight's Eurocopter A-Star-B2 to the coordinates Beth gave them, high in the Montana Mountains northwest of Lennep. Flying at 150 mph, the

EMS helicopter would reach its destination in less than 30 minutes. The *Golden Hour* clock, critical to Alec's survival, was running, and time was running out.

"Tell me about the wound." The thoracic surgeon at Benefits Healthcare was talking with Beth Phillips, Alec's friend whom he was planning to marry and who was now carrying his child

*   *   *

Elizabeth Beaumont-Phillips had been married to Secretary of the Interior, Jerome Phillips when the helicopter in which they were traveling had been shot down over a remote area in the Selway-Bitterroot Mountains of Idaho a year earlier, severely wounding the Secretary. Their marriage had been a sham for years, but in support of his political career, she had not filed for a divorce.

The President's national security advisor had tasked Alec to find the downed helicopter and determine the cause of its crash. The incident was first thought to be the work of Middle Eastern Terrorists, but Alec was able to uncover evidence that pointed in another direction. The secretary had been assassinated in cold blood at the crash site, but the shooter, who had other ideas for his wife's use, had spared her life. Alec was able to rescue Beth, the only survivor of the crash, and together, they determined the reasons behind the hit, sanctioned by a Chicago based Mafia family with ties to the gaming industry in Nevada and New Jersey.

*   *   *

"It's a *through and through*, Doctor. As best I can tell, it didn't hit any bone and exited his lower back right of his spinal column, but it must have pierced his lung because the blood around the entry wound is bright red and frothy. Based on the location of the entrance and exit wounds, the would-be killer was above him when he made his shot."

"You're correct. The blood tells us it's a lung shot. Is he losing any blood now?" the surgeon asked.

"No, I've stopped the bleeding, which was mostly from the exit wound but he may be bleeding internally. The exit wound is a little smaller than a silver dollar. The entrance wound is very small, and I could hear air passing through it every time he inhaled. I've dressed both wounds, but he seems to be under considerable stress. I believe his right lung has collapsed. His breathing is labored and very shallow, and he's loosing his color."

"It's called a pneumothorax, Ms. Phillips. If the bullet pierced his lung, air escaping from his lung into the pleural cavity would offset its normal negative air pressure and force the thin lung membrane to collapse. The lung may not bleed enough to create a problem if it wasn't torn up by the bullet, but with a collapsed lung, you're going to have to stabilize the situation now or he won't last long enough for the EMS people to get to him. They're on their way now and should be there in about thirty minutes or so. How long has Mr. Caldwell been down?"

"Almost thirty minutes, I think. I really don't know. I haven't been keeping time."

"With a little luck they can get there in time, but you're going to have to act quickly to buy him some extra time. You said he's showing signs of being under distress. His breathing is labored. Correct?"

"Yes, and he almost passes out every time he takes a breath. It must be painful for him to breath. And his breathing seems to be getting more shallow with every breath."

"OK. We're going to have to stabilize him. If we don't, his lungs will continue to collapse until he has no more breathing capacity left. He will die from suffocation if we don't do something.

"Ms. Phillips, tell me about the first-aid kit you're using. Does it contain a syringe and needle? And surgical gloves?"

"Hold on a minute." Beth took the canvas bag and dumped the contents out on the rock ledge. "Yes, it does. It's one Alec takes with him every time he goes out into the mountains. It looks like it's government issued. It's a dark green canvas bag with U.S. stamped on the flap. It's like the medical kits you see in the war movies used by field medics. The needle is about two inches long and is attached to a syringe. The gloves are latex, and they're all in sterile paper containers."

"Good. If you didn't have a syringe and needle, I would have told you to use some type of cellophane to seal both the entrance and exit wounds. Zip-Loc bags are good for that. You could burp the entrance wound every time he takes a breath. When he inflates his lungs, you would open the dressing on the entrance wound and the displaced air in the plural cavity as the lungs expand would be allowed to escape through the hold. You would reseal the wound as he begins to exhale. This would relieve some of the pressure on his breathing and his level of distress would lessen. But, since you have the needle and syringe, I want you to put on the surgical gloves and use iodine to sterilize an area on his chest about three to five inches above his right nipple. If you have extra iodine, pour it on the gloves and needle. Do that, then tell me if you can feel his ribs in that area."

A minute later, "OK, done. The area is sterile. And yes, I can feel his ribs, but not very well. He has a well-developed chest."

"All right. Now move your fingers around until you locate the top or first rib. Then move your fingers down slowly towards his nipple. When you come to the space between the second and third rib, stop. This is where I want you to insert the needle. Feel it?"

"Yes."

"Good. Now, place the needle on the syringe and remove the plunger. The space you located earlier between the second and third rib is called the second intercostal space. Insert the needle into his chest there, as close to the top of the third rib as possible. You want to avoid hitting the nerve bundle just below the second rib. His right nipple should be directly below the point of insertion. Do it slowly. The pleural cavity lining is tough and you'll feel some resistance as the needle comes in contact with it. Don't stop. Just keep pushing. When the needle punctures the pleural cavity you're going to hear a "pop" and hear air escaping through the syringe, so keep your ear close to it. It's going to sound somewhat like opening a carbonated drink can, but not as loud. As soon as you hear the "pop," stop! Don't push the needle any further into the cavity. But, don't worry if you do. A two-inch needle is long enough to penetrate the pleural cavity but won't go deep enough to do any harm to the lung. Anyway, it's already collapsed.

"Now, place your finger over the opening in the top of the syringe. When Mr. Caldwell begins his intake breath cycle, remove your finger. His lungs are going to expand and put pressure on the air inside his pleural cavity, forcing it out through the needle and the syringe. At the top of his breathing cycle, when the lungs are fully inflated, cover the top of the syringe with your finger. This seals the opening and eliminates more outside air from being drawn back into the cavity as his lungs deflate. This will help begin establishing a negative pressure environment in his pleural cavity. And, that's got to happen before his lung will begin to re-inflate itself."

"OK, I'm going in."

"Tell me when you penetrate the pleural cavity."

"I'm through! I wasn't sure I could get the needle through the lining into the cavity, but I did. And, I heard the pop and the rush of air like you said."

"Great. You're doing fine. Now stay with his breathing rhythm. Open and close the syringe air vent with your finger just as I told you. You should begin to see some improvement in his level of distress almost immediately. His breathing should become easier and more rhythmic and his color should begin to return. He's going to be thirsty, but give him only small sips of water, and keep him awake. There's still a chance he could go into shock. The EMS people will hook him up to an IV when they get there to increase his fluids level and upgrade his electrolytes. I sent one of our thoracic surgeons and an RN with the helicopter; the surgeon will insert a chest tube in Mr. Caldwell's pleural cavity when he gets him aboard the helicopter and will remove your needle and syringe. But, know that what you are doing will probably save his life. There is no way he could have survived this trauma otherwise."

*   *   *

Alec survived the assassination attempt on his life and remained in the hospital in Great Falls, Montana for just over ten days, first in the intensive care ward and then in a private room on the surgical ward. Beth stayed by his side throughout the entire stay.

His would-be assassin, George Henderson, a rogue FBI agent who had *gone off the reservation* when his career began to toilet for the second time, blamed the CIA, especially Alec, for his personal failures and attempted to assassinate him. He would have been successful if not for Beth, but, he died himself when the rocks under his feet gave way as he was about to put a second round into Alec's prone body lying on a rock ledge below him. Henderson plunged over the rock precipice onto a large granite boulder a thousand feet below.

When Alec was discharged, Beth drove him to his small house outside of Lennep, Montana and moved in with him. She was eight-months pregnant when they were married in the small Episcopal Church in White Sulfur Springs. Alec's brothers and sisters and their families attended, as did Alec's long-time personal friend and college roommate, Don Armstrong, Central Intelligence Director. Alec's CIA handler, Rob Downing also attended as did Beth's brother and his wife. It was a very private ceremony. Little did the locals know that such a powerful federal official was in their midst or that a federal agent lived among them.

That was six months ago.

Alec & Beth's Home
North of Lennep, Montana
Wednesday, April 11 – 5:15am

It was already eight o'clock on the East Coast where Rob Downing was sitting at his desk in CIA headquarters in Langley, Virginia, drinking coffee and smoking his fourth cigarette of the day in spite of the *No Smoking* policy imposed by the Company on its headquarters staff several years earlier.

Alec heard the soft ring of the telephone beside his and Beth's bed. *Nobody calls at this time of the morning except someone out on the East Coast who has no concept of the ungodly hour out here*, he said to himself, reaching over Beth to answer before the next ring woke her up. Rob Downing's familiar voice was on the other end of the line.

"What in hell are you calling me for at this time of the morning, Downing. Don't you know that with a baby in the house nobody gets any sleep around here anymore?"

"Yeah. Sorry, Chief. Been there, done that! But I need to talk to you, now, rather than later. By the way, how's Alexander doing? And Beth?"

"Both are fine! The kid is up every four hours to feed, but he's already passed eighteen pounds and growing like a weed. Looks like his mom, but he has my eyes."

"And you, Alec. Are you healed yet?"

"Fit as a fiddle. Walking five miles a day now. Even jogging a bit to get my lung capacity back."

"Are you ready to get back in the saddle? The Company has a need for your expertise down in Mexico, but I don't want to rush your recovery. If Beth can handle your newborn and the household chores for a week or two, we want you to do a little job for us down there. Nothing you can't handle. Nothing too strenuous."

"I'm ready. What's the job?"

"Let me first tell you that a chopper's going to pick you up in a couple of hours, probably around 0700, and take you to Boise for a commercial flight down to Cabo San Lucas. We've already got your reservations set up, knowing you would be anxious to get out of the house.

"A military courier will meet you at the airport in Boise with your papers: passport, and driver's license from New Jersey, credit cards, those sorts of things. He'll have some tapes for you to listen to. They were made by one of the players in this game, but more on that later.

"You're flying commercial this time. But Don did authorize business class. You're going down there as William LaCrosse, an American journalist working for *Hotel Magazine* on an assignment to write an in-depth review of the Melia San Lucas hotel, its accommodations and cuisine. The magazine is for real and is based in Manhattan, so we have you living in Jersey. That cover should keep the police from looking too closely at what you're really doing down there, so, you shouldn't be shadowed. But, if they check you out, *Hotel Magazine* is on board with your cover. Don has a friend on the magazine's staff, and we have used them a few times in the past. Your name and address belong to Don's friend, and should anyone call, they will say he's down in Mexico doing a story."

"O.K. So what am I supposed to be doing down on the Baja?"

"First some background. A guy named Horace McKenzie, who seems to have the ear of President Hunt, put this in motion. He's from a well-to-do banking family in Boston, old money, and was a friend of Hunt's at Harvard years ago. According to this guy, his daughter and some of her Bostonian teenybopper friends flew down to Cabo San Lucas for a spring break holiday away from their parents, and she got snatched."

"Snatched? What do you mean, snatched?"

"Right now it's a kidnapping, but the worst part is, it's doesn't look like a ransom situation. Seems like the word on the streets down there is she's going to be put in the white slavery pipeline and sold to a buyer over in Saudi Arabia as a sex toy. We're told there's a real market for young, pretty, American girls in Cabo with a degree of breeding and a taste of the good life. It's a very selective process, we're told. Only Caucasian girls from money, and evidently McKenzie's daughter fit the bill on this particular buy contract.

"But, this contract is a good thing as well. At least, if it's true, the girl is still alive, and whoever has her will keep her alive until she's unloaded and the payoff made.

"Director Armstrong wanted to brief you on this himself, but he was called away early this morning before your normal wakeup time, so I got the duty. Lucky me! Don met with the President and this McKenzie fellow late yesterday afternoon out at Andrews. McKenzie must be a heavy hitter around D.C. because the President got him a clearance to land at Andrews, and instead of ferrying him over to the White House, Hunt hopped his chopper and met McKenzie out there. You've got to have a lot of juice for Hunt to do that."

"What else do you know about this guy? What did you say his name is, McKenzie?"

"Right. We understand that he and Hunt don't share the same political ideologies now, but they did early on before Hunt switched parties and moved over to Pennsylvania Avenue from Capitol Hill. But, it seems McKenzie has maintained his loyalty to Hunt and Hunt to him. He's been a member of Hunt's Economic Roundtable for a few years, serves on the Board of Governors for the First Federal Reserve Bank up in Boston, and we're told he's slated to be appointed to the Federal Reserve's big board if the Senate approves him. And that's probably a slam-dunk.

"Anyway, McKenzie flew down to Cabo when he got word his daughter was missing and did some intense interviews with his daughter's friends and with the police. Her friends are safely back in Boston now. McKenzie was smart enough to wear a wire and he made the tapes I mentioned earlier. I haven't had a chance to listen to them but we made copies here and our specialists will be going over them this morning. If they find anything that may be interesting, I'll call you down there. You do the same after you've listened to them.

"According to the Director, this McKenzie fellow was really pissed off when they met out at Andrews. You couldn't tell it in his speech, but Don said he was ready to go back down to Cabo and take the whole police force on. He had thought the local police down there would bend over backwards to help him find his daughter, but instead they treated the affair as nothing more than a teenage gringo sowing some wild oats. He was smart enough not to get in their faces, but he knew he was being conned. Evidently he kept his cool and the locals have written him off as a distraught father with nowhere to turn. Boy, are they in for a surprise."

"Could this be just what the locals say it is?"

"Armstrong doesn't think so. McKenzie developed some information that seems to implicate three local boys in his daughter's kidnapping. And, he believes the local police are protecting them. He thinks these boys are involved in more than just the white slave trade. Word on the streets, according to his information, is they also run the drug trade in and around Cabo."

"I didn't know there was any organized drug ring down on the Baja, just some retail street sellers."

"We didn't either. Neither did the DEA. We checked."

"Anything else I should know?"

"Yeah, McKenzie has established a contact for you. He tells the Director he trusts this guy completely. He's the hotel's general manager and he'll pick you up at the airport. His name is Jorge Campo, and McKenzie says you can trust him as well. But, you know better than me that you can't trust anyone in this business. He tells McKenzie he thinks some members of his staff are dirty, so be careful whom you question. The word could get out and blow your cover. Be sure no one is listening to your conversations, and don't trust their telephone system, either. Use the satellite link. Don thinks the police may have bugged the phones. He suspects they're up to their asses in this mess.

"Like I said, this guy, Campo, will meet you at the airport. He knows who you are and the cover you're using. He's agreed to treat you as he would treat anyone who holds his cahonies and the future of his hotel in his hands. Enjoy the royal treatment, Chief. It should be first class all the way."

"Since you've planned my itinerary and done everything short of packing my bags, should I call you when I get down there to ask what I do next, Mother?"

"Screw you, Caldwell. Just go find the girl and bring her home," Rob said, jokenly.

"You never told me why we're getting involved in this. This sounds like a personal favor for the President, and I know Don doesn't hold that toad in any high regard."

"You're right on both counts. The Director thinks he's a poor excuse for a President, but he wants him in his debt. Job security, maybe. I don't really know. Hell man, I'm just the messenger here. Just remember, the clock is running. Don doesn't think this girl has much time left."

"By the way, you never told me anything about the FBI's reaction to Henderson's attempt to take me out up in the mountains. What was their take on the whole sorry mess?"

"The FBI never could figure out why Henderson targeted you, but I understand they got hold of some of his computer records and I was also on his hit list. He must have disliked you more than me, since he went after you first. Anyway, Vanessa's name never came out so her identity is secure. As far as we know, they don't even know she exists. We used her on a job about a month ago, and she walked through it as if she was born with a gun in her hand. I think she rather likes working for the Company. She's a good asset, thanks to your intuition. I would never have thought to try to turn her from the dark side."

"Yeah, she's a good girl. I'll touch base with her sometime. And, I'll be ready when my ride shows up. See you around, Downing. Don't smoke too many of those cancer sticks. I don't want to have to go to Washington to put you in the ground."

"I'll be around to harass you for a long time to come."

Alec smiled, replaced the receiver and lay back down beside Beth who was sleeping like a baby. *This should be interesting*, he thought as he closed his eyes.

*   *   *

Vanessa Van Pelt—CIA Contractor
A brief biography

Vanessa Van Pelt was a Chicago native, raised by well-to-do parents who had pampered her during her childhood, and as she grew into womanhood, sent her to the best finishing schools in the Midwest and on to the halls of one of the nation's most prestigious Ivy League universities. There she met and married her husband who was to become a renown cardiologist whose inquisitive mind led him to the discovery of a non-rejection drug that virtually eliminated the body's rejection of both mechanical heart valves as well as those made from swine and bovine tissue. His drug was now being mass produced by one of Britain's largest pharmaceutical companies, and its worldwide acceptance by the medical profession was making Vanessa and her husband a very rich couple, in addition to the family wealth she had brought to the marriage.

Vanessa had borne two children-a boy and a girl. Tragically, while the couple was living in Baltimore, her infant son was kidnapped by two teenagers who demanded a small ransom to support their drug habits. When the child suffered an asthma attach during his captivity, the kidnappers beat him to death with a baseball bat for fear that his crying would lead to the discovery of what they had done. They buried the child's body in a shallow grave, which was later discovered. The two teenagers confessed to the crime, but an unscrupulous attorney got their case thrown out of court on a technicality. The arresting officers had not read the confessed slayers their Miranda rights.

Over time, Vanessa's sadness turned into a feeling of frustration and ultimately she fell into a state of mental depression due to the loss of her son. She vowed she would gain justice for her slain child, and with a renewed sense of purpose, she began a dedicated regimen of study and practice that gave her the tools she would need to complete the task she had set for herself.

Ultimately, Vanessa orchestrated the deaths of both of the boys, now young men pursuing respectable professional careers, and took their lawyer out as a bonus. Her execution plans were so meticulously carried out that none of the three deaths were ever ruled as homicides. She made sure, however, that the two killers knew only moments before their deaths that they were being executed at the hands of the mother of the child they had kidnapped and bludgeoned to death.

Vanessa enjoyed both the planning and the execution of her newfound talent, and worked her way into the ranks of Chicago's Mafia as a non-family assassin for hire. Who would have ever suspected that a lady considered one of Chicago's most socially respectable citizens was secretly a hired assassin in the employ of the Mafia.

Vanessa had completed three contracts for the family of Chicago's most famous crime boss when she ran up against Alec Caldwell, who was working a case for the CIA that pitted his talents against hers. Alec immediately recognized her exceptional potential as a contract assassin for the Company if she could be turned from the *dark side*, and was able to convince Rob Downing to assist him in her recruitment. Vanessa liked the idea of pursuing her chosen profession as a paid employee of the government, and was persuaded to join the Company as Alec's partner.

*   *   *

Los Cabos International Airport
Cabo San Lucas, Mexico
Wednesday, April 11 – 12:15

The American flight arrived at Los Cabos International on schedule just after noon. Alec stepped off the Boeing 727 into the heat of the Baja sun, shaded his eyes with his hand and walked to the terminal gate entrance. The temperature had already reached 100 degrees, and the heat waves shimmering off the tarmac distorted the images in front of him.

Two members of the Municipal Police, armed with automatic weapons slung over their shoulders, were standing beside the terminal door, smoking cigarettes and looking over the disembarking passengers. They didn't give Alec a second glance. He was sporting a two-day growth of beard, wearing a wrinkled blue blazer and his customary jeans and cowboy boots. His tie was untied and he was carrying two cameras and an oversized briefcase. He was either a businessman or a reporter, certainly not a CIA operative.

Getting through customs at Los Cabos International was a joke. The customs agents were standing aside, smoking and talking among themselves as the throngs of tourists streamed through, none being checked. Alec shook his head and walked over to the luggage area to join the other arriving passengers waiting for the handlers to bring their luggage inside.

"Are you a reporter?" the man, obviously of Spanish descent standing beside him, asked.

"Yes and no." Alec responded, smiling down at the man. He was short, just over 5' 4" with a graying mustache, receding hairline and a potbelly. He looked to be in his mid-forties, and quite out of shape. "I work for a magazine so I go where they tell me to go and write about subjects they tell me to write about. Not a very glamorous job, actually boring at times, but it pays the bills."

"You are *Senor* LaCrosse of *Hotel Magazine*?"

"Uh, yes. I mean*, si*?"

"*Buenas Tardes, Senor.* I'm Jorge Campo, manager of the Melia San Lucus Hotel." He extended his hand. "*Senor* McKenzie asked me to meet you here. I already have your luggage, so you don't have to wait. The hotel has a car for us outside at the taxi ramp and your luggage is there. If you will come with me, *Senor,* I'll drive you to the hotel and get you settled in. The Land Rover will be available for your use whenever you wish. Welcome to Cabo San Lucas, *Senor* LaCrosse."

"*Gracias, Senor* Campo."

The man sitting on the bench just inside the exit doors didn't look at them as Alec and Jorge Campo passed him and strolled out the building. The small camera concealed in the folded newspaper he pretended to read and the small parabolic mic he concealed in his hand

and pointed at the two men, had done their jobs. He would soon be back in the office of the police captain where the pictures would be scanned out of the digital camera and the conversation recorded between the two men would be analyzed. An international search would begin to determine the true identity of the man in the hotel manager's company. Certainly he was not a writer for a snobbish magazine specializing in hotel reviews. But, they would find nothing that would lead them to Alec's true identity or his real reason for being in Mexico.

*　　*　　*

Melia San Lucas Hotel
Cabo San Lucas, Mexico
Wednesday, April 11 – 1:42pm

Alec settled in his penthouse suite that occupied the entire roof of the hotel. In addition to living and dining quarters, the penthouse sported an Olympic size pool and beautiful tropical gardens. He called room service for a bucket of ice and a bottle of water, although the quarters were well stocked with everything he could want in snacks and drinks. It was the code he had been instructed to use if he wanted to see Jorge Campo in his suite. Campo was there in three minutes. Before Campo arrived Alec used a small hand-held electronic device to quickly scan the suite for listening devices. There were none. However, he could tell by the distinct background noise when he lifted the phone receiver that a listening device was monitoring all calls in and out of the suite. He had confirmed this by holding the receiver in front of the television. As he passed the phone in front of the TV, static lines appeared on the screen, confirming that an electronic force was present within the phone. This information could be useful. He felt it wasn't the hotel monitoring his calls since his identity was secure. *Probably the police,* he reasoned. He would use this source to feed false information to the police, keeping them in the dark about his real mission.

Alec had noticed the man sitting on the bench at the airport when he stopped to find his luggage and met Jorge Campo. He knew he was being photographed and his conversation with Campo recorded, but he didn't alert Campo. Without training, he would probably overreact and expose the fact that Alec was aware of the surveillance. Alec had seen the small camera and parabolic microphone as he and Campo walked by the man. He had tried to hide them but he wasn't quick enough. Alec had purposely stayed away from discussing the real reason he was here until out of range of the mic for just that reason. *Probably a cop doing what he was told to do,* Alec thought to himself. *Unless someone slips up on our end, their photos won't do them any good. And if the man were a local cop, they wouldn't know the slightest thing about voice print analysis. Everything the guy collects will have to go to Mexico City to be processed, and that will take days. I'll be long gone before anyone there knew who I am or what I'm doing here.*

Alec knew the local police would follow him at a discreet distance until they could verify his identity as William LaCrosse, feature writer for *Hotel Magazine.* Or worse, discover his real identity. He would let them play their silly little game of hide-and-seek for a while, then lose them when the time was right.

*   *   *

The staff had been alerted that a writer for a magazine would be visiting the hotel for a stay of several days, and what he had to say about the establishment, its food, its accommodations and especially about its staff could mean the difference between the hotel's success and failure. When he was spotted in the company of the hotel general manager, who personally drove him from the airport, the word spread fast. Whatever he asked for, he was to have, no questions asked.

Jorge Campo arrived on the quick, knocked softly on the door and was ushered into the suite by Alec, who had already found the private bar and was drinking a Corona.

"Want a beer, Jorge?"

"*Ningun gracias*, senor. I'm on duty."

They sat on the veranda, overlooking the turquoise waters of the Sea of Cortez. It was late evening, and the sun was setting behind them across the Pacific. With the glass French doors closed, Alec felt his conversation with Jorge Campo would not be overheard or recorded.

"OK, first, let me tell you what I know about this mess, and you can fill in the blanks. The prime suspects in the McKenzie girl's kidnapping are three boys who run a dive shop just off the beach here in Cabo San Lucas. Mr. McKenzie gave us their names and we've been able to identify two of the three. They're from Ville de Bravo, a village just west of Toluca near Mexico City. And, they have extensive arrest and conviction records for petty crimes, mostly robbery and petty larceny. Nothing unusual there, but the interesting part is, since they arrived in Cabo San Lucas, their records have been clean. Not so much as a speeding ticket. Leopards don't change their spots overnight, Jorge. I would bet my last dollar that they're still dirty, but they've bought their way out of their crimes with the local police. That theory substantiates the word that they are protected. Money buys respectability everywhere, Jorge, not just down here. But what I can't understand is why the police protect such petty criminals? It sounds like it goes much deeper than we're seeing on the surface.

"As for the leader of this little group, Antonio Mendez, there isn't a record anywhere, at least not one we can find, and we have the most sophisticated information gathering systems in the world. Plus, we have worldwide cooperation from just about every law enforcement agency. He's supposed to be from the same village as his two buddies, but we can't find any trace of his existence. No birth record, no school records, nothing in the name of Antonio Mendez from there. Our people have spoken with the Federal Agency of Investigation in Mexico City, and even they can't find a trace of his existence. Mendez isn't a family name associated with the village he is supposed to have come from. It's like he doesn't exist. And maybe this Antonio Mendez doesn't. Maybe it's a fictitious name, one he made up to conceal his true identity. But why would he do that? Is he trying to protect someone, his family maybe? But why?"

Alec continued, "So we expanded our search for the Mendez name in a two hundred mile radius and came up with more than five thousand Mendez males. Just under five hundred had the given name, Antonio, but only ninety were in our suspect's age bracket, and all of them were accounted for. None matched the description of our man. We even had a recent picture of this Antonio Mendez but no one the FAI talked with could identify him. So, we're back to the theory that he's using a name he invented to disguise his real identity. We're going to have to find out why. It could mean everything to this operation.

"So, Jorge, what can you add to this?"

"Not much, *Senor.* The streets are quiet. No one is talking. It's like the girl never existed. I have asked those on my staff who I think are on the take from these three gangsters, but they swear they know nothing. I'm afraid they know if word gets around that they have been talking about this kidnapping, they will disappear. Not even my offer of money has loosened their tongues. And these are poor people. They will usually tell me anything I want to know if I offer enough of a reward, but in this case involving these three boys, they will say nothing. They are afraid."

"OK, I expected that. What can you tell me about their movements, their habits, Jorge? Where they go, what they do, who they pal around with, things like that. And routines, what schedules do they generally keep? Are there any patterns they seem to follow?"

"*Si, Senor*, there I can help. They are, how do you say, creatures of habit, I think."

*   *   *

Alec listened carefully to what Jorge told him about the habits of the three young men. He decided to concentrate on the one called Chico since he was the youngest, and consequently would be the most vulnerable. He was seventeen, and under the right circumstances could probably be convinced to give Alec the information he wanted without too much persuasion.

Chico's older brother was twenty-one, and would probably be harder to break. His criminal record was much more extensive than his younger brother's. Although Alec would have liked to interview both brothers, he didn't have the time. The girl had been missing for four days now, and if he didn't act now, they could move her and kill his chances of bringing her home. Also, the longer he stayed in the area, the more the chances of his real identity being discovered increased.

Jorge's information was correct. The one they called Chico left the dive shop just after 5:00 PM, walked to the rear of the shop and got into a white Porsche 911 Turbo, the 480-horse power performance machine that takes you from zero to sixty in 3.7 seconds. At a price tag of around $122,000, it was a little out of the reach of a dive shop employee, unless he had another source of income. And, Chico, like his older brother and Antonio Mendez, had another very lucrative source of income.

Alec decided to put his plan into action the next afternoon, the fifth day of the girl's disappearance. He had rented a Ford panel van from a car rental agency at the airport and would pick it up tomorrow morning. He would have to ditch the cops before then, since he couldn't afford to be associated with the van in case it was discovered before he could have it cleaned up and returned. In the van, he put a folding card table, two folding chairs, a propane lantern, a length of rope, and several blankets, a first-aid kit and a bucket for water that he had asked Jorge to get for him. He also included stainless steel surgical instruments he had purchased at a local drug dispensary. He wouldn't need anything else.

The boy called Chico would be returning from a roll in the hay with his girlfriend late tomorrow afternoon and would stop to see what Alec was doing on the back road to her parent's home. His curiosity would get the best of him when he found Alec on the ground next to the van with blood all over his shirt, as if he had been the victim of a shooting. He wouldn't suspect a set-up for a kidnapping. Chico would be an easy target.

With Jorge's help, Alec had located a vacant building on the outskirts of Cabo San Lucas with a twelve-foot chain-link fence to keep vagrants out. The gate was padlocked, but that wouldn't slow Alec down. The building was made of corrugated metal sheeting and had once been used as a storage warehouse for an area grocery chain, then abandoned several years earlier because of the high crime rate in the immediate area. There were no lights, and no guards-a perfect place to conduct an interrogation.

CHAPTER FIVE

Eastern Cape Road
North of Cabo San Lucas, Mexico
Thursday, April 12 – 5:18pm

ALEC FOLLOWED CHICO out of town on the beautiful Eastern Cape Road leading north along the Sea of Cortez until he turned west into the hills on a little used unnamed dirt road. He didn't immediately follow the boy, but drove past the intersection in case he was watching his back. Alec doubled back about a mile beyond the intersection of the dirt road and retraced his route back to the turn-off. He wanted to be sure he had not been spotted. Jorge had told him the boy would take this road, as he did three times each week to see his girlfriend who lived on an isolated ranch in the hills. Her family lived there and worked as ranch hands. It was the back entrance to the ranch and little used. Jorge had given Alec a detailed map of the roads in the area, and it was clearly marked. The dirt road meandered through the low scrubby hills, presenting Alec with several good locations to spring his trap. It was a perfect place to take the boy down when he came back from his rendezvous with his girlfriend.

Chico's abduction went just as Alec had planned. He had positioned the van across the one-lane dirt road leading to the girl's home, just enough to almost block any vehicle from passing what seemed to be a disabled vehicle. He left the vehicle's front and rear doors open, as though it had been cleaned out, and positioned himself against the front driver's-side tire to wait for the boy's return. He had smeared catsup on the front of his white deliveryman's uniform, and with his head slumped forward, appeared to be dead or seriously injured.

As expected, Chico's Porsche careened down the road at a speed much too fast for the road conditions. Chico saw the disabled van just in time to slide sideways to a stop. He swore and got out of the car just as Alec knew he would. Alec had counted on his being curious. Not that he would care if the driver, bleeding and sprawled beside the front wheel, was alive or dead, but there could be something of value in the van he could steal, maybe the driver's wallet. Alec had also counted on his sense of greed to bring him close enough to spring his trap.

"Hey you stupid gringo, you're in my way. You sleeping or something? You got a lot of blood on you, Hombre. You look pretty messed up. Let's see what you got on you. Maybe a good watch and a few pesos," Chico said, getting out of his Porsche and taking out his switchblade.

As the boy walked over to where Alec was slumped against the wheel, his head down and his eyes almost closed, Alec kicked out as hard as he could, knocking the boy's legs out from under him. Chico screamed, in pain as his left knee buckled and he went down in the dirt, face first. Alec was up in a second, like a snake coiling to strike. He grabbed Chico's head and slammed it into the side of the van. The boy was caught totally off-guard and was out like a light.

Alec quickly tied his ankles and wrists with heavy plastic ties and used duct tape as a gag after stuffing an old rag in the boy's mouth. Although the road was seldom used, someone could come along the road, and he didn't want to have to deal with collateral damage at this stage of his plan, so he worked quickly. He threw the boy into the rear of the van, slammed the rear doors, got in the Porsche and drove it into the brush behind a slight rise beside the road, high enough to hide it from anyone driving by. He covered the car with a camouflage cover he had purchased from an army surplus store earlier in the morning and piled brush over it. Even from the air, it would be impossible to see. Alec took a piece of brush and carefully erased the vehicle's tire tracks in the sandy soil from the edge of the road to the vehicle's hiding place. When he drove away, the scene looked as though nothing had happened there.

*   *   *

Abandoned Warehouse
Cabo San Lucas, Mexico
Thursday, April 12 – 10:30pm

When the boy awoke, he was sitting in a chair in front of a table, his hands and feet still bound, but his gag had been removed, as had his shoes. The only light in the drab, empty warehouse was from the propane lantern on the table in front of him. As he began to focus more clearly, the boy could see Alec sitting quietly across the small table from him. He was looking into his eyes and smiling. On the table next to the lantern were a pair of latex gloves and surgical scissors, the smooth chrome finish reflecting the lantern's light like a mirror. Chico knew what was about to happen. He had been on the other end of similar interrogations before. He was scared, and rightfully so. It wasn't going to be one of his better days.

"I have several questions for you, young man," Alec began, when he felt the boy was fully conscious. Some are simple *"yes or no"* questions. Others are going to require some explanation. You know the answers to all of my questions. But before you give me your answer, you should think about what you're going to say. Right answers have their rewards, wrong answers have their penalties. In every case, the answer you give me is your choice. But, let me point out that the penalties for wrong answers are much more severe than if you tell me the truth. Tell the truth and I'll let you live. Tell me a lie and you will suffer the penalty.

It's simple, really. And, the penalty for a wrong answer is immediate and severe. You won't have the opportunity to change your answer before the penalty is administered, so think carefully before you answer, my young friend. Oh, your refusal to answer a question is considered a wrong answer. You see, young man, I know the answers to most of the questions I will ask you, especially the yes and no questions. So, are you ready?"

"Go to hell, *Gringo*. I ain't gonna tell you nothing." Chico's voice was filled with venom. He tried to spit across the table in Alec's face. Alec only smiled but said nothing, letting the boy feel the moment. He knew the boy was now realizing how helpless and vulnerable he really was.

Alec continued to wait, staring at the boy across the table and smiling. He knew the boy's show of defiance was a cover for the fear he was feeling. He could see it in his eyes. Perspiration had begun to break out on the young man's forehead. Alec waited, letting the severity of the situation continue to play on the young man's mind.

"Not a good sign, young man," Alec finally said. "Don't be so hostile. I could have your *cohunes*, you know. And I might, if you don't lose the attitude. Now, first question: Did you and your brother and Antonio Mendez lure Katherine McKenzie and her friends to a club in Cabo San Lucas on the night of April 14th, and did you three boys drug and kidnap her?"

"To hell with you, old man. I'm going to cut you up in little pieces and feed you to the crabs."

"Suit yourself, son. Oh, that wasn't the correct answer. Sorry."

Alec slowly put on the latex gloves, letting the thought of what would come next play on Chico's sense of fear. He picked up the surgical scissors and held them close to the lantern turning them slowly in its light, as if admiring the precision that went into their making, all the time smiling and shaking his head. He remained silent, letting the severity of the moment continue to sink in. The look in Chico's eyes told him the young man knew what was coming next. He was sweating profusely now. *This isn't going to take as long as I had thought*, Alec said to himself as he stood, the light from the lantern casting shadows across his face.

He moved around the small table to a position behind the boy whose hands were tied behind his back and placed the gag in his mouth and taped it again. Chico turned his head trying to see what Alec was doing, but he couldn't. Alec waited about a minute as the boy squirmed around in the chair, his eyes wide with fear. Alec selected the little finger on Chico's right hand, massaging it gently to help the young man realize what was going to happen next. He quickly severed it at the first joint. The pain was excruciating, running up the young man's arm like a hot poker. He screamed at the top of his lungs, but the sound was not heard outside the building because of the gag and tape over the boy's mouth. He slumped in the chair and was about to pass out when Alec jerked his head back and poured water over his face. Chico was sweating profusely now, and the color was quickly draining from his face. Alec had hoped the boy would not go into shock. A small pool of bright red blood was forming on the concrete floor beside his chair. Alec cut the tie binding Chico's wrists so he could see the damage to his hand and the blood flowing from the wound. He casually walked back around the table, ripping the tape from his mouth and removing the gag. Facing the boy, he dropped his severed finger on the table in front of him, still continuing to smile.

"The penalty for a wrong answer, son. Would you like to try that question again?"

"*Si, Senor,* I will tell you. Yes, we kidnapped her. Antonio put a drug in her drink that made her sick. He told her friends that he would take her to the restroom. My brother and I were to stay with the others so none of them would follow him. Instead of taking her there, he took her out the back door and put her in his car. By that time the drugs had taken effect and she had passed out."

"Good boy, you finally got it right. See, that wasn't so hard, was it? Now, let's move on. Question two, where did you, your brother and Antonio take her? And remember, wrong answers tend to hurt."

"I don't know, *Senor,* honestly. It was dark and I was sitting in the back seat with the girl. She was out cold, but I was watching her, not where we were going."

"Sorry, Chico, wrong answer. You're a slow learner, aren't you? This wasn't the first young American girl you've snatched, but you can damned well bet it's going to by your last." Alec walked back around the table, and was going to put the gag back in his mouth, but Chico kept his mouth closed. Alec took the boy's hand and touched the damaged finger. When he opened his mouth to scream, Alec shoved the gag into his mouth and placed the duct tape over it. He knelt down at Chico's right foot. In one quick motion, Alec severed the boy's little toe. Chico tried to scream, but the gag and tape across his mouth stopped the sound. His eyes, now as big as saucers rolled up into his head and he passed out. But Alec had anticipated that and doused him with cold water from the bucket sitting beside the table. When he raised his head, Alec held the boy's toe in front of his face, and, smiling, chanted, "This little piggy went to market, this little piggy stayed home, this little piggy had roast beef, this little piggy had none. And, this little piggy cried wee, wee, wee all the way home," as he dropped the toe he had just removed from Chico's foot onto the table beside the severed finger.

"Want to play again?"

"No, *por favor, Senor.* I will tell you everything you want to know."

"Good. So let's begin again. Did you and your friends rape the girl?"

"*Si, Senor.* But she was passed out from the drugs Antonio gave her. He has been back to check on her and he says she is all right."

"OK, what are Antonio's plans for her?"

"He has a contract to furnish a young American girl for one of his clients. In Saudi Arabia, I think. This girl is supposed to be what the man is looking for. He is a prince or something. Antonio has furnished him with other American girls in the past. His clients give him descriptions of the girls they want, and we find them among the thousands of tourists who come here. They always pay us in drugs, cocaine mostly. We are supposed to take the girl out to the place where we always meet the drug ship from Panama. We will exchange her for the drugs next Wednesday. The 23rd I think. The drug ship is supposed to deliver her to the buyer."

Damn, I don't have but two days to get her out, Alec thought to himself.

"Only two more questions, Chico, so get them right on the first try. First, who is Antonio Mendez? And remember, no more wrong answers. I don't think you could stand the pain if I had to cut off your big toe. And, I know you know his real identity, so don't be coy with me, son. I don't have time to play games."

"No, *Senor,* please. I will tell you everything. Antonio's real name is Felipe Hernandez Garcia. Do you recognize the name?"

"No, go on."

"He is the son of Jose Manuel Garcia."

"The Minister of Energy? He's the minister's son?"

"*Si, Senor.*"

Well, I'll be damned. No wonder he doesn't want anyone to know his real identity. His family is one of the most respected in Mexico, They would be disgraced if he was caught and his real name came out and was traced back to his father. Hell, his father pretty much controls Mexico's economy. That's a piece of information worth knowing, Alec said to himself.

"OK, last question. Where is she?"

"I will draw you a map, *Senor.* It is difficult to find, but not impossible. The girl is in a shack in the hills. There is no real road to the place, just a path. An old woman lives there. Antonio knows her and she is guarding the girl for him. She has done this for him in the past. No one ever goes there."

"Can we get there with 4-wheel drive?

"*Si,* but it is a very bad road, not even a road, *Senor,* just a path."

"OK, here's a first-aid kit. Bandage your foot and hand. You're going with me."

"Where, *Senor*?"

"To hell if you've lied to me, boy."

* * *

Friday, April 13 – 2:18am

Alec put the boy in the front seat of the panel van parked outside the abandoned warehouse and drove out the gate, stopping to close and lock it before driving away. There was nothing outside the building to suggest anyone had been there recently. He had carefully repacked everything he had brought with him to interrogate Chico and had spent some time cleaning the blood from the warehouse floor. He left no evidence inside that it had been the scene of an intense interrogation. Dust would soon cover everything. Alec was counting on that.

Although the boy had bandaged his hand and foot, blood was beginning to seep through the bandages. Alec covered the bandages with a waterproof material that would prevent blood from getting in the van. Chico was unable to walk on his damaged foot and would need to see a doctor soon to repair the wound Alec had inflicted on him, but that could wait. Time was running out for Miss McKenzie, and she was Alec's top priority. Alec gave Chico a shot of morphine to dull his pain. He needed him awake and alert to guide him to the old woman's isolated shack where the girl was being held.

Alec drove the van to the rendezvous location Jorge had recommended. It was adjacent to a pier used to offload commercial freight next to a customs warehouse in a darkened part of Carbo San Lucas' industrial area. The Land Rover was there as Jorge Campo had promised. Alec left the van for Jorge to pick up the next morning, and had instructed him to wash it, inside and out, and wipe it down to eliminate fingerprints and any trace of blood before returning it to the rental agency the next day. Alec did not replace Chico's gag, but the boy knew if he tried to escape, Alec would kill him without a second thought.

Alec really didn't care if Chico lived or died. Personally, he would have preferred the latter. The boy had lived a life of petty crime before coming to the Baja. Here, he and his brother had met Antonio, and had graduated into a life of criminal activity far worse than their former transgressions. How many lives these boys had ruined with their drugs were too numerous to count. And the families torn apart by the loss of a daughter to their white slavery trade couldn't be measured in terms of the human suffering they had caused. In Alec's sense of right and wrong, running drugs and white slavery-selling young women into bondage-were offences punishable by death, and not necessarily quick and painless. As far as he was concerned, Chico's death wouldn't cause even the slightest ripple on the pool of human consciousness.

*   *   *

Alec drove out of the commercial waterfront district of Cabo San Lucas and onto the dark streets of the city. It was 2:45am, and this part of town was deserted, except for an occasional truck delivering fish and other seafood to restaurants throughout the city beginning to prepare for the onslaught of tourist staying in the hotel district.

To be sure no one was following him, Alec varied his speed as he drove through the city towards the hotel district where he would pick up Highway 1 and head north. On occasion, he would pull the Land Rover over to the curb and shut down the engine, listening and watching for anything out of place, especially a vehicle traveling in his direction. He got out of the vehicle several times in areas where a view of the sky was unobstructed to scan for the presence of aircraft, especially a helicopter, which could be used to track his route. There was no evidence of a tail, either by vehicle or by aircraft, and he knew there would be no one on foot doing surveillances, since not even Jorge knew the route he would be taking to the rendezvous point or his route out of the city.

*　　*　　*

Eastern Cape Road
Baja California Sur, Mexico
Saturday, April 14 – 3:30am

As the boy had suggested, they drove out of Cabo San Lucas on Highway 1, the four-lane Transpeninsular Highway that carries most of the commercial and tourist traffic down the Baja peninsula from Tijuana to Cabo San Lucas. Some thirty-two miles into their trip, just before reaching San Jose del Cabo, they exited onto the Eastern Cape Road that runs along the east coast of the Baja north towards Cape Pulmo. The road was dirt and gravel now, down to two lanes, but easily negotiated.

They had driven for about an hour when Chico pointed to the low hills to their left.

"There, *Senor*! That is where you must go."

Alec pulled over to the left side of the road and killed the engine. They were well south of Cabo Pulmo and the Los Frailes airstrip. The road was flanked on the left by low hills, barren of any vegetation. Beyond the hills, low mountains dotted the horizon. In the light from the stars overhead, the scene reminded Alec of a stark moonscape.

On the right, waves continually rolled into the small cove from the Sea of Cortez, gently lapping at the rock-strewn beach. There was no sign of civilization for miles. No lights anywhere that he could see. They had been on the road for almost two hours and had seen very little traffic since leaving San Jose del Carbo.

The road was dark except for the eerie light cast by the millions of stars overhead. According to Chico, this was the entrance to the path that led to the old woman's shack where Katherine McKenzie was being held. "See those mountains over there?" Chico asked. "The shack is in the hills just before you get there."

Alec stepped out to listen for the presence of another vehicle either behind him on the coast road or in the nearby hills. He heard nothing but the night sounds of a desolate moonscape. Nor did he hear or see any evidence of aerial surveillance. From what he could tell, he and

Chico were the only humans in the immediate area. Using his small LED flashlight, he found the tracks of another vehicle that had left the road about a hundred feet from where he was parked. They disappeared into a flat depression between two small hills. Looking closely, Alec could tell that the depression had been used to gain access into the hill country beyond the highway. He got down on his hands and knees to observe the tire tracks more closely. From the tread design and thrust of the tire prints, he knew they had been made by a vehicle that had been put into four-wheel drive just after leaving the road. He also noted that the tracks were made several days ago, and no one had bothered to try to hide or obliterate them. Chico had mentioned that Antonio had gone back to the cabin to check on the girl a day or so after they had put her there, and Alec reasoned he had made the tracks. *Evidently he isn't concerned that someone might see the tracks and follow them to the old woman's shack,* he thought, as he bent closer to get a better look. *Probably thought the constant winds off of the sea would cover them quickly. Off-road vehicle tracks are seldom visible more than a couple of days out here.*

Alec decided that Carlos was telling the truth. *Trying to cooperate to save his hide,* Alec speculated, smiling.

"Are you absolutely sure this is the place Antonio turned off the highway when you brought the girl out to the old woman's shack?" Alec asked.

"*Si, Signor.* This is the place. The old woman's hut is about five miles into the hills. You will be able to find it without me. Just follow the little path. You can let me out here and I'll catch a ride back. You don't need me to help you anymore."

"Don't think so, huh? Well, guess what, son. You're going with me all the way, and if I can't find your hostage, I'm going to leave you out here in the hills for the coyotes and rattlesnakes to feed on. How long do you think you would last bleeding all over the place? Did you know a pack of coyotes can smell the scent of human blood three miles away?"

"*Por favor, Senor,* don't do that. I will help you find her, but you must get me to a doctor so I don't bleed to death."

"You won't bleed to death, boy, unless we don't find the girl. If we don't, or if she has been harmed any more than the gang rape you confessed to, you will wish I only cut off your finger and your toe. What I will take next, you don't want to even think about."

The three-quarter moon had set earlier in the evening eliminating much of the sky's natural light. But Alec's night vision was excellent, and he could see well enough by the faint starlight. He couldn't afford to use the vehicle's headlights once on the path that meandered through the neighboring hills. They would be easily spotted if the old woman was up or if someone else was guarding the place or looking for him. As he did on the highway, he stopped frequently, killing the engine and listening. All he could hear was the gentle whisper of the wind through the rocky, barren, hills, an occasional pack of coyotes on a distant ridge celebrating their kill, and the scream of a small mammal which had unfortunately been caught out in the open by a winged predator, and was about to become its next meal. *The cycle of life, and death, is never ending*, Alec thought, as he continued his trek into the hills.

When Chico touched his arm, Alec stopped the Land Rover, killed the engine and looked at him. Chico pointed to a hill several hundred yards beyond their position. "The cabin is beyond that hill, *Senor.* You can't see it until you get to the other side of that hill."

"OK, you stay here, boy. I have the keys so you won't be able to drive out of here. And you surely can't walk out with your missing toe, so be nice and you'll survive. Since I trust you just about as far as I can throw you, I'm going to handcuff you to the steering wheel. Oh, if you decide to blow the Rover's horn or flash its lights to warn the old lady, I will come back and cut off your dick, together with your *cahonies*! I don't know how I can be more explicit. I presume you understand my meaning?" Alec said, smiling at the boy.

"*Si Senor,*" I understand," he said, cringing at the thought of losing what he considered his most precious possessions.

* * *

Somewhere in the hills west of the Eastern Cape Road
Baja California Sur, Mexico
Saturday, April 14 – 4:38am

Alec crept slowly around the low hill, straining his eyes to find the old woman's cabin. It was still dark, but dawn would be breaking over the eastern horizon soon. He was using his small 10 x 26 Steiner Predator binoculars. Even though they were designed with superior light gathering power, there was very little light to magnify.

The shack was just where Chico had said it was, a couple of hundred yards beyond, sitting on the side of a ravine that divided two high hills. It looked like it was about to collapse, but it was an excellent location to view the lower surrounding hills and several possible approaches. It was tucked in the ravine to make it less conspicuous. It would have been impossible to spot in the dark environment except for light from the stars overhead reflecting off a few places on the tin roof that had not rusted. There were no lights in the cabin and Alec assumed the old woman was asleep because of the lateness of the hour. His eyes had adjusted to the lack of light as he picked his way through the rocks and boulders. Chico had reluctantly told him about the phone Antonio had left for the old woman to use if anything happened he needed to know about.

Alec had thought that a means of communication would have been established between the old woman and the kidnappers, but he didn't realize cellular service would be available this far out into the hills. A threat to remove another finger was all it took to get that piece of information. He was not surprised that, with no cellular towers in the area, the kidnappers would use a satellite activated phone system. His first task had to be to find and hide the device.

Alec had slowly made his way up the hill to the rear of the shack when he first heard the noise. It sounded like an animal in pain. He knew immediately it was the girl. He stopped and dropped to a crouching position. He didn't know if the old woman was armed or not, and the sound could have awakened her. He remained motionless, but when no light or additional sounds, except the girl's moans, came from the cabin, he resumed his slow recon of the outside of the building and the area surrounding it.

The phone was where Chico had said it was, lying on an overturned rusty bucket. He picked it up, turned it off so it would not ring and wake the old woman, and placed it out of sight under the bucket. *If I get the girl out I'll tell the boy where the phone is so he can call in some help to get him out before he bleeds to death,* he said to himself. If the boy can muster the strength to make it to the shack from the Rover, the old woman could take care of his wounded hand and foot before his friends get here. Alec figured the other two boys would come as soon as Chico called, but he and the girl would be long gone by then. *They can get him to a hospital, and that will slow down their search for the girl and me. What the hell, he could die of gangrene for all I care.*

Alec continued his recon of the outside of the shack. When he reached the only door he turned his flashlight on, removed his Glock automatic from his waistband at the small of his back, and kicked the door into the building. The old woman had been sleeping on a straw mattress in a corner of the room. It was pitch dark inside, but Alec detected the woman's movement and bathed her in the light of his flashlight. She had a kitchen knife in her hand but was not able to move quickly enough to surprise Alec.

"Move and you'll die," he shouted in Spanish, hoping she would understand his threat. "Drop the knife or I'll shoot you now," he screamed. He hoped his voice would frighten her into submission. She was old and weak, and Alec knew she would have little desire to resist.

The old woman dropped the knife on the stone floor and cowered in the corner on her mattress, a look of mortal fear on her face. Alec knew he would not have any problems with her. He retrieved the knife and moved through the doorway into the second room of the shack.

"Are you Katherine McKenzie?" He asked.

The girl was on the floor, sitting in the corner of the room. She was dressed in a loose fitting black garment that covered her body, much like those worn by Moslem women. Like the old woman, she cowered when Alec bathed her in the strong beam of his LED flashlight. Her face was dirty and her blond hair was in tangles.

"Who are you?" she asked.

"Your father sent me to bring you home. He's been worried about you, Kathy. Can you stand up?"

Kathryn McKenzie burst into tears. "Where is my daddy?" she sobbed.

"He's not here just yet. I'll call him when we get back to civilization and you can talk to him. Do you know if the old woman has any weapons around here other than the kitchen knife she wanted to use on me?"

"I don't think so, but I really don't know. She has a phone though. She is supposed to call if there is any trouble."

"OK, I found that. We're leaving here now. I have a vehicle down the wash a ways. Here, let me help you up. You can lean on me. It's dark and we have to be careful not to fall in these rocks."

"I can't walk out there. They took my shoes," she explained.

"That's all right. I'll carry you on my back."

Katherine McKenzie put her arms around Alec's neck, kissed him on the cheek and clung to him for as long as she could. Her relief to finally be free and with someone who would protect her from her nightmare of the past week was so overwhelming that she again began to cry. Alec stroked her dirty hair and held her close, but he really didn't know what he should do. He knew that they had to leave as soon as possible. With Chico missing, his brother and Antonio could become suspicious and be on their way to the shack even now.

"I don't think I've ever been so happy to see anyone who didn't want to harm me as I am to see you. They were going to sell me to someone over in Saudi Arabia, they said. Why would anyone do something like that to someone else? This has been the worst time of my life. I just can't believe people would do something like that. I want my daddy," she cried.

"I wish I could tell you this has all been a bad dream, Kathy, but unfortunately I can't. From what I understand, you match the description of a young girl a member of the royal family over in Saudi Arabia wants, and evidently he felt his money could buy him anything or anybody, regardless of the human misery it could cause.

"You can bet this isn't over yet. From what I understand, your father said he's not going to turn this thing loose until he extracts his pound of flesh from the people who did this to you. What your dad doesn't seem to realize is that people are sold into bondage every day, mostly young girls for sexual reasons, but in many cases, young boys are the victims. The people who provide this white slavery service are well organized and as ruthless as they come. They will stop at nothing to have their way. Your father will be up against a formidable foe. I just hope he has the resources and the guts to stand up to the challenge."

"Are you going to help him?"

"I don't know. I just might! You just relax now and let me pick my way down through these rocks. The vehicle is about a half mile down this path.

"The boy who calls himself Chico is handcuffed to the steering wheel. I'm going to put you in the back seat, and I don't want you to say anything to him. I know you would like to scratch his eyes out, but just do as I say. We want to make as little noise as possible. His friends may be on their way here now, and I don't want to give our position away if we see them coming first."

"I promise."

Alec eased his way back down the hill to where he had driven the van off of the road into some low growing brush and placed Kathy in the back seat. "I want you to lie down and stay quiet, please."

"I see you're still here," he said to the boy handcuffed to the steering wheel. "Did you have a nice quiet time while I was away? Alec unlocked the handcuffs, setting the boy free.

"Get out!"

"Please, *Senor.* Take me with you. I need to go to a hospital."

"Get out, or I will drag you out. If you want someone to make the pain go away, you had better start crawling up to that old lady's cabin. I put the cell phone under the bucket and covered it with rocks so she couldn't find it and call your friends. If you make it that far you can call them to come and get you. By that time we should already be out of Mexico. Just be glad I don't shoot you right here, or better yet, open up your wounds so the pack of wolves I heard earlier can smell your blood and use you for their next meal."

"Please, *Senor*. I beg you."

CHAPTER SIX

El Conquistador Hotel
San José del Cabo
Baja California Sur, Mexico
Saturday, April 14 – 8:28am

“**I**'VE GOT HER, Rob! Miss McKenzie is safe, at least for the moment. But she's not out of danger. We've got to get her out of Mexico as quickly as possible.”

Alec was using his Falcon II AN/PRC-117F Manpack radio, linked to CIA headquarters through three of the U.S. military's twelve communications satellites on stationary orbit over North America. It was the only means of long distance communications he trusted, and it was in wide use for command, control and communications within all the branches of the military. The CIA had given his unit to him for a mission several years earlier in which his team had saved the life of the Queen of England.

Too many countries have the technology to intercept and listen to just about any unprotected satellite conversation they please. The NSA has earned the reputation of spying on U.S. citizens through monitoring telephone conversations in and out of the U.S. and is already in hot water with Congress. Alec couldn't afford the risk of anyone knowing his location except Rob Downing, his personal friend and CIA handler who had sent him down to Mexico to rescue Kathy McKenzie.

"Great, Alec. Brief me, please."

"Your Intel assessment was right, Rob. The three men who operate the dive shop in Cabo lured the girl and her friends to a local club, then drugged and kidnapped her. They were going to sell her to a Saudi royal family member who had put out a contract for a young white American girl. Evidently Kathy matched the description they had. I found her stashed in the hills up the coast from San Jose. The boys were waiting for their payoff and her overseas ride out of there."

"I'm sure that kind of information wasn't readily available on the streets down there, Alec. Any bodies lying around that we need to make go away?"

"Not really. It was a clean sweep when my snitch and I parted company. After I found the girl, I turned him loose. I suspect he got word to his brother after I left him in the hills, and things went downhill from there. He was the younger of the two brothers who worked for one Antonio Mendez. When I cut him loose, he was suffering a little pain from the fact that he didn't have all the fingers and toes he had when we sat down for our little chat. But, he would have healed if given half a chance."

"What do you mean, would have?"

"Unfortunately for him, his buddies found out he had dropped a dime on them. I'm not sure who took him out, probably not his older brother, but someone did, and the police have me pegged for the deed. His throat was cut, and he had a bullet in his head, so the papers say. Someone left him in an alley behind a hotel on the Resort Corridor. I'm sure the cops are in this as deep as the dive shop boys, probably deeper. They may have even finished him off. If so, they're part of the cover-up to frame me for Chico's murder. The only person who maybe could tie us together is the old woman who was guarding Kathy. But, she never saw Chico and me together. If someone else did, the police could possibly make a case against me."

"Do they have a weapon?"

"No, but they could manufacture one if they wanted to.

"According to the boy, the white slavery payoff is always in drugs, primarily large quantities of cocaine. In the two hundred plus kilo range. At 2.2 pounds per kilo, that's at least four hundred pounds of uncut coke, Rob. Just think what the street value for that much coke would be, especially after it's cut. That's big business down here as you well know, and I doubt the dive shop kids have the operations needed to cut the stuff, repackage it, and move that much product up the Transpeninsular Highway to the U.S. border. I seriously doubt they have the connections needed to get the drugs to the wholesale distributors up in Texas and California. At best, that's a day and a half drive if someone's at the wheel twenty-four hours. And that's along a two-lane road through some desolate country. Nothing commercial runs that highway without some sort of protection. So, the police have to be involved, probably running the whole show from down here, but having the boys fronting for them in case there's some backlash. And, if you ask me, this probably goes up the food chain much higher than the local police. It's just too big to be local.

"And from what research I've been able to dig up on the Internet, none of the seven major Mexican drug cartels operates on the Baja except the Tijuana cartel, and their bases of operation are in the towns just south of the U.S. border. However, I would suspect this operation has some ties to that group. These people would need them if they're getting their product across the border safely.

"Now, here's the big surprise, Rob. Our dive shop owner, Antonio Mendez, is really the son of Mexico's Oil Minister, one Jose Manual Garcia. He's using a fictitious name down here."

"Well, I'll be damned! Do you think the kid's father is involved in this?"

"Don't know, but it's an interesting thought," Alec replied. "Maybe worth pursuing!"

"Well, if he is, it could be hard to prove. He's reported to be a pretty sharp politician. Even been mentioned as a possible candidate for the

Mexican presidency. It's a fact that he's tight with President Montoya. And it's rumored he's also close to President Hunt, so who knows."

"Yeah, if he's a political friend of Hunts, there's a good chance he could be dirty."

"You're right, it is an interesting thought to play around with," Downing commented. "I'll see if I can dig up anything. If I do, I'll let you know."

"What do you think about McKenzie? He's supposed to be a very close friend of the President. Could he be part of this?"

"No, we checked him out. His friendship with Hunt goes back to their college days at Harvard. McKenzie is a died-in-the-wool Republican, and Hunt is a bleeding liberal Democrat. They're on opposite ends of the political spectrum, and we know they don't share political philosophies. McKenzie always contributes heavily to Hunt's campaigns, but he's never stumped for him. We think he has considerable personal integrity, and if it came to a showdown, McKenzie would do the right thing. But, he's smart enough to know that money can buy power, influence, and accessibility, and we just may be able to use his accessibility to the White House down the road.

"So, Alec, what's your situation now?"

"Dicey at best! The local police know I'm not a feature writer for some travel and leisure magazine, so I'm on the run, so to speak. They've got an APB out on me for Chico's murder. Even have a couple of traffic checkpoints on the Resort Corridor between Cabo and San Jose, so they're out there looking hard. At least that's what the local news is reporting.

"Miss McKenzie and I are keeping a low profile for now, but I think the word has gone up the food chain that I may know more than these people want me to know about their operations. If I slip through their net, their little operation could just fall apart. Chico didn't tell me much about their operation here, but I think they suspect he spilled his guts, and that's why he was killed. From what Jorge Campo told me, there're a lot of folks out there looking for me. This isn't just a kidnapping, Rob, it's a well organized, and well—funded organization that, if we take it down, could take a lot of important people with it. The white slavery scam is just the tip of the iceberg. It's just a sideline for the dive shop boys."

"So, where are you?"

"Right now, we're holed up in the El Conquistador resort hotel in San Jose, since the police are all over the Melia. It's off the beach a couple of blocks. But, we can't stay here forever. And the two remaining dive shop boys have a pretty big reward out for both of us. They evidently have a lot of juice with the cops, and you know as well as I that down here people will sell their mothers for the right amount of money, so it's just a matter of time."

"How are you keeping your cover with so much heat out there?"

"Before I left home I packed a couple of extra passports and corresponding credit cards, just in case I needed them. I'm registered under a fictitious name matching the passport, and Miss McKenzie is posing as my daughter. All I had to do was fill in the blanks and paste in a digital picture I took of her and it all looks legitimate. The passport I'm using is right out of your documents section, so it will pass inspection with no problem. Since Kathy is my daughter, the customs people will hardly give her a second look.

"I think we're safe for the moment, but someone's going to recognize us once the police get pictures of us in circulation. I've let my beard grow some, and we've cut and dyed her hair dark brown. Bought her some glasses too, so that will buy us a little more time, but probably not much."

"OK, how do you want us to get you out?"

"Los Cabos International is out. Campo tells me the cops are all over it. And with the APB out on me, security is tight as a drum. He tells me everybody leaving here is scrutinized and their papers checked as never before. We would never get through their net. So, I want Kathy's father involved. Contact him with the good news about his daughter, and have him fly down to Tucson, Arizona. That's where you get back in the picture. We need a small plane to fly out of Tucson to make the extraction. Use one of the agency's four-place single engine aircraft-one registered to one of your dummy corporations so there won't be a link to the Company or to McKenzie. It needs to be fast and have the fuel range you'll need for the return trip, since there's no fuel at the airstrip. And, the plane has to be able to land on a 2,800-foot dirt strip. The pilot should be one of your agents just to maintain confidentiality and for protection, if needed. McKenzie should be the only passenger. His face and name aren't known in the area where we'll make the extraction, but his brief encounter with the police in Cabo concerning his missing daughter may have generated some photos. So, give him a bogus passport in the name of Michael Dempsey, and give him a mustache, just in case. The name will dovetail with the names Kathy and I are using, and he'll only need the disguise if the authorities are onto us. This should be a *stop and go* extraction, Rob, but if the police aren't there, I may want to spend a few minutes with McKenzie.

"Rob, your pilot's destination is a public airstrip just west of the village of Los Frailes. It's at least 625 miles from Tucson, and the last part is over the Sea of Cortez. I would refuel in Ciudad Obregon just to be safe. It's another 300 miles to Los Frailes and there's no fixed base operator or fuel there. You should be able to get back to Ciudad Obregon to refuel on your return leg. I don't have the GPS coordinates, but since Los Frailes is a public airstrip, they should be published. The strip isn't paved, but at just 35 feet above sea level, a small aircraft shouldn't have any trouble getting off before it reaches the end of the runway, even with four people on board. It's used primarily by private aircraft bringing people out of the U.S. to visit their vacation properties, and it's a pretty desolate area around there.

"Remember, I want to talk to McKenzie if time permits, so be sure he's on board. He and the pilot only, just in case I decide to fly back with them. Kathy will definitely fly back, but if this thing goes as I suspect it will, I just may hang around here for awhile."

"Why would you want to hang around down there when so much heat is on you?"

"Idle curiosity, I suppose. Nothing official. At least not yet."

"OK, that's your call. Just lie low for now and we'll start working on this right away. Call me again in two hours. I should have an aircraft lined up by then and know the approximate ETA. Tomorrow is the target date to do this."

*　*　*

At precisely 10:30am Alec made the call. Rob Downing picked up on the first ring.

"It's a go, Alec," was Rob's response. "We're going to use a four-place single engine Beachcraft Baron G 58 and fly it out of Tucson like you suggested. At sea level, it has a takeoff requirement of only 2,300 feet, so we can get in and out of your airstrip without any trouble, even with four people and some extra fuel on board.

"Our pilot and Mr. McKenzie will clear customs in Tucson, but you'll need to stamp the passport his daughter is using with U.S. exit and Mexican entrance stamps so she can use it when she returns through Tucson. I'm presuming she no longer has her real one. You'll also need to stamp their passports with Mexico exit stamps before they leave Los Frailes unless they have a customs agent there. I presume you have your visa kit with you."

"Affirmative."

"Good. Their ETA at Las Frailes is 6:30 tomorrow morning, unless bad weather slows them down. We would have liked to do this earlier, if possible, less visual contact with the locals and the police if they're watching. But, first light will have to do. According to published information, Las Frailes airstrip has radio signal activated landing lights, so if we're early, we can land safely if we need to use them.

"I know you'll check out the area thoroughly before our aircraft gets there, but the pilot will do that also, so you'll see him circle the area a couple of times. If he sees anything suspicious, he'll contact you. You do the same. But if it appears to be a go, no contact with the aircraft, please. Let's keep this as quiet as possible. Someone could be monitoring the aircraft communications channels."

*   *   *

Sunday, April 15 – 12:28am

Just after midnight, Alec and Kathy, dressed in stylish jogging togs, slipped out onto the hotel's loading dock at the rear of the resort, eased off the platform onto the concrete drive and began jogging around the resort's perimeter road as though they were finishing up a late night jog before retiring to their villa. They jogged through the guests' parking lot several times before he spotted the car. They stopped, seemingly out of breath, holding their knees. Alec knelt as though he was retying one of his running shoes and confirmed the license plate on a dark blue compact Ford he had rented from the Alamo agency in downtown San Jose with one of the credit cards issued in the name he was currently using. He had asked the agent for the license number when he placed the order, and was able to pick it out of the dozens of cars parked in the well-lighted lot. The rental agency had delivered the car to the parking lot the day before as he had requested. *Now, if the keys are on top of the right rear tire, we can get out of here,* he thought.

Before approaching the car, Alec and Kathy continued their jog around the guest parking lot. He was looking for anything out of place: a car with its lights out and someone behind the wheel, the presence of a police car or van, or anyone looking at the two of them with more than a casual interest. The lot was empty of people and nothing aroused his suspicions.

Alec retrieved the keys, unlocked the car and started the engine. He waited for a few moments, the windows down so he could hear if the engine of another car in the lot was started. There was no other sound. He checked his watch. It was now 1:27am He drove through the resort complex with the lights off, stopping occasionally to listen for anything unusual. At the resort's main entrance he switched on the lights and headed north. He avoided the Transpeninsular Highway because of possible police patrols. Instead, he took a side road to the Eastern Cape Road that runs along the Sea of Cortez. It would be slower, but safer. He was some three hours from the Las Frailes airstrip and wanted to be there at least two hours before the planned ETA of the aircraft that would take Kathy away from her terrible nightmare. He needed that much time to do a thorough recon of the airstrip, the village and the surrounding area.

*　　*　　*

Kathy had spoken with her father twice since her rescue, and after a couple of nights of rest, she seemed to be focused on her survival and avoiding the Mexican police who had now posted an All Points Bulletin on both her and on Alec. Posters of the two were everywhere, and hotel employees up and down the Grand Strand had been interviewed. No one seemed to be talking until a large reward had been offered. Then, tips began coming into the police stations in record numbers. It was time to get out of Mexico.

As usual, the Eastern Cape Road was deserted. Alec was a little concerned that driving on a road usually devoid of traffic at this time of the morning would arouse suspicions if they were spotted, especially in the villages and small towns where he would have to slow his speed. But at this hour there were very few people up and about, and there was really no other route to his destination.

*　　*　　*

Before Alec left San José, he used his laptop computer to connect with the Internet and logged onto the Google Earth website. He maneuvered the world map to Mexico's Baja peninsula and brought the Las Frailes airstrip general area onto the screen. He brought the area in as close as he could before the satellite-generated photo began losing its focus, and looked for roads not on the topo and road maps he had picked up in San Jose. There was only one he could identify in the Las Frailes area. The unchartered road was hardly a path that wound through the hills for about three miles. Located at its terminus was what appeared to be a dilapidated building with a rusting tin roof, partially ripped away by the winds off the Sea of Cortez. Alec rotated the image to a near horizontal plain to get a better view of the lay of the land. He could see the building in the low hills. It was about two hundred feet above and overlooking the airstrip, situated on a higher plane, an excellent vantage point for someone watching the airstrip. Alec couldn't tell if a vehicle could be hidden in the building, but its existence caused him concern. *If a vehicle could be hidden there, the police could launch a surprise attack on him after the plane had landed. I've got to check that out,* he said to himself as he downloaded a copy of the topo and printed out a hard copy for reference later.

*   *   *

Alec's recon of the Los Frailes area had yielded nothing. He and Kathy had driven slowly through the village several times. At 4:30am no one was stirring, not even the dogs and chickens that would wonder aimlessly through the dirt streets and alleys during the hot day, scratching fleas and pecking at flies.

Before approaching the airstrip, Alec checked the topo and found the location where the dirt path up into the hills intersected with the unpaved road leading into the village. He decided to drive up through the hills towards the dilapidated building but stopped far enough away so his presence would not arouse anyone who might be there. "Kathy, you stay in the car. Get some shuteye while I take a look around. But, lock the doors when I leave."

Alec walked the last half-mile towards the building, stopping often to listen to the night sounds. He heard nothing that would arouse his suspicion, so he continued until the old building was in sight. All seemed quiet as he moved cautiously forward until he was standing at the side of the building. Still no sound from inside. As he looked in, he saw two green eyes staring at him. The guttural growl caught him by surprise. He jumped back just in time to avoid a coyote that sailed out the paneless window he was looking through. The animal jumped past Alec and scrambled into the hills. Alec was so startled he had to sit down for a minute to regain his composure.

As soon as he could steady his legs, Alec decided to use his flashlight to see why a coyote would be in the building. As he entered, he knew. Someone had been there, and he had been there recently. The coyote had been feeding on food scraps the person, or persons, had left behind. Food wrappers were everywhere as though the occupants had been there for several days. He walked over to the side of the building facing the village of Las Frailes and the airstrip below. The window and its frame were missing. But, using his flashlight, he discovered scrape marks on the window ledge.

Looks like someone has rested a rifle here, probably going through targeting exercises, checking distances and winds, Alec said to himself.

In addition, he found tire tracks outside the building as though a vehicle had been driven there and parked. He found where the vehicle had been turned around and driven out of the area. The convincing evidence were the many boot prints outside the building. Alec recognized them right away as military issue, the type issued to Mexico's police S.W.A.T. teams.

"*Damn, they have this airstrip covered. I didn't count on that. And this is a hell of a place to set up a sniper's nest. It overlooks the airstrip, and it's just over a mile away. If they have a qualified sniper, he could make a kill shot from up here. Or better yet, take out the aircraft and strand the occupants in his field of fire. They've been here, probably a daylight observation post. So, they'll be back, and soon. I've got to get Kathy out of here in a hurry,*" he swore, as he left the building and raced back to the car.

Alec knocked on the car window. He had tried to open the door and realized Kathy had locked them as he had instructed. Kathy awoke to the knock and quickly opened the door for him. She had been asleep in the passenger's seat.

"We're in trouble, Kathy. The police have been watching the airstrip from a building overlooking the area. It's a perfect place to set up a sniper's post. We've got to contact the aircraft and turn it around so it doesn't get caught in an ambush."

"What are we going to do?" she asked, a worried look on her face.

"I'll have to think that through. In the meantime, we'll have to lie low today and have the plane come in under cover of darkness later. Right now, we have to get out of here before these guys return," he said, as he started the car's engine and spun the vehicle around facing the way they had come in. He floored the accelerator, spinning the car's front wheels and throwing up a dense cloud of dust and stones, not worrying about the police noticing that someone else had been there. *Maybe they aren't savvy in looking for signs*, he thought.

The airport, a long strip of reddish brown dirt running north and south, was deserted. The single building adjacent to the airstrip, once a small hangar covered on three sides with rusting corrugated tin, was on its last legs. The roof was supported by wooden poles fashioned from small trees that, at one time, must have grown near the airport. The building was empty and the windsock, which had once flown on a pole above the hangar, was in tatters. An old 1950s model Cessna 140 was parked next to the building. The cowling covering its small Continental engine was wrapped with an old piece of torn canvas. Both tires had dry rotted and were flat. Alec thrust his hand under the canvas. The engine was cold. No one had bothered to start it in a long time. Just as a precaution, he opened the drain cock on the fuel line. Both wing tanks were dry.

"Well, we won't be able to use this old relic to get out of here, Kathy. Chances are the police have the roads around here covered as well," Alec said as he took his radio out of the car's trunk and began setting it up on the car's hood.

*   *   *

Alec keyed the mic and dialed Rob Downing's special office number that he had memorized years ago.

Rob picked up his phone on the first ring. "That you, Alec?"

Alec didn't mince words. "Rob, turn the plane around. You've got to do it now. Their ETA here is just five minutes away. The airstrip has been compromised. If the plane gets here after daylight, there's a good possibility a sniper could take the plane out and put the pilot and McKenzie in his field of fire. I found the sniper's nest a few minutes ago, and it's getting light here, so I think the snipers will be back at their post in a few minutes to do their daylight recon. Looks like they leave at night; probably stay in the village. Kathy and I are going to make ourselves scarce. We'll hide out on one of the deserted beaches south of here today, and contact you once we get out of here and set up somewhere else. Just keep the plane out of here until I can think this through."

"OK, I'm on it. Just hope I can reach them in time. Call me as soon as you can."

Alec cut his conversation with Rob Downing, threw the Man Pak into the back seat and drove out past the old hangar building with its tattered windsock and away from the village. As he intersected the main road, he heard the sound of a single engine aircraft approaching from the northeast.

"Damn, I was too late. That's our ride," he said to Kathy, pointing towards the aircraft approaching the airstrip. As he entered the Coast Road he turned south and lost sight of the plane.

Kathy had her head out of the window, looking at the plane. "Alec," she yelled. "It's turning, it's turning! It's going away from the airstrip, back over the water. Your friend must have gotten in touch with the pilot in time."

Alec sank into his seat. *Saved again*, he said to himself. *Now to get the hell out of here.*

Dawn was just breaking as the aircraft, flying low over the water, melted into the haze rising from the Sea of Cortez.

*   *   *

Alec drove south towards a small village with a name he couldn't pronounce. They had driven through it on their way to Las Frailes earlier in the morning. Kathy picked up some food at the local cantina, and they exited the main road down towards the beach, and spent the better part of the day there until just before dark. "We're going to sneak back into Las Frailes, and watch for the snipers to drive out the road leading from their nest. If we can find out where they're staying, we can get a better handle on their routine. With luck, we may be able to disable their ride, which would give us a better change of getting you out of here tomorrow. In the meantime, I'm going to call Rob again."

*   *   *

CIA Headquarters—Langley, Virginia
Sunday, April 15 – 8:45am

"You and Miss McKenzie OK?"

"Yeah, we got out just in time. I stopped up the road from the airstrip and parked behind a building to watch the old shack up in the hills the police were using to stake out the airstrip. They set up about ten minutes after we left the airport. They were on their way up when I was talking to you, but I don't think they were on station when the plane was on its final. They probably didn't see it, maybe didn't hear it, but I don't know that.

"I think there may be two of them. One of the guys is using a long rifle and the other is his spotter. It's a sweet setup they have up there, Rob. They have a perfect view of the airstrip. If they can make the shot, they can disable the plane. The pilot and McKenzie won't stand a chance. Like shooting ducks in a barrel

"And, man, you were cutting it close with the plane. They were on final, flaps and landing gear down when they turned back out to sea. They would have landed just as the snipers were setting up. We just got lucky again, Rob."

"That's the name of the game, Alec. Stay one step ahead of your enemy. Then turn around and burn their butts! By the way, the Beachcraft 's safe, gassed up and ready to go. It'll have enough fuel on board to haul the four of you back to the States if you want a ride."

"I'll probably hang around down here for a while. I haven't made that decision yet."

"OK. So, how do you want to play this?"

"Let's just wait and see. I left a couple of bricks of C-4 with an electronic detonator under an old rusted out bucket below the window they're using to scope out the airport. If our ride is late and they're there when it lands, I'll detonate the charge and blow them to hell. In the meantime, we'll just wait and see what happens."

* * *

Los Frales Airstrip
Baja California Sur, Mexico
Monday, April 16—Dawn

The eastern sky was just beginning to turn a light shade of pink when the Beachcraft Baron approached the Los Frales airstrip for the second time in as many days. The pilot was flying at an altitude of five hundred feet to stay below any radar surveillance the Mexicans could be using in the area. At about half a mile out, Alec picked up the aircraft in his binoculars and verified its "N" number. As it approached the strip, the pilot began to execute a slow clockwise circular pattern to check out the area before committing to his final approach. A counter-clockwise approach was the internationally recognized approved landing pattern, but the opposite had been agreed upon to help Alec identify the plane as the CIA aircraft if there was other air traffic in the area using the airstrip.

The pattern took the aircraft out over the dilapidated building Alec had identified as the sniper's nest. Had the pilot seen anything suspicious, he would have flown out of the area and contacted Alec so he could leave as well. He saw nothing out of the ordinary, and on his second pass, lined up with the runway, lowered the landing gear and dialed in sufficient flaps to float the aircraft onto the airstrip in a three-point landing just beyond the barrier marking the leading edge of the runway. The time was five-thirty in the morning, an hour before the sniper pair would leave the little hotel and make their way up to their nest if they maintained their routine. The aircraft's pilot had a half hour before Alec's party had to be out of there.

*　　*　　*

Alec had parked the Ford inside the dilapidated hangar and was waiting with Kathy when the pilot taxied the Baron up to them, locked the wheel brakes, and idled the aircraft's single engine. Alec ran his index finger across his throat as a sign for the pilot to shut down the engine.

"Welcome to Mexico," Alec called, as Horace McKenzie stepped out of the aircraft and ran to his daughter who had been standing beside Alec, but was now crying and running towards her father.

"I didn't think I would ever see you again," she sobbed, looking up at him. "They told me they were going to sell me to somebody so I could have his babies. Oh, Daddy, it was so horrible. I wanted to die!"

"You're safe now, Sweetheart. I need to talk to this man for a minute. I want you to go get in the plane. I'll be there in a minute and we'll be on our way home. Mom and the boys are waiting for us in Tucson. Go on, Honey. I'll be right there."

*　　*　　*

"I'm Horace McKenzie," he said extending his hand to Alec. "Thank you for saving my daughter's life. I'll always be in your debt, Sir. Please tell me your name. Your director wouldn't tell me who you are."

Alec grasped McKenzie's hand in friendship. "I'm sorry Mr. McKenzie. I could give you a name, but it wouldn't be mine. Maybe sometime in the future we can be formally introduced. You know, Mr. McKenzie, Kathy was close to being a statistic."

"What do you mean, a statistic?"

"Well, Sir, there are some 800,000 people sold into bondage each year, mostly children, and all against their wills except those too young to know what is happening to them. I'm just glad we were able to get Kathy out before it was too late. We were lucky, Sir.

"You have a wonderful daughter there, Mr. McKenzie. She's been through a lot these last few days. More than you could ever imagine. Maybe she'll tell you everything, but I suspect she will be too embarrassed to do that right away. Give her plenty of space and time. If she loves you like I think she does, she'll confide in you some day. In the meantime, love her and keep her safe."

"I will, Sir. Thank you. There's something I would like for you to do for me. I'm not sure if what I'm about to ask you should be an official CIA act. That would be up to you and those to whom you answer. If not, I'm willing to pay you whatever you want as an independent contractor to get this done."

"Please continue, Mr. McKenzie."

"What I want is simple, Sir. I want the people who inflicted this dastardly thing on Kathy to go away. I don't care how it's done, I just want it done. Do you understand the anguish I'm going through to ask someone to kill other human beings for me? It's a vengeful act, I know, and it goes against everything I have lived by through my entire life. I have anguished over this ever since Kathy was lost. But I know in my heart, I won't be able to let this thing go until it's done. Does that make sense to you, Sir?"

"Yes, it does, Mr. McKenzie. But, you have no idea how big this situation is, and how dangerous it could be. The boys who kidnapped Kathy to sell her to some Saudi prince are just the tip of the iceberg. They are small time players, pawns in a much larger chess game than you could possibly imagine exists. Big time drugs are involved, and the people playing this game may go all the way to the top of the Mexican government."

"Sir, pardon my vulgarity, but I don't give a rat's ass who down here in Mexico is involved. I want the rats' nest cleaned out and I have two important assets I can offer you. First, all the money you need to get this job done, and second, I have influence with important people in very high places in the U.S. I can bring this influence to bear if and when you ask. All you need to do is to ask!"

"Mr. McKenzie, I really appreciate your offer. It's very tempting, but I work for the U.S. government and I have to do what I'm told to do. I believe we have exposed a major drug syndicate down here, one we and the DEA didn't know existed, and I believe if we can shut it down, it will go a long way in stemming the rising flood of illegal drugs moving across our border with Mexico. The DEA is doing all they can, but they're spread too thin. I'm going to suggest to my superiors that we move on this situation immediately. But, the only reason I'm telling you this is I need a pledge from you that you will not mention any of this to anyone. Trust me on this. You trusted me with the life of your daughter. Now, extend that trust to what we've just talked about."

"You have my word, Sir. And I don't give my word lightly. He handed Alec his business card. This is my private number. It's a secure phone. Call me, day or night if I can help. As I said, you have all of my assets and my influence available to you anytime. And I mean that sincerely."

*   *   *

Monday, April 16 – 8:35am

The Beachcraft Baron powered off the runway into the cool morning air, trailing a stream of red dust in its prop wash as the first rays of the sun broke across the tranquil turquoise waters of the Sea of Cortez. *Kathy is safely on her way home, probably in the arms of her father, a powerful man, and a possible ally I may need to call on,* Alec thought as he walked towards the old hangar building. He had decided to stay behind: "To take care of business," he had said.

Alec backed the Ford out and began to retrace his route back to San Jose. The sun was just climbing above the distant horizon now, and the air was beginning to warm. It was going to be another hot day on the Baja.

As Alec turned out of the dirt road into the airstrip the side-view mirror on the driver's side exploded, sending mirror glass chards through the open window into his face. His sunglasses saved his eyes, but the glass exploded with such force that small pieces were driven into his cheeks and forehead. Alec instinctively ducked to a position that allowed him to barely see the road ahead through the steering wheel and floored the accelerator. He glanced up at the old shack on the hill above the airstrip as he roared down the road at full throttle. For only a split second, he noticed a reflection of the sun on something at the side of the cabin.

"It's the sniper. They must have just gotten there and saw the plant take off, but weren't ready to take the shot they wanted, so they decided to try to take me out," he said out loud. "Damned lucky the car was moving when he fired. Otherwise, I probably wouldn't have my head attached to my body. Think I'll finish this little game before this guy gets lucky." At that moment a round penetrated the windshield and embedded in the seat next to him, only six inches right of Alec's shoulder. Damn, he's pretty good, especially since I'm hauling ass!"

The windshield took another round, also off target, before Alec could reach over to the glove compartment, open the door, and take out the electronic detonator. He pushed the button on the small black box and instantly, the old shack that had served as the sniper's nest just moments ago, was reduced to a pile of rubble, splintered by the blast of the C-4 Alec had hidden under an old rusted out bucket he had placed just below the shack's window.

I would drive up there to see how many pieces the sniper and his spotter were blown into, but I just don't have the time. Plus, I don't need any locals seeing me and identifying me later. Unless someone goes up there, it's going be a while before those guy's remains are discovered. I guess the buzzards will eventually get someone's attention, Alec thought as he sped away from the village of Los Frailes.

*   *   *

El Conquistador Hotel
San José del Cabo, Baja California Sur, Mexico
Monday, April 16 – 11:45am

"Rob, by now I'm sure you've heard from your pilot. I presume they made it back to Tucson."

"They did. Your young friend and her father landed there several hours ago and immediately boarded his jet for Boston. I'm told her mother and two older brothers were there to meet them. I would think they're in Washington by now."

"Washington?"

"Yeah. Armstrong tells me McKenzie is planning to stop in D.C. to personally thank the President for sending you down to rescue his daughter."

"Damn. That's not good. I hope he doesn't mention I stayed down here to look into the possible drug trade connected to his daughter's kidnapping."

"Why?"

"The close ties between Hunt and President Montoya are well documented, Rob. You know Don doesn't trust either one of them, especially Hunt. No telling where Hunt's allegiance might lie if giving me up would benefit him personally."

"Good point, but that's a long shot, Alec."

"Yeah, you're probably right. But I don't like loose ends when it comes to my life, and that's a loose end."

"And speaking of loose ends, I buttoned one up for the good guys this morning. Kathy and her dad has just lifted off and I was leaving when evidently the sniper and his spotter arrived at their hide up on the hill and began taking pot shots at me. The cabin isn't there anymore and neither are the two men who had been sent there to stop me from getting Kathy back home."

"Good, chalk one up for us. And, I'm glad you're still with us. It's too late now to contact McKenzie, but I'll make a discreet call when he's back in Boston, and if he mentioned it, I'll let you know so you can watch your back. You have enough heat on you as it is.

"Anyway, everything else seems to be in good order regarding the McKenzie affair. The President asked Don to handle this for his friend, and you did just that. Hunt is in the director's debt, especially since this had to be done *off the books,* so to speak.

"But, it's you I'm concerned about, Alec. With this possible leak by McKenzie, do you think it wise for you to remain down there? We've made some inquiries and you're right, the police have a murder warrant out on you. They're saying you killed the young man who told you where you could find McKenzie's daughter. They don't know who you are or where you are. At least they didn't when the information reached me several hours ago. They don't know you work for us either. So they really don't know who they're looking for, or what your motives were. But, if they catch you, I'm sure they'll use every means available to them to find out. We could pull you out in a matter of hours, Alec. Think it over."

"What these people don't know is how much the boy told me during his interrogation. I suspect that has them scared, because they don't know how much he knew. Hell, I had no idea the amount of drugs coming ashore here on the Baja and being funneled up the coast to the U.S. It wasn't until after I found Kathy and turned the boy loose so he could call in some medical help for himself that I realized the quantity of cocaine he was talking about was far more than would be associated with a simple white slave exchange. He didn't elaborate on the drug side of the equation, and it didn't dawn on me until later that there was such a disparity between what he and his two friends were doing and the cocaine they were getting in exchange. I'm sure the boy didn't know what the drugs were worth. I did a quick mental calculation, and damn, the uncut value was in the millions, far in excess of what a white slavery contract would normally bring in today's market. Cut the stuff and get it ready for shipment to the wholesalers in El Centro and the value skyrockets. And that's the value before it gets to the retailers in L.A. and is cut again, then repackaged for sale on the streets. Sure, there're a lot of fingers in the pie, but the street value is staggering.

"So, here's my take on the situation down here. As far as these three boys are concerned, I guess I should say two boys now, they're just unsuspecting pawns in a game much bigger than they realize. They're the risk takers. They're expendable. They go out to meet the drug boat every week, generally at night, according to my source. They pick up the drugs and bring them back to Cabo San Lucas in their yacht the same night, and hold the stuff until they're told to make the drop. They then deliver the drugs to someone else, always at night, and always in a safe area. Their contact is a low-level, but trustworthy flunky in the organization. He's also expendable. The boys are paid in drugs and that ends their involvement. Except, they use the drugs given to them in the payoff to support the retail drug trade they've developed in Cabo San Lucas and San José del Cabo. That's where their real money comes from. The kidnapping and selling of young white girls is just a means to an end for them.

"So, where's the risk, you ask? It's in the pick-up and delivery timeline. If they were caught with the drugs, picked up by the Coast Guard for instance, they would have no idea who's running the game or where the money comes from for the drug delivery payoff. The real drug runners aren't caught because their identities aren't known that far down the organization's chain of command. They are never seen. They just fade into the night and begin operations again as soon as another supply is available. And there are always guys like Antonio Mendez and his friends who want in on the action because they think they're too smart to get caught, and the payoff is too big to ignore. Dumb!"

"Plausible, Alec, but who iced the boy, and how did you get framed for the kill?"

"Probably the police, or at least those members of the force who are a part of this operation. I suspect when the boy crawled up to the old woman's shack and found the phone, the first person he called was his brother or Antonio. They probably came out and got him, but then they had to tell the police who were working with them that the girl had escaped. When the police learned that someone from the outside was involved, and the boy had given her up, they panicked. They didn't know how much he had talked, or who he was talking to, so they started sweating him. He probably told them the truth, which was that he told me next to nothing about the drugs, but I doubt they believed him and kept torturing him until he died. Then they slit his throat and dumped him behind a hotel on the Resort Corridor and decided to have me take the fall. And, there was logic in their plan. I was the last person to see him outside of his immediate circle of friends, I waylaid him and interrogated him and cut off his finger and toe. They just did the rest and blamed me. Fortunately for me, they don't know who I am. That makes it even more convenient. Blame an unknown, end of story!"

"Sounds like you got yourself in a world of hurt, my friend!"

"Well, maybe not. Why would I dump the body in the hotel district? If I had iced the boy, wouldn't it be more logical for me to leave him in that God forsaken moonscape where the old woman lived and let the coyotes feed on him? Any logical judge would certainly see the rationale for that argument."

"Maybe so, but if you're caught, who says you'll even see a judge? And even then, who says the judge would be logical, or even honest."

"Point taken. I'll stay low for a while until this blows over. You know they're going to stop looking after awhile."

"For your sake, I hope so. Let me know if we need to get you out of there. You know the drill if it has to be a surprise party!"

CHAPTER SEVEN

Rob Downing's Office
CIA Headquarters, Langley, Virginia
Thursday, April 19 – 7:33pm

"ROB, MR. CALDWELL'S transmitter just went active!"

"What? When?"

"Caldwell's transmitter just . . ."

"I know what you said, Jim. When did it activate?"

"Six minutes ago, Sir. Signal Control says it went active at 3:27, Cabo time, 7:27 here." Rob Downing's senior assistant had burst into his office and picked up the in-house phone on Rob's desk with its "active" light blinking red.

"Control is on the line now, Sir. When they first intercepted Alec's signal, they tried to contact him. No response. They think the transmitters were triggered on purpose."

"Damn. Is the signal stationary?"

"Yes, Sir. Here, Control wants to talk to you." Jim Crowder tried to hand the phone to Rob.

"Where is he?"

"There're trying to triangulate the signal now."

"How long before they get a fix?"

"They say they should have a fix in seven to nine minutes."

"Are both transmitters active?"

"Just a second." Jim Crowder spoke softly into the phone. "Yes, Sir. Control confirms the second transmitter went active within forty-five seconds of receiving the first signal."

"Which transmitter was activated first?"

"Why?"

"Don't answer my question with a question, Jim. Which one?"

"The transmitter embedded in the grips of his Glock, Sir."

"OK. That tells us Alec knew he would have to give up his weapon so he activated its transmitter first. He must have been in a situation with no time to execute an escape plan. If he had activated the transmitter in his radio first, we would have known he was planning an escape and would be taking his weapon with him. If the transmitter in the weapon had not been activated, we would assume he had either been killed, or had escaped. It's a sequence code we use in the field, Jim."

"I didn't know, Sir."

"Of course you didn't. Not many here know his codes and their sequences. I suspect by allowing himself to be taken peacefully, he's trying to buy as much time as he can. He knows we'll pick up his distress signals. We're going to go with that scenario for now.

"And Jim, stay on the line with Control. They don't have to talk to me. I've got to make another call. But, I want to know if and when the signals begin to move. I know they're going to triangulate, but tell them he was probably in the El Conquistador hotel in San José del Cabo on Mexico's Baja peninsula. That will give them a starting point and speed up the location process."

The door to Rob's office was still open. "Helen," he yelled. "Get me General Hollins at Special Operations Command South. I think he's at Homestead Air Reserve Base just out of Miami. Tell him we have an Alpha One Alert. I need to speak with him now!"

Twenty-seven seconds later Helen said, "Sir, General Hollins is on your secure line."

Rob grabbed the phone. "Leon, where are you?"

"Good afternoon to you too, Rob. It's been awhile. I'm in the air somewhere over Virginia. The big boys have a Joint Chief's meeting at the White House, and I've been ordered to attend. Evidently whatever they have up their sleeves is going to involve Southern Command.

"An Alpha One Alert, you say! Sounds serious enough. How can I help?"

"It is, Leon. One of our agents has gone missing down in Mexico. We think he's been taken down."

"Rob, you know Mexico isn't in our area of focus. All of South and Central America and the Caribbean islands are, but Mexico is supposed to be *hands off*. Another one of Hunt's dictates."

"I know, Leon. We're not supposed to be down there either, and we aren't, at least not officially, but Hunt asked us to go and we went. Now one of my men is missing and I'm asking you to help us."

"Well, since you put it like that. Do you know if he's alive or not?"

"We're not sure. We're waiting to see if his transmitter signal begins to move. If so, he's probably still alive."

"So how did he get caught? Do you have a leak over there, or did he just get sloppy?"

"This guy doesn't get sloppy, Leon. He works *off the books* for us, so to speak, and he knows he can't afford to get caught. He's a former field agent, and one of the best. Maybe even the best."

"OK, then it sounds like you have a leak."

"Not in this agency. Only our director, my senior assistant, and I knew he was in Mexico or what he was doing down there. He went down there to rescue a girl who had gotten caught up in a white slavery ring. We didn't know any particulars about the girl's kidnapping until he got there and had a conversation with a local who was a part of the organization. That's when he learned about a major drug connection not involving any of the known Mexican cartels. So if we have a leak, it's in the White House. No telling how many people over there knew about this mission."

"Knowing how you fellows do things, I suspect he's down there without the Mexicans knowing he's there. Can you go to the Mexican authorities to negotiate a release?"

"Unfortunately, no. As I said, we initially sent him down there on an unofficial mission to rescue a young lady who had gotten caught up in the white slavery trade that operates out of Cabo San Lucas. He got her out, but decided to stay and investigate what appears to be a major operation picking up drugs out in the Sea of Cortez and running them up the Baja peninsula into California. From the amount of cocaine moving through that area, it's probably something you folks may have an interest in. We checked with the DEA and the Drug Intelligence Center, and they didn't even know it exists. So, we agreed to let our man stay and see what he could develop for them. Never know when you may need to call in a favor with the DEA."

"That's for sure. If you aren't using the Mexican government to get your boy out, I have to assume you think there may be some involvement up the political ladder."

"That's affirmative. And we don't know how far up it might go, to the top possibly. The operation seems to be too big to just be local. We're sure the locals are involved, but we think it goes much higher than that. One of the people involved in both the drugs and white slavery aspects of the operation is the son of Mexico's Oil Minister. He's using a false name, so we assume he doesn't want his family's name to surface. With that link, his father may be involved, and there's only one other person down there who outranks him. Get my point?"

"Loud and clear! How did you guys get involved in this anyway? Rescuing damsels in distress isn't usually a part of your bag of tricks."

"That's true. The President asked Don Armstrong to send someone down to pull the girl out. Nothing official, just a favor for one of his personal friends and well-heeled supporters. I asked Armstrong why he agreed, and he told me he had the President's promise that doing this would go a long way in our appropriations battle with Congress. The President told Don that if the CIA got her out, he would use his considerable influence with Congress when they begin talking about budgets later this year. You know as well as I that the Democrats are itching to cut our budget, as well as yours."

"I'm very much aware of that, my friend. But I also know Hunt rarely honors his promises unless there's something in it for him, personally."

"True, I suspect this McKenzie fellow whose daughter got caught up in this mess will be beholden to him for a long time. Hunt will take credit for saving her life. I'm sure this is going to cost this guy dearly some day."

"Can't Hunt intercede for your man? From what I hear, he's pretty chummy with President Montoya."

"That's the problem, Leon. This thing may just go all the way up to the top of their political ladder. If it does, our agent's identity would be exposed and he would probably just disappear. And if it's leaked that he is CIA, that would be one hell of an embarrassment for Hunt if the Mexicans wanted to capitalize on that piece of propaganda. Hell, he may even be getting a piece of this action. I wouldn't put it past him."

"Good point, Rob. OK, I should be free around noon tomorrow. I'll change my plans and stay over a day longer in D.C. and I'll drive out to Langley tomorrow afternoon. We can discuss this in more detail then. In the meantime, I'll ask my people down at Southern Command headquarters to put together a scenario we can chew on tomorrow when we get together. I'm also going to get Bill Cook over at Bragg involved. I'm thinking we may need his expertise, maybe some of his boys."

"Thanks, Leon. I knew I could count on you. So, you're thinking about bringing Delta into this?"

"Don't know at this point. Bill will tell me if it's something he thinks his people should get involved in. I suspect it'll be a joint effort, since our people in Special Operations Command know the country and have a shitpot full of reconnaissance information on that area. I'll make a call to a friend of mine over in our Joint Interagency Task Force and have their J2 Directorate take a *look-see.* See you tomorrow."

*   *   *

El Conquistador Hotel
San José del Cabo,
Baja California Sur, Mexico
Thursday, April 19 – 1:57pm

"Who is it?" Alec was responding to a soft knock on the door of his suite at the El Conquistador hotel.

"Room service, Sir."

The response sounded an alarm in Alec's subconscious. He hadn't ordered room service, and immediately realized he had been exposed. Someone had recognized him even with his disguise and forged passport, which he had been required to use when buying his and Kathy's running togs with one of his credit cards issued in his bogus name. *The police probably have my photo from the shots taken by the plain clothes cop at the airport when I flew down*, he thought. *The store clerk must have seen a resemblance in my new passport photo to the APB sheet the cops have been circulating. But how could they have traced me here? The only person who knows my location is Rob.* Alec thought a moment. *Damn, Kathy knows, and I bet she told her father, and he told the President. I'm screwed.*

Alec looked around the suite for an escape route. There was none. He had counted on evading the police, if necessary, by leaving his suite by way of the pool area. The heavy curtains on the French doors leading to the pool were open, and through the closed sheers he could see several men dressed in uniforms standing outside. They were all looking up in the direction of his suite. People around the pool were beginning to notice. He knew they were members of the special police and were covering his escape route.

"Go away, I didn't order room service," he shouted, stalling for time as he activated one of the miniature transmitters, a special GPS tracking device the CIA had planted under the grips of his Glock automatic. Alec knew that when he did so, the Company would know his mission had been compromised and would spring into action. He was counting on the police taking the weapon wherever they took him. The transmitter would emit a signal that would be picked up by satellites overhead, triangulated and pinpoint his location, or at least, the location of his handgun.

But he knew the transmitter might soon be discovered. The police wouldn't be so stupid as not to think he had an emergency means of contacting those who had sent him on his mission to find the girl, but he hoped the transmitter would remain active until he was taken to where they would conduct his interrogation. It was a long shot and he needed a backup, but he didn't have one. Time was running out. He had to stall for time until the extraction team could get to him.

"Open the door, Mr. Dempsey, or should I address you as Mr. LaCrosse, or whoever you are today. You have ten seconds or we'll break the door down and drag you out."

Well now, this seems to be an educated man, Alec reasoned. *He'll be less likely to do something rash, like shoot me in the head before he gets the information he wants.*

Alec decided to let them work for their prize. He activated the second transmitter hidden in his Man Pak radio and laid it on the coffee table. He sat down in one of the overstuffed chairs beside the fireplace in the living room, faced the massive door and waited. If the police were going to break the door down, it would take some time. He smiled at the thought.

He didn't have to wait long. A key turned in the lock and the door suddenly swung open, slamming against the inner wall. Five men, dressed in full SWAT gear, rushed into the room, automatic weapons at the ready. Alec immediately recognized their insignias as a specialty division of the Federal Judicial Police, an organization once noted as much for its involvement in criminal activities as they were in combating organized crime.

Alec continued to smile, but slowly raised his arms above his head to indicate he was unarmed and would not resist. He had laid his Glock .45 caliber automatic on the coffee table in front of him with the slide open and the clip removed. His special radio was also on the table. He wanted to be sure the police took both items when they left. But Alec didn't stand as three of the SWAT team grabbed him and threw him to the floor, binding his hands behind his back with a heavy plastic tie as the other two team members went from room to room searching for anyone else who might be in the suite.

Alec recognized the plastic tie as being identical to the one used to bind Kathy's hands and feet. *That can't be a coincidence*, he thought.

"Mr. LaCrosse, or Mr. Dempsey. We know neither of these is your real name. Would you like to tell me just who you are, or are you going to force us to learn your true identity the hard way?" The man, dressed in an immaculate dark blue suit, spoke perfect English. Alec knew he was not the run-of-the-mill undercover cop he had expected to see come through the door following his storm troopers.

"Your command of the English language tells me you were educated north of the border, Sir. Would that be correct?" Alec was stalling for time.

"True enough, Sir. I was raised in Tucson and attended Arizona State on an academic scholarship. My parents were dirt poor so I had to get a scholarship if I was going to rise above my upbringing. My mother cleaned the houses of the gringos and my father picked vegetables for the truck farmers outside Tucson until he died in a lettuce field of a heat stroke. I was seventeen, and since I was born in the United States, I was allowed to stay, but when my father died, my mother was deported. They were illegal aliens, as your people call them, bogus green cards. The people for whom she had worked like a slave all her life didn't even bother to come to her defense when she was put on a bus and driven over the border. They just began looking for someone else to do their dirty laundry and clean their dirty houses. She died several weeks later. I swore I would never live under the thumb of the gringos, and after graduating I proudly walked back into Mexico, renounced my U.S. citizenship and enrolled in the Mexican police academy in Mexico City.

"My specialty, Mr. whoever-you-are, is interrogation. And, I must say, I am very good at it. I work for the Center for Research and National Security. We deal principally in intelligence matters. Being here is a real vacation for me, you know. I normally work out of Mexico City, but you must be someone very special for my superiors to send me all the way over here to the Baja to visit with you."

Or, what they think I know about their little drug game has some people high up the food chain pretty worried that their game just may come unglued, Alec thought as he continued to smile at the man.

"Get him up, Gentlemen. Let's take him out through the pool entrance so we don't alarm the other guests. And release the ties on his wrists, but bind them in front. Our exit will look more socially acceptable if he's cuffed with his hands in front. And, drape his coat over his wrists so no one will suspect he's our prisoner. This is a very up-scale resort hotel, and we don't want anyone asking questions about an American being led away in handcuffs by police dressed in full combat SWAT uniforms. It could give the resort a bad name."

"You are very considerate, Sir. What shall I call you?" Alec asked.

"I'm not sure my name is important to you, Mr. LaCrosse. I'm afraid you won't be around long enough to be able to use it for any real purpose."

"Humor me, please. I may have heard of you."

"I doubt that, Sir. Very few people know me. Yes, there are many who may know of me, rumors mostly, but my identity is a well-kept secret. I apologize if you think me rude, Sir, but anonymity is very important in my line of work."

"So, where are you taking me?"

"Let's not discuss that, Mr. LaCrosse. People may be listening. Your people, that is." The man turned to one of the uniformed SWAT officers. "Sergeant, take his gun with you, but leave the radio. If there is a bug, he has already activated it, and it's probably in his radio. We don't want this man's people knowing where we're going, do we?"

Alec continued to smile. *It's working,* he thought.

*   *   *

Rob Downing's Office
CIA Headquarters
Langley, Virginia
Thursday, April 19 – 4:43pm

"Rob, the signal's beginning to move." Downing's senior assistant, Jim Crowder, had remained in his office during his telephone conversation with General Hollins, monitoring communications with Alec's control section.

"Both signals?"

"No, Sir. Just one. The transmitter in Mr. Caldwell's weapon."

"OK. Looks like they're on the move and taking Alec's weapon with them. How about the signal from the transmitter in the radio?"

"Stationary, Sir. No movement."

"OK. That's good and bad."

"What do you mean, good and bad?"

"Bad, in that it reduces our ability to stay on these people by fifty percent. Two signals are always better than one. Let's just hope we don't lose the signal from the transmitter in the weapon."

"And good, Sir?"

"Yes. By leaving the radio behind, the likelihood of their finding the transmitter in the weapon is reduced by the same margin. If they had been smart and carried the radio with them, they could have found the bug, and would have been alerted to the possibility of there being other signaling devices hidden elsewhere, like in his Glock. But without the radio, no one would ever suspect that a tracking device would be hidden under the grip covers, especially in a standard-issue weapon. So they have no leads as to who he is or what he does. May even be an independent contractor hired by the girl's father to get her out. Regardless of who they may think he is, or for whom they may think he works, his chances of survival are very limited if we don't get him out fast.

"What has Control established as the take-down position, and where's the weapon going?"

"You were right, Rob. They've pinpointed the location to the living room of Alec's suite in the El Conquistador hotel. The radio's transmitter signal remained there, but the weapon's signal began to move while you were on the phone with General Hollins.

"Control has a detailed map overlay of the resort, and the signal initially began moving at a walking pace out of what appears to be Alec's pool exit towards the parking lot. Once whoever has the weapon is outside, we may be able to get a satellite image of the number of people involved, and possibly be able to identify Alec if he's with them. Unfortunately, we just don't have enough time, nor do we have any UAVs down there to generate real-time streaming photos.

"The good news is, when you mentioned where Mr. Caldwell was staying, Control contacted the National Security Administration. They have a Signal Intelligence satellite in stationary orbit over that part of Mexico, and its visible area covers the lower portion of the Baja. They were working with DEA on drug smuggling down there some time ago, but lately they haven't been asked to do any imaging in that part of Mexico. So, the bird has been in "sleep mode" for several months. They're powering it up now and are repositioning it to take continuous photos of the San José and Cabo San Lucas areas. It should be up and running in a matter of minutes.

"They're telling us that the photo resolution of the pics produced by the new digital cameras they've installed on these birds has really been enhanced since the incidence in North Africa where the Marines took out the Hezbollah camp for us. They can now read images as small as the numbers on a credit card. If they have the bird operational by the time whoever is carrying the weapon makes it out of the hotel, they should be able to see how many people are involved and possibly determine who they are. We've already given them the frequency our bug is transmitting on and they've linked it to their satellite, which will automatically track the signal as it takes continuous photos.

"The bad news is there's a lag-time of about seven minutes between the time a photo is taken and the time it reaches the National Photographic Interpretation Center. It's digital now, but it's not instantaneous. Space time lag I suspect. But, the NPIC is on board with us and we're setting up a video/audio conference center downstairs to view the photos when they come in on a real time basis."

"Good work, Jim. Let's see what happens!"

* * *

El Conquistador Hotel
San José del Cabo,
Baja California Sur, Mexico
Thursday, April 19 – 2:43pm

Alec was escorted out of his suite by two of the SWAT team members, his hands cuffed in front of him, two of the team members holding him by his upper arms. The cuffs weren't visible under his coat draped over his hands. The other three members of the SWAT team walked in front, their automatic weapons strapped across their chests, their right hands on the trigger guards. Their black facemasks gave them the ominous look of terrorists.

The interrogator, who had engaged Alec in conversation when he was taken down, walked several steps behind, his fingers laced behind his back. His head was bowed as though he was in deep thought and he wore sunglasses. He wasn't sure if anyone was watching from space, but to protect his identity he kept his head bowed as he followed Alec and his two guards. Alec couldn't see the man. If he had, he would have known what he was doing. The man's suspicions were correct!

They walked by the ornate pool and out the gate into the surrounding courtyard on a path that led through a beautifully landscaped area of palm trees and tropical flowers. They continued on to the parking area and placed Alec in the rear of a black unmarked Chevrolet van. The interrogator moved past the group and walked over to a white Lincoln Town Car. The rear door was being held open for him by a uniformed person sporting an automatic pistol strapped to his left side in a quick-release shoulder holster.

*   *   *

Space – Far Above San Jose del Cabo
23 deg. 03' 55.85" N & 109 deg. 40' 40.12" W

The NSA's spy satellite, anchored in stationary orbit over the Mexican Baja, had been repositioned and was now powered up and fully operational. The first digital photographs of events below were flowing in and were being patched through the National Photographic Interpretation Center in Arlington, Virginia to CIA headquarters in Langley. There was a seven-minute space-time delay.

*   *   *

Situation Room 13-B
CIA Headquarters
Langley, Virginia
Thursday, April 19 – 5:15pm

"There they are, Rob!"

"You're right. Focus on that group of people over there on the left side of the pool. Even though it's a still photo, you can tell they're walking. Looks like they're heading towards one of the exits leading out to the parking area. They certainly aren't dressed to be hanging out around the pool like the other people down there. I think they're wearing some kind of uniforms. Their headgear and facemasks suggest they're either terrorists or a SWAT team. My money is on SWAT.

"Get in tight on those three people, please. The one in the middle is dressed differently. He's in civilian clothes. That could be Alec. I think the other two are holding him by his arms. Nobody walks that close together. And look at the guy in the middle. His hands are together in front of him like they're cuffed. Nobody walks with his hands out like that unless they're cuffed. That's got to be Alec. Can you get in closer? We need to identify him, please."

"Sorry, Sir. That's the best resolution we can get on this shot. Any closer and we lose resolution. The pic gets too fuzzy to do us any good. Maybe we can get closer in this next series."

Another photo flashed on the screen. "Good. That's great. That looks like Alec in the middle, all right. See, he's looking up to give us as much of a facial shot as we can get from overhead. He knows we're up here. Look at that nose, that's Alec. I would bet my life on it," Downing exclaimed. "And whoever has him is hustling him out of the hotel. They're going to take him somewhere to question him. For God's sake don't lose him. And Jim, contact Director Armstrong and tell him we know where Alec is. He'll know why you called. It's personal.

"OK. Now focus on that guy walking behind them? He's part of that group, probably the leader. He's dressed in a suit, not a uniform like the others, and he has his head down like he's trying to hide his identity in case someone is watching from above. Smart move. Get in tight on him too. We need to know who he is! His identity could tell us a lot about just how far up the political ladder this thing goes. If I had to guess, he's probably not local.

"Jim, get a blow-up of that guy in the suit over to the FBI. Tell them we think he may be either a Mexican government official or someone connected to their current administration. See if they can identify him from the photo. If they have a jacket on him, ask them to send it over electronically. Tell them it's a priority request, ASAP please. And check our files also. Something about him seems familiar, but I can't put my finger on it."

*   *   *

El Conquistador Hotel
San José del Cabo,
Baja California Sur, Mexico
Thursday, April 19 – 2:51pm

The van sped out of the parking area of the El Conquistador luxury hotel in San José del Cabo and headed northwest into the older part of the inner city. The white Lincoln Town Car took up a position behind the van and a second van, also black, without identification markings on its sides, fell in behind the Lincoln.

The spy satellite was taking continuous pictures of the area, sending them down from space to the Virginia countryside, one by one, where each was scrutinized by Rob Downing and select members of his special operations section assembled around the teleconference setup.

*   *   *

Situation Room 13-B
CIA Headquarters
Langley, Virginia
Thursday, April 19 – 2:55pm

"Where do you think they're heading, Jim?"

"Looks like they're going into the old part of San José."

"OK, what do we know about that part of town?"

"Well, Sir, we have a detailed map of the town as it is today. Back in the early seventeen hundreds it was just a Jesuit mission. The Spanish saw the area as a vital military outpost, and later set up a presidio there to house and protect their soldiers from Indians and English pirates, but in the mid-19th century, they turned it over to the Mexican nationals. Most of the town's architecture is eighteenth century. The area was little more than a military outpost, a backwater, until the nineteen seventies when it gained the reputation for some of the best marlin fishing in the world. When the "Sun and Sand" set began invading the area, San José grew, almost overnight, to what it is today, over 40,000 residents."

"Thanks for the history lesson, Jim, You sound like the damned Chamber of Commerce. That's not what I had in mind. If Alec is being taken into the old part of town, where would they be taking him?"

"Sorry, Sir. The only building in old town that could be used to imprison someone is the presidio. It's really the only structure in that part of town that seems plausible. It's in a run-down area where most of the buildings are in poor condition at best."

"Tell me about this presidio."

"Better yet, a picture is worth a thousand words, Rob. Here's a satellite photo of what it looks like today." Jim handed Rob Downing an 8 x 10 black and white digitally enhanced photo. "Note the walls. They're massive. They're more than ten feet thick, and the moat was built to protect the Spanish soldiers from attacks from the local Indians. No water in it now, just trash. See the open courtyard inside. It's surrounded by that high stone wall in an octagon shape. Rooms are built into the wall, accessible only from inside the fortress. They're only eight feet deep, which is why the wall appears to be so thick. They originally housed the soldiers, but could easily be used now as holding cells or interrogation rooms. Each is supposed to have a small window, not big enough for a person to crawl through. We're told the wooden doors are more than four inches thick. If you wanted to detain and question a person in San José and not use their modern police station and jail complex, this is where you would take them.

"Since the presidio was built on the highest ground around, and because of the section of town it's in, a person could suffer a hell of a lot of physical torture before anyone would ever hear his screams. If I had to guess, I would say that's where they're going, Rob."

"OK, Jim. We'll go with your theory. Thanks."

* * *

San José del Cabo,
Baja California Sur, Mexico
Thursday, April 19

Satellite generated photos were beginning to download more frequently now. The van and Town Car targets had been identified by the satellite's TARGET-LOK laser system automatically keeping all three vehicles in the center of the camera's focal plane, now dialed down to a screen size equal to less than half a city block. Photo clarity was ultra-sharp.

The numbers on the vehicle license plates were easily discernable, and had been identified as Government Issue. The CIA had already begun tracking the plates through the Mexican bureaucracy to determine to which department they had been assigned. They knew they could be raising a red flag. If someone wanted to know the ownership of a government owned vehicle, that person most likely would be onto their interrogation mission in San José del Cabo. The question was this: would they be so suspicious as to flag the information? Rob decided the risk was worth taking.

The three vehicles continued deeper into San José's inner city, making several unnecessary turns to determine if they were being followed. At one point, the three vehicles split up and were driven in different directions as though they were each heading to a different location. But, the LOK-ON lazar system had painted each vehicle as a separate target and continued to follow. The video screen switched from a single image to a split screen format with each vehicle pictured in a separate frame.

The convoy continued away from the hotel section of San José for twenty minutes, slowed by the unnecessary turns, seemingly meandering through the city at random. Soon they again merged into a single file and began to slow their pace.

*   *   *

Situation Room 13-B
CIA Headquarters
Langley, Virginia
Thursday, April 19 – 5:05pm

"Looks like you're right, Jim. They've just turned off the paved road. I think they're heading up the plateau to the presidio. Now, if we can confirm they drive through the gate, we should be able to see which room they put Alec in. With that information, extraction should be a breeze."

Rob's pager vibrated on his hip. He took it off his belt and looked at the message. General Hollins was waiting for him on the third floor.

CHAPTER EIGHT

Rob Downing's Office
CIA Headquarters
Langley, Virginia
Friday, April 20 – 12:14pm

BRIGIDEAR GENERAL LEON Hollins was ushered into Rob Downing's office.

"Leon, come in. I've been expecting you." Rob was standing in front of his desk and extended his hand to an old friend with whom he had worked many times in the past on missions that never made national headlines, mostly in Columbia and Venezuela, and all top-secret covert military operations.

"How did the meeting go between the Joint Chiefs and the President, yesterday?"

"Same old, same old," he replied. One of these days maybe we'll get a President with a set of cahonies who will give us the green light to go down to Venezuela and take Hugo Chavez out for good. First, he bands our surveillance flights, then he suspends bilateral anti-drug cooperation. I would think since it's a well known fact that ninety percent of all the drugs that reach our shores are funneled from

Colombia through Venezuela before they get here, we would be justified in taking that son-of-a-bitch out and closing his drug pipeline."

"We tried that back in '02 and the coup failed, you know."

"Wrong time, wrong people, Rob. They should have given the job to us. Those bureaucrats over at the State Department didn't know what they were doing. They were more concerned about setting up a new government than taking out the real problem. Eliminate Chavez first, then let the people of Venezuela set up the government they want, not what we want. All they needed was one man with a silenced rifle and a good trigger finger. Bureaucrats always screw up a good thing if you give them half a chance. Case in point.

"Anyway, Hunt has no backbone. He's worried about his legacy. Wants everybody to love him, regardless of what's best for the country. Wants to be remembered as the President who took care of the little people, never mind that he's doing it on the backs of those citizens who are willing to work hard for a living, make something of themselves and are paying their taxes.

"If you ask me, he's probably on the take anyway. But you'll never prove it. The dirty money funneled his way comes out of a Swiss bank account and goes directly into an offshore account in the Cayman Islands."

General Hollins pulled a handmade Cuban Cohiba from the breast pocket of his neatly pressed uniform, and used a .270mm casing to make a hole in the end. He thrust it in his mouth as he reached for his lighter. "I see you still smoke those cancer sticks, Rob. Hasn't anyone ever told you cigarettes can kill you?" He took a long drag on his contraband cigar, letting the cloud of blue smoke slowly rise to the ceiling.

"Do you know that for a fact?"

"What? The advice about smoking cigarettes, or the fact that Hunt's on the take?"

"The Hunt revelation, of course!"

"Well . . . yes. As a matter of fact, we do," he said, looking Downing squarely in the eyes. "Some of our people have snooped around and know more about it than I do. But, yes. It's real. Just proving it would be the hard part."

"I may want to talk with you later about that. Maybe we can put together a sting operation or something. But now, let's discuss the problem at hand.

"First, some good news. We've confirmed that our man is alive, or at least was alive yesterday afternoon. Also, we know where he is. And, you're going to like the setup. Here's a blowup of a photo taken by one of our satellites in stationary orbit over Mexico's Baja. The fortress is the old 17th century presidio built by the Spanish. It's in the old part of San José del Cabo. The photo was taken yesterday just after the three vehicles you see parked in the courtyard arrived. See the guy in civvies? That's our man. He's handcuffed and we have a visual of his face from an earlier photo, so we've confirmed his identity."

"Are you sure they didn't do a body switch on you? Dress one of their people in your man's clothes to make you think you're monitoring your guy?"

"I don't think they know we're up there looking down. So far, nothing they have done would suggest that except we noted the only member of the team not in uniform kept his head down when they took Alec away from the hotel. That could be his normal walking posture, or he could have been trying to conceal his identity. We just don't know.

"They did executed a few avoidance maneuvers on their trip from the hotel where they snatched him, but that looked like standard textbook stuff to spot a tail, not something someone would do to hide from a spy satellite."

"Could be you're being played, Rob. Those avoidance maneuvers could have been for your viewing pleasure. Just to make you think they don't know you're looking down on them. All I ask is that you keep that in mind as we go through this thing."

"I don't think so, but that's a good point, Leon. We did a hairline analysis of the guy in the fortress with one of the photos of our man at the hotel when he was first taken into custody. They matched, so we're reasonably sure it's our man. You should have been a spook though. You're as paranoid as we are!"

"Hell, man, what do you think I am? Don't let these stars fool you."

*   *   *

Old Spanish Presidio
San José del Cabo,
Baja California Sur, Mexico
Friday, April 20 – 7:26am

The small room was dark, damp, and smelled as though it hadn't been cleaned in years, almost the size of a holding cell. The floor, walls and ceiling were solid rock and a single naked bulb hung from a short frayed electric cord in the center of the ceiling. It was not lighted and there was no wall switch. The walls were at least ten feet high, preventing anyone with tampering with the light. *I know what that's for,* Alec thought. A small speaker was mounted in one corner of the room next to the ceiling. *That too, sleep depredation. They've used this place for interrogations before. Maybe torture.*

A small window, no more than ten inches square, had been chiseled into the rock wall facing the interior courtyard. A small amount of light was filtering through the window, but it was positioned too high for Alec to see what was going on in the courtyard. There was no furniture, just a dirty canvas bag filled with straw in one corner of the room. *My mattress,* he thought. A chipped porcelain chamber pot was in another corner, its lid missing. "How about some toilet paper in here!" he yelled. He knew no one would respond. *If I didn't know better, I would swear I'm back in the Hanoi Hilton,* he thought, as he surveyed his quarters in the old fortress.

*   *   *

"Let's see, what shall we call you today? Would you prefer Mr. LaCrosse or Mr. Dempsey? Or have you invented a new name for us today?" The interrogator, who had been dressed in a suit yesterday when Alec had been taken to the fortress, was now dressed in tan slacks and a cotton golf shirt. He wore dark glasses so Alec couldn't see his eyes. *Smart move*, Alec thought. *What do they say-the eyes are the portals to one's soul. He's probably wearing them because he doesn't want me to know he has no soul.*

The interrogator continued to stand in the doorway of the tiny cell, smiling, as Alec pretended to rub the sleep out of his eyes.

"Sleep well last night?" he asked, continuing to smile. The light bulb in Alec's cell had been left on all night with the rheostat dialed up to bathe the small room in blinding light. Latin music had blared through the speaker the entire time, making sleep impossible. But Alec wasn't about to acknowledge that the sleep deprivation was beginning to have an effect on him.

"Slept like a baby all night. I appreciate your leaving the light on. It's an old habit from when I was a little kid. I've never been able to break it. I've always had to sleep with a light on. By the way, what's for breakfast? If I remember correctly, you did introduce yourself as *room service* when we met at the hotel yesterday."

The smile on the interrogator's face faded into a frown. He stepped back out the door and slammed it shut, cursing in Spanish.

"Latin temper. One point for my side," Alec said under his breath. He was smiling.

Alec remained in solitude for the balance of the day. No food or water, just oppressive heat and humidity. Every two minutes, the ceiling light turned on and off as if on a timer. And the music continued, the same tune repeating without a break.

That afternoon, as the last rays of the sun seemed to be pulled below the Pacific horizon, the door to his cell opened again. This time two men in uniforms identical to those worn by the SWAT team that had taken him down the day before entered the room, grabbed him by his arms, and dragged him out the door into the waning evening light. A table with two straight wooden chairs had been set up in the middle of the courtyard. His interrogator was sitting in one, smoking a cigar and drinking a cup of coffee. He was forced into the other chair, facing the other man.

"Doesn't it say somewhere in the Geneva Convention that a prisoner can't be denied sustenance?" Alec asked, smiling at the man.

"Sustenance? Such a big word from such a learned man. I'm impressed. But, what makes you think you have earned the privileges provided by the Geneva Convention? Those privileges are reserved for prisoners of war, not civilian spies. You, my friend, are not entitled to a military tribunal to decide your fate. You will never see the inside of a courtroom. Understand that I am your judge, your jury, and possibly your executioner. I will decide what happens to you. But, you can earn your freedom if you will tell me just what the innocent young man told you. The boy whose finger and toe you savagely removed before you murdered him."

"Sorry, Pedro. I don't have the slightest idea what you're talking about."

"Well, let me give you some idea of what's in store for you tomorrow morning if you continue not to know what I'm talking about. First, the sleep deprivation will continue, day and night. Maybe even a little water boarding this evening for the entertainment of my men. After they have dinner, of course. I understand your government considers that as inhumane treatment. Some of your more vocal liberals say it's a form of torture.

"But, my friend, that's the least of your worries. I'm a nice guy, so I'm going to give you until tomorrow morning to think this over. Ever heard of the non-sedating antipsychotics drugs such as haloperidol and droperidol? They cause akathisia, and I suspect you already know of that condition. The amount of these drugs we will administer into your body will cause you to experience an intense sense of anxiety, a total inability to sit still and finally an indescribable sense of terror and doom. I'm told it's like chemical torture from the inside out. You'll experience violent mood swings from fits of rage to uncontrollable panic attacks. These attacks will come from so deep in your body that you can't isolate the pain no matter how hard you try. The muscles in your jawbone will go berserk so that you bite the inside of your mouth. Then your jaw locks and the pain throbs. The pain will grind into your every fiber. You'll experience uncontrolled restlessness, an urge to walk, but when you do, you will collapse from a feeling of fatigue. It will continue like this, day and night. You will be in constant pain. A pain you can't locate. You will have such wretched anxiety you will be overwhelmed, because you cannot get relief, even in breathing. The end result: you will want to take your own life. Want me to continue, Mr. LaCrosse?"

"No thanks, I know what those medications can do."

"Good, I thought you might. Your knowledge confirms my suspicions that you also are in this business. I don't know for whom you work, but I will before the sun sets tomorrow. We can avoid all of this, you know, if you will just tell me what the boy told you, and one other thing, whom you may have told. You have until tomorrow morning to think this over. Then the pain begins, Mr. LaCrosse, in earnest.

"But there is good news, my friend. I have an antidote! I have always used Klonopin and in most cases it has worked effectively for me in the past. I am sure it will soothe your restless soul if you force me to administer these drugs, then decide to come clean. But, tell me now what I want to know and we can avoid all this pain. We could even become friends."

Alec remained silent, a slight smile on his lips. *Bull. I'm not going to let that bastard get the best of me, at least not yet. Let him sit around and wonder if his lecture had the effect he wanted it to have.*

Alec was dragged back to his cell as the sun sunk below the Pacific horizon. An evening breeze had kicked up and the Baja peninsula was beginning to cool. He knew when the sun rose again tomorrow, it would mark the beginning of his last day alive unless his rescue had been set in motion. It would be a most painful ending. He wasn't even sure the CIA was aware of his capture and imprisonment. He had no way of getting in touch with them other than through the signals emitted by the tiny transmitters concealed in his radio and hand gun. And he had no way of verifying that they had been picked up, or even worked, for that matter. Both had been confiscated.

If he could only tell Rob Downing that tomorrow would be his last day on earth. If only he could see Beth and Alexander just one more time before he dies, just to say goodbye. *Damn it, anxiety is already setting in*, he thought. He had never personally experienced the effects of akathisia and he didn't want to. But he had seen the videos taken by CIA operatives of hardened terrorists to whom the drugs had been administered. He had watched in horror as they had begged to die as they lay on the floor, screaming and shaking uncontrollably. He decided he would never allow himself to be subjected to such perverted torture.

*   *   *

Rob Downing's Office
CIA Headquarters
Langley, Virginia
Friday, April 20 – 2:15pm

"OK, Rob, here's what we're going to do." The general walked over to the large conference table and rolled out a map of Mexico's Baja capes. He also laid out current and historical weather charts, wind and tide data sheets, and close-up photos and topography maps of the general land mass and surrounding sea floor.

"Getting your man out will be a joint effort which is going to involve Air Force South, a part of the U.S. Southern Command. They're headquartered at Davis-Monthan Air Force base in Arizona, but normally stage out of Homestead. The other part of the joint effort will be the First Special Forces Operational Detachment-Delta. As I told you yesterday, I talked to Colonel Bill Cook at Fort Bragg about the situation as best I knew it. He agreed his people would probably be the best choice to do the rescue. So, Air Force South will deliver a five-man Delta extraction team to the target area at an hour that will allow sufficient dark time to get your man out. The Delta team left for Homestead Air Reserve Base last night. That's going to be their staging point.

"Here's how it's going to go down. The insertion team will be a five-man Delta, all of Latin descent and all with an excellent command of Spanish. I'm told they look, act and talk like Mexicans. In fact, the team leader is. Under their jump suits, they'll be dressed in civvies, because after they get your man, they may have to melt into the local population if transportation isn't available in the presidio to get them to their rendezvous point. We're hoping one of the vans will be there. Our J2 people identified them as '07 Chevy Suburbans. GM gave us a master key that will unlock and start any '07 Chevrolet vehicle produced. We made duplicates even though you aren't supposed to be able to do that, so each team member has one."

"How about weapons?"

"Weapons will be Chinese. The kind most of the middle-eastern terrorist groups use as back-ups for their Russian hardware. Mostly automatic rifles and side arms. They'll have plastic explosives and fragmentation and flash grenades, but the theory is that this is going to be an *up close and personal* encounter.

"The deployment is going to be a HAHO maneuver: high altitude, high opening. The Delta team will jump from an altitude of some 28,000 feet, about twenty-five miles west of the target site."

"That's over the Pacific Ocean, Leon! Why not over the target? Wouldn't it be safer?"

"No. Our meteorologist people tell us the winds tonight will be out of the northwest. Winds aloft will be stiff, estimated at twenty knots, but surface winds will only be in the five knot range. They've calculated that if the team jumps at the designated altitude and open their chutes at 24,000 feet, they'll be able to fly to the target with sufficient altitude remaining to travel several additional miles, if needed. Since conditions can change, that safety margin is necessary. They plan to drop into the presidio's courtyard, take out the guards, blow the lock on your man's cell, get him out, and get the hell out of there as quickly as possible.

"J2 tells us there are eight guards, but only two are on duty during night hours. That makes it easy. These must be the five SWAT guys that broke into your man's hotel room, and the three guys we saw leading the group out to the vehicles in the hotel's parking lot. They're staying in tents set up in the presidio's courtyard.

"The guy running the show leaves every evening in the white Lincoln and returns every morning. He's not local, and neither are his men, but he likes his creature comforts, so is probably staying in one of the resort hotel in San José. If we had the time, we would set up a secondary mission.

"Our people have seen this guy before. They know his work. He's a sadistic bastard. Likes to use chemicals on his prisoners, and if they don't work, he goes for body mutilation, first the genitals, then the eyes. It gets worse, Rob. We know of an incident where he inserted the barrel of a small caliber handgun up a man's rectum and pulled the trigger. It tore the man up inside and took him two hours to bleed out. Two hours of excruciating pain before you die. That's way over the top. You interested in hearing some more stories of his sadistic torture?"

"No, I don't. Let's get back to the situation at hand. You're doing this mission at night, Leon. How can five guys with fully deployed parachutes and all their weapons and other gear stay together as they drop 24,000 feet vertically over a twenty-mile horizontal plain? What makes you think some of your team won't get lost in the dark?"

"They're a team, Rob. Team is the key word. They live together, train together, eat together, and stay together, both in military and in civilian environments. When they do this HAHO deployment, they'll form up as a stack: five guys, the team leader on the bottom with the other four stacked above him. The team leader will have a compass and a GPS unit with the target coordinates locked in, so he sets the travel course and acts as a guide for his other team members. He'll have to make course corrections from time to time because of wind direction and velocity changes, so he has to be familiar with the general terrain to be able to know the team's exact position related to the target during the descent. Each team member has an altimeter strapped to his wrist, so they always know how far they are above the ground. They also have closed circuit communications devices in their helmets so they are in constant touch with one another."

"Yeah, but opening their chutes at that altitude, how can they get enough oxygen in that thin air so they don't get hypoxia? And, it's got to be cold as hell that high up. How can they survive?"

These boys go through a pre-breathing period for about forty-five minutes in the aircraft just before they deploy. They breathe 100% oxygen to flush out as much of the nitrogen in their blood as possible. They'll also employ an oxygen bottle during the initial part of the jump, but jettison those when they reach an altitude where they can breathe normally, around 15,000 feet. To answer your second question, their jump suits are heated so their body temperatures don't fall to critical levels."

"Wait a minute. I didn't catch it at first, but didn't you say *tonight* when you were explaining winds aloft or something? Is this mission on for tonight?"

"As a matter of fact, I did." General Hollins glanced at his watch. "The timetable has the team leaving Lakeland just about now. They'll make a direct cross-country flight over the Gulf and across Mexico to the Baja and should be over their deployment zone at 0230-tomorrow morning, local time. We're using a C-130 Hercules to get them there, so they'll need only one in-flight refueling going in."

"Won't the Mexicans know what we're doing if we fly over their territory?"

"Why should they? We fly surveillance and recon flights over Mexico all the time, day and night. They know we do it, but they don't complain. If we see anything unusual, we notify them, so it's a win-win situation. Anyway, their radar systems aren't sensitive enough to detect the deployment of the team, so they'll never know we dropped our boys over their territorial waters west of the Baja. Plus, the team's equipment is pretty stealthy as it is. They're using the high performance Intruder Ram-Air chute system designed specifically for HAHO jumps. And, these guys know what they're doing."

"So, how do you plan to get them out?"

"If one of the vans is available in the presidio, the team will use Plan A. They'll stay together, keep their weapons, and hopefully just drive away. But, they're prepared to fight their way out if it comes to that. Plan B calls for the team to split up into three groups of two, which includes your man assigned to the team leader. In that case, they'll ditch their weapons and other gear, except their handguns, and will appear just as normal citizens of the area. They won't have passports, but each has papers indicating local addresses in San José. They also have papers for your man.

"By the way, he's already been assigned to our team leader who's actually from San Felepi, up the Baja peninsula a ways. He knows the general area quite well. He lived there until he was a teenager, came to the U.S. with his parents some fifteen years ago, and joined the Army. The rest of the story is boilerplate.

"If they have to separate, each two-man team will work its way through the town to the resort hotel district, steal a car and drive north. Their rendezvous point is the same if they are able to stay together or have to split up, but the timeline is longer with Plan B. In either case, we're using the airstrip you used to get the girl out. They'll be rendezvousing there with a couple of MH-53M Pave Low IV helicopters out of Phoenix. Only one refueling, in and out. We should have your man out by tomorrow afternoon. The next day at the latest."

"Leon, you haven't asked who our man is. Aren't you the least bit curious?"

"Of course, but I know how important anonymity is in your game. And there's no good reason for me to have that information anyway. The description you gave me will suffice. If we can get him out, so much the better. If something happens and he doesn't make it, then no one out of your circle will ever know your man was lost, not even me."

"Except his wife and new born son," Downing said, a look of deep concern on his face. He looked General Hollins square in the eyes. "Leon, we have no choice. This mission has to succeed. Our man has to be brought back alive!"

* * *

28,000 feet above the Pacific
Baja California Sur, Mexico
Saturday, April 21 – 2:18am

The C-130J Hercules was holding an altitude of 28,000 feet. Although bucking a head wind of just over twenty-five knots, the aircraft had made the trip from Homestead Air Reserve Base in South Florida in good time and was on schedule over its designated drop zone.

The Hercules was flying due west at its full throttle speed of Mach 0.59 when it crossed the Pacific Coast of Mexico's Baja. The pilots reduced the power to the aircraft's four turboprop Rolls Royce engines and began executing a slow, wide 360-degree turn while maintaining altitude. As the operations officer announced that the aircraft was approaching the drop zone, the cargo bay door began to descend. The backdraft was strong enough to suck a man out the rear of the aircraft.

When the jump light turned red, the five team members stood and began helping the member next to him with his knapsack and parachutes, checking and rechecking to be sure all were in order. Each team member had secured his weapon, explosives and other hardware to his chest so his hands and arms would be free to maneuver his chute when open.

The jumpmaster, secure in his safety harness, stood in the middle of the open bay and, over the roar of the wind, yelled the Sustained Airborne Training Points of Performance while each of the five combat-equipped troopers went through the mandatory drill: proper exit, proper body position, and don't forget to count. The jump light began to blink red fifteen seconds before turning green. The troopers donned their full-face helmets and gloves and turned on the personal oxygen bottles they would use during their descent until they passed through the critical breathing altitude limits.

As with all Delta air deployments, this would be a no static-line jump. The jumpers would free-fall until they reached 24,000 feet, then deploy their chutes and form up in their stacked formation to follow the team leader to the target zone. Each knew his position in the maneuver. They had practiced the jump multiple times and were ready.

The jump light turned green, the jumpmaster yelled, "go" and in assigned order, the troopers exited the rear of the aircraft, arms and legs spread to maintain position and balance as they fell through the frigid night air towards the ground and their uncertain fate waiting below.

*   *   *

Old Spanish Presidio
San José del Cabo,
Baja California Sur, Mexico
Saturday, April 21 – 2:45am

Alec saw it. At least he thought he did. He had not been able to sleep since being brought to the presidio two days ago. He looked down at his left arm, forgetting they had taken his watch when they took his shoes and belt. He shook his head in disgust. "How could I forget," he said out loud.

He had no idea what time it was, but the moon had crossed over the yardarm, so to speak, so he felt it was early morning, probably around 0300. The sleep deprivation was working. Without rest, the human mind becomes more susceptible to making mistakes in judgment. Reasoning power is diminished, and, with no food or water, the body becomes fatigued more quickly, adding to the danger of falling into the trap that sleep deprivation sets for those who are untrained in resisting the effects of this subtle torture. And although it might not seem so, Alec knew that the glaring light from the single bulb hanging from the ceiling of his cell, and the constant annoying music were wearing on his nerves. He knew it would just be a matter of time.

The water boarding he had been forced to endure earlier in the evening had not helped either. Regardless of a man's training, it was a very effective means of mental and physical torture. It produced the sensation of drowning, but just as he felt he was going under they would jerk him back into reality. The mental aspect of this rather mild form of torture was his knowing he would be going through it again, night after night until he broke. And he knew he would break, given enough time.

Alec had begun to lose hope of rescue. He knew if his interrogator administered the chemicals he had mentioned earlier in the day, he would go over the edge. It was just a matter of time.

But what had he seen? What sailed across his view of the moon while he was staring out the little window in his cell?

He was standing barefoot on the stone floor, wet from the humidity in his cell created by the intense heat of the day. His back had been against the far wall and he had been looking at the full moon through the tiny window in the front wall of his cell. Occasionally he would move slightly as the moon worked its way into the western sky, on its way to disappearing below the far horizon of the Pacific.

A shadow? What had just crossed in front of the moon, momentarily blocking it from his view? A cloud? He didn't think so. There were no clouds in the night sky, at least none he could see. Or was it just a figment of his imagination, something he thought he saw but really didn't. Or did he just blink, and for a brief moment lose his vision. Not likely. Alec moved across the room closer to the front wall so the light going on and off in the ceiling of his cell would not affect his vision but he could see nothing from that angle and he had nothing in the cell to elevate his position. And, he hadn't heard anything over the constant annoying music that played non-stop in his cell day and night. *Maybe my mind's playing tricks on me,* he thought. *That can happen, regardless of how well I'm trained to resist. I must be going off the deep end.*

He walked back over to the far wall and sat down, again trying to concentrate on the full moon, shading his eyes from the glaring light in his cell. He could see little else out of his window. Fifteen minutes passed. Suddenly, his view out the little window was blocked by something, he didn't know what. He rubbed his eyes.

"Hablas Ingles, Signor?"

"What?"

"Do you speak English?" Someone was speaking to him, looking at him through the window. He could recognize a man's face hidden by a black mask with only slits for his eyes.

"Yes, I do," he yelled. "Who are you?"

"A more appropriate question, Signor, who are you?"

"I'm an American!"

"Are there any other prisoners here?"

"Not that I know of. I haven't seen anyone else except the people who brought me here. Where are the guards?"

"Dead!"

"Dead! Damn, I didn't hear anything. Can you get me out of this hellhole?"

"Roger that, Sir. Can you walk?"

"You bet."

"OK, then come over to the front wall and crouch down in that corner away from the door. I'm going to blow its hinges. And, cover your ears. There's going to be a hell of a concussion in there."

Alec did as he was told. The explosions blew the door off its hinges, slamming it against the back wall of the cell. He stepped out into the moonlight, his ears ringing from the concussion of the blast. Five men dressed in black jump suits, faces covered by black knit masks, were facing him, automatic weapons at the ready.

"I don't know who you are, but I'm damned glad to see you. Just don't shoot. I'm unarmed."

"We suspected that," one of the men said, smiling. The others laughed.

"I don't know who authorized this mission, Signor, but it was a cakewalk."

"Who are you guys, anyway?"

"We're Delta, out of Bragg. Left Homestead yesterday afternoon and made a HAHO drop into this courtyard about ten minutes ago. We had been told to expect eight or more guards on you, but nobody knew what resistance we would come up against. We were told small arms mostly. Fortunately, there was none. There were eight guards. Two had been posted, the other six were in their tents. All eight were sleeping."

"Did you take prisoners?"

"We aren't equipped to take prisoners, Sir. It isn't in our playbook. So what do we call you?"

"LaCrosse will do. What's yours?"

"Julian will do. Now we've got to get the hell out of Dodge. People out there must have heard us blow that door to your cell. Somebody's going to get curious and call the law, so let's move, men.

"You're not wearing shoes, Mr. LaCrosse?"

"No, they took them when they brought me here."

"Well, find some. We're going to be on the streets for a while. Check those guards over there near the tents. One of them probably has a foot your size. And pick up a handgun from one of them. You may need it before this is over."

The five Delta Force troopers stripped off their black jump suits and piled them on top of their automatic weapons. Under their suits they were dressed in street clothes matching those found among the poorer class of people on the streets of San José del Cabo. None of the men had passports, but all carried papers identifying them as citizens of the town. Julian handed Alec his forged papers and a hat to hide his sandy gray hair. "You're not quite Mexican enough. We need to tone your face down a little. Here, put this makeup on and keep your head down if we see any law enforcement officers," he said.

Gasoline was poured on the pile of weapons and clothes and set ablaze as two members of the team set up several explosive charges at the entrance gate with trip wire activated detonators to discourage the local populace from looking too close at what had gone down inside the presidio. They know word would spread quickly, but the explosives would slow things down a little. They had to get as far away from the presidio as possible before the police came looking.

"We were told one of the Chevy Suburbans might be here, but I see we're going to have to hoof it out of here and find our own rides," the team leader commented to Alec.

The team split into three units of two members each with Alec and the team leader, Julian, making up the third team. They left the presidio going in different directions.

"Since a van isn't here for us to use, we're going to activate Plan B. We're going to split up to appear less obvious. A group of six men walking together could arouse suspicions. We'll all go in separate directions, but once away from ground zero, we'll double back and all make our way towards the hotel district on the Sea of Cortez, steal vehicles, and rendezvous with our ride at our extraction point. We have until 0200 tomorrow to get there, so time isn't a factor just now. We've ditched our weapons except our handguns, so we should look innocent enough."

The team members didn't have maps of the town, but had memorized the names of the streets that would take them to the hotel district. They also had memorized the most direct route to their rendezvous point.

*   *   *

The first light of the new day was painting the eastern sky a pale orange, a sure sign that rain was on the way. The westerly breeze off the Pacific had freshened, bringing a slight smell of salt to the air. "It's going to rain before noon," Alec said to his partner who looked more like a Mexican peasant than an American soldier.

"What makes you think so?" he asked.

"I can smell it," Alec replied. "Look at the eastern sky. We'll have rain clouds all over us by mid-morning and rain by noon."

"So, you're a weather man?" Julian quipped.

"Nope. But I've been around long enough to know when it's going to rain. By the way, what's your plan to get us out of here?"

"Once we get to the resort hotel area, we look for a nondescript General Motors car we can steal to drive to our rendezvous point. We each have a key that will start any GM vehicle from 2005 up. Simple."

"Do you mind if I make a suggestion?"

"Be my guest."

"Why steal a car when I have the keys to one?"

"Keys? You don't have car keys on you. The only thing in your pockets is a handkerchief."

"Correct, but the keys are hidden in the car."

"OK, let's hear your plan."

"Simple. I was staying at the El Conquistador Hotel when I was taken down and brought to the presidio. I don't think the people who found me knew I had rented a car, since I rented it in another alias I use from time to time. As far as I know, it's still there in the parking lot. The lease was open-ended so there would be no reason the rental agency would have come looking for it. Let's go over to the El Conquistador, pick it up and see if we can find any of your other team members. If we just happen to get stopped by the police, we could use the extra firepower. Beats running the risk of getting caught stealing one."

"Agreed. Another alias, you say? So LaCrosse is also an alias?"

"Afraid so. We're all better off if no one, not even you, knows my real name."

"OK, Mr. Secret Agent Man. Lead on."

*   *   *

El Conquistador Hotel Parking Lot
San José del Cabo,
Baja California Sur, Mexico
Saturday, April 21 – 7:05am

Alec and Julian stood on opposite sides of the guest parking lot for several minutes, observing the constant activity of vehicles entering and leaving. They were careful to avoid the security cameras that panned across the lot taking photos every six seconds. When they were convinced the lot wasn't under human surveillance, they both casually walked over to the car from their respective observation points. Alec retrieved the keys, hidden on top of the right rear tire, unlocked and started the car as Julian got in the rear seat.

"What are you doing back there?" Alec asked.

"Just a precaution. If we come under fire, I want a clear shooting path out of both sides of the car. If I were in the front seat, you would be in my way if I had to shoot out the left side. And, give me the handgun you took off the guard back at the presidio. You can't shoot accurately if you're driving.

"By the way, you suggested we try to find the other members of the team. We're not going to do that. Your face is too well known in this town. And by now, you know the police are all over the presidio. Next they'll reestablish their net and begin looking for you again. You need to be gone.

"Besides, the other team members have keys to start any '05 or later model GM product. They'll find their way to the rendezvous point. Right now you're my biggest concern. We've got to get you out of this area as quickly as possible."

Since it was early-morning, Alec drove out of the hotel grounds with several other private vehicles and cabs, and merged onto Grand Avenue leading to the Los Cabos Corridor, the six-lane thoroughfare along which most of the luxury hotels are built between Cabo San Lucas and San José del Cabo. He turned north on the Transpeninsular Highway towards Los Cabos International Airport.

Fearing he may be followed, he did not turn onto the Eastern Cape Road, but continued on through San José Viejo north. Several miles into the hills, he turned northeast on Palo Escopeta Road, passed through the village of Santa Catarina and stopped briefly in the village to watch for a possible tail. No vehicle slowed or stopped in the vicinity of the Ford, so he continued on through the village until reaching Palo Escopeta, where he turned east again towards Vinorama on the Sea of Cortez.

Several miles out, he turned right again and headed south towards La Fortuna. If anyone were following, they would be completely confused as to where he may be heading. When he reached La Fortuna he stopped again, pulled into a small parking lot and watched traffic pass for thirty minutes before continuing again. Traffic was heavier here on the Eastern Cape Road. He and Julian agreed that they had not been tailed, so Alec continued north along the Sea of Cortez until they reached a small bay with white sand beaches and craggy outcroppings just north of Boca del Salado. He parked the car, locked the doors, took the pair of binoculars he had left in the car several days ago, and walked out towards the beach. They would wait there for several hours before going on to their rendezvous point, the airstrip at Los Frailes where they would be picked up by two Army Bell UH-1Y tactical utility helicopters and flown back to the States.

There was no reason to suspect that the police had the airstrip under surveillance since they had missed their chance earlier to stop Alec from getting Kathy out of Mexico. They had tried to kill him after the aircraft on which Kathy McKenzie was being transported left the airstrip before they could get set up in their sniper's nest. But Alec turned the table on them when he activated the detonator that set off the charge of C-4 he had hidden in their nest.

*   *   *

U.S. Southern Command
Special Operations Command South
Homestead Air Reserve Base, Miami, Florida
Saturday, April 21 – 1:15pm

"They've got him, Rob! Your man is with our Delta team. He's a little shaken, but they don't think he's suffered any mental or physical damage that won't heal over time. He hasn't had anything to eat or drink for a few days so he's a little dehydrated. Otherwise, he's OK.

"He suffered some water boarding and sleep deprivation though. He says his interrogator was going to begin some sort of chemical torture this morning. Looks like we got him just in time."

"Great, Leon! Casualties?"

"No casualties, at least none on our side. And no resistance. Just eight guards, all asleep. In fact, they're still sleeping, if you know what I mean. No evidence of heavy weapons, just light arms. No sign of the interrogator you mentioned though. He must be sleeping somewhere outside the compound. Wish we could have stuck around and taken him out when he came to work this morning. But, that would have been putting the team at too much risk. We got your man, so the team leader decided to pick up our chips and get out of the game. I personally think he made the right command decision. We'll get the bastard some other time.

"Like our team leader said, it was a cakewalk, Rob. Your man identified himself as an American. Later he identified himself as a Mr. LaCrosse. I sure hope we got the right man. Other than the guards, he was the only person there."

General Leon Hollins had just completed his conversation with Colonel Bill Cook, the Delta Force Commander he had contacted two days earlier regarding what was then a proposed mission to rescue Alec Caldwell from his captors in Mexico. Since the extraction team had left all their military gear burning in the presidio, except their handguns, the team leader had reported to his unit's headquarters on a cell phone he had bought on the street in San José del Cabo when he and Alec were on their way to the El Conquistador hotel to pick up the rental car Alec had left there. His conversation with Colonel Cook seemed innocent enough, mostly regarding the Marlin fishing in the coastal waters off San José. The conversation was quickly decoded at Fort Bragg, revealing the information Cook was looking for about the success or failure of the mission. Without knowledge of the embedded code words, anyone listening would have had no idea it contained a very important hidden message.

General Hollins had immediately dialed Rob Downing's direct line at CIA headquarters in the heavily wooded countryside near Langley, and delivered the good news.

"That's fantastic, Leon," he said with a sigh of relief. You did get the right man. LaCrosse is the name we sent him down there with. Are they back in the U.S. yet?"

"Not yet. They rendezvous with their ride tonight and should be back on our soil before the sun comes up tomorrow. We'll ferry our people back to Bragg, but drop Mr. LaCrosse off at Andrews if you guys want to debrief him there. They should be touching down at Luke Air Force Base outside Phoenix around 0600 Mountain Time. We can have him at Andrews by noon tomorrow. Luke is their closest touchdown point on U.S. soil, so we're directing them there. The C-130 Hercules they rode down on is waiting for them and will bring them back East."

"That works for us, Leon. I'll have a car there to pick him up. By the way, we owe you one. A big one, and I won't forget it."

"Our pleasure, Rob. We're on the same side, you know. But, it's great to have you in my debt. How about a steak dinner the next time I'm in the DC area. We'll call it even."

"You got it, General. Stay safe."

* * *

Don Armstrong's Office
CIA Headquarters
Langley, Virginia
Monday, April 23 – 8:30am

"Alec, glad to have you back. Rob brought me up-to-date when his contact in Southern Command called with the good news. I understand the boys over at Bragg sent us a crack Delta Force team. I'm just glad they got there when they did. Those chemicals Rob tells me they were prepared to use on you would have been the worst possible torture they could inflict. You wouldn't have survived, but you would have told them everything before they killed you. Welcome home, my good friend." Don Armstrong grabbed Alec's shoulder and gave his college roommate a one-arm hug.

"But, we need to talk before you fly back home. We've learned some things that you're not going to like."

"What the hell is going on, Don? It must be critical to bring you over here for a routine debriefing."

"Nothing routine about this, Alec. Sit down, my friend. I'm going to give it to you from the beginning.

"First, when McKenzie stopped in Washington to thank the President for sending you down to Mexico to rescue his daughter, Hunt seemed overly inquisitive about you. At least that's what McKenzie told Rob. When I met with both of them out at Langley before your mission began, I purposely didn't give them your name, not even the alias you would be using down there. Unfortunately, when you met with McKenzie the two of you discussed the drug connection you had uncovered when he asked if you would do a little job for him on the boys who kidnapped his daughter. You declined, of course, but he knew you were going to remain in Mexico to look into the drug connection so he had that information. When McKenzie and his daughter were meeting with the President in the White House, she mentioned your name, quite innocently of course, but evidently Hunt picked up on that piece of information. You would think it would have ended there, but there's much more to the story.

"Let me digress a bit. When Rob and his friend from Southern Command, General Hollins, were discussing the overall mission, Hollins indicated that Southern Command's intelligence section had information that supported the theory we have had since Hunt took office: that he was dirty, on the take, so to speak. When you went missing, Rob began to wonder how the Mexican police could have found you, so he checked in with General Hollins and learned they have some pretty creditable evidence that Hunt and the President of Mexico are in the drug business together. Not involved directly, of course, but at least profiting from it. Turning a blind eye to what's going on, for a price. And, according to the records Hollins' people have, Hunt has been getting regular payoffs through one of his accounts in the Caymans for years. Rob was about to contact Mr. McKenzie to determine if he had told the President about your plans to investigate the drug ring you had uncovered, when McKenzie called him. He was concerned that the President had been too curious about who you are and what you would be doing now that the rescue had turned out OK."

"Damn! I specifically asked McKenzie not to mention anything about this to the President."

"Hold on, Chief. Don't blame Mr. McKenzie. It was his daughter who mentioned the name you were using and the fact that you had stayed behind when they brought her out. She had wanted you to come with her. According to her dad, it was a comment she made in praise of what you had done for her, in no way meant to cause you harm. She just didn't know. But, according to McKenzie, it opened up the subject, and the President kept pressing for more information. That's why he called Rob. He felt the President's curiosity was over the top.

"So, we put the National Security Agency on alert to concentrate their covert listening program on calls in and out of the White House. We had to do a lot of explaining, and had to call in a lot of favors, but we finally got their OK. But, they insisted on limiting their recordings to calls only to and from Mexico City. They were convinced we were barking up the wrong tree. That is, until they intercepted a call from the White House to President Montoya in Mexico in which the President told him who you were and what you were doing down there. That really got their curiosity up. Then, another telephone call. This time from the President of Mexico to Hunt. Montoya told him the situation had been taken care of, and nobody would be the wiser. Montoya said he had personally sent his best interrogator over to San José to interview this Mr. LaCrosse, and that would be the end of it. I believe those were his exact words.

"But let me play the tapes for you. There are only two conversations. The first from Hunt identifying you by the name you were using down there, and telling Montoya that you had uncovered the drug operations out of Cabo San Lucas. He must have thought his conversation was private because he expressed concern that you might turn off the spigot. We believe he meant your investigation might dry up his source of illegal funds, the protection money he and Montoya were getting. The second call is from Montoya to Hunt telling him you had been taken care of. As far as Hunt was concerned, you were dead."

Alec listened to the tapes in silence, playing them over and over, but revealing nothing in his body language or facial expressions. Finally he shut off the recorder and stood, saying nothing. He walked over to the window and looked out at the forests beyond the expansive CIA compound. Armstrong and Downing sat in silence, waiting for what Don had said and what Alec had heard to sink in. Alec turned slowly to face his friends and smiled. "So, the President betrayed me."

"Yes, but just as bad, he betrayed the Company as well. It's bad enough when it gets personal, but when you betray an agency of the federal government, you step on a lot more toes than one person's. And there's more."

"More?"

"Yes. We also know the identity of the guy Montoya sent down to interrogate you."

"Rub me out is a better description, wouldn't you say? Who is he?"

"His name is Carlos Ortega. He works exclusively on special projects for President Montoya. Keeps his people in line. Also, keeps his enemies at bay. He's ruthless. Quite a few political enemies of the President have suddenly disappeared while in his custody. His specialty is chemical torture. Most people down there have no idea what he does. Or at least won't acknowledge what he does. Socially, he's quite respectable. He's often seen in the company of President Montoya, especially at social functions and political rallies."

"How did you identify him?"

"We had a pretty good shot of him from the satellite when he and his people were taking you out of the hotel down there. We didn't have anything on him, so at General Hollins' recommendation, we sent it over to the J2 Intelligence Directorate of Southern Command's Joint Interagency Task Force. They had a world of information on him, and had his ID back to us in thirty minutes. Seems he's been active down in Guatemala, and their government had been complaining to Montoya's people with no response. So the Joint Interagency Task Force got involved, spoke with Montoya, and in the course of dealing with the situation, built a rather impressive dossier on him."

"So, what are you going to do about all of this, Don?"

"Right now, nothing. I know what you would like to do, and so would I, but let's not go off half-cocked. You and I need to think this through first. Then put together our plans. Whatever we do, we must not harm the office of the President nor cast a shadow on this agency. We go after the man, not the office. It has to be personal, and it has to be complete. And, we have to walk away from it once completed. No looking back. Just you and me, and maybe Rob if he's interested."

Don and Alec looked over at Rob Downing. "I'll use a saying the Delta team leader told Colonel Cook that Alec used when he asked him if he could walk: *You bet your sweet ass*," Rob said with a smile.

"Good. Well, if you're through with me, I'm going to catch a flight out to Montana, hug my wife, kiss my boy, hang around for a few days, then pack for a few days solitude in the high country. I need some time by myself to work out how I think we should play this. I won't be taking the radio, so please don't try to reach me until I come down. I'll call you then. In the meantime, you put together what you think we should do and we can compare notes. And, give me a copy of those tapes. I want to listen to them some more."

"OK, but only because it's you. You have to promise me you'll destroy them when you are through. Otherwise, I can't give them to you. If they got into the wrong hands we would all be history. Are you going to be OK with all this, Alec? Keep your cool and let's do this right."

"I'll be fine, and I'll destroy the tapes, Don. I promise. See you two soon."

*   *   *

Alec and Beth's Home
Lennep, Montana
Monday, April 23 – 6:45pm

Alec arrived home to the loving arms of Beth, his wife of only a few months and the innocent eyes of their young son, less than a year old, born as a result of a passionate moment when he and Beth had been thrown together amid the chaos of an intense rescue mission in the mountains of Idaho.

The sun had begun to set behind the looming Castle Mountain to the west of their tiny home, casting long gray shadows across the small green valley that stretched south towards the village of Lennep. A slight breeze had freshened, spinning the leaves of the nearby aspens as they caught the last rays of the sun and reflected the fading light like millions of sparkling Christmas ornaments.

"We have to talk, Alec. I need to do something with my life."

"I'm not sure I understand, Sweetheart."

"Well, I fell in love with you the first time I saw you standing outside that cabin just after you shot the Mafia soldier holding me captive. You were standing there bigger than life, with your rifle cradled in your arms. You looked like John Wayne or Jeremiah Johnson. I would have sworn it was one or the other. I was like a schoolgirl on her first date. I don't know how else to describe how I felt.

"I knew right then we would be married and I would have your children. I also knew you would be away a lot on your covert CIA missions, and I accept that. But, it seems our love life now is pretty much limited to the phone sex we seem to engage in every time you call. But even though you call just about every day, your absence really isn't very satisfying. I want you here with me, in my arms, more often, but I know that's not going to happen if we don't make some changes in our commitments to each other. If you were here more often, I would be happy being with you wherever we are, in this cabin out here in nowhere or in the middle of some big city. But, since you won't be here as much as I need you to be, I want to discuss my ideas with you.

"First, I want to move to a larger house with neighbors and sidewalks. We can keep this place as somewhere we can get away to when we want to be by ourselves. And, you can use it as a hunting cabin and take little Alec here to hunt elk and deer. I know you want him to grow up like you, and I want that also. He needs to be self-reliant when he's old enough to be on his own. But I also need a life of my own, and I can't have that out here in the woods.

"So, in addition to moving to more civilized surroundings, I plan to open a small law practice and begin using the talents I spent so many years in law school developing. I gave up my practice in Idaho Springs after I married Jerome and he became Idaho's governor, because he felt the wife of the governor shouldn't be involved in the workplace. And when he was appointed Secretary of the Interior any plans I had to return to the law had again to be put on hold. His death freed me of that, and I think now is a good time to take up the law again as part of my life. Since you are away so much of the time, it will give my life purpose again."

"I thought our child was just about all you wanted to concentrate on these days."

"He's a handful, and I love him to death. And I plan to take him to my office every day. In fact, if we can find the right house, I would prefer to work out of our home. Then I wouldn't have to bother about finding and outfitting an office.

"I plan to start out doing corporate and personal tax work, as well as title work. I'll hire a secretary who can double as a nanny when I'm working at the clerk's office or Register of Deeds office. That way, I can be a mother and a lawyer at the same time, and when you do come home from your adventures, I can also be a lover. Personally, I don't think Alexander should be an only child. But that's something we can work on together when you are at home."

"Where do you want to move to, Beth?"

"Well, since White Sulfur Springs is the County Seat I think it would be good to live there if we stay in Meagher County. Of course, we could always go to Idaho Springs where I was in practice before I married Jerome. But, there are some memories there that I don't want to revisit just now. So, as I see it, the only place I think you would be happy in is Big Timber over in Sweet Grass County. It's the County Seat, and your friend, Bill Hawks, lives there.

"I've also done a little research. Sweet Grass County is getting ready to burst wide open with new developments, ski resorts, golf courses, dude ranches, all the trappings that attract tourist and real estate growth for second homes for the filthy rich. And real estate growth means a lot of title work for enterprising paper trail attorneys like me.

"Your friend, Hawks, got in on the real estate boom when it was first beginning and made a small fortune over there. Now it's time for someone with my talents to cash in also. I know you don't believe in all the developments that are springing up all over the Rockies, but it's something that you, nor anyone else, can stop. Only God, and a major earthquake, can slow it down, but nothing can stop it. And you always have this little house and these mountains to retreat to when the walls begin closing in on you."

"OK. I agree. You take care of the details. I'll go along with your plans on one condition: we retain ownership of this property and don't rent it to anyone. It's going to be our little get-away place, and a place Alexander can grow up in and learn what living in the mountains is all about. Just call me so I'll know where to find my family when I return."

"It's a deal, lover. Now let's slip in the house while you-know-who is sleeping and work on making his little sister."

CHAPTER NINE

Billings, Montana
Billings International Airport
Saturday, May 12—5:47am

IN THE EARLY morning hours of May 12th, Alec Caldwell boarded United flight 1123 at Billings Logan International Airport for his short hop to Denver. He was dressed in his usual attire: jeans and plaid work shirt, black, hand-tooled cowboy boots, and his ever-present Stetson over his graying unruly mane. With a two-day growth of beard, he looked the Mountain Man image that had made him legendary in the agency through which he served his country.

The flight to Denver, Colorado left Billings at 6:10am Unfortunately, the second leg of his flight to Washington didn't leave Denver International until 10:20, and there were no earlier flights out of Denver to the DC area he could take to avoid the delay. He could have taken an earlier flight through Atlanta, but Hartwell International is one of the more congested and hard to navigate airports on the Eastern Seaboard. Since the delay was of little consequence, he elected to stay with his direct flight into Reagan National.

Alec used the down time to review the action plan he had put together several days earlier while camping alone in the Bob Marshall Wilderness west of his home in Lennep, Montana. He had arrived home to the loving arms of Beth, his bride of only a few weeks, and to his newborn son. The timing of the birth of their son wasn't a concern to either of them, although both would have preferred that Alexander had been born at least nine months after their nuptials. Circumstances beyond their control had thrown them together in a dangerous and unpredictable environment that left them little time to be concerned about traditions. Both had endured hardships in their former marriages. Alec had lost his wife of many years to breast cancer only a couple of years before meeting Beth. And Beth had been forced to watch her husband, the Secretary of the Interior, be murdered in cold blood after a Mafia family targeted him for death. There was no love left in their marriage, and there was nothing she could do to save him. She had then been taken hostage and raped by her husband's assassin before Alec found her in the mountains of Idaho and shot the man as he tried to kill Alec.

Together, Alec and Beth had broken the back of a deadly allegiance that went far beyond just the assassination of her husband. In doing so, they had fallen in love. She was eight months pregnant with Alec's child when they were married.

Beth understood why he had to leave so soon after coming home from his last CIA mission. It wasn't over. In fact, it had hardly begun. Alec needed time to think, time to clear his head of the thoughts of revenge generated by having been betrayed by the President of the United States. Time to plan the next phase of a dangerous game into which he had unwittingly been brought. He needed the solitude he could find only alone in his mountains.

Alec knew Rob Downing and Don Armstrong were developing scenarios they felt would achieve the goals they had agreed upon after his debriefing of the Mexican mission several weeks ago. Now, all he had to do was to convince his two associates that the way he wanted to play the new mission would be the most likely plan to achieve their goals.

Alec was good at details and good at covering all the bases. After all, it would be his butt on the line, at least in the initial phase of his two-phase plan to take out those people down in Mexico who had made and Kathy's lives hell. He would accept what Don and Rob wanted to do to take down the President of the United States, but the first phase had to be his call.

*   *   *

Regan National Airport
Washington, DC
Saturday, May 12 – 2:25pm

United Airlines Flight 316 to Reagan National Airport left Denver on time and arrived fifteen minutes early, riding a tailwind at an altitude of 27,000 feet. Alec moved through the crowd of people on the concourse, entered the main terminal and rode one of escalators downstairs to the baggage carrousels where several United flight numbers were flashing. He picked up his tan, soft-sided garment bag and hurried out one of the exits marked for taxi and limousine pickup and took his place in the queue. The cab took him to CIA Headquarters in Langley, Virginia. His meeting with Don Armstrong, CIA director and Rob Downing, his section chief was scheduled for late afternoon. Alec had a lot to say and little time to say it.

It was now 6:30 in the evening of the same day. Rush hour traffic around Dulles International Airport was heavy as daily commuters fled the concrete canyons of Washington to their condominiums scattered throughout the northern Virginia countryside.

A man using a passport issued by the U.S. State Department in the name of Samuel Cowen called for a cab to pick him up at a prestigious residential address hidden in a heavily wooded area just off Dominion Drive in the rolling countryside outside of McLean, Virginia. The clean-shaven man, dressed in a smartly tailored business suit, black captoe lace-up shoes, his dark brown hair neatly trimmed and combed showing no hint of gray, was carrying a black leather briefcase and a tan soft-sided garment bag when he exited the cab at Dulles and hurried into the terminal serving British Airways flights to the U.K. His late evening flight to Heathrow, outside London, was scheduled to depart U.S. soil at 8:45 in the evening and he was late. His flight was being called when a senior customs agent waved him through without inspecting his luggage. Someone had made a well-placed phone call. He made it to his gate as the door was being closed.

*   *   *

Heathrow Airport, Terminal Three
Outside London, England
Sunday, May 13 – 9:45am

The Boeing 777 touched down on English soil at 9:45 the next morning. The nine-hour flight to Heathrow was smooth, and most of the passengers in business class, including the man calling himself Samuel Cowen, were able to get a few hours of well-deserved sleep.

The man boarded the Piccadilly Line outside Heathrow's Terminal Three and rode the train to Green Park. There he switched to the Victoria Line out to Oxford Circus and on to Regents Park on the Metropolitan. Anyone following him would have been lost in the crowds of people using the London underground.

The man strolled into Regents Park through York Gate, stopping briefly to photograph St. Marylebone Parish Church before crossing over Regents Canal by way of St. Marks Bridge Gate. He stopped in the Feng Shang floating Chinese restaurant on the canal just long enough to enjoy a cup of green tea and study his surroundings, then moved on past the entrance to the London Zoo and into the park's inner circle, slowly making his way to the twelve-and-a-half-acre Winfield House estate, the official residence of the U.S. Ambassador to the U.K. As best as he could tell, he was not being followed.

He walked up to the massive wrought iron gates with imposing white pillars on either side, and spoke briefly with the armed Marine guard as he handed him his passport. The guard glanced at the man's passport and checked the name against a list he retrieved from the concealed guardhouse next to the gate. After making a quick call to announce the man's arrival, the guard opened one of the two iron gates, allowing the man to enter. The gate was immediately closed and locked. A telephone call two days earlier from the U.S. State Department assured the man and Sir Timothy Sutherland the privacy they would need for their important meeting.

*   *   *

A bit of history
The novel: The Irish Conspiracy

Sir Timothy Sutherland had flown to the U.S. as the Prime Minister's representative to a secret meeting held several years earlier in a remote cabin in Montana with Mason Novak, a high-level civilian advisor to the U.S. Secretary of State. The two men had been tasked to develop a plan to protect the British Crown from an assassination plot discovered by Interpol, devised in Ireland and involving a splinter group of the Irish Republican Army and a Hezbollah death squad. The death of the Queen would supposedly disrupt the fragile peace existing between the U.K. and the Irish Republic. The theory had been that the assassination would make England appear weak and spark an armed rebellion in Northern Ireland to rid it of English rule and again unite the island under the rule of the Irish Republic.

Alec Caldwell had been dispatched by the CIA to provide protection for the two men attending the meeting in the vast expanse of Montana's high country, much of which very few white men had explored. He was the only safeguard between the two men and a possible assassin sent to kill them. A secretary to the President's intelligence director, Dr. Louise Betters, had leaked word of the secret meeting to a friend with connections to the IRA. Fortunately, using his mountain man skills, Alec was able to locate and flush out the would-be assassin before he could complete his mission.

Because of his skills, Alec had been asked to join Sutherland and Novak in developing and executing their plan to protect the Queen and ferret out the mastermind behind the assassination plot. Although successful in protecting the Queen and taking out the Hezbollah death squad and the IRA cell, they were unable to identify the person behind the assassination plot. It was feared he might strike again.

*   *   *

Because of their friendship, Alec knew he could trust Sutherland with information about his current mission to eliminate the people responsible for his recent capture and torture in Mexico. His plan would ultimately include the President of the United States, and it was this part of his plan that would involve Sutherland.

At the appropriate time, he would ask Sutherland to begin anonymously planting stories in the U.K. that hinted of illegal and illicit acts committed by Hunt and some of his associates at times during his long political march to the White House. The CIA director maintained a secret file on President John Hunt spanning several decades, involving drugs, prostitution, money laundering and even murder. Alec and the Director of Central Intelligence were college roommates and fraternity brothers at William and Mary College and had maintained a close personal relationship since their college days together. Alec knew the DCI would give him access to the files, and he planned to use as much of this information as necessary to sink the political career of the man occupying the highest office in the nation, the one man who betrayed Alec to further his own political career.

*   *   *

U.S. Ambassador's Residence
Winfield House, Regency Park
London, England
Sunday, May 13 – 4:32pm

The two limousines eased out of the circular brick driveway
through the main entrance gates in the black wrought iron fence
that provides security for Winfield House, and merged into evening
traffic, each going in different directions. The gate was immediately
closed and locked by the Marine guard. The first limousine was
being driven by a chauffeur who knew his way around London like
the back of his hand. His section chief had assigned him to this
driving detail, although it wasn't a part of his job description. He
was an MI-5 agent, and a damned good one. He had been told that
the PM had made it abundantly clear that no harm was to come to
his passenger while he was on British soil, and he planned to provide
the protection required to honor that order.

The man in the limousine was dressed in the style of the Scottish
landed aristocracy. He wore a smartly tailored brown tweed sports jacket
with brushed leather patches on the elbows and a soft leather recoil
pad above his right breast pocket. The coat's buttons were also covered
in calfskin. He wore a silk maroon ascot around his neck, which he
had tucked into the open collar of his tattersall-patterned button-down
collar shirt, a style more common to an older generation of Scots, and
rarely seen today on the streets of London or Edinburgh. A simple tan
handkerchief was barely visible in the left breast pocket of his coat.
His light tan woolen trousers were double pleated and cuffed over tan
brogans and hand-knitted Argyle socks. A handlebar mustache had
been a last-minute addition. In effect, the man was dressed as though
he would be attending a casual garden party or possibly a fox hunt in
the Scottish countryside, a sport still enjoyed by Scottish aristocracy,
but which was banned in England and Wales by the Hunting Act of

2004 because of neighboring land-owner complaints, and protests by animal rights groups such as the League Against Cruel Sports.

There had been a time, not so long ago, when fox hunting was considered a national sport among the aristocratic landowners of England. But as increased wealth filtered down to the middle classes, many of the larger estates were divided and sold to pay the burdensome taxes imposed on the wealthy by the liberal-leaning government. These smaller tracts of rural English countryside were gobbled up by persons with newly acquired wealth, wanting to escape the crime and pollution of the cities, but unaccustomed to the traditional ways of the landed gentry. They were much more liberal in their views and were easy targets for the animal rights and green groups organized by the socialist-leaning political leaders of England's *new age of reasoning.*

In addition to his tan soft-sided garment bag, the gentleman carried a rather sporty tan leather gun case with the initials JMC tooled into the top above the embossed Coat of Arms of the Scottish Sutherland Clan from the country's northern highlands. The initials matched the first letters of the name he was using: James Michael Connors. Inside, cradled in a soft red-velvet fabric were two weapons: a highly-prized sixteen-gauge double barrel Fox Sterlingworth shotgun with open and improved cylinder bore barrels, and a Remington 700 bolt action rifle with Walnut hand-checkered stock, chambered in .22-250mm caliber with a high powered sniper scope. He knew his gun case would be opened and inspected by both British and Mexican Customs agents, and a lot of questions asked, but through diplomatic sources, permission for him to personally carry the weapons on his flight to Mexico had been secured. The man's papers were in good order and he had memorized the answers he would need to make his passage go smoothly.

According to documents he carried in the breast pocket of his jacket, the man had booked a two-week hunting safari on the Mexican Baja Peninsula with the highly respected outfitters, Del Sol Safaris. The outfitter was located on an expansive private ranch bordering the lush game-rich Parque Natural San Ignacio near Punta Abrejos, a thriving village on the Pacific Coast of the Mexican Baja, popular for its marlin fishing. A wealthy American industrialist, whose products were used extensively by the United States military, supposedly owned the ranch. Although the outfitting business was legitimate and actually did book hunts, its clientele was limited to a very select group of political and administrative people in the U.S. government and the governments of friendly nations. Hunts through Del Sol Safaris were impossible to book unless you had the right credentials. Many of its clients never fired a weapon while visiting the ranch. In effect, it served as a heavily guarded and very secure location for high-level meetings among the several known and unknown agencies that make up the U.S. intelligence community. No uniformed guards could be found along the ranch's perimeter, but the most technically advanced monitoring systems developed exclusively for the CIA had been installed throughout the ranch. After all, it was the CIA's Mexican headquarters.

Everything that moved on or above the lands was instantly picked up on the security system, identified, and continuously monitored if it seemed to pose a threat to the ranch or its inhabitants. The systems were monitored 24/7 by CIA personnel housed in underground steel reinforced concrete bunkers, constructed without the knowledge of the Mexican government or the local populace. Access was by a four-mile unpaved road, mostly sand, monitored by hidden video cameras and motion sensors. A small airstrip had been carved into the lush grasslands surrounding the main lodge and guest quarters, which afforded long low-level approaches for smaller jet aircraft flying below the Mexican radar net. A fully armed AH-6J "Little Bird," the Army's Special Operations variant of the OH-6A helicopter, was housed in what appeared to be an old barn next to the main hacienda. In reality, it was a hardened mini hangar built specifically for the "Little Bird," its crew and its ordnance. The helicopter was designed to carry six men for quick insertion and extraction, and it was armed with Hellfire and Air-to-Air Stinger missiles and two 7.62mm M134 miniguns, one each mounted on its two fuselage hard points. Six military-trained pilots were housed on the ranch and could bring the gunship's armament to bear at a moment's notice.

According to the itinerary prepared for him in the U.S., but given to him in the U.K., the man would be hunting doves in the subtropical highlands of the Sierra de la Laguna during the mornings, and in the afternoons he would hunt pintails and widgeons which winter in the area by the millions around the watering holes that pocked the expansive green valleys. His quest for record-book whitetail deer would take him higher into the Sierra Columbia Mountains and was the justification for bringing his high-powered rifle with him. The man's booking papers and licenses had been given to him in London along with his passport, airline tickets, credit cards and safari itinerary that legitimatised his reason for bringing weapons into Mexico.

*   *   *

The MI-5 agent drove the man to the North Terminal at Gatwick International Airport twenty-eight miles outside of London where he cleared customs under the name, James Michael Connors, a British born citizen residing in Glasgow, Scotland. He boarded American Airlines Flight # 79 to Dallas-Fort Worth International Airport. Not a word had been exchanged between the agent and his passenger. No words were necessary.

The flight left Gatwick as scheduled and arrived in Dallas ten hours and twenty minutes later. It was 6:55am, and although the man had traveled in first-class accommodations, he had not slept during the entire flight from England. Having cleared customs in England, and traveling on a non-stop transatlantic flight, the man's fellow passengers passed through the U.S. customs arrival gates without being detained by the agents, although each was scrutinized as they filtered through the Dallas/Fort Worth arrival gates. However, because the man was carrying weapons, he was required to go through a thorough customs search again. "Damned bureaucrats," Alec said under his breath.

He waited patiently in the American Airlines Admiral's Club lounge for the airline's next flight to Los Cabos International Airport outside of San Lucas del Cabo, his gun case on his lap. He was holding an A/Advantage Executive Platinum Club card given to him in London with his other documents. It too was a forgery. No one asked the man what he was carrying, but everyone in the club gave him a wide berth and continued to stare at him until he departed the lounge to catch his flight. Behind his dark glasses, his eyes were smiling. The three-hour flight departed DFW at 9:40am. It was on time.

*　　*　　*

Los Cabos International Airport
Cabo San Lucas, Mexico
Monday, May 14 – 12:45

Los Cabos International Airport wasn't busy this time of the day. Most tourists planned their vacations around weekend arrivals and departures, and the mid-week arrival of American Airlines Flight 875 was only partially filled. The man walked across the tarmac towards the main terminal and through the door marked Customs. Two Mexican agents searched his garment bag, while the customs supervisor opened his gun case and examined his weapons.

"Beautiful Fox Sterlingworth," he commented, holding the rare and much prized weapon up to the light. "Bird hunting in our fair land, *Senor*?" he said, smiling at the owner.

"Ducks and doves," the man replied, twisting the end of his mustache. "And, a friend has a giant whitetail tied to a tree up in the mountains. Been feeding him corn for the last month, I'm told." The man's attempt at humor didn't seem to impress the customs supervisor who frowned and looked away.

"A Remington Model 700, I see." The customs supervisor did not lift the rifle from its case, but rubbed his hand over the well-oiled checkered stock. "Looks like a very heavy barrel, *Senor*. It must be a large caliber."

"It's a 308. I need a big gun that shoots long distances if I'm going to bag that big buck my friend has tied to a tree." Still no response from the customs supervisor who continued to frown.

Actually, the rifle the man had brought with him into Mexico was chambered for the small .22-250 mm Remington center-fire cartridge. To the untrained eye, its very heavy free-floating barrel made it look as though it was chambered for a much heavier cartridge. However, its cartridge was designed for target shooting and hunting varmints at very long distances. The 40-grain Ballistic Tip bullet had a muzzle velocity of 3,680 feet per second and 1,654 foot pounds of muzzle energy. Although it was a very fast and hard-hitting projectile, it was susceptible to windage problems in uncontrolled environments. That wasn't a problem for the man. Its flat trajectory was just what he wanted for the rather easy shot he was planning to make. And if the shot were placed correctly, it would kill the target outright.

"Looks like a sniper's rifle, Senor. I'm told the Remington bolt action rifle is used by you Americans to kill people at long distances." The customs agent frowned as he continued to admire the rifle. The man was counting on the customs supervisor not bothering to take the rifle out of its case to examine its heavy barrel more closely. The customs supervisor looked the man in the eye. "Are you a sniper, *Senor*?" He was not smiling.

"My name is James Michael Connors, and I'm from Scotland. I'm not a Yank. Check my passport if you wish. Your two stooges have it over there. And hell no, I'm not a sniper. I hunt animals for sport, not people. Are you through looking at my weapons?" The man's anger was beginning to show.

"My apologies, *Senor*. I didn't mean to offend you." The customs supervisor closed the leather case, fastened its leather straps, and slid it across the counter to the man. "Have a nice stay in Mexico, Senor. And I hope you kill lots of game."

"Thank you. I usually get what I come after," he replied.

The man walked out of the room housing the customs check-in into the main terminal lobby and out a side door where he had been told to go to meet the person who would transport him to the ranch. The customs supervisor was already on the phone as he watched Alec life.

As he did, he noticed a Cessna 172-R, four-place aircraft displaying the orange and yellow Del Sol Safaris rising sun logo on its fuselage moving towards him at idle speed. He stopped and waited, setting down his tan garment bag but continuing to cradle his gun case in his arms.

"Mr. Connors? Are you James Michael Connors?" the pilot shouted out of the aircraft's window over the noise of the plane's engine.

"Yes," Alec replied.

"Welcome to Mexico, Sir. I'm your ride out to The Ranch." The pilot idled the Cessna's Textron Lycoming engine, applied the wheel brakes and swung his muscular body out the left side door of the aircraft. He was dressed in tan slacks and a short-sleeve checked shirt and tan penny loafers. Alec instantly noticed the excessive wear on the left side of the pilot's trousers just below his belt. *Wears his weapon there*, Alec reasoned, *but takes it off when he goes off the reservation. He's young, probably in his late twenties, and built like he works out every day*, he thought. *But, this is where they send the young recruits to get a taste of the world they will be working in after they get their first real assignments.*

"The weather forecast down here is supposed to be perfect for hunting. Not anything like what you're used to in the U.K. I'm your guide for the dove and duck hunts you booked, but your hunt for big game is in another guide's hands." The young pilot walked over to the man who was shouldering his garment bag and extended his right hand. "Bill Parsons, Sir. Good to have you aboard. Here, let me get that for you." Parsons took the man's garment bag and reached for his gun case.

"I'll hold on to this, thank you."

"Your call, Sir. You can set it in the back seat while I put your bag in the aft storage compartment. We'll leave directly unless you need to relieve yourself. Flying over the Sea of Cortez can be a pretty bumpy experience at times."

"I'm fine, thank you."

Alec opened the right passenger side door and sat down in the seat next to the pilot, who was boarding the plane and buckling his four-point seat harness. The pilot increased the engine's revolutions so that the engine sound would mask his comments to the man who had just entered his aircraft.

"I need your identification, Sir."

Alec reached into the breast pocket of his sports jacket, drew out his British passport and handed it over to the pilot.

"Thanks, but no thanks. Your real identification if you please, Mr. Caldwell, your CIA credentials. I know who you are, Sir. Everyone at The Ranch knows who the Company's Mountain Man is. But, I have to verify that you are who you say you are, but you know the drill as well as I."

"Yes, I do, Mr. Parsons. But since I don't know you personally, and anybody can put a logo on the fuselage of an aircraft, I trust you'll return the favor."

"Of course. But if I wasn't the real deal, you would already be dead, Mr. Caldwell."

"There you have me, young man. My agency credentials are hidden in my gun case. It'll just take a moment. In the meantime, let me see yours."

"While you're back there, you may want to take off your coat. It's hot down here, and it's going to be getting hotter before the day's out. And, you can lose the mustache. It's got to be hot wearing that thing. And, it makes you stand out like a sore thumb!"

"Direct, aren't you, young man?" Alec said, exchanging his CIA credentials for the pilot's and giving him a stern look while checking his official photo.

"Sorry, Sir. Down here the first thing they teach us is to say what we think, and say it with as few words as possible to get the point across."

"Point taken. I remember those days, but my training began before you were born. Things really haven't changed all that much in the Company. Rules are rules. It's just that the environment we work in now is totally different."

"Roger that, Sir. Strap yourself in, Mr. Caldwell. This little puddle jumper is a great toy to drive. We're going to fly out over the Pacific a few miles, then turn north and run up the coast so we can approach The Ranch low and fast out of the west. Great fishing just off shore here, Sir. You'll probably see a few big marlin out there from this altitude. Maybe you can get in a little fishing before heading back to wherever you came from."

"Out of Scotland by way of London, young man. But no time for fishing on this trip. But the hunting should be interesting. No duck or dove shooting though. And no big game hunting either. At least not the four-legged kind."

"You're just as blunt and to the point as I am, Mr. Caldwell."

"Same employee, same rules, Mr. Parsons."

CHAPTER TEN

The White House
1600 Pennsylvania Avenue
Washington, D.C.
Tuesday, May 15 – 10:45am

" C OMEINMR.Armstrong. The President will see you now." Hunt's personal secretary smiled and opened the heavy oak door leading into the Oval Office.

Bitch, Don thought, returning the smile. *She loves to play the role just like her boss."*

She stood back for Don Armstrong to enter and closed the door silently behind him.

*   *   *

Don Armstrong, DCI, had called the President earlier that morning, and after being put on hold by his secretary and waiting for fifteen minutes, the President had answered the phone. Armstrong knew full well that Hunt purposely made him wait, just to remind him who his boss was. *My turn will come,* he reminded himself, smiling at the thought. He had been tempted to hang up, just to piss him off when he picked up the phone and found the Director of the Central Intelligence Agency had hung up on him. *One of these days*, he thought. But, he knew he had to play the game today, even though he had again waited outside the Oval Office for another ten minutes before the President finally buzzed his secretary to send him in. This was going to be a very important meeting, one where Armstrong would bait the trap that would put into play the plan he and Alec had agreed on that would work to avenge the President's betrayal and expose his treachery.

"Mr. President, thank you so much for taking the time out of your busy schedule to see me this morning. I apologize for the short notice, but I believe you should be apprised of what I'm going to tell you, and I preferred that it come from me, one on one."

"Come in, Don, you old rascal. You know I always have the time to see you. Sit over here on the sofa with me. How are things in Langley? You want coffee?"

"No thank you, Sir. I reached my limit early this morning."

"So what's so important that you had to come all the way over here to see me? That's what telephones are for, Don."

"True, Sir. But you never know who may be listening."

"Agreed. And your people are some of the worst offenders, Don. I'm not sure you don't know what I'm thinking even before I have the thought," he laughed, patting Armstrong on the knee. Just kidding, my friend. What's on your mind?"

"Sir, we don't do that anymore. Transparency is the name of the game these days"

"Of course. I know that. I'm just pulling your leg, Don. Don't be so serious."

"Well, Sir, as to why I asked for this audience . . ."

* * *

National Security Agency headquarters
Fort Meade, Maryland
Tuesday, May 15 – 2:15pm

"Hi, Bill. Don here."

"Well, if it isn't the nation's number one super spy. You keeping everything aboveboard over at Langley?"

"Just as transparent as the contaminated waters of the Potomac. But I understand you fellows up there at Fort Meade are even listening to the cell phone conversations of the downtown DC hookers these days. Miss Deborah Jean isn't on your payroll, is she? I understand our DC Madame has a world of dirt on quite a few of our elected officials. You boys are way overpaid, you know."

"Well, it looks like you finally got the goods on me, Don. To what do I owe the honor of a phone call from the esteemed Director of Central Intelligence? Not another breach of our congressional mandate not to listen to conversations of U.S. citizens, I hope."

Don Armstrong and Bill Davis had been friends since they both joined their respective agencies just out of college. Armstrong had graduated from the College of William and Mary in 1959 and Davis had graduated the same year from Rutgers University. Their friendship had grown stronger as the years passed, and had served as a catalyst in cementing good relations and information sharing between the two largest spy agencies in the U.S. They had kept up their friendly banter over the years, their friendship moving beyond the workplace and spilling over into their social lives.

"Well, yes and no. Bill, you remember those conversations between the White House and the President of Mexico you monitored for us a few weeks back?"

"How could I forget? I couldn't believe the guy holding the highest office in the land would rat out a CIA agent on a mission he actually thought up and authorized. Let me assure you, the tapes are in our archives should you ever want access. I assume you destroyed the copies I gave you."

"Yes, I gave them to the agent who we sent down to Mexico and he returned them to me. I know he didn't make extra copies. But, right now we've set up a sting operation to take down the guy sent by President Montoya to squeeze my agent who was down there. Some folks down in Southern Command's intelligence directorate let it be known that they had some dirt on our chief that probably was the reason he went to Montoya with what we were doing down there in the first place. That wouldn't have been so bad, but when he learned our agent had uncovered a sizable drug cartel operating on the lower Baja that was otherwise unknown to any of the people over at DEA, and our man was down there sniffing around, he must have realized we had opened his lunch box. So, he dropped a dime on my man to keep his involvement quiet. Fortunately his little squeeze play didn't work, and a Delta team out of Bragg went down, kicked some ass, and brought our man out.

"So, I need a repeat of the work you did for us initially. I know you aren't supposed to monitor conversations originating in the U.S., so like last time, use the same *cover your ass* scenario and log the operation as listening to conversations involving someone down in Mexico. You're still going to catch both sides of the conversations, regardless of where they originate. Anyway, what could you do if your people are listening to calls in and out of the President of Mexico's office and just happen to pick up a conversation or two between him and our President? We've got to know how much of the information I gave to the President this morning reaches Montoya. Whatever Hunt tells Montoya will be passed on to the man we're after."

"Jesus, Don, you're going to put my ass in somebody's crosshairs for sure this time."

"Nobody will ever know NSA was involved in this. You know we don't talk out of school, and the President surely isn't going to tip his hand. It's already too far down in the cookie jar for him to recover if the press gets wind of his little skimming operation and his treachery.

"But, his reaction to our agent's safe return was quite interesting, and the news I laid on him that our man was now back down there putting the final touches on a plan to take out the drug cartel seemed to shake his cage. He had thought our agent was history, and I know he was prepared to express his condolences for our loss of a top agent. I thought he was going to shit a brick right there in the Oval Office when he learned we were still pursuing the drug operation. He made some lame excuse to end our little meeting, hustled me out and told his secretary he didn't want to be disturbed for at least a couple of hours. When I left, she was frantically trying to cancel meetings he had committed to. It was hard to hold back my laughter until I got outside the White House.

"Just as a heads-up, we've turned the drug information over to DEA, and they'll handle that end of the equation. We're not involved in that, and they don't know the President is, either. That's really none of their business, so as far as we're concerned; that information is *need to know* only.

"We, on the other hand, are going after one Carlos Ortega."

"Never heard of him."

"He's the executioner Montoya sent to take our man out after he was through administering some very professional torture. The son-of-a-bitch is a sadist. Fortunately, his little plan was interrupted before any physical or mental harm was inflicted on our man, but, we were just hours ahead of his execution.

"It's more than just a personal vendetta with us, Bill. We've just learned this Ortega lowlife has been linked to some pretty horrific drug-related deaths down in South and Central America, according to intelligence given us by Southern Command. We know now that some of the agents we've lost down there over the past several years fell by this shithead's hand. So, like the man says, *what goes around comes around*."

"OK, you've convinced me. We'll use our facility at Sugar Grove, West Virginia. They cover all Intelsat satellite traffic for the whole of North and South America. These satellites mostly carry civilian traffic, but they also carry some diplomatic and governmental communications. Even if they use a secure communications system, one or more of the

Intelsats satellites following a geo-stationary orbit will carry the signals, and we can intercept and monitor their conversations.

"I'll set this operation up on one condition, Don. If we nail the bastards, you've got to come clean on this. Together we'll go to General Alexander and give him all the details. Then you and he can decide where this goes from there. I suspect it will end there. Me, I'm just going back to being an underpaid civil servant and hopefully hang on to my job for a few more years."

"Done. And, as always, I owe you, Bill!"

"That you do my friend, big time!"

CHAPTER ELEVEN

The Ranch, CIA Covert Operations Center
Baja California Sur, Mexico
Monday, May 14 – 2:36pm

ALEC PUT AWAY the disguises and forged papers he had used on the circuitous route he had taken from his home in Montana through the U.K. and back to the U.S. before arriving in Mexico, the CIA's covert operations station located on Mexico's Baja peninsula. He dressed in shorts, a pullover short-sleeve knit shirt and tan loafers without socks, looking the typical single male British tourist on vacation in one of Mexico's most popular resort areas. He had removed the wedding band from his left hand and had washed the temporary dye out of his graying hair. In the little town just beyond The Ranch he had found a barber shop and had his hair cut in the style he had worn before beginning the mission to rescue Kathy McKenzie that had led to his discovery of a major drug ring operating out of the Cabo San Lucas area and his near-death experience. The haircut was not what one would classify as professional, but it really didn't matter.

His new identity, the same name that Don Armstrong had given to President Hunt earlier in the day, was supported by new papers

and another forged passport with a week-old entry stamp indicating
he had crossed the U.S./Mexican border at Nogales and had driven
down access-controlled, Highway 15 through Hermosillo, and on to
Guaymas where he supposedly took the ferry from the mainland across
the Gulf of California to Santa Rosalia on the Baja. There he took the
Transpeninsular Highway north to The Ranch. Alec was given dated
fuel, lodging, and toll receipts, including a ferry ticket, generated along
the route he supposedly took to The Ranch.

The car Alec was to use while in Mexico, a Nissan "Z" Roadster,
befitting his new identity, had actually been driven on Alec's route
by another agent whose looks had been radically altered through the
use of a plastic face mask expertly molded to match Alec's facial
characteristics as closely as possible. The agent's name was Vanessa
Van Pelt. Since she didn't have to leave the vehicle, her body features
didn't require alterations. Her picture had been taken at the border
crossing and again as she drove onto the ferry to Santa Rosalia, but
she knew that photos were being made at both points and hid her face
sufficiently under the cap she was wearing that no one looking at the
tapes could say for certain who the driver was.

Alec's new identity as John Majors, a single British pharmaceutical
salesman on vacation in Mexico, was complete. His next task was to
check in at the Casa Del Mar resort hotel on Medano Beach in Cabo
San Lucas where reservations had been made for him through a travel
agency in London, used occasionally by the CIA. The reservations, in
the name of John Majors, were made on the day Alec left the Washington
area for England, the same day Don Armstrong had sanctioned his plan
to take down Carlos Ortega, the sadistic executioner, working for
President Montoya, whom he had sent to the Baja to torture Alec and
ultimately erase all traces of his life.

Alec had purposely not discussed his entire plan with Armstrong,
because he knew he would not have agreed with what he planned to
do. But, he had already set the plan in motion. After all, there was more
than one culprit in the events that lead to Alec's capture and torture;
and he had decided, as he sat alone in Montana's quiet mountain

wilderness, that everyone involved would ultimately pay, at least those within his grasp.

The next day, Alec drove the "Z" the eighty-five miles northeast to Route 1 and turned south down the winding and sometimes treacherous Transpeninsular Highway back through Santa Rosalia on the gulf shore where he supposedly had arrived by ferry on the Baja. Beyond Mulege, the highway continued southeast through the coastal town of Loreto, but further south, turned inland, winding through the beautiful panorama of Bahia de la Concepcion. Here, the highway turned southwest moving inland again through the rugged Sierra de la Giganta, then descended into a wide agricultural valley and through the quaint inland towns of Ciudad Insurgentes and Ciudad Constitucion. Another one hundred and twenty miles past the historic village of Santa Rita, the highway turned back towards the beautiful coastal town of La Paz on the Sea of Cortez before winding through green coastal hills via the steep Sierra de la Laguna and on through quiet fishing villages along the Bahia de Palmas. The highway then wound through low coastal hills before reaching San José del Cabo. The next twenty miles, called the Golden Corridor, had white sandy beaches and craggy coves to the east and wall-to-wall resort hotels and time share condominiums to the west. The highway here hugged the coast to its terminus on the extreme southern tip of the peninsula at the touristy town of Cabo San Lucas.

Alec exited at Medano Beach and pulled into the valet parking entrance to the Casa Del Mar resort hotel and spa. A corner suite on the hotel's top floor with a view of the north beach and neighboring Dreams Los Cabos resort hotel had been requested and reserved. Alec checked in during the early evening and later strolled over to the Mango Deck for a tequila shooter or two.

*   *   *

The Mango Deck
Cabo San Lucas, Mexico
Tuesday, May 15 – 5:18pm

"You alone, Handsome?" The voice was female, soft and seductive, but contained a note of refinement. He knew it wasn't one of the local prostitutes who circulated among the more up-scale bars, it was too familiar. The attractive lady was wearing a pleated silk chiffon skirt that ended just above her knees, showing off her deeply tanned and well-sculptured legs. She wore no slip, exposing her shapely hips and buttocks through the folds of the sheer fabric, attracting the gaze of most of the bar's male patrons, none of whom were locals. Dressed as she was, her full breasts seductively exposed just enough to draw every man's gaze away from her striking face; she appeared much younger than her age. She approached Alec from the rear, but had waited a few minutes in a dark corner of the bar to be sure no one else was joining him before walking over to his table.

"Not if you join me," he said, standing and turning around to greet a smiling Vanessa Van Pelt, a fellow CIA operative whom Alec had recruited several years earlier. *She looks very comfortable in the role she's playing,* Alec thought. *In fact, she always seems to be comfortable in any role we've asked her to play. Remarkable lady.*

Although from a well-to-do family whose roots had been traced back to the earlier settlers of Virginia, and married to a very famous cardiologist who invented a heart valve anti-rejection serum that continued to generate gobs of money far beyond their wildest dreams, Vanessa had decided to take the law into her own hands after her infant son was kidnapped and brutally murdered by two teenagers who needed money to feed their drug habit. A technical legal maneuver by their attorney had freed them, although they had confessed to their heinous crime.

After months of schooling and practice, she had become an assassin, avenging her son's death by taking the lives of his two killers and their corrupt attorney in such ways as to leave no incriminating evidence. The adrenalin rush she got from her new endeavor gradually led her into the life of an assassin-for-hire.

Instead of turning her over to the FBI after she successfully carried out the assassinations of two associates who had fallen out of favor of her Mafia employer, Alec decided, because of her exceptional talents, to turn her from the dark side and bring her into the CIA as a free agent. Under Alec's tutelage, she ultimately took down the head of the Mafia family who had contracted the death of Alec's wife's former husband, the Secretary of the Interior.

"Sorry to be a little late, darling. Took me longer to get here from The Ranch than I figured it would," Alec said, embracing his friend and associate; he kissed her as though she were his lover. They held the embrace for a sufficient time so anyone watching them would assume they were.

"I checked in yesterday at Dreams Los Cabos resort," Vanessa whispered in his ear, still in Alec's embrace. "And if we don't back off this embrace, I'm going to begin to think there may be something between us and decide to get up real close and personal. You know this old girl may have a couple of years on you, Alec, but there's still a little fire left in the furnace."

"Now what would your husband say if he heard you talking like that?" Alec teased, slipping his hands down from her waist and patting her on the buttocks.

"He's off in Germany on another speaking tour. That's what he gets for being such an important cardiologist. Everyone wants some of his time, which leaves very little for poor little me," she said, pouting. "He's been away for almost a month now, and this lady is getting a bit lonely, if you know what I mean. Anyway, he's probably already enticed a fraulein or two into his bed by now. He's good at that. So, what's good for the gander is also good for the goose!"

"You do make a convincing argument, Lady. Something I'll be thinking about these next few days," he whispered.

"Don't wait too long, Alec," she quipped, whispering in his ear. "You know what they say about striking when the iron is hot. Your iron, that is!"

They both laughed.

*   *   *

CIA Headquarters
Langley, Virginia
Wednesday, May 16 – 10:32pm

"Hey Rob, heard anything yet from Don's friend over at NSA?" Alec and Vanessa had returned to his suite after an early dinner at one of Cabo San Lucas' better beach restaurants noted for its almond crusted grouper and unique frozen margaritas. Even though it was late, after ten on America's east coast, he was betting Rob Downing, his contact at CIA headquarters, would answer. Alec knew he kept late hours. It went with the territory.

"Nothing yet, Alec. But we expect Hunt will make contact before the evening is out. He won't keep this under wraps long. And as soon as they get something, they'll let me know. That's why I'm still here. I'm waiting for their call.

"But to give you an update, Don met with the President first thing this morning and gave him all the disinformation he would need to pass on to President Montoya about your current activities in Mexico. He told him the truth about the hotel you're staying in and the alias you're using this time, so if this sting works, they'll know where to come looking for you. Or, at least they'll think they know.

"Don said when he told the President you had survived the torture somebody put you through and escaped before they could kill you, he seemed overly surprised, even disappointed, as though he was prepared to tell Don how sorry he was that you had been captured and killed. Don didn't give him any of the particulars about your escape, just that you had escaped and returned stateside to brief the CIA, before heading back down there to wipe out the drug runners you felt were behind your capture and torture. Hunt has no idea we have his conversation on tape with Montoya where he gave you up. We guess he felt if you could get the information you needed to rescue the McKenzie girl, you could also learn enough to take out the cartel. And that would end his meal ticket. So, he sold you out."

"Yeah, the son-of-a-bitch will pay for that act of treason," Alec said angrily.

"After leaving the White House, Don immediately called his friend, Bill Davis, the deputy director over at NSA, and he agreed to have all conversations between President Hunt and President Montoya monitored and taped as he did earlier when his people picked up the conversation where Hunt gave you up initially and told Montoya what you were doing, where you were staying, and what alias you were using. Unfortunately, all that information came from McKenzie's daughter by accident, but you know that.

"Hunt has no idea we're on to him, and the information Don fed him this morning, if he contacts Montoya and gives you up a second time, should give you the target you asked for.

"By the way, just so you know, Don's a little pissed at you for not letting him in on the fact that you were going to use Vanessa as a back-up on this mission. And I didn't think it was my place to tell him, so you be thinking how you're going to get out of that when the two of you get back. Not that he isn't pleased you finally agreed to use some help. He just likes to know where his people are."

"Well, just so you know, Rob, that's not the whole story either. When Vanessa and I get through with this first gig, we have another in the works."

"Jesus, Alec. Don't tell me you two are going on a killing spree down there. You could set our relations with Mexico back a hundred years if you take out Montoya. You may even spark a war."

"Montoya's scalp is safe for the moment, Rob. I'll let the honest politicians down here take care of him after this is over. Once the Mexican press gets hold of what he and Hunt have been doing-skimming and protecting a drug cartel-he won't last long on the political scene.

"As for us, we'll be going after the two remaining assholes in the dive shop gang who kidnapped and raped Kathy, then ratted out the boy I interrogated. Hell, they just may have slit his throat for all I know. That's going to be a little favor for McKenzie. I'm going to need a favor from him after we return and I want him in a position where he can't refuse. Anyway, eliminating the other two guys just might slow down the white slave trade down here for awhile. But, I'm not so naive as to think that someone else won't jump in and take their places as soon as word gets out that they aren't around anymore."

"Ok, Alec. When I know, you'll know. Just cool your heels. It'll come."

"We're standing by down here waiting for your call, Rob"

* * *

Casa del Mar Hotel
Cabo San Lucas, Mexico
Thursday, May 17 – 9:38am

"Can you see me over here?" Alec was talking on his cell phone to Vanessa from inside his suite on the top floor of the Casa del Mar. He was looking north through his binoculars at Vanessa standing on the balcony of her top-floor suite at the Dreams Los Cabos. The resort hotels were located side by side, but separated by an extensive and beautiful courtyard filled with tropical gardens, pedestrian walkways and occasional open-air bars with thatched roofs and decorative gas lanterns, all designed to promote a festive atmosphere for the throngs of tourist that frequently this high-end tourist destination.

The built-in range finder measured the distance at six hundred twenty yards. Although there was an on-shore breeze off the Sea of Cortez, the air was dead calm in the expansive courtyard between the two resort hotels. Alec knew it would be. Before selecting the two hotels, he had checked this out by placing wind velocity meters at strategic locations throughout the gardens within the courtyard.

"Yes, I can see you, but you're going to have a problem if the target is standing inside your suite. Too much shadow over there this time of day to get off a kill shot. This thing has to go down in the morning, Alec, when the sun's in the east and there's plenty of light filtering through the rooms of your suite. In the afternoon when the sun's in the west, your suite's living room is in shadows. You're going to have a tough time making the shot if your target's inside unless you have a night scope. We've got to find a way to lure him outside onto the balcony if we have to wait until afternoon. We have to create a reason he would want to go outside."

Vanessa was standing outside the glass French doors that led onto the balcony of her suite. She was holding her cell phone in her left hand and a pair of binoculars with a built-in range finder to her eyes in the other hand.

"What's your reading?" Alec asked.

"Six hundred twenty-three yards," Vanessa replied.

"OK. I'm going out on the balcony to a position I want him in when this thing goes down. So, you go back in the room and take another reading from a position in the shadows. I'm going to need that cover so he or his men can't see me and mark the location of the shot. Mark the position in the room and give me another reading."

"Six hundred sixteen yards, dead on."

"OK, I'm coming over. Stay put."

"Yes, Bwana," she said, mockingly.

Alec rode the elegantly decorated elevator to the fifth floor of Vanessa's hotel and walked down the hall to her suite. She was standing in the doorway, seductively leaning against the doorframe, still wearing her revealing skirt.

"If you don't take that outfit off, I don't think I'll be able to concentrate on our mission." Alec said, smiling at his associate.

"So, are you telling me you can't handle two missions at one time? And, if I do take off this skirt, I know very well you won't be able to concentrate on your primary mission," she said, fluttering her eyes and smiling at him, seductively. "Your eyes will be glassed over."

"Jesus, I didn't mean now, at least not in front of me. You're too damned seductive, woman. If I weren't married . . . ." He shook his head, all the time eyeing her slim, firm body, and the sensuous pose she had struck. "And after those tequila shooters, I'm not sure I could stop myself if you keep playing this game. So, please, let's just concentrate on what we're here to do."

"OK, Lover. I'll give you a rain check. But don't forget, we haven't finished this conversation."

Alec walked out on the balcony, shaking his head as Vanessa watched him walk out. "Nice ass," she thought as she smiled and turned to go to her bedroom to change her seductive dress for shorts and a loose fitting blouse.

*　　*　　*

The White House
1600 Pennsylvania Avenue
Washington, DC
Tuesday, May 15 – 8:30pm

President John Hunt was used to telling his secretary to ring whomever he wanted to speak with, but it was nearing midnight and the regular White House staff had long since gone home to be with their families. For most of the staff, the day began at six in the morning, and a good night's sleep was a rarity. But this was an international call Hunt needed to make himself in the privacy of the Oval Office with no one around except the Secret Service agents stationed outside and strategically throughout the west wing, none within hearing distance. He opened the left top drawer of his massive desk and withdrew the Red Phone, the one instrument he had been informed was so secure that not even the NSA could monitor his conversations. Of course it had been the Director of the National Security Administration who had told him that.

Hunt punched in the numbers, and within seconds, the call was answered by the familiar voice of a person who seemed to have just been awakened.

"Yes?"

"President Montoya, this is John Hunt."

"President Hunt. Why are you calling at this time of the night?"

"I had to be sure I could make this call in complete privacy. There are just too many eyes and ears around the White House during working hours. I hope your line is secure."

"It is, Mr. President. What's on your mind?"

"I just learned this morning from my DCI that his agent, the one we sent down to the Baja to rescue the daughter of a very good friend of mine, escaped your men and returned to the U.S. to tell the DCI all about the little drug ring he had discovered down there. You assured me, Juan, that he would be taken care of and I would be expressing my condolences to his boss, not congratulating him on his agent's safe return. Just what the hell happened, Juan?"

"I was going to call you, John, but I wanted to find out how he escaped before I did. I really don't know what happened at this point. My interrogator had the CIA agent imprisoned in an old presidio in San José del Cabo with eight guards bivouacked there just to prevent such an escape from happening. When my man returned to the presidio in the morning to continue his interrogation of your agent, he found the police already there and his prisoner gone.

"Someone heard a loud noise in the presidio in the night, like an explosion, and had called the police the next morning. They found all of the guards dead, each shot multiple times as though they had been killed with automatic weapons. They were all laid out on their backs in a row, faces up. Strange, but a guard's shoes were missing, and his sidearm, according to my man's report. The door to the room where your agent was being held had been blown off its hinges. That's probably what the person heard who called the police. And, the police found the remains of what looked like parachutes, jump suits and various weapons, all burned. But, they were able to identify the remains of the automatic weapons as having been made in China. Using Chinese weapons doesn't sound like a U.S. operation, but personally I think it was a military operation launched from the U.S. Probably used Chinese weapons just to confuse the issue. But, there wasn't enough left behind to support any ironclad conclusion.

"The police fanned out across the town looking for anyone who seemed out of place, but with so many American tourists there it was futile to even think they could find the people responsible. No one living in the area saw anyone who looked like they didn't belong there, and everyone the police checked had their papers.

"But, Carlos is still down there looking into what happened, and he'll report to me as soon as he knows anything."

"Well, Juan. I have a little news for you. The CIA agent your man let escape is already back down there, and I understand he's planning to take out everyone connected to the drug ring for what he believes they tried to do to him. And that includes your executioner. From what the DCI tells me, this man is capable of doing just that. The one thing we have going for us is the DCI doesn't suspect I have any involvement and gave me all the information your man will need to locate and take out his agent."

"Excellent," exclaimed the President of Mexico. "Carlos will have an opportunity to earn a reprieve of his own execution for failing me the first time. That is, if he kills your agent like I told him to do the first time. He's such a perfectionist. He wanted to know what your agent had learned, and to whom he may have talked, before killing him. So, now that he has returned, I will instruct him to kill him first and not to take chances that he may escape again. After he's dead he can ask your agent any questions he wishes.

"But what I don't understand, John, is how your agent got word to whoever came down and got him out, that he had been taken and where he was being held. He didn't have contact with anyone on the outside, and Carlos swears by his men, so there wasn't a leak there."

"I asked my DCI the same question. Seems he had two miniature transmitters on him. One in a communications device he always carries with him, and the other embedded in his handgun. It's supposedly molded into the composite grips and can't be found unless its signal is picked up and the grips are broken apart. When its battery is depleted, he just discards the grips and screws on another pair identical to the original."

"That explains it. Carlos told me when he took down your agent he took his gun with him. I guess he wanted a souvenir. So, that's how his buddies found him. Very clever people, your CIA agents, John."

"So, Juan, tell your man, Carlos, he got off lucky this time, but there aren't going to be any more second chances. You and I can't afford for him not to be successful this time. It's just dumb luck we're getting this second chance, so tell him to make it good, or I'll personally send the whole damned CIA down there to screw his life up, royally."

"All right, John, calm down. But let's be sure we understand each other. If you keep your people off our sovereign lands, we'll do likewise. But, if you send your people down here again without telling me first, I'll personally supervise the release and transport of our worst criminals across your Texas and Arizona borders. And, my friend, you haven't seen bad until these boys slip into your country."

"OK, Juan, I get the point. I apologize for what I said. I just can't afford to have this thing get out. It would ruin me here, and it would ruin you down there, so let's just try to cooperate and get this guy under the dirt before he does us in."

"Agreed. So what else can you tell me?"

When President Hunt had finished his discussion with President Montoya of Mexico, he had Alec's current alias and where he was staying in Cabo San Lucas. What he didn't have was the fact that Alec;

a.k.a. John Majors, had a back up-one Vanessa Van Pelt-and a plan they had already put into play.

*   *   *

CIA Headquarters
Langley, Virginia
Tuesday, May 15 – 8:45pm

"Green Light, Alec! Hunt made the call thirty minutes ago. You'll love the tapes. By the way, your target, this Carlos fellow, is down there in your back yard. He's up in San José del Cabo trying to figure out how you slipped out of his grasp and wiped out his little army. And, he's got your name, or at least the one you're using now, and where you're staying. Of course he doesn't know Vanessa is there so he doesn't know you have a backup. We believe he'll put another team together and go after you right away, probably in the next two days.

"When President Montoya got off the phone with Hunt, he called this Carlos person and chewed his ass out. Told him if he screwed this up, his head would adorn the flagpole outside the capitol building in Mexico City. Sounded like a general dressing down a private. So, my friend, like Larry the Cable Guy says, *Git er done!*"

"You're the man, Rob. I'll keep you posted."

*   *   *

Dreams Las Cabos Resort Hotel
Cabo San Lucas, Mexico
Wednesday, May 16 – 9:45am

Alec was sitting in Vanessa's suite in an overstuffed chair he had placed over a mark on the carpet. Vanessa had marked the spot when he instructed her to give him the target acquisition yardage from a fixed point deep in the shadows in her suite at the Dreams Las Cabos hotel. The shot would be made to a fixed point on the balcony of his suite at the Casa Del Mar hotel a few hundred yards north. The yardage was six hundred sixteen yards. For some, it would be a long shot, for others, impossible. But for Alec, it was an easy reach. He had selected a Remington 700 bolt-action rifle chambered for the small, but swift 22-250 caliber cartridge propelling a forty grain ballistic tip bullet at a muzzle velocity around 3,700 feet per second. For weapon stability and accuracy, he had affixed a very heavy free-floating barrel to the receiver, designed for long-range competitive target shooting. Normally, his greatest fear would have been windage with such a light bullet, but in selecting the kill zone he had virtually eliminated this factor. His wind velocity meters had been active since yesterday, and none of the six units had registered winds of a velocity that would have an impact on the bullet's trajectory over this distance.

Depending on the hour, the courtyard and gardens separating the two hotels could be filled with people. There were two outdoor bars in the gardens sporting thatched roofs over open bars featuring frozen margaritas and daiquiris, two for the price of one, all day, every day. He couldn't afford to have the people strolling the gardens or drinking at the bars hear the shot. It had to be silent, and there could be no flash to attract anyone's attention. However, timing was a factor over which he had no control.

Because of these environmental drawbacks, Alec had decided to use a suppressor. The silencer would not decrease the accuracy of his shot, and would suppress the muzzle report and virtually eliminate the weapon's flash signature, both factors that could assist in identifying his location if someone were looking in his direction when he made his shot, or if a second shot were needed to complete his mission.

Alec decided to make the suppressor in his machine shop in the basement of his house outside of Lennep, Montana, rather than purchase one on the open market. The unit he made was an 8-½ inch, thread-mounted tube, almost two inches in diameter and machined entirely from welded 304 stainless steel. The unit's baffle stack was designed to create a substantial sound frequency shift and produce a muzzle report equal to the ballistic crack of the bullet in flight. Just a dull thump, barely audible more than twenty yards away.

The suppressor also would reduce the weapon's recoil to the extent that Alec would be able to see the bullet's impact through the riflescope. The slightly added weight of the suppressor would assist in reducing the barrel's harmonics, thus increasing Alec's shot accuracy.

Alec mailed the suppressor to himself at The Ranch and picked it up on his way through. He knew the Mexican Customs inspectors would open the package, so he inserted it into the hollow aluminum leg of a tripod designed to support a camera with a heavy telephoto lens for outdoor long distance photography. The Mexicans never knew it was hidden there.

*   *   *

The day before Rob called confirming the conversation between President Hunt and President Montoya of Mexico, Alec and Vanessa worked through their plans until Alec felt comfortable with the setup. He had stationed Vanessa on his balcony well out of the way of a thick cardboard box filled with newspapers he had positioned where his target would be standing, reading the note Alec planned to leave for him. The newspapers inside the box would stop a projectile the size of the bullet he would be using. He was in Vanessa's suite, deep in shadow, in the position he was now occupying, communicating with Vanessa on a hand-held CB radio. She couldn't see him, even using her binoculars.

He used the back of a sturdy chair to steady the rifle's heavy barrel. Sighting his target through a 10 x 42 fixed power Super Sniper scope with mil-dot reticule, manufactured by SWFA Optics, he placed three shots in a two inch circle he had drawn on the face of the target box from over six hundred yards away. After each shot, he and Vanessa scanned the neighboring suites in both hotels and the people below in the courtyard park and at the bars to see if the reports had attracted any attention. No one below was looking up in his direction and no one had appeared on the neighboring balconies. Alec was satisfied with the setup, and with the functioning of his suppressor. The pair met in the courtyard between the hotels and walked over to one of the open bars for a drink.

*   *   *

Thursday, May 17—Dawn

It was the second day of Alec's vigil. Dawn was just breaking over the calm waters of the Sea of Cortez. The sun would be rising in another thirty-five minutes. He was sitting motionless in the overstuffed chair placed deep within Vanessa's suite, his binoculars trained on the balcony of his suite on the same floor as Vanessa's, but in the Casa del Mar Hotel across the expansive courtyard. His arms were bracing the weapon lying across his lap. He was invisible to anyone who might enter his suite just over six hundred yards away. Nothing was happening, no movement in the target zone. He continued to wait and watch.

Vanessa was sitting by the Casa del Mar indoor pool, having coffee, her bikini tracing a well-defined tan line that suggested she had recently spent a good deal of time in the sun. She was a beautiful woman, and her tan accentuated her beauty. Her vantage point gave her an unobstructed view through the thick glass partitions of the bank of elevators in the La Casa Del Mar hotel that took guests up to their suites. When the target arrived, she would warn Alec through the hand-held CB radio, using a coded word in case someone was tuned in to the public channel they were using. The advance warning would give him sufficient time to prepare for the shot he knew he would make today. She was only to key her mic and say the word, *Showtime*. Alec would know.

*   *   *

When talking with Alec the previous day, Rob Downing had mentioned that he and Don Armstrong felt the man, known to them as

Carlos Ortega, would put a team together once President Montoya told him that Alec was back on the Baja. He would be coming after Alec with instructions to kill him as quickly as possible. Alec assumed he would be dressed as he was when he and his men had taken Alec down the last time he was here. Alec's assumption was dead wrong.

*   *   *

Vanessa had been sitting at her out-of-the-way table for better than two hours, seemingly reading a book, but behind her sun glasses, watching the movement of the hotel's guests in and out of the bank of elevators behind a glass partition separating the indoor pool area from the corridor leading from the lobby to one of the hotel's wings. She was looking for a person matching Carlos' physical description and dressed in a smartly tailored suit, surrounded by a cadre of men in military uniforms. She paid no attention to the darkly tanned man wearing a light blue open-collar knit shirt and white tennis shorts, no different from many of the other tourists staying at the resort. A white towel was draped over his head concealing his face from Vanessa and the other guests waiting for the elevators to arrive. He was wearing tennis sneakers with white half-socks and was carrying a tennis racket, a tube of balls and a small leather case, as he waited patiently for one of the elevators to return to the hotel's lobby. He appeared to be returning from the hotel's tennis courts, on his way up to his suite to take a shower. It was a perfect cover for an assassin bent on killing another guest of the hotel.

*   *   *

Vanessa's Suite
Dreams Las Cabos Hotel
Thursday, May 17 – 11:30am

It was going on noon of the second day of Alec and Vanessa's watch. His suite at the Casa Del Mar resort hotel was bathed in sunlight, filtering through the glass panels separating the suite's living quarters from its outside balcony. It was a clear day, cloudless, and the temperature was steadily rising-another beautiful day for the well-heeled beautiful people visiting this very expensive vacation paradise.

Alec continued to focus his full attention on his suite, but having done so for the past three hours, he was beginning to tire, his mind beginning to wander. Initially, the slight movement of the sheers covering the glass panels didn't register on his mind. Then a quick shadow moved slowly, deliberately. Someone had entered the suite. Alec knew that when the door to his suite was opened, even slightly, the air pressure differential between the suite and the entrance hall would make the sheers move if the French doors leading to the balcony were open. Air would be sucked into the suite from outside through the open doors causing the sheer curtains to move.

"Probably maid service," he said to himself. "Vanessa would have warned me if it were Carlos." Then Alec remembered; he had left word with the front desk that he didn't want maid service today. *Did they disregard my request, or has someone else entered my suite?* He asked himself.

Alec's pulse quickened as he lifted his rifle, centered the scope on the French doors leading into the suite from the balcony, and tried to identify any movement. *Why hasn't Vanessa warned me? Has something happened to her?* He picked up his hand-held CB radio, keyed the mic and spoke into the unit. "Vanessa, are you there?" His call was answered immediately. "I'm here, Alec. What's happening?"

"Somebody just entered my suite. I saw the sheers inside the windows move. And, then a shadow. Did our target get by you?"

"I didn't see him if he did. No one dressed like your description of Carlos has used the elevators. Everybody has been dressed in casual clothes. And no group of men, at least no more than a group of three have gone up since I got here."

"OK, stay put, but keep your eyes open."

"What are you going to do?"

"I'm going to sit and watch. You do the same."

Alec continued his scan of his suite through his high-powered riflescope, looking for movement. Nothing. The first hint that someone might be in his suite had brought him back to full alert. A minute slowly ticked by, then another. There it was again. Something or someone in the very back of the suite was slowly moving from room to room. It was a person and he was casing the two bedrooms. He would come out into the main room, then slip back into one of the adjoining rooms. He was now in the main room of the suite but remaining in the back shadows moving slowly, stopping often to look and listen, taking in every aspect of the suite. As he slowly emerged from the back shadows, Alec could see his right arm was crooked. He was holding a semi-automatic handgun in such a way as to be able to bring the weapon to bear quickly. He could see a suppressor attached to the barrel. The man was dressed in tennis shorts and a knit shirt. "No wonder Vanessa didn't recognize Carlos, he's dressed like a tourist, not like I described him to her," he said out loud.

Alec grabbed his CB radio, keyed the mic and spoke softly. "He's here, Vanessa. He's in the suite. And he's alone. Or, at least I haven't seen anyone else. And, it's Carlos. He's dressed in tennis shorts, but it's Ortega all right. I would recognize that scar on his right cheek anywhere."

"I've seen several men wearing tennis shorts and carrying rackets at the elevators but since I didn't have a photo of Carlos, I didn't have any point of facial recognition to use other than the scar on his cheek you told me about." Vanessa responded. "But I didn't see anyone with a scar. Sorry."

"That's not a problem," Alec responded. "We're ready to move into phase two. I want you to go up to the top floor. Take the elevator and be sure you're loaded down with the packages we made up yesterday. In the hall you'll be able to determine if there's anyone else with Carlos. If so, they would possibly be loitering around in the hall, or ready to burst into my suite with weapons drawn. If anyone's there, go to the suite two doors before mine and unlock the door with the key card

I gave you. Go in and get rid of the packages, and be ready to step out into the hall if you hear anyone out there. If no one is in the hall, discard the packages and stand away from the door to my suite so you can block Carlos' escape if he makes it that far. Shoot him in the head if you have a shot. Even though he's dressed in tennis togs, he could be wearing body armor, so if you have to shoot him in the chest, be sure you follow up with a head shot. With body armor, it'll take him a few seconds to recover from the impact of your chest shot, so you take him down permanently with the head shot before he recovers enough to shoot you. If he's in the hall, drag him into the suite. Then, get the hell out of there."

"What if someone comes while this thing is going down?"

"You really don't have a choice, Vanessa. If you can get away without being recognized, you know what to do. If you can't, kill the witness," Alec responded. "You can't afford to be recognized or get caught."

"Hey, Lover, nobody said anything about collateral damage. I'm not in to wasting innocents."

"I hope it doesn't come to that, Vanessa, but you're on a mission, and sometimes innocents get in the way. You're in the real world now, Sweetheart, and it isn't pretty. Sorry, but you don't have a choice. Let's just hope this thing goes off without a hitch and you can maintain your innocence."

*   *   *

Alec's Suite
Casa Del Mar Resort Hotel
Cabo San Lucas, Mexico
Thursday, May 17 – 11:51am

Alec continued watching the man in his suite move about the living room, now in full sunlight. There was no question as to his identity.

Alec had moved the large glass-top table on the balcony to a position just forward of where he wanted Carlos to stand when he ultimately came outside onto the balcony. He had also arranged the four chairs in a fashion that would place the man at just the right distance and just the right profile. In addition, he had placed an open briefcase on the table positioned so anyone reaching into the briefcase would have to be against the table's edge to reach it. All of these minor details were very important. Nothing could be left to chance.

The briefcase was empty except for a sheet of paper, folded twice. He knew Carlos would never open a briefcase to see what was inside for fear of triggering an explosive device. He wouldn't be that stupid. Even before lifting and unfolding the paper, he would check to see if a miniature switch had been placed below the paper. He would be careful, because he was smart. His intelligence had taken him this far. Would it be enough this time?

*   *   *

Carlos remained within the confines of the suite and didn't venture out onto the balcony for close to half an hour. He sat in one of the side chairs, his weapon in his right hand extended across his lap, seemingly waiting for Alec to return to his suite. Alec continued to wait, his finger on the trigger of his weapon. Finally Carlos got out of his chair and began pacing around the room. Suddenly, he stopped and looked out the glass windows towards the balcony. Alec moved his scope to see what he was looking at. It was the briefcase. He was staring at it as though he was seeing it for the first time. Carlos walked over to the door, still focusing on the briefcase on the glass-top table, and moved out onto the balcony, walking slowly towards the table. He looked at the briefcase from underneath the glass top table to see if a compression switch to activate an explosive charge was positioned underneath. There was no switch. He looked down into the empty briefcase, which contained only the folded paper that Alec had placed there. He looked at it for a moment, but didn't pick it up, turned and walked back into the suite.

"Shit." Alec said out loud. "Thought I had him." He eased his finger off the trigger and continued to watch.

Carlos opened the center drawer of the writing desk in the living room, took out a long yellow pencil, and returned to the balcony, looking in all directions before he ventured beyond the entrance.

Careful SOB, Alec thought. He continued to watch through the scope as Carlos walked over to the table and carefully inserted the pencil's sharpened end below each corner of the folded paper, lifting it slightly and looking beneath the corner to determine if the paper could be another trigger that, if lifted from the briefcase, would set off an explosion designed to kill him. Alec smiled to himself. *The moment of truth has arrived*, he thought.

When Carlos was satisfied there was no hidden pressure switch, he took the paper out of the briefcase, unfolded it into a single sheet, and read the words written inside. As he did, he glanced up, a look of total surprise on his face.

He was still holding the sheet of paper in his left hand when the bullet struck him in the soft tissue of his right eye. It mushroomed, then fragmented, and scrambled his brain, but didn't exit the back of his skull, its kinetic energy spent. Carlos Ortega was dead before he fell backwards onto the tiled patio floor. The only blood leaking from his dead body was from the socket where his right eye had been, and from his right ear. The sheet of paper he was holding floated out of his hand on a gentle breeze, remained suspended in the air for just a moment, then floated over the edge of the patio towards the well-manicured grounds below. It would be picked up by a maintenance employee of the Casa del Mar resort hotel and innocently deposited in a nearby trash receptacle. No one else would ever read the cryptic note.

Alec placed his rifle beside his chair, casually retrieved his hand-held CB radio and spoke these words: "The door has been closed." Vanessa responded: "Excellent, I'll see you in fifteen minutes."

*   *   *

Vanessa had been standing in the hall outside Alec's suite, her back pressed tightly against the wall adjacent to the suite's door, waiting for

Carlos to come out or to receive word from Alec that he was dead. As soon as she had received Alec's message that the man was down, she burst through the door, her silenced Walther PPK at the ready should anyone else be there whom Alec had not seen while following Carlos through his riflescope. She quickly checked all the rooms; no one was there except Carlos Ortega, whose prone, very dead body was lying on the hard tiled floor of the balcony, leaking a small amount of blood from his destroyed right eye socket and his right ear. He was lying on his back, the force of the bullet having knocked him backwards. A small amount of blood had drained onto the patio floor, which she would remove before leaving.

As Alec had instructed, she had put on surgical gloves before entering the suite to eliminate fingerprints. She dragged the body into the suite, and turned him over on his stomach so what blood drained out of his eye socket would stain the carpet. The police would think the man had died in the suite and would not check the balcony too closely for blood evidence. She next went out on the balcony and retrieved the briefcase from the glass-top table. Alec had wiped it clean of prints before setting it on the table, hoping Carlos would pick it up, leaving his prints. He hadn't, so Vanessa placed it in Carlos' dead hand, pressing his fingers around the handle to be sure the prints would take, then placed it on the writing desk.

Out of the bag she had brought with her, she removed several brochures of area points of interest, a local map, and the return portion of a round-trip airline ticket back to London listed in the name of John Majors, the name Alec was using on this mission. She also had the passport in Major's name that Alec had given her. It had been prepared just for this event and didn't contain a photo. She found the dead man's passport in his jacket pocket, removed his picture, and glued it into Alec's passport. She placed all of these items in the briefcase on the writing table and left it open. She also placed a worn leather wallet in the left rear pocket of the dead man's tennis shorts. The wallet contained a U.K. issued drivers license in Alec's fictitious name, several bogus credit cards, and other papers, all designed to convince the police that the body lying face down in Alec's suite, was John Majors, a pharmaceutical salesman from the U.K., the target Carlos Ortega was hunting.

After wiping it clean, Vanessa removed the silencer and placed her Walther PPK in Ortega's right hand, his thumb through the trigger guard as though he had used it to take his own life. The Walther PPK was a favorite of British MI-6 agents, which added a touch of reality to the British agent cover that Alec wanted the Mexican police to believe. A British agent traveling as a pharmaceutical salesman was the icing on the cake.

The day before, Vanessa had fired a round from the weapon, picked up the spent cartridge, wiped it clean and slipped it in her pocket. After pressing it between the thumb and forefinger of Carlos's right hand, she placed it on the carpet next to his dead body lying on the floor. The fingerprints would confirm that the cartridge had been fired from the gun in the dead man's hand.

Vanessa had no way of adding powder residue around the entrance wound made by Alec's shot, but she reasoned the local police were not so sophisticated in their forensics procedures that they would even consider looking for residue, always found on close-in shots like suicides. She turned to look back at the scene she had staged as she softly closed the door and took the elevator to the lobby where she would meet Alec.

*   *   *

Alec placed the CB radio on the table next to his chair, picked up his binoculars, and focused on his suite's balcony in the Casa del Mar hotel across the gardens, some six hundred yards away. He watched as Vanessa entered the suite and meticulously began putting the finishing touches on a situation he had put into play five minutes earlier. When he saw Vanessa leaving, he took the rifle apart and placed it and his binoculars into the golf bag he had purchased from the hotel's pro shop the day before, zipped the cover that concealed its contents, and slung it over his shoulder as he left Vanessa's suite for the lobby. He would walk over to the Casa del Mar to meet Vanessa and leave these two resort hotels for good. It was time to celebrate, and put the next phase of his plan into play.

*   *   *

Cabo San Lucas
Baja California Sur, Mexico
Friday, May 18

The story was relegated to a three-inch column on page six of the local newspaper and didn't even rate prime time reporting on either of the two local television stations. Excluding national happenings, the local news concentrated on what the tourist wanted to see and hear. No one seemed to be interested in the suicide of a male tourist, just another Brit on holiday who had lost his way.

According to police reports, John Majors, a U.K. tourist, traveling alone, had committed suicide in his suite on the top floor of the Casa del Mar resort hotel in Cabo San Lucas. No one came forward to claim the body, and after all legal requirements had been met and the British Consulate in Mexico City had been notified, it was cremated, as are all unclaimed bodies in Mexico.

*   *   *

Presidential Palace
Mexico City, Mexico
Friday, May 18 – 4:00pm

One person, sitting alone in his opulent office in Mexico City, was very interested in the news of the under-reported event of Major's suicide. He had been waiting, patiently, for word to reach him. The little-read news item brought a smile to his weathered face. Juan Montoya, the President of Mexico yelled at his secretary, "Get me a secure line to the U.S. President in Washington, DC, and hurry."

"Well, my friend. It's over. Your Mr. Majors is nothing more than a small pile of ashes."

"Ashes?" questioned President Hunt.

"Yes, his body was cremated this morning."

"What are you saying?"

"My man, Carlos Ortega, shot him. Evidently he walked up to this Mr. Majors' suite, knocked on the door, and when your agent answered it, he shot him in the face. He made it look like a suicide. At least that's what the coroner's report says, *Death by Suicide*."

"What does your Mr. Ortega say?"

"I haven't talked with him. I told him, if he's successful, he must immediately go underground. No contact with me or anyone else. He had to disappear for at least two weeks. He did exactly what he was told, so I haven't talked to him. He'll turn up in Ecuador in a couple of weeks. I have some work for him down there."

"Are you absolutely sure of this, Juan? Remember, your man didn't get the job finished last time. Maybe he didn't get it finished this time either."

"It's done, John. Trust me. If you wish, I can have his personal effects sent to you. The police are holding his wallet and passport plus his watch and his wedding band. The watch is inscribed to him from someone named Beth, probably his wife, but it's not to your John Majors, a British Pharmaceutical salesman. It's to someone named Alec. I suspect that name can be traced to your agent's true identity since we both know Majors is an alias he was using."

"No, don't do that. Have it burned. I want every bit of evidence of his existence eliminated. Don't send anything that belonged to him up here. Nobody down there can know I'm involved in this, you either, for that matter.

"By the way, Juan, you know you've made my day. Now I can call this man's boss, my Director of Central Intelligence, and tell the bastard that word is out down in Mexico that his agent has been killed. I'll play the sorrowful bearer of bad news, but it tickles the shit out of me to put that screwball down. Armstrong has been a thorn in my side ever since I became President. It's my turn to lay a little whoop ass on him for a change."

"Goodbye, John, and good luck. Our people over on the Baja have been lying low ever since your man arrived back on the peninsula. I'll get the word to them that their threat has been eliminated and to get back into full distribution. We want those money transfers to keep coming."

*   *   *

The Venetian Restaurant
Cabo San Lucas
Baja California Sur, Mexico
Friday, May 18 – 7:45pm

"So, Lover, just what did you write on that piece of paper that so startled Mr. Ortega that he dropped his guard?" Vanessa asked Alec as they sat in the dimly lit bar waiting for their dinner reservations to be called.

"Just one word: *Goodbye*! When he read it I think he realized he was about to buy the farm. The look of surprise on his face was worth everything we had to do to put him in that position. I believe he was looking directly at me when the bullet hit him. His mouth was open as though he was asking someone a question. So, we've successfully written the first act of this play. Now, let's see what we can do to write the final chapter."

Both Alec and Vanessa knew this wasn't the end; it was hardly the beginning.

CHAPTER TWELVE

Hotel Finisterra
Cabo San Lucas
Baja California Sur, Mexico
Saturday, May 19 – 9:45am

V ANESSA CHECKED OUT of the Dreams Los Cabos resort hotel that afternoon, paid her bill with an American Express credit card in the alias she was using and instructed the concierge to have a taxi pick her up and drive her to the airport for her return trip to the U.S.

At Los Cabos International Airport, instead of going into the terminal building to check her luggage, she waited on the curb for the few minutes it took Alec to arrive. He was driving her vehicle, and the trunk was already full of equipment she had brought with her when she initially drove the car across the U.S./Mexican border at Nogales. She had flashed a fake U.S. Border Patrol ID when crossing into Mexico, and was waved through by the Mexican border guards without having her vehicle searched. So she placed her two bags in the back seat and buckled up for the ride back to Cabo San Lucas where she picked up the car Alec had been given at The Ranch and followed him to the Hotel Finisterra. Alec had made reservations for both of them in separate, but adjoining, rooms when he first arrived on the Baja, and only had to confirm their arrival two days earlier than anticipated. The first phase of Alec's plan had finalized two days earlier than he had expected.

The Finisterra is a luxury hotel located at the tip of the Baja peninsula, overlooking the Cabo San Lucas Yacht Club to the north and the unique rock outcroppings rising from the sea to the south. It is here that the Sea of Cortez merges with the Pacific Ocean. The point is known as Lands End.

The hotel's location was important. It put Alec within easy walking distance of the boat slip where the young men from the dive shop berthed the yacht they used to make the blue-water runs to the drug ship that arrived each month some thirty-five miles off the Baja's east coast. The rendezvous point was well outside the area covered by the coastal radar net, even beyond the normal patrol routes of the Mexican Coast Guard cutters.

* * *

Hotel Finisterra
Cabo San Lucas
Baja California Sur, Mexico
Monday, June 4

For over two weeks, Alec and Vanessa had watched and recorded every movement of *The Emerald Pelican*. On day trips out into the Sea of Cortez the yacht always carried passengers, usually young men and women dressed in wet suits. Alec watched their departures and arrivals through his binoculars as he sat on the veranda of his third floor suite in the Hotel Finisterra. SCUBA equipment was always present, and the trips were relatively short, stopping at various points along the barrier reef several miles beyond the mouth of the harbor to allow the guests to don SCUBA equipment and plunge into the cool emerald green waters.

Alec used the time the yacht was out to make regular visits to the Coast Guard station and the Harbor Master's office, both located at the entrance to the harbor. The Harbor Master monitored and logged all water vessel traffic in and out of the harbor, recording the name of the vessel, the flag under which it was sailing and the names and number of people on board. The Coast Guard monitored all large vessel traffic once it passed outside the harbor and kept detailed records of each vessel's travel route within the statutory limits of Mexico's territorial waters. *The Emerald Pelican*'s length was sufficient to require Coast Guard monitoring. Vessels with a length of twenty-eight feet or less were exempt, but many captains of smaller vessels registered their trip information with the Coast Guard for safety purposes.

Alec was supposedly conducting research on the coastal waters of the Sea of Cortez at various points along the east coast of the Baja for the shipping company for which his papers indicated he worked. Because of his credentials, and the plausibility of his inquiries, he was given access to the route information of all watercraft plying the coastal waters out of the Cabo San Lucas harbor. Alec was interested in only one of these vessels, *The Emerald Pelican*. And, he was interested only in their trips made during non-daylight hours. According to information logged by the Harbor Master, *The Emerald Pelican* generally carried only three persons on these night excursions: the vessel's owner who served as her captain, and two employees, his mate and the new member of his dive shop operations. There were no passengers logged with the Harbor Master.

Unfortunately, the vessel's midnight voyages continued past the outer limits of Mexico's territorial limits and the Coast Guard's radar net, and its signature would be lost beyond this point, only to be reacquired several hours later as the vessel returned to port. The Coast Guard station commander had initially been curious about the timing and duration of these trips and kept precise route and time logs, but when he began making inquiries, he was instructed to cease and desist, and had taken the inquiry no further.

According to the commander's log, *The Emerald Pelican* would make these midnight runs once each week, always on Thursday, and always just after midnight. The vessel, according to the Coast Guard logs, would run the same route, always at an average speed of sixteen knots, relatively slow for a vessel with twin screws that could easily travel at twenty-seven knots without taxing its engines. The Coast Guard had recorded these trips for three years. His logs showed one trip each week at precisely the same date and time each month, even during inclement weather.

Alec reasoned that if the vessel maintained the same speed beyond the radar net as when it was within Mexico's territorial waters, and returned on average two hours later, it could have traveled a little more than sixteen nautical miles beyond the radar limits before making the return trip. Allowing for a half-hour rendezvous time, Alec figured *The Emerald Pelican* would rendezvous with the coastal freighter carrying the supply of cocaine some twelve nautical miles beyond the radar net. But, he had to be sure.

Alec's plan required knowing the general route information *The Emerald Pelican* would follow after its signature was lost to the coastal radar net. He assumed it was a straight-line course where the captain would dial in the GPS coordinates and put the vessel on autopilot, which would automatically compensate for tides and winds. He knew the vessel's captain was aware of the radar's search limits, and that what he was doing out in the Sea of Cortez in the dark of night had to be done beyond the prying eyes of the Coast Guard. Alec knew the *what* of this question, but he didn't know the *where*, and that information was crucial to his plan.

Alec had the Company's pilot, Bill Parsons, fly the Cessna 172 down from The Ranch to a small local airstrip west of Cabo San Lucas to pick him up just before midnight on Thursday, the 16th, the evening *The Emerald Pelican* would normally make its weekly drug run. The four-place Cessna, with Parsons in the left seat, Alec in the right, and Vanessa in the back, lifted off just before midnight on a warm breeze that filled the darkened sky with the scent of tropical flowers. The full moon had risen and the sky was ablaze with millions of stars as they flew over Cabo San Lucas and banked right towards the harbor and the Sea of Cortez beyond.

They were flying at only two thousand feet when they arrived at the mouth of the harbor leading into the Cabo San Lucas Yacht Club, the bright lights of the surrounding hotels and tourist attractions making it seem almost like day. Alec scanned the boats moored in the general vicinity of the slip used by *The Emerald Pelican*.

"It's not there. It's gone. We're too late," Alec said, dejectedly.

"Could you recognize the yacht from the air if we were to fly over it?" Parsons asked, looking inquisitively at Alec.

"Yes, I think so." Alec continued to scan the hundreds of large yachts moored in the harbor.

"OK, let's check out the vessel that was leaving the harbor as we flew over a few minutes ago. Maybe it was your friend," Parsons said, glancing out the left side window as he dipped the Cessna's left wing and applied slight left rudder on the pedals, putting the plane in a slow left bank back towards the mouth of the harbor.

"See down there," he said to Alec, pointing to a large yacht just crossing the first harbor marker buoy into the Sea of Cortez. "Check that boat out, Alec. I'm going to stay at this altitude and come up on his stern. When you can verify the name of the vessel on the stern, say so, and I will turn the aircraft away as if we are going north up the coast."

"That's her," Alec said after training his binoculars on the vessel's stern. The apprehension was gone from his voice, replaced by a note of triumph. "She's right on time, and making the same track the Coast Guard says she always does. This should be interesting."

As anticipated, *The Emerald Pelican* continued on a straight-line track out to sea. Parsons continued to fly the Cessna in a crisscross pattern well behind the stern of the yacht, at varying altitudes, but never below two thousand feet. The three men on the yacht never knew the aircraft was plotting their course.

The yacht was being steered on an easterly track with her running lights off. Alec anticipated this, but he knew they would be able to see the vessel's wake from their altitude by the light of the full moon. The phosphorescence in the water, disturbed by the passing yacht, left a glowing trail of emerald green as the vessel sailed eastward. This was a trip that the yacht owner did not want recorded by the Coast Guard. Without running lights, once the vessel passed beyond their radar net, they would vanish into the night. At least that's what they thought.

Each time they would cross the yacht's path, Alec would log the longitude and latitude coordinates in his hand-held GPS unit, creating a route matching the exact route the yacht was on. He would need these coordinates later to plot the course of another craft.

The captain began to decrease the yacht's speed until it was dead in the water, waiting. The outline of a much larger ship a mile or more off the yacht's bow was now barely visible. It seemed to be anchored, although the smoke drifting from its stacks indicated its diesel engines were running at idle. There were no deck or running lights visible.

"That's a coastal steamer if I remember its general outline correctly, probably a dry bulk transport. Great for transporting drugs for offshore pick-up," Alec commented. "Probably drifting, waiting for the rendezvous."

"Look out there." The pilot was pointing towards the bow of the freighter. "That's a blinking light near the bow, probably a flashlight. They're signaling the yacht. Do you read Morse code?" he asked, looking at Alec.

"No, sorry. It's been too many years since I had to use it," Alec replied, a disappointed look on his face.

"I do," Vanessa said from the rear seat of the aircraft. She was using her night-vision binoculars. "The larger ship is signaling an *all clear* message to the yacht," she said. "The yacht should begin its approach now."

"I assume they aren't going to light up their radar," Parson observed. "If they do, their signature will be picked up by the Coast Guard patrol planes and their location will be given away. They don't want that to happen, so I assume they don't know we're out here either."

"Good. Let's stay well away from both vessels until we see the yacht leaving," Alec responded. "When we put the next phase of our plan in place, it will be on their return trip to the Mexican coast. I want to take out the yacht after it's loaded with their weekly supply of cocaine."

*   *   *

The Emerald Pelican retraced the route it used to reach the drug ship and slipped back into the harbor. The Coast Guard picked up its radar signature when the yacht entered the area covered by their sweep and tracked it to the mouth of the Cabo San Lucas harbor. It was nearing dawn, and the full moon was moving across the Pacific Ocean towards the distant horizon. Although the night sky was full of stars, the harbor and yacht basin were far too dark to discern any activity there with the naked eye.

Alec and Vanessa were back in their hotel when the yacht completed its return trip. They were sitting on Alec's veranda watching the yacht's captain maneuver it into its docking slip through their night-vision binoculars. Although the scene seemed to be colored in a light green phosphorus color, they could easily make out the mate throwing the bow and stern lines to two men standing on the dock. They secured the yacht and backed a panel delivery truck to the side of the yacht where all hands, except the captain, began offloading brown, cellophane wrapped square packages into the back of the panel truck. There was no other activity at the yacht basin, no prying eyes watching the men unloading the drugs. It was 5:30 in the morning, and as far as they were concerned, there was no one else there.

"We've got a lot to do before next Thursday," Alec said. "If they keep to the routine they've used these past several months, they'll make their next blue-water drug run then and we'll be ready."

Alec and Vanessa watched the panel truck drive off the docks and onto Boulevard Marina, which meanders around the yacht basin and merges into Lazaro Cardenas towards San Jose del Cabo. The driver flicked on the truck lights as it entered the deserted thoroughfare and headed north.

* * *

Georgetown, Washington,
District of Columbia
A Look Back

The name he used was Henry Rothrock. It really didn't matter what his real name was since he never used it anyway. In his business, names weren't important as long as they were fictitious.

Henry Rothrock possessed three traits that were very important to the line of work chosen for him: his military prowess, an ability to kill without hesitation or remorse, and an undying loyalty to his employer.

They had tracked him down in Somalia in East Africa six years ago. He was working with a rag-tag group of mercenaries using hit-and-run military styled incursions into Ethiopia, their mission was to harass the Ethiopian government to the extent that they would invade Somalia, which had a much superior army and was itching for a fight. Somalia had long converted the suspected oil and gas deposits deep in the sands that lay beneath Ethiopian territorial waters. Of late the food his group was able to glean from the countryside was poor, living conditions were terrible, and their pay even worse. He had been an easy recruit.

Rothrock had acquired his special military talents during his twelve-year stint with the Army Rangers assigned to Southern Command's teams of deep cover personnel deployed in South and Central America to interrupt the flow of drugs into the United States. The Army's Southern Command called it *interdiction.* He called it a waste of time. His definition was closer to the truth. Nothing they did put even a small dent in the flood of drugs streaming into the United States from South and Central America.

Earlier, his parents had convinced him to continue his formal education. He had been an exceptionally bright student, so acceptance at Davidson College in North Carolina was no problem. However, after only three months there, it became apparent, at least to him, that spending hours studying subjects that held little or no interest for him was a waste of his time and a waste of his life.

On spring break that same year, he hitched a ride with a friend down U.S. Route 29 to Charlotte, walked into the Armed Forces recruiting offices, and joined the Army on the promise that he would be called up for duty within thirty days. Without telling his parents, he had left school. He left for basic training at Fort Jackson in Columbia, South Carolina two weeks later, and went on to Advanced Infantry Training at Fort Benning in Columbus, Georgia. There, after AIT, he enrolled in Ranger School and was assigned to the 75th Ranger Regiment with which he saw combat in Saudi Arabia in 1991, during Operation Desert Storm, and again in 1993 in Somalia. Later, he served in Kosovo as a member of the Regiment's Reconnaissance Detachment Team 2. In 2002, he was discharged and disappeared off the face of the earth. Not even his parents knew his whereabouts.

Rothrock had no strong political convictions and embraced no known political ideology. He was in it for the money, but equally important, he relished the adrenalin rush he got when engaged in close combat situations. He was the perfect candidate for the work they wanted him to do.

Over the next six years, Henry Rothrock had become the leader of a team of five men, all, except he, in their early thirties. They all had extensive military training that qualified them for the black operations they were employed to carry out. All were single and without strong family ties except to one another. Rothrock had reached forty, and although he kept his body and mind in top physical and mental condition, his age was beginning to show.

The five men worked exclusively for the President of the United States, and no member had ever retired from the team. When a member was killed, another younger recruit would take his place. Longevity, as a member of the President's *Black Hawks* team, was not one of the perks of membership. But wealth was.

The team was financed with funds generated through grants awarded by the Spartan Foundation, established by one of Hunt's corporate holdings to support deserving community medical endeavors. Applications were taken each spring and fall, and the single most deserving applicant received funding based on his needs. Somehow, a grant application from the Georgetown Community Medical Center was always on file along with the other applicant and was always the successful candidate. The Internal Revenue Service never seemed to question the foundation's so-called philanthropic endeavors. Hunt's political machine made sure of that.

* * *

Hunt was a wealthy man, but his wealth was old family money, generated first by his grandfather, Joshua Hunt, whose skill and cunning during the Prohibition era of the 1920s took the family from its poor Irish roots to a lifestyle they never had imagined. Joshua's theory was quite simple. *Give the people what they want, the law be damned, and give them the very best products available at a reasonable price, and you will succeed.* Although he was not an educated man, he possessed a keen sense of economic logic, realizing that what a government prohibits its populace from having is always the one thing they crave the most. And, he was prepared to take advantage of what he knew to be a most lucrative endeavor. He also was well aware that if he kept his operation small, those men who controlled the passage of illegal goods between Canada and the U.S. would not interfere with what he was doing.

Prohibition was in full swing when Joshua set up his base of operations on the U.S. shores of Lake Erie just across the New York border in Pennsylvania where he unloaded Canadian whiskey from his small boat each night. Joshua's two sons, one of whom was John Hunt's father, helped him with his small enterprise. The boys, both in their teens, would take the skiff over to the Canadian side of Lake Erie during daylight hours, load it to its gunnels with brands of Canadian whiskey in demand in the U.S., and would sail across the lake under cover of darkness, their only navigation aid being an old compass their father had brought with the family when they fled Ireland years earlier. Joshua made the daily rounds of the clandestine speakeasies that dotted the many waterfront towns along Lake Erie, taking whiskey orders from the owners. He would extend credit to his best customers, but not without collateral. And, he didn't "cut" his products with water as many of the larger purveyors did. His initial operation was so small and insignificant that the rum runners didn't see him as a threat to their booming business, and they left him alone. Before anyone in the trade knew he even existed, Joshua commanded a fleet of nine sailing barks to support the transportation requirements of his growing business. When prohibition ended, John Hunt's grandfather was a very rich Irishman. John's father's shrewd investment skills quadrupled the family's wealth, primarily through investments in real estate, which provided the family with a substantial cash flow. Hunt inherited his family's fortune.

*   *   *

John Hunt organized his secretive *Black Hawks* team in his early political days as a junior member of the U.S. House of Representatives-actually, some six months before being elected to his first term. Their clandestine work had contributed significantly to his election to Congress. Hunt had no credentials on which he could base his campaign, so he created the *Black Hawks* team to smear the image of the incumbent. In fact, fabricated stories that surfaced during his first run for Congress were credited with turning the popular vote against his rival candidate, who had held the office for six consecutive terms, and who was innocent of the charges fabricated by Hunt's people and fed to the news media, hungry for dirt of any kind to print.

The team had continued to function as Hunt's private *army of dirty tricks* as he rose through the House, then the Senate and ultimately moved into the White House. Not even the President's Chief of Staff, although a close friend of twenty-plus years, knew of their existence. Hunt planned to keep it that way.

Hunt maintained a residence on Evergreen Avenue, West, just off 39th Street, NW in the Georgetown suburb of Washington. Evergreen is a quiet residential one-way street in the northern section of the village, shaded by large maples and oaks whose roots were beginning to buckle the cobblestone sidewalks and street surface. It was tucked away from the trendy shops and restaurants that lined K Street, the main thoroughfare into Georgetown. Most homes on Evergreen were considered substantially above modest, but not so large as to attract the wealthy politicians who lived in the more exclusive areas of Georgetown, down towards Canal Road.

The property had been acquired by a DC based law firm with political ties to the Hunt administration, and purchased under the name of a shell corporation whose ownership was shrouded in secrecy. The house was large compared to most houses in the neighborhood, bordering on estate class, with a high colonial-styled brick wall surrounding its one acre wooded and well-groomed gardens and lawn. The only public entrance into the heavily fortified compound was through a wrought-iron gate, continuously guarded by one of the President's *Black Hawk* members, and monitored from within, using the latest technology.

Hunt used the compound for two purposes: to meet with his *Black Hawks* team members when their services were needed, and as a sugar shack to bed his many female companions whose visits had increased significantly since his wife's passing. However, their numbers had dwindled recently in favor of the charms of one prostitute who worked exclusively with an escort service whose clients included many Washington-based politicians and lobbyist willing to pay thousands of dollars for the favors of these Ladies of the Night.

The one fly-in-the-ointment of which Hunt was not aware was that a few selected members of the Central Intelligence Agency knew who owned the property and for what purposes it was being used. Activities there were under constant surveillance and reported periodically to the DCI. To make matters worse for the President, the escort service he used was secretly run by the CIA

CHAPTER THIRTEEN

Apartment 301, Fairgate
209 Hamilton Boulevard
Georgetown, District of Columbia
June 5

H ER STREET NAME was Patricia, a name most would associate with a young, attractive, housewife with children, driving her Volvo SUV to a school PTA meeting or taking one of the boys to soccer practice. It was certainly not a name you would associate with a highly paid and well-educated prostitute who could hold her own in every level of Washington's social structure. Prostitutes in downtown Washington used street names such as Candy or Sugar, but these women were never found in the social circles frequented by the clients and employees of Stepford Escorts, a well-funded and highly-organized escort service created by the Central Intelligence Agency which used its employees as conduits for information gathering from its Washington based political clients.

Patricia hailed from Lawrence, Kansas and had attended the University of Kansas, located in her hometown, as a day student. Although participating in their honors program and majoring in pre-law, she decided to spend her last year of undergraduate studies at American University in hopes of being accepted into their Washington College of Law, where she wanted to specialize in International Studies and work towards a dual LLM/MBA.

Living costs in Washington, DC were much more expensive than in Kansas. The same was true for tuition at American University. When she found herself short of funds, she succumbed to the suggestions of one of her friends and classmates and became an employee of Stepford Escorts, Washington's most prestigious escort service. And, Patricia was well qualified for her new part-time employment. She was extremely attractive, tall, slim, just under six feet with sparkling eyes, a winning personality, and a broad smile that melted the hearts of all of her clients. And, she loved the act of making love, as long as she could choose her partners. After all, who from Lawrence, Kansas would ever know she had a part-time job as a highly paid and very successful prostitute?

Financially, she was doing well in her new profession and seemed to be losing interest in the legal profession, the one goal that had brought her to DC. But she had developed a propensity for spending beyond her means. The CIA knew this, and continued to feed her spending habit. They had plans for Patricia and would capitalize on this vulnerability at the appropriate time.

Since entering *the life*, Patricia had limited the men she would entertain to just three, one of whom was an older, widowed Senator looking only for companionship, someone to talk with and be on his arm for the many social events he was forced to attend as the Senate Majority Whip. Another was a very handsome lobbyist just a few years older than she, whom she thought she could truly love if circumstances were different. And, there was the most eligible john in all of Washington, the President of the United States, John Hunt.

What none of her clients knew, or even suspected, was that Sarah Jacobson, known to them only as Patricia, was writing a diary, keeping meticulous notes of her activities, and recording every word spoken by her clients, especially those uttered by the President. She was surprised at how freely he talked about political matters when in bed with her. She had branded him as a braggart the first time they were introduced at a social gathering on the well-manicured grounds of one of his well-to-do and loyal contributors on the Virginia banks of the Potomac, well below the District. She had been ordered to attend the gathering even though a male escort did not accompany her. She and another coworker from the agency had been driven there in one of the escort agency's stretch limousines. Both had been instructed to mingle with several highly placed politicians whose photographs and biographical information had been provided well in advance of the event, one of whom was President Hunt. She had been talking with one of her targets when she caught the eye of the President. She had smiled at him as he strolled among the guests, glad handing those with the deepest pockets. He had literally walked up to her, introduced himself, taken her arm and whisked her away from the man with whom she had been talking. Hunt had been so infatuated with Patricia that he had not allowed the Secret Service to check into her background, other than to confirm that she was an undergraduate student at American University, hailed from Kansas, and that she did indeed work for the well known Stepford Escort Service.

The Director of Central Intelligence was ecstatic when he read the report of Patricia's latest conquest. He had never dreamed she could cultivate such a high value target so quickly. The one thing the DCI didn't know was that this was not the first meeting of the prostitute known as Patricia Simpson and the President of the United States.

* * *

Delmarva Peninsula
Earleville, Cecil County, Maryland
Some History

Maryland Route 282 begins just east of the Delaware-Maryland state line off US 301 near the village of Warwick, winds its way west through Cecilton and Earleville, and ends some seven miles west of

Earleville at Grove Point on the Chesapeake Bay across from the Army's Aberdeen Proving Ground.

Cecil and Kent Counties, which lie along the eastern side of the Chesapeake, are dotted with small towns and villages, most hardly larger than wide spots in the road, but all very important in the support of the agrarian economy of the Delmarva Peninsula.

The land is flat, and for the most part, is farmland dedicated to the production of corn and soybeans. Outside the mid-western Corn Belt, the fertile farmland on the eastern shore of the Chesapeake Bay produces some of the highest corn and soybeans yields in the nation.

People living here fall into two major groups, either farmers or watermen. Those who work the land now do so primarily for the very rich, or for large corporations, both domestic and foreign, who, over the last half-century, have purchased most of the small family-owned farms that once dotted this patchwork landscape.

The watermen, living in this area, are a breed unto themselves. Hardy, self-reliant, and fiercely independent, are just a few of the many adjectives that describe these men. They work the waters of the Chesapeake Bay and its tributaries, during both fair and adverse weather, tonging oysters, working their crab pots in the shallows, trawling for shrimp, and fishing their pound nets during the runs of blues and trout. These hardy seafarers grow old before their time, and by tradition, are locked into a lifestyle from which there seems no escape.

*   *   *

Stanhope Plantation
Earleville, Cecil County, Maryland

Stanhope Plantation is a three thousand acre farming operation located off Route 282 west of Earleville on the banks of the Sassafras River. The Sassafras feeds the upper reaches of the Chesapeake Bay, and has become a yachtsman's paradise, anchored in the small village of Georgetown, some ten miles upstream. Most of the sailing yachts here are owned by families living in and around Baltimore, located across the bay from the mouth of the Sassafras.

Stanhope Plantation is owned by the W. George Stanhope family. The patriarch, who was christened with the same name as his father and grandfather, represents a major portion of Maryland's Eastern Shore in the U.S. House of Representatives. Three generations of the family have laid claim to the political fortunes of this area, and in the minds of most residents, have served them well over the years.

The plantation's manor house, a two-story Georgian mansion with massive white columns rising above the first and second floor front porches, is located on a well-manicured grassy knoll that overlooks the Bay and the mouth of the Sassafras River. Guests lounging on the front porches of the mansion in the late evenings can see the lights of Baltimore on the western horizon, a stark reminder that civilization is closer than one cares to acknowledge in such a pristine setting.

The estate has served for three generations as the center for political gatherings of some of the most powerful and influential people who reside in the nation's capital, just a two-hour drive from DC by way of U.S. 301 through Annapolis and over the Bay Bridge. Guests exit Route 301 at Maryland Route 213, and drive west on the scenic two-lane road that meanders through the villages of Centerville and Chestertown to Cecilton, or remain on Route 301 until they reach Warwick. The only land approach to the estate is by way of Maryland Route 282 originating at Warwick through Cecilton and Earlville, and ending at Grove Point.

The graveled entrance to the estate, through large iron gates suspended between two massive brick columns, runs approximately two miles through fields of corn and soybeans interspaced occasionally by cypress swamps and patches of hardwoods. Years ago, cedars had been planted along both sides of the private drive, interspaced with manicured George Tabor azaleas. The cedars and the azaleas have grown to enormous size in the fertile soils of the area, and they present an inviting and beautiful welcome to guests to the estate.

During the warm days of spring through the blustery days of fall, sailboats of all sizes and descriptions dot the Chesapeake Bay waterscape. Many, including motor yachts, anchor in the protected cove at the river's mouth where the Stanhopes maintain their private docks if they are invited guests to what is taking place in the manor house up on the hill.

Behind the main house, three immaculate red stables house eleven of the finest thoroughbreds in eastern Maryland. Each morning, the horses are allowed to romp in the expansive green pastures surrounded by miles of white board fences.

If the President of the United States is planning to attend, he can leave the White House in Marine One, his Merlin EH 101 helicopter, and be at the estate in seventeen short minutes. A circular concrete helipad has been strategically located adjacent to one of the stables where the President's helicopter remains during his stay, constantly guarded by the members of the four-Marine contingent that always accompany the helicopter whenever the President is present.

*　　*　　*

The Hans Jacobson Family
St Augustine, Cecil County, Maryland

The Jacobson family ancestors settled in Cecil County, Maryland during the great European migration of immigrants escaping oppression and looking for a better life in the U.S., generations ago. Over the years they farmed the land and established a well-run family farm, one of hundreds that dotted the landscape through the sixties. But as the value of the dollar continued its fall against other world currencies in the seventies, most of the area family farms were gobbled up by European and Asian interests looking for good investments in the U.S., as well as by major American corporations that could take advantage of the economies of scale to produce products at lower costs than smaller concerns.

In effect, the farming families of the area who remained loyal to the land, took on the roles of farm supervisors and manual laborers, working for hourly wages, rather than for the pride of ownership. This was the fate of the Jacobson family.

Hans Jacobson worked on the Stanhope plantation as one of two farm supervisors, responsible for the planting, cultivation and harvesting of the corn and soybean crops that were annually rotated through the hundreds of acres of tillable soil on the plantation. He was also responsible for the thousands of dollars of modern farm equipment that was used to create the economies that make large scale farming on the Chesapeake a very profitable venture. His wife also worked for the Stanhopes as part of the house staff that swelled to three times its normal size during weekend festivities. His two sons, when not in school, worked as part-time laborers with the staff that maintained the grounds surrounding the manor house, and Jacobson's daughter, Sarah, also worked part-time with her mother as a member of the house staff during summers and weekends when not attending high school.

*   *   *

Stanhope Plantation
Earleville, Cecil County, Maryland
Six Years Earlier

On this particular weekend, the President had decided to attend the festivities at Stanhope. It was fall in the later part of his first year in office, and his wife had just been diagnosed with cervical cancer and didn't feel up to trying to maintain an up-beat image of the supportive wife of the most powerful man in the world. She had decided to remain in the White House on this particular weekend.

When the house staff heard the beat of the rotors of the President's helicopter, word of his arrival spread with considerable excitement.

At the Friday evening dinner, served in the master ballroom, a young and very pretty sixteen year old serving the table, caught the roving eye of the President. With his wife's frequent absences from Washington's social gatherings, he had already begun to establish a reputation of an errant spouse. But, presidents and kings are not necessarily held to the same moral standards as other less important men.

At 7:00am on Saturday morning, the President was sitting at the writing table in his upstairs suite, drinking coffee delivered earlier, and looking out over the Bay as the colorful oak and maple leaves of fall swirled around the manor house on a gentle October breeze. He was wearing a royal blue robe, especially tailored for him with the Presidential Seal and his name embroidered on its left breast. He wore nothing else except his watch.

The evening before, President Hunt asked his host to have the staff serve his breakfast in his suite at seven, because of calls he had to make. He also insisted that the young lady who had done such a masterful job serving his dinner, bring his food to him.

John Hunt knew who was at the door to his suite when the soft knock came. He glanced at his watch *Right on time*, he thought, as he rose to open the door. Sarah Jacobson was standing at the door behind the serving cart, smiling, her new soft white cotton uniform, which ended just above her knees, revealing the outline of her young and well-proportioned body.

The President returned the smile and stood aside as she rolled the serving cart into the room and began to set up the service on the writing table. Hunt admired the outline of her firm breasts and tight buttocks as she walked past. He knew what he was going to do. He had planned it since first seeing her at dinner the previous evening.

As Sarah walked over to the side of the writing table where the President had seated himself, he slipped his hands under her short skirt and massaged her thighs. She tried to step back away from his grip, but his hands were already on her buttocks as he stood up and pulled her up close to him.

Sarah Jacobson didn't know what to do. If she screamed and someone came to her rescue, the President would likely say that she had tried to come on to him. After all, he was the most powerful man in the world, and his word would be taken over hers. So, she remained silent as he pushed her skirt up and put his hand into her panties. Then he bent over and kissed her. Sarah thought she was going to throw up from the smell of stale cigar smoke on his breath and his rough unshaven face. She wanted to run and hide but knew it would do her no good-probably get her and her family fired if she resisted.

Sarah Jacobson remained passive as Hunt pushed her onto his unmade bed, pulled down her panties and entered her. She bit her lip from the pain of his forceful entry but did not scream out. She lay on the bed and let him have his way with her. Fortunately, Sarah was not a virgin. She was having an on-and-off affair with her current boyfriend, but she was far from experienced in the act of making love. And this wasn't love making. It wasn't even just rape. It was statutory rape. Sarah was only sixteen.

John Hunt's rape of the young girl didn't last long. He had been thinking of the act since dinner the previous evening and had even masturbated once during the night. By the time Sarah arrived he was already in a state of heightened excitement and couldn't hold back his moment of climax.

When he was through with her, he got up without saying a word and walked into the bathroom to take a shower. Sarah lay on the bed for a few moments asking herself why this awful thing had happened. Her thoughts of pity quickly turned to anger, and then to hate. She pulled herself off the bed, put on her panties he had partially ripped when he tore them off, smoothed her hair and uniform as best she could, and began to leave, when she saw Hunt's wallet on the bureau. He was in the shower, singing, when she opened his wallet and removed five one hundred dollar bills and stuffed them into her pocket.

"That's what it's going to cost you to rape me, you Son of a Bitch," she said, focusing her voice towards the partially closed bathroom door as she walked out of the suite, not bothering to close the bedroom door.

Sarah told her father about the rape that evening when they had gone back to their small rental home in St. Augustine. The next morning he drove up Route 213 to Elkton, the County Seat and informed the county sheriff of what had happened to his daughter. He filed an official complaint against President Hunt in his daughter's name. Since she was a minor, he had to sign the statutory rape charge.

Of course, nothing happened. The sheriff first called Congressman Stanhope to report the incident. He scoffed at the accusation, dismissing it as a fantasy concocted by an adolescent with too much imagination and loose morals. The sheriff agreed, and burned the complaint. Sarah's father called the sheriff several times during the following weeks, only to be told that *we're working on it*. Finally he gave up in frustration. There was no one else to help him vindicate his daughter.

That was just under six years ago.

*   *   *

The story of the rape of Sarah Jacobson was kept under wraps for several weeks, and, since the sheriff had personally burned the records, would have remained so, had it not been for a Cecil County off-duty deputy drinking far too much in a neighborhood restaurant/bar in Chesapeake City who began to recount the story as told to him by the sheriff. A man sitting at the bar a couple of stools away offered to buy him another beer, which he gladly accepted. When the man left, the deputy had consumed several more, compliments of his new friend, and was well on his way to his usual weekend state of inebriation.

During that short time span, the man had learned every detail of a very interesting story. That man was Don Armstrong, Director of the Central Intelligence Agency. He had taken U.S. 50 out of DC, had picked up U.S. 301 west of Annapolis on his way to his fishing cabin on the Delaware River, but had decided to drive a few miles out of his way to Chesapeake City for some locally famous crab cakes and bisque before traveling on to his cabin. As it turned out, his encounter with the deputy sheriff was a stroke of pure luck.

Armstrong did not complete his trip to the Delaware. He immediately retraced his route back to Washington and spent the remainder of the weekend working on a plan to learn just how promiscuous President Hunt really was.

Initially, he set up a watch detail that concentrated on Hunt's evening guests, especially unescorted ladies who accessed the White House by way of the private family entrance. The CIA was getting nowhere fast until one of the watch details observed a nondescript automobile leaving the White House grounds late one evening by the private entrance, and noticed that the person sitting in the front seat next to the driver looked a lot like the President. They decided to follow the vehicle, which drove west on Pennsylvania Avenue, and seemed to be driven aimlessly through the city for forty-five minutes, probably to determine if they could spot a tail.

Evidently satisfied that they were not being followed, the car turned up Evergreen Street and entered the walled grounds of a home with a large iron double gate in the Georgetown section of the District. The gates were opened as soon as the vehicle arrived, probably pre-arranged, and closed as soon as the car drove through.

The CIA was later able to learn the compound's ownership, plant sophisticated audio and video devices throughout the estate, and set up an observation post across Evergreen Street. Over the ensuing years, the set-up provided much of the evidence they were able to gather supporting the Washington rumors of Hunt's indiscretions.

*   *   *

As the weeks following the rape of Sarah Jacobson passed, rumors began to surface that pictured her as a girl with loose morals who had slept with the President and was paid five hundred dollars for her services. Although some of her girlfriends thought it was cool, among their parents, she was branded a whore. None of the boys in her school could raise that kind of money, so they didn't try to score as they did with her friends.

Rumors continued to swirl around the Jacobsons, questioning the moral fiber of the entire family. Hans decided to move his family out of the area. His older brother lived in Lawrence, Kansas, and worked for a large cooperative grain elevator and storage operation owned by several local ranchers. He got his brother an interview with a large rancher whose spread was only a few miles west of Lawrence. With his farming experience, Hans was offered the job as ranch supervisor over the phone.

The Jacobson family left St. Augustine late one evening, several months after the rape incident. Neighbors were surprised to see the "For Rent" sign in the front yard of their small home the next morning, and no one could determine where the family had gone. The real estate agent was sworn to secrecy.

*　　*　　*

Apartment 301, Fairgate
209 Hamilton Boulevard
Georgetown, District of Columbia

Patricia considered her diary an insurance policy that would provide her a long and prosperous future when she decided to give up her chosen profession for a quieter and more genteel life. She had abandoned her room on the American University campus and established a residence in an old brownstone, now an upscale apartment house in the Georgetown area of the District where she entertained the young lobbyist and the aging Senator when they were not out on the social circuits. She had discreetly placed recording devices throughout the apartment, but the President insisted on using his Georgetown compound for their rendezvous, so planting bugs there was impossible. But, she had managed to plant three small state-of-the-art listening devices in her apartment that produced excellent sound quality. The tiny devices produced clear signals that were picked up and recorded continuously on the equipment she had hidden in her bedroom closet, even when she was not in residence.

CHAPTER FOURTEEN

Hotel Finisterra
Cabo San Lucas
Baja California Sur, Mexico
Wednesday, May 23 –7:30pm

IT WAS WEDNESDAY evening. For over two weeks, Alec and Vanessa had spent long and boring hours watching *The Emerald Pelican's* travels, in and out of the yacht basin. As the yacht would begin backing out of its docking slip, they would leave their hotel together, and drive out to the small airstrip west of Cabo San Lucas on the Pacific coast, where they would loosen the tie-downs and remove the wheel chocks on the Agency's Cessna that Bill Parsons had left for them. Alec had been qualified in small Piper and Cessna single engine aircraft since his early days with the Company, and had kept his license current. Their route was always back over Cabo and out over the Sea of Cortez where they would observe the yacht and its passengers snorkeling and SCUBA diving on the shallow coral reef that protects the shoreline of the lower Baja.

*　*　*

"OK, Vanessa, it's time for me to do my thing. Those boys should be making their weekly drug run just before midnight if they follow their normal pattern. I haven't seen anyone down at the yacht basin for the past three hours, so it's time to go." Alec was looking at his watch. It was 2:30 Thursday morning. He was dressed in casual tan pleated shorts, no belt, leather topsider boat shoes without socks and a tee shirt with a huge blue marlin silk-screened on its back. It hung loosely outside his shorts, playing down his excellent physique. Anyone seeing him would think he was a tourist on his way back to his hotel after a night of drinking and carousing in the late-night bars and tourist traps that line the harbor. "If you see anyone at the yacht basin, or anything out of place, call me on the CB and use the codes we rehearsed. I'll break off and come back. I'm going to drive your car down to the dock and park it away from our friend's yacht. I'll stroll over to his slip. Be alert, and let me know if anything is going on. Do a wide sweep, Vanessa. This is a time we can't afford any surprises."

Alec locked the driver's side door of Vanessa's car which he had parked adjacent to one of the gated entrances to the southern section of the yacht basin, slung the backpack he had packed earlier over his right shoulder and entered the planked walkway that led out above the murky waters of the basin made turbid by the many boat propellers that churned up the muddy bottom and all the human waste collecting there for years. *The Emerald Pelican* was moored in its slip three spaces from the end of the catwalk. Other larger yachts were also moored there, but all were dark. No one was around at this late hour, at least no one he could see. Alec continued his slow and what appeared to be somewhat unsteady walk towards the end of the pier. To a casual observer, he seemed to have had too much to drink and was on his way back to one of the yachts. But, no one was there to see him. Vanessa was keeping him informed through his CB radio. He was using a remote mic and earpiece to eliminate any conversation that could be overheard by someone in the area whom they may not have seen.

Alec stopped in front of *The Emerald Pelican's* slip and checked his watch as he looked around the area. Still no one loitering about. He walked around to the side of the yacht and entered the aft deck through the passageway on the starboard side. He slipped quickly past the rows of air tanks used by the recreational diving customers and past the air compressor to the doors leading into the main salon. The two sliding doors were locked, and he used two thin wire-like tools from his lock-picking kit to quickly gain access. There were no lights on inside the main salon, and he could see no reflections from lights below. He quietly closed the outer doors to the main salon and drew the curtains so no one who might pass by outside would be able to see the light from his flashlight. Alec was looking for a hiding place, one where no one would have any reason to look. His search took him down into the galley, then the head, and finally into the rear stateroom. He did not investigate the forward and midship staterooms, because even if he could have found the perfect hiding place in either, they weren't in the appropriate area of the yacht to inflict the damage he felt was necessary.

Alec made his way down into the bilge and aft towards the engine compartment in the yacht's stern. This was the first time he had been inside the yacht, and he noticed the loading platforms built in the midship bilge. *Great storage area when you're bringing in a couple of tons of coke,* he said to himself. *Easy access and good ballast in rough seas.* He continued aft, knowing if he could find an appropriate hiding place in the engine compartment, his mission would have a successful ending.

There it was, below the battery compartment, a small rope locker, which looked as though Antonio Mendez had not opened it since he purchased the yacht. Eight massive batteries were lined up on the port side of the engine compartment on a shelf above the locker. The small, concealed area would be ideal to hide five bricks of C-4. Alec positioned the explosives in such a way as to direct the blast sideways, both into the engine compartment towards the two massive diesel engines, and outward through the port fuel tanks, blowing a large hole in the port side of the yacht below the water line and turning the vessel into a fireball. Seawater would rush into the engine compartment, and if the blast didn't take out the engines, the seawater would, in a matter of seconds. The water rushing into the aft compartment would destabilize the craft, and what was left of it would go down intact, in less than a minute, stern first. The three crew members would have no time to launch the yacht's dingy or put on life preservers. If they were far enough away from the drug ship they wouldn't survive, even if they had time to jump ship. They would be miles from shore and well outside the Coast Guard's patrol area.

Alec slid the backpack off his shoulder, snapped it open, and removed the five bricks of C-4, carefully placing the explosives into the space below the line of batteries before replacing the front panel. He had waited until the last minute to plant the charges to lessen the chance of anyone finding the explosives and foiling his plan. Anyone entering the engine room would not be able to see the little present he was leaving for the crew. He had inserted electronic detonators into the two end bricks. The detonation of the two armed bricks of C-4 would instantly set off the other three. The yacht's transom, its backbone, would literally be blown apart, and even if the crew survived the blast, the boat would sink quickly. Any distress signal the crew might try to send over the disabled radios would not be heard and would go unanswered.

Alec climbed the carpeted teakwood steps back to the yacht's main salon and up through the glass-sliding door into the pilothouse. He had one more present for the crew, and it had to be placed in a location that would give someone outside the vessel access to the signal it would begin generating before he left the yacht.

Alec finished his work, slipped off the yacht, and in just under an hour was back in his suite with Vanessa. They spent Tuesday strolling among the many shops on the waterfront and continuing their casual observance of the yacht. No one came near or boarded the yacht during the entire day, except a yacht club attendant who pulled a heavy hose from a fuel truck to the yacht and filled the tanks with diesel fuel. *The Emerald Pelican* was ready for her next blue-water drug run.

*   *   *

Thursday, May 24 – 11:38pm

Thursday passed with very little activity around the yacht. It was approaching midnight, the time Alec had been waiting for. He sat motionless in the lounge chair on the veranda of his suite, overlooking the Cabo San Lucas Yacht Club. He had been there well over two hours. It was the time Antonio Mendez usually put to sea with his two-man crew on his yacht, *The Emerald Pelican*. Alec was waiting for the yacht to weigh anchor and head out to sea. He would wait until the yacht reached a pre-determined position in its route to the Panamanian drug ship before he would call Vanessa and authorize the launch of the unmanned aerial vehicle. Timing was critical. With only so much life in the batteries that powered the UAV he had to be sure not to launch too soon for fear that it would lose power and go down before it accomplished its mission.

Alec held a pair of night vision binoculars in one hand and a Harris Falcon III, tactical military radio he had procured from the U.S. Central Command, in the other. On the table at his side was a sophisticated tracking unit equipped with a directional antenna. A laptop computer with full-image screen was beside the tracking unit, all part of the equipment Vanessa had brought with her when she crossed the border into Mexico at Nogales several weeks earlier. When the UAV was airborne and its cameras switched on, the images it was looking at would be projected onto the computer's screen, giving Alec a bird's eye view of what was happening within the camera's visual plane.

Days before leaving the States for Mexico, Vanessa had spent a week with the United States Joint Forces Command in Norfolk, Virginia with their special weapons unit, thanks to General Leon Hollins who had also engineered Alec's Delta Force rescue. She was there to learn the technical aspects and launch sequences of the Marines' newly upgraded Dragon Eye Unmanned Aerial Vehicle, a modular, twin-engine battery-operated UAV weighing only nine pounds with a wingspan of only 26 cm. The UAV's engines had been upgraded with higher capacity batteries giving it an enhanced flight endurance of three hours and a cruise speed of over 130 km/h. The Dragon Eye is one of several reconnaissance, surveillance and target acquisition UAVs in the Navy's Interim Small Remote Scouting System arsenal supporting Marine Corps operations. Its detachable video payload contained an IR 360 Pan tilt zoom platform supporting its black hot/ white hot night vision imaging camera system. Alec had specifically asked for this UAV, and Rob Downing had obliged.

Vanessa would bungee launch The Dragon Eye from the abandoned airstrip west of Cabo San Lucas, located on the Pacific side of the peninsula. The prevailing winds were always offshore here, supporting a westerly launch out over the steep cliffs at the end of the airstrip.

They had found the location by accident on one of their many scouting trips around the area. The overgrown dirt road into the abandoned strip appeared not to have been traveled in years. Just after the launch, when the UAV had gained altitude and speed, she would program the GPS coordinates into the drone's guidance system, and the Dragon Eye would automatically fly to a point south of Cabo over the rocky coast where the Pacific Ocean and the Sea of Cortez collided, generating enormous waves crashing against the rocky crags protruding from the eroded and rock strewn cliffs. Alec would take over the flight on Vanessa's command, and using his remote controls, would manually fly the UAV towards Cabo.

Earlier in the day, some five miles south of Cabo San Lucas, Alec had placed an innocent-looking cardboard box among the rocks, containing a single five pound brick of C-4. As the UAV approached the target zone he would test the remote detonation switch that would send a signal to the tiny receiver attached to the explosive's detonator. The explosion would be heard all over Cabo San Lucas. If the trigger worked, he would then reprogram the coordinates to direct the UAV out over the Sea of Cortez towards the primary target area. The drone's guidance system would automatically make course corrections to its flight plan to compensate for the aircraft's wind drift.

The hunt was on!

The plan was perfect, except for one factor over which Alec had no control. NOAA had announced only hours earlier that an unexpected weather front had begun to form some five hundred miles west of the Mexican Baja out over the Pacific and had begun moving towards the region. If it continued to gain speed and increase in intensity, as anticipated, it could reached the coast during the drone's flight and could easily blow the Dragon Eye off course to such an extent that it would be unable to reacquire its primary target. In his mind, Alec was praying for the front to be delayed until his operation was over.

*　*　*

It was just after midnight. The stars that had illuminated the sky earlier in the evening were now hidden from view by the dark clouds approaching from the west, giving the images he was watching through his night vision binoculars on *The Emerald Pelican* an eerie, almost translucent appearance as though each movement was being made in a shadowy slow-motion green haze.

The approaching storm didn't seem to dampen the spirits of the tourists strolling around the yacht basin and drinking in the bars that lined the streets around the harbor. Music of every description flowed on the night breeze, which was beginning to freshen as the storm approached. From Alec's veranda, high above the merriment below, the harbor appeared as a large black hole surrounded by bright lights and throngs of people, all in a party mood.

Vanessa had left Alec's suite two hours earlier, and headed towards the abandoned airstrip to assemble the components of the UAV and set up its launch system. She had given herself time to spare. Even though she had been through the assembly and set-up routines several times before, she wouldn't get a second chance to get it right this time. This time, it was for real.

The drive was just over an hour, and the assembly would take about twenty minutes, sufficient time to get the UAV into the air and turned towards Cabo. Alec had watched her car leave the hotel guest parking lot and merge into the late hour traffic flowing into Cabo. In a moment she was lost in traffic on the boulevard encircling the yacht club.

Alec turned his attention back to *The Emerald Pelican*. He recognized Antonio Mendez, the yacht's owner and leader of the three young men who ran the cocaine ring in Cabo-the same man who had tried to have him killed, and who kidnapped Kathy McKenzie. Alec smiled as he thought of the fate that awaited these profiteers who were living off the American tourists who used their cocaine for recreation highs while partying in Cabo, and who profited off the misery of the poor population of Cabo who were hopelessly hooked on the drug.

Antonio Mendez was standing at the ship's wheel on the yacht's bridge, yelling at his two-man crew. Alec was too far away to hear what he was saying, but he knew. They were getting ready to cast off. Little did Antonio know that only inches away was a well-hidden transmitter that Alec had placed there before he left the vessel the night before. Alec reached down and clicked one of the switches on the unit beside his chair as he continued to scan the yacht with his binoculars. *Show time*, he said to himself, as the yacht's location coordinates appeared on the screen of the GPS receiver built into the sophisticated unit on the table. It was part of the advanced technologies the military had included with the drone that he and Vanessa were going to use to deliver his message to Mendez and his partners as they celebrated on their return trip from the drug ship, now anchored far out in the black Sea of Cortez.

Alec heard the yacht's diesel engines respond to the electrical ignition, first coughing oily water and blue smoke out the port exhaust, then the starboard, as they roared into life and quickly settled down to an even throb. Answering the thrust of the starboard engine, one of Mendez's crew slackened the bowline, allowing the yacht's bow to swing to port, as the port engine remained idle, the hydraulic clutch disengaging its propeller. As the yacht continued its slow arch to port, the crewman jumped on board the yacht and released the bowline that he was playing out in response to the yacht's swing, throwing it onto the dock. The other man simultaneously loosened the stern line, allowing the yacht's stern to move slightly away from the dock as it continued its swing in its counter-clockwise arch. At just the right moment, the crewman also jumped on board the yacht, and threw the stern line onto the dock, freeing the yacht from its mooring. The yacht's bow continued to arch to port as the starboard engine was thrown into reverse, allowing the stern to swing free of the dock. Mendez increased the port engine's forward revolutions, completing the maneuver and bringing the vessel's bow into the open water of the yacht basin. With *The Emerald Pelican* free of its mooring, Alec watched as Mendez pushed the controls of both engines slowly forward, increasing the revolutions of each simultaneously, his practiced eyes on both the black sea ahead and the engines' tachometers. *The Emerald Pelican* began cutting through the water at an impressive speed, trailing a wake of luminescence as its bow began to rise, answering the powerful thrust of its twin diesel engines. They were underway. It was 12:25 Thursday morning, May 25.

The yacht's running lights remained on, but the deck and cabin lights had been extinguished before it reached the mouth of the harbor and began its run along the breakwater. It would be impossible for anyone looking at the yacht to see who was aboard and where they might be positioned on deck or inside. The breakwater had been designed to keep the constant movement of sand traveling down the coast with the prevailing current, out of the ships' channel leading into deep water. Alec watched as *The Emerald Princess* moved beyond the breakwater. He saw her running lights go out, and knew Mendez was purposely running the yacht in defiance of Coast Guard vessel lighting requirements. He could have been stopped and boarded had there been any patrols in the area at this late hour, but he knew Mendez was very familiar with Coast Guard regulations a well as their routines. There were no late night patrols here.

Alec watched the yacht's position constantly change on his GPS readout as it moved further out into the Sea of Cortez. His equipment was also producing a slow-running paper chart, constantly logging the yacht's position as a red line on the flowing stream of paper that likewise reflected the vessel's coordinates every thirty seconds. Alec checked his watch. It was 12:49, and *The Emerald Pelican* had left her mooring just after midnight. *"Right on time*, he thought as he leaned back in his deck chair and cut the end off his Cuban Cohiba, his favorite cigar, considered contraband in the U.S., but readily available in Mexico's better smoke shops.

Alec had called Vanessa at exactly 1:00am on the tactical radio, just as they had planned. "They just left the harbor, Vanessa; so far, so good. I've mapped out their route in a timeline and, according to my calculations, at 2:45 they should be beyond their point of no return. We are still on schedule to launch in about an hour. How close are you to having the bird ready?"

"I'm on schedule over here. It's assembled, and I've run up the engines and both seem to be in good order. I'll check the battery packs with a voltmeter before I launch, just to be sure we have full charges. Several spare packs were in the kit, so I'll replace them if I need to.

"I set up the bungee launch about a hundred yards back from the cliffs. If we get a system failure, at least the bird won't go over the cliffs into the surf. I've checked the launch bands, and I don't think we'll have a problem there. Just give me the word when you want the launch and our little Dragon Eye will fly.

"By the way, what's the weather supposed to be like out there with this storm moving in? I don't have any wind over here yet, but the clouds have moved in and so have the mosquitoes. It's also black as hell; so let's get this show on the road as soon as we can. I'm ready to get back to the Cabo night life."

"Nobody said this was gonna be a cakewalk, Vanessa. Just stay in the car or put on some insect repellent. I'll call you about fifteen minutes before launch time and follow that up with a five-minute heads-up so you can get the bird and the launch system ready. We'll do a one-minute check and then a ten-second countdown. We've got a pretty critical window of opportunity with this bird's limited battery pack life, so if the wind picks up a little out of the west, it'll give us a little increase in our time-over-target. But, if it comes at us hard, it could affect our ability to fly the bird and stay on target."

"You still think they're going to follow the same trip-pattern they have in the past?"

"Sure. Why shouldn't they? They left at the same time they have every Wednesday since we began monitoring their movements out to pick up their drugs. And every time they've followed the same coordinates and every time the drug ship has been anchored in the same place. Nothing's different tonight. They've been underway for a while now, and they're following their previous course like clockwork. They probably have their waypoint coordinates locked into their navigation system and have the boat on autopilot. But keep your fingers crossed anyway."

"Will do. I'm ready, so give me a call."

*   *   *

Abandoned Airstrip west of Cabo San Lucas
Baja California Sur, Mexico
Friday, May 25 – 1:45am

Storm clouds had engulfed the lower end of the Mexican Baja, bathing Cabo San Lucas in a light rain, a mist really. The wind, out of the west, had freshened to a steady ten knots, not strong enough to be a factor that would affect the Dragon Eye's flight pattern, but enough to curtail much of the partying that had been in full swing earlier. It seemed as though Cabo was shutting down to wait out a blow that had been upgraded to tropical storm status only moments earlier by the National Oceanic and Atmospheric Administration's Weather Service.

Alec had begun to worry. If the wind increased to twenty knots, it could affect the UAVs control surfaces and blow it off course far enough so the guidance system couldn't bring it back to its preprogrammed heading. If it increased even more, the fragile components of the aircraft could be damaged or could even be torn apart.

"It's 1:55am, five minutes to launch, Van. Are you ready?"

"Yes. It's really socked in over here, Alec. And the wind's picking up. If we don't get this bird off the ground soon, it may be too late."

"I agree. Launch when you're ready. And don't delay, Van. This wind worries me, and the National Weather Service has just upgraded this front to tropical storm status, so we can expect this thing to get worse before it blows out. But, the good news is that once airborne, the Dragon Eye will have a good tailwind and can stay ahead of the worst part of the storm if it continues to move eastward at its current pace. Right now we need a little luck to go our way."

"OK, Alec. Stand by. I'm using the headset, so I'm hands-free to launch. Wish me luck. I've been through this a dozen times, but this is for real!"

Vanessa switched on the UAV's two electric engines, and, cradling the Dragon Eye by the handholds designed into the aircraft below the wing mounts in her left hand, and keeping her right hand on the rear of the fuselage, as the launch instructions indicated, began walking backwards along the dirt runway. She was watching for the marker she had placed on the ground that would indicate the bungee cords, which would propel the UAV into the air, were stretched to their proper tension based on the surface winds she was experiencing. The bird's engines were at full revolutions, providing additional thrust to that created by the bungee cords. As instructed, she was launching into the wind, which was now blowing at just over six knots. The wind was a plus because it would help get the UAV airborne quicker than if it were dead calm.

It was 2:05. "She's away, Alec, and she's gaining altitude. Looks like a good launch. Hell, it looks like a great launch. As soon as the altimeter readout indicates she's reached five hundred feet, I'm going to put her into a one hundred eighty degree turn, and keep her climbing up to one thousand feet. I launched her due west so she will be heading straight for you when she completes her turn. You should be able to pick up her signal at that altitude and take over the controls. Oh, the cameras are on, and the video feedback is excellent. Let me know when you're ready to take over, and I'll pack everything away and head back to Cabo. I'm getting a little rain over here now and the wind is increasing. Your weather any better?"

"No, conditions are going downhill over on this side also, but it's still good enough to keep this project running. The rain doesn't bother me, the bird is waterproof, but let's just hope the wind doesn't increase too much. If we can stay out ahead of any major increase, we can keep this bird in the air."

Alec had turned on his monitoring equipment and was waiting for the signal that would tell him the UAV had reached the altitude they had programmed into its miniature computer embedded in its fuselage just aft of its wings.

*   *   *

Hotel Finisterra
Cabo San Lucas
Baja California Sur, Mexico Friday,
Friday, May 25 – 2:10am

"I've got her, Van. Pack up and get back here as soon as you can. I'm going to need you over here. Right now the bird is about three minutes out from the test target. I'm activating the trigger now, and when she gets over the target, I'm going to test this thing. According to the military, we can set it off as far away as two miles, but I want to be dead over the target when we do the test."

"See you in a few minutes. I'm already on my way. Keep her on course, Alec."

"Roger, Mother!"

"Don't get sarcastic with me, young man. You don't want me to take you over my knee, do you? No telling what might happen between us with you in that position," Vanessa said, laughing at what she knew was an embarrassing moment for Alec.

"Like I said, get your good looking butt back over here as soon as you can, Missy."

*   *   *

Alec continued to track the Dragon Eye as he watched its progress on the GPS screen. The black light night vision video camera showed the terrain below almost as though it were in full daylight. He could see the waves crashing against the rocks as the currents from the Pacific and the Sea of Cortez collided at the point that made up No Man's Land on the end of the Baja peninsula.

The UAV was advancing on its target as it passed overhead at an altitude of one thousand feet, its two electric engines emitting a slight hum, inaudible to the untrained ear, almost in total silence. Alec waited until the camera picked up the marker below, checked the drone's coordinates on the GPS, then activated the remote trigger, sending an electrical impulse to the UAV, which turned it into a command to the detonator imbedded in the charges below. The explosion of the two C-4 bricks he had hidden in the rocks just up from the crashing waves was instantaneous. He saw the explosion through the eye of the video camera mounted in the belly of the UAV forward of the wings. But, he couldn't hear it. He was too far away, and his suite faced north overlooking the harbor, not south towards the explosion.

"We got ignition, Van! The trigger works perfectly. I didn't hear anything but a slight rumble. Sounded like distant thunder, but I saw it on the video. It detonated just as promised. Now, on to our real target. What's your ETA?"

"Fifteen minutes."

"Good. We're just about an hour out from *Showtime!*"

*   *   *

Somewhere off the coast of Cabo San Lucas
Baja California Sur, Mexico
Friday, May 25 – 3:00am

It was the same routine on every trip. Antonio slowed *The Emerald Pelican* to a four-knot crawl, then disengaged the propellers as he neared the coordinates where the coastal freighter carrying his cocaine was suppose to be anchored. He was almost forty miles off the Baja coast, well outside any interference from the Coast Guard's blue water patrols. The weather was deteriorating quickly, and as the winds freshened, he knew the swells would increase, adding another element of danger to an already dangerous enterprise-off loading his precious cargo of cocaine from the Panamanian registered drug ship. He waited, *The Emerald Pelican* wallowing in the black water, waiting for the signal from the freighter that he should approach, but he could see nothing in the black overcast night.

A light rain had begun and his two-man crew had joined him in the yacht's wheelhouse. He checked the coordinates again. He was where he was supposed to be according to his GPS, but he couldn't see the ship, not even through his night vision binoculars. The night was just too black with the overcast. A sea fog had moved in, shrouding his vision even more. But, he knew he was early by about thirty minutes. He was tempted to try to raise the freighter on his ship to shore radio, but he knew his call would be overheard if anyone was listening on the frequency he would use. He couldn't take that chance, so he waited, growing more impatient by the minute as the weather continued to deteriorate.

*   *   *

Hotel Finisterra
Cabo San Lucas
Baja California Sur, Mexico
Friday, May 25 – 3:05am

Vanessa didn't bother to knock, but slipped through the door into Alec's suite, using the key card he had given her. He was sitting in a lounge chair on the balcony under an open umbrella watching the video screen on his tracking equipment. The mist had turned into a light rain, so he had opened the large umbrella over the table where he had set up his equipment. He was studying the paper readout on which he had scribbled the coordinates of the many waypoints he had previously noted for the route of *The Emerald Pelican.* His plan was to fly the Dragon Eye down the identical route the yacht had taken to reach its rendezvous point with the coastal freighter. As the UAV crossed a waypoint, Alec crossed it off the chart and fed the coordinates of the next waypoint into the system. The Dragon Eye responded immediately to each set of instructions, flying down the exact path the yacht had taken. With deteriorating weather conditions and varying tides influencing both the path and the speed of the yacht's trip out into the Sea of Cortez, and its return, Alec needed to be sure he didn't miss the yacht on its return trip. As soon as the drone was close enough to intercept the constant signals coming from the transmitter Alec had planted in the yacht's wheelhouse, the Dragon Eye would lock on the yacht's position and fly directly to its location, but until then Alec would continue to fly the bird down the route the yacht had taken on this trip out to the drug ship. The only way his plan could fail was if the small transmitter Alec planted on the yacht was discovered and the signals interrupted. He knew Antonio always took the same route back from his rendezvous with the drug ship that he used to get there. Somewhere on the yacht's return trip, *The Emerald Pelican* and the UAV would cross paths, and Alec had to be ready.

*   *   *

Somewhere off the coast of Cabo San Lucas
Baja California Sur, Mexico
Friday, May 25 – 3:05am

"There it is, Antonio! Look over to the left, about one o'clock. It's the signal from the ship. You can just make it out through the fog."

Antonio saw the small blinking light some five hundred yards out from *The Emerald Pelican*. "You're right. Start the engines and head towards the light. Slowly, please."

The Emerald Pelican's engines came to life quickly, its propellers were engaged, and she began to move off towards the blinking light. As they approached the coastal freighter, Antonio took the wheel and maneuvered the yacht up to the port side of the freighter, his partners catching the two lines that were thrown to them from the foredeck, and secured the yacht.

Although a rope ladder was thrown over the gunnels to the yacht below, Antonio did not go aboard the freighter to talk with the captain. Their deal had been made and the less personal contact the better. The three waited as a large cargo net was slowly lowered onto the yacht's foredeck. The young men quickly removed the wax impregnated cardboard boxes wrapped in heavy plastic to prevent seawater contamination and worked then through the forward hatch into the guest room below where they stacked them on the king size bed. It was a routine repeated each week, and one they knew well. When the last crate was secured, the captain of the freighter saluted Antonio as the lines securing the yacht were released, and she drifted away from the side of the ship. Before they could restart the yacht's engines and get underway, the freighter's anchor was being raised, and black smoke began billowing from its stacks. In a matter of minutes, the only thing in that precise location would be the black sea.

*   *   *

Hotel Finisterra
Cabo San Lucas
Baja California Sur, Mexico
Friday, May 25

It was 4:17am and the Dragon Eye was some thirty-eight miles from the coordinates Alec felt was the rendezvous point where *The Emerald Pelican* had met the drug supply ship. If his estimates were correct, the yacht would now be thirty minutes into its return trip, steering west to Cabo. The bird would be intercepting the yacht at any moment, but as yet had not locked on the signal from the transmitter hidden in its wheelhouse. Alec planned to manually override the yacht's signal and fly the Dragon Eye over the yacht at an altitude of one thousand feet, do a one-eighty and release the signal override allowing the UAV to lock on and fly back down the yacht's return route until he overtook it. He would then activate his little surprise.

Alec had left nothing to chance. To be sure the UAV would not pass over the yacht and he not see it through the video feed, he had earlier activated the location transmitter he had hidden in the yacht's steering controls as soon as *The Emerald Pelican* passed beyond the breakwater protecting the entrance into the yacht basin.

Alec and Vanessa watched intently as the Dragon Eye closed rapidly on the yacht, seemingly on a collision course. Of course, the UAV was a thousand feet above the ocean's surface as the yacht plowed through the heavy waves on its return trip to Cabo and the safety of the yacht basin.

The ferocity of the storm that had hit the Mexican Baja had forced Alec and Vanessa to move their base of operations inside his suite, abandoning the rain-soaked veranda. Vanessa had moved in closer to Alec so they both could watch the monitor as the Dragon Eye's black-light night vision video camera surveyed the churning waves of the black sea below. They watched the tracking of the location transmitters on the UAV and the yacht as the two crafts closed.

The rain, now coming down in steady sheets in Cabo, was much lighter fifty miles east over the Sea of Cortez. Alec knew it wouldn't be a factor of concern. The wind was another matter. It had already reached a steady thirty-four knots in Cabo, and was increasing every moment out over the Sea of Cortez.

Around midnight, small craft warning had been hoisted over the Coast Guard station at the mouth of the bay, and Cabo San Lucas had virtually shut down, awaiting the hurricane force winds promised by NOAA's National Weather Bureau. What had been categorized earlier as a storm front, then a tropical storm had been upgraded to the area's first hurricane of the season. The storm, now referred to as *Fay*, had reached a Category One designation and gained phenomenal strength over the warm waters of the Pacific, west of Mexico in a very short period of time, catching the National Weather Service and their hurricane hunters by surprise. The hurricane warning was issued too late for the throngs of people vacationing in the several tourist spots on Mexico's lower Yucatan Peninsula to flee. Everyone was hunkering down to wait out the full force of the storm, which was predicted to cross the Yucatan quickly and gain further strength over the Sea of Cortez before slamming into Mexico's primary land mass around what was called the Mexican Riviera.

When the two locator transmitters' signals came together, Alec and Vanessa shifted their attention solely to the video pictures streaming from the UAVs night vision camera. Some thousand feet below the camera lens they saw the yacht pass by on its trip to its homeport. The camera locked onto its target immediately and followed it for a few seconds before it was lost to the camera's view.

The Dragon Eye had reached its target well before originally planned. In computing its original flight plan Alec had not factored in the substantial tail wind the UAV was riding since there had been no early warning of the storm they were now experiencing.

Vanessa quickly checked the winds aloft through the satellite weather monitoring system developed by the National Oceanographic and Atmospheric Administration which monitors weather conditions around the world, especially in areas where U.S. federal agencies or the military have an interest. As CIA operatives, Alec and Vanessa had access to a classified website unknown to the public, but with proper access, open to selected members of certain federal agencies.

"Winds aloft over the target have increased to twenty-three knots and are holding," Vanessa said, looking at Alec quizzically. "Will the UAV hold together in its turn back west? And, how about its backtrack?"

"Hell, I don't know. What do the UAV's instructions say?"

Vanessa grabbed the UAV's instruction book off the table and began checking the index. "When I looked this over, I concentrated on how to put the damned thing together and get it off the ground. I never thought we would be facing structural stress problems.

"Here it is. Oh crap! The manufacturer says the bird shouldn't be flown in winds in excess of fifteen knots. But the structural stress tolerances of the various components differ. Generally, though, they all redline at fifteen knots of wind. They even underlined this section so we would know. And, I didn't catch it. Evidently they've had some failures in winds above these tolerances. They say the UAV's components could come apart or the strong winds could render the bird uncontrollable. Hell, the thing is built out of reinforced Styrofoam so you can't expect much if conditions aren't right. At least its engines are waterproof. We may have a problem here, Alec," she said, shaking her head at her mistake in not noting the UAVs structural stress tolerance limits earlier.

"Well, we don't have much of a choice now, do we?" There was a slight edge in Alec's voice, and she feared he would blame her if the mission failed. But what could she have done, even if she had known the front was going to turn into a full-blown hurricane? When she launched the UAV, winds aloft were not a factor.

"If we fail, we fail," he said, looking up at Vanessa and smiling. He knew she had caught the slight trace of anger in his last statement and wanted to be sure she didn't blame herself if anything went wrong.

"These guys don't know we're up there looking down on them, so they'll probably continue to repeat their same old routine if our plans go south. If we need to, we'll use one of the spare UAVs and do this again until we get it right."

"Not an option, Alec. We don't have a spare camera and platform, nor do we have spare transmitters and triggers. They're not necessarily a part of the standard Dragon Eye package. The manufacturer figured the military would always fly these birds back to their bases, not run them until they run out of fuel or their batteries die and drop them in the sea like we plan to do with this one. Unless we get these components shipped out to us, we better get this right the first time."

"OK, but I'm not sure this is anything we can control. I've locked the bird's tracking system onto the signal of the miniature locator transmitter I hid on the yacht. She will execute the one eighty on her own, and fall into the yacht's line of travel. She should be able to track the yacht and remain at altitude unless something goes wrong. Since the UAV is flying faster than its target, she should catch up with the yacht in about ten minutes. That is, if the wind doesn't tear her apart before she gets in range."

*　　*　　*

Somewhere off the Coast of Cabo San Lucas
Baja California Sur, Mexico
Friday, May 25 – 4:28am

Several miles behind *The Emerald Pelican*, and couched in the thick cloud cover blanketing the Sea of Cortez a small, very fragile, unmanned aircraft was homing in on the signal being broadcast by a miniature transmitter hidden in the yacht it was tracking. The relentless winds of the approaching storm buffeted the small airframe unmercifully as it continued to overtake the yacht.

Antonio couldn't see beyond the bow of his yacht. The rain had increased, beating down in wind-blown sheets, distorting what few images he could see out of the front windows of the yacht's wheelhouse. Fog had moved in and swirled around the yacht as it plodded westward through the heavy seas towards Cabo. The oncoming waves had increased in height, keeping the yacht in constant up and down motion as the bow plowed into the black water, then sprang free and drove on above the wave crests, propelled by her two strong diesel engines. Conditions were perfect to induce seasickness, and Antonio was feeling the effects. His two partners were already over-the-rail.

*　　*　　*

Hotel Finisterra
Cabo San Lucas
Baja California Sur, Mexico
Friday, May 25 – 4:30am

The atmosphere in Alec's suite had become tense as they neared the end of their long-awaited goal. What had begun as a slam-dunk mission looked like it was heading for failure. They had not factored in the possibility that weather could easily destroy their plans.

"What's the distance between the UAV and the yacht?" Vanessa asked, looking over at Alec, an expression of concern on her face.

"Not sure yet. It took the bird longer to do its one-eighty turn because of the wind, so I won't have a true reading until it picks up the yacht's line and falls in behind it. If I had to guess, though, I would say about three miles max. At least it didn't break up on the turn."

"One hurdle down and one to go. So, with a two-mile maximum trigger range, when will we be in shooting range?" Vanessa asked.

"Hard to say just now. I'll have to factor in the increased wind speed. That's going to slow us down somewhat, but it won't slow down the boat. I hope this thing can close on the target sufficiently for us to get a shot. It's just going to take a little longer than I calculated. The bird's flight line is getting a little erratic now, so the wind is having an effect. Just keep your fingers crossed that this thing doesn't break up before we get in range to shoot."

"How about a short prayer?"

"I'm not sure a prayer would be the answer. Especially since we're attempting to blow up three people, even though they're killers and purveyors of death. But, what the hell, give it a try!"

* * *

Friday, May 25 – 4:35am

"OK, Van, we're just under three miles from the target. I'm not sure the bird is going to make it. Its flight pattern is getting more erratic every minute.

"Come on, baby, give me a little more push. Just a little more push, please. Just stay together through this," Alec yelled at the monitor.

Things were getting more tense in Alec's suite as the UAV continued to close on its target. The weather outside was raging, and the wind whistling around the high-rise hotel almost made it impossible to carry on a conversation without yelling. Both Alec and Vanessa were worried, and the expressions on their faces reflected their concern. They had put so much time and planning into this mission, and it looked as if all their work might go down into the black sea raging below the UAV.

"We're two and a half miles behind the yacht, Van."

* * *

"Oh, hell, the drone's rolling over on her back. One of her wings must have been sheared off by the wind. She's going to spin down into the ocean. I can't override the autopilot to manually control her flight, Van. She's going in! We're more than two miles behind the target. We're too far away to trigger the charges!"

"You don't know that, Alec. That's just what the military says. To hell with the distance, just activate the trigger before the bird crashes. We just may get lucky. Shoot it, Alec!" Vanessa said calmly, resting her hands on his shoulders. "Who knows, this thing just may have a little more range than the manufacturer says it has. So, shoot, and let's see what happens!"

Instinctively, Alec flipped the trigger switch on his remote guidance equipment, and the LED above the switch glowed *green* for only two second,s then went back to *red*.

"Did it activate, Alec?"

"Yes. At least I think so. The LED went from red to green, then back to red, so I assume the trigger activated. Since we're too far away from the target to see the explosion, we just don't know if the signal activated the charges. The drone's camera was going to confirm that for us but in its flight configuration, it couldn't acquire the target at the time I activated the trigger.

"Let's just hope that even though the drone was in a steep dive with its wing torn off, it was close enough to the target to detonate the charges I planted on the yacht. Unfortunately, the camera was feeding us pictures of the black sky as it rolled over just before going in, so we may never know."

"There's got to be a way we can confirm this, Alec."

"We'll just have to wait and see if they make it back to the yacht basin. If not, we'll assume the yacht went down with all hands lost. Plus a hell of a lot of cocaine."

*   *   *

Somewhere off the Coast of Cabo San Lucas
Baja California Sur, Mexico
Friday, May 25 – 4:35am

Antonio and his two partners in his white slavery and drug smuggling business had no warning of what fate lay ahead for them. He was at the wheel making course corrections as the wind continued to buffet the yacht. The hurricane had gained strength as it moved across the Baja and into the Sea of Cortez, heading towards the Mexican mainland.

The two boys were still hanging their heads over the yacht's port rail, throwing up and wishing they could die. Their wish came true an instant later.

The explosion of the C-4 Alec had placed in the yacht's engine room blew through the yacht like a monstrous clap of thunder, shaking every timber in the entire boat, shattering its fiberglass hull as it blew a gigantic hole in its port side. Seawater rushed into the engine room drowned the engines instantly, and shorted out the electrical circuits to the bilge pumps. Without power, the yacht began to wallow in the turbulent seas, its forward motion lost when the engines shut down, the monstrous waves driving down on her bow, slowly turning the yacht to starboard.

She began to list to port as seawater quickly filled the engine room in seconds and blew up through the aft hatch, ripping it from its hinges and sending it skyward. In less than a minute the three bedroom suites located in the lower section of the yacht filled with water, forcing the yacht down into the surging waves until its decks were awash under the black seas that crashed over her bow.

The explosion, just below the two boys hanging over the rails, sent them into the surging waves as the suction created by the water rushing into the yacht through the hole in its side sucked both young men back into the boat. With no air inside the engine room, both drowned immediately. Their wish had been granted.

When Antonio lost steering, he knew the yacht was in trouble. He reached for his ship-to-shore radio, but before he could press the distress signal button, which would give the Coast Guard the yacht's position and would begin transmitting the recorded distress signal, the yacht began to roll onto its port side, throwing him out of his seat and sending him across the wheelhouse deck out of reach of the yacht's electronic gear and into the rising water now pouring out of the lower decks through the stairwell and into the wheelhouse. He crawled to the storage locker where the life preservers were kept, but it was locked. As The Emerald Pelican sank below the raging sea, taking him, and his partners trapped below, to their watery graves, Antonio's last thought was that he had decided to keep his private stash of coke in the life preserver locker. He had installed the lock to be sure his partners didn't learn he had been skimming their product since they entered the drug running business years earlier. His greed had sealed his fate. He could not survive in the raging sea with a life preserver.

* * *

A crewman, standing on the open deck of the small coastal freighter that had only minutes earlier delivered a cargo of cocaine to the yacht, reported to the captain that he thought he had seen an orange ball of fire on the water after they were underway, but he wasn't sure because of the dense fog and sheets of rain now enveloping the ship. And the location of the fireball was generally where he thought the yacht should have been. The captain scanned the horizon but could see nothing through the fog and blowing rain. Against his better judgment, he switched on the ship's radar, knowing it would produce a signal that would pinpoint their location should anyone be in range of the signal, but he could find no surface targets. He became concerned when the radar couldn't locate *The Emerald Pelican's* signature, which, he reasoned, would have been well within the radar's range and should have been easily identifiable. His concern quickly grew into a state of panic. He immediately switched off the radar, ordered the ship's running lights doused, reversed course, and headed for the Pacific and the safety of his homeport in Panama.

"Those boys can look out for themselves," he said out loud as he instructed the engineer to give the old freighter all her engines had. The captain was in a hurry to leave the area.

*   *   *

Coast Guard Station
Cabo San Lucas
Baja California Sur, Mexico

At 1:53am on the morning of May 25, the Coast Guard Petty Officer, pulling the night shift duty, had logged the passage of *The Emerald Pelican* through his control zone and out into the open sea. At that time, only small craft warnings had been posted. The Weather Service had not yet alerted the Coast Guard and the general public that the weather was fast building into a much more serious threat, so the watch commander felt there was no need to communicate with the passing vessel, especially since its captain had not bothered to inform the Coast Guard of its trip and the persons on board. *The Emerald Pelican* had left port on many previous occasions in weather worse than what they were now experiencing and had never bothered to register their trips with the Coast Guard. *To hell with them,* the Petty Officer thought as he sipped his cup of coffee and watched the yacht fade into the heavy fog now blanketing the coast.

The Coast Guard's logs would later show that the yacht made the same passing every week on the same day and at the same approximate time.

At 02:45 NOAA notified the Coast Guard that they were going to upgrade Tropical Storm Fay to a Class One Hurricane, and suggested they notify all coastal shipping immediately of the deteriorating weather condition on the Baja and its coastal waters. The storm was heading directly for Cabo San Lucas and was gathering speed as it blasted into the west coast of the Baja.

The Coast Guard issued its initial alert at 2:51am, and repeated the broadcast continuously for the next six hours. Although the captain of *The Emerald Pelican* had noted the warning, he was in the process of taken on his cargo and was about to begin the trip back to the safe harbor of Cabo San Lucas, the closest port to their location. He was confident that his vessel could weather the storm and was looking forward to the challenge. He was in for a rude awakening.

When the yacht didn't return in the early morning hours, as was normal, the watch commander waited until daylight and dispatched a Coast Guard HH-60 Jay-Hawk rescue helicopter to search for the missing vessel and her crew. Although *The Emerald Pelican* had not notified the Coast Guard of her proposed destination and the number of souls on board, as is customary, she had failed to do so on many previous occasions. The captain had been warned about this failure to register its travels, but he had blatantly refused to cooperate. There was always the possibility that the yacht had gone elsewhere and had not planned to return, but the Coast Guard couldn't confirm this since *The Emerald Pelican* had not filed its itinerary before leaving port. Their inquiries to the harbormasters of other nearby ports were of no help. *The Emerald Pelican* had vanished.

At that point, concern began to mount that the yacht may have gone down in the raging seas churned up by Fay as it swept across the Yucatan Peninsula and out into the Sea of Cortez, heading straight towards the coordinates where *The Emerald Pelican* was thought to be.

The Coast Guard later reported that their rescue effort yielded only a single hatch cover that seemed to have been ripped off its hinges. But there were no identifying marks that would suggest it was part of *The Emerald Pelican*. No other evidence of the yacht was found and no bodies of the crew were discovered. Since the Coast Guard station at Cabo San Lucas had not received any distress calls from ships in danger during the early morning hours when the yacht was beyond their command area, they closed the case a week later as unsolved.

A short story regarding the mysterious disappearance of *The Emerald Pelican* ran on the front page of the local newspaper several days later. It was as though the brooding sea had swallowed up the vessel. In fact, it had, with a little help from a charge of C-4.

Alec and Vanessa read the article with interest. They had remained in Cabo San Lucas for a few more days to see if they could confirm the yacht's sinking. To satisfy their curiosity, they had earlier asked the pilot of the CIA's small plane, stationed at The Ranch, to fly them out over the area where the yacht had supposedly gone down. They had the exact coordinates. Like the Coast Guard, they found nothing to indicate the area could have been the site of a sinking, no debris and not even an oil slick.

Alec convinced the Coast Guard to let him photograph the hatch cover the rescue helicopter had picked up out of the sea, on the pretense that he may have a source that could identify the manufacturer of the vessel from which it came. Since the Coast Guard had no means of gathering that information, they readily allowed Alec to take as many pictures as he wanted, providing he would alert them if he could identify the vessel.

While photographing the hatch cover, Alec noticed a series of seven numbers and letters under the flanged rim where the hatch's neoprene sealing material had once been attached. *If the CIA has information in its database on parts numbers from various private boat manufacturers, they just may be able to give me the name of the manufacturer, and possibly the very yacht the hatch cover came from*, Alec thought as he recorded the numbers.

In less than three hours from the time he called Rob Downing, his cell phone was ringing. "Sorry to hold you up on this, but our data base for yachts manufactured outside the U.S. is somewhat limited. Your suggestion that we look first at Italian manufacturers, and specifically Azimut Yachts, paid off in more ways than one. First, you were correct. The hatch cover was a standard item on their sixty-eight foot Evolution series yachts. Also, the sequence of numbers and letters you gave me were matched to a specific yacht delivered to Yacht Sales of Aruba, Mexico this past year. It was a special order for one of their customers who had specified several changes in their basic interior décor. We made a call to Aruba Yachts, and with a little prodding, they gave us the name of the purchaser, one Felipe Hernandez Garcia."

"So, that wraps it up. *The Emerald Pelican* did go down after all," Alec replied. "And the captain, who we knew as Antonio Mendez, owned the yacht. He was using that alias to keep his family name out of what he was doing, but he must have had to register the yacht in his real name in order to get it licensed and insured.

"No need for me to stay down here any longer, Rob. I'm heading back to Montana. Vanessa is already on her way to Boston. I dropped her off at the airport this morning, and I'm up at The Ranch now. As far as the police are concerned, I'm dead, so the pressure is off and I'm using another alias. I'm going to catch a flight out tomorrow for Montana and spend a few days with Beth and my son. I'll fly over to DC later and fill you and Don in on the details of what we accomplished down here. In the meantime, do me a favor. Ask Don to contact the President about some made-up situation and casually mention that I'm back in the U.S. That should frost his rear end. That bastard set me up to take a fall down here, but we turned the tables on him and his buddy over in Mexico City. We got their assassin as well as their stooges who kidnapped Kathy McKenzie and were running the drug market down here. Now, it's my turn. I want to meet with you and Don when I get there, I've already been working on a plan for the next phase of this payback. It's going to involve using a pal of ours over in the U.K. Do you remember Timothy Sutherland?"

"Yes. You mentioned Tim Sutherland before you left on your last trip down there. Did you meet with him on your way through London?"

"I did, and he's on board. All I have to do is get him copies of the information that Don tells me he has in his files. Got to go, man. See you in a few days."

CHAPTER FIFTEEN

The White House
1600 Pennsylvania Avenue
Washington, DC
Monday, June 4 – 10:30am

"OH, MR. PRESIDENT, on another matter and just for your information only, our agent down in Mexico who rescued your Mr. McKenzie's daughter is back, safe and sound. Seems, with the help of a few of our Delta Force boys out of Bragg, he escaped from a rather sadistic interrogator who had learned who he was, or at least the alias he was using, and that he had helped the McKenzie girl escape. We have no idea how he learned our agent was still down there, but he did, and trapped him in his hotel room. He was planning to kill him after a lengthy interrogation, but we were alerted and watched from overhead as the man and his little army took our agent to his interrogation quarters. With the help of some military types, we set up our agent's release. Unfortunately, the interrogator wasn't there when our boys arrived, so our agent took him down on his own later.

"He set the man up and took him out with a shot between the eyes. He tells us the newspaper down there reported our agent's death, not the man hired to kill him. Our man did a good job switching identities. To top that, he also took out the boys who were running the cocaine trade down on the lower Baja. The only evidence of that last deed was a hatch cover recovered by the Coast Guard far out at sea that came off the yacht belonging to the leader of that gang, who, by the way, was the son of Mexico's Oil Minister."

Don Armstrong, the DCI, had called the President on another matter, and as Alec had requested mentioned Alec's remarkable return, but avoided mentioning his name. He was enjoying the dead silence on the other end of the conversation. "Are you still with me, Mr. President?"

"Yes, my apologies, Don. You caught me off guard. Somewhere back in my memory, I remember someone telling me you had lost an agent down there. I didn't think much about it since I didn't have the details and I know you people in the spy trade don't talk about such losses, so I didn't call you."

You son-of-a-bitch, you damn well did know the details. Your buddy down there, President Montoya, gave you all the particulars of Alec's escape and you gave him up—the name he was using as well as where he was staying. The one thing you didn't know was that Alec had given your shooter his identity so the press would think Alec had been killed. Montoya bought the ID switch and so did you, Don said to himself, smiling at what he knew the President was thinking.

"Don, I've got another call I have to take, so I'm going to ring off. Thanks for the information. I'm glad your man is safe. By the way, I would like to contact him to thank him for helping rescue my friend's daughter and taking out the drug runners. Those drugs make their way up here, you know."

"Sorry, Sir. You know I can't reveal the names of our agents to anyone, even you. It could compromise their work. I know you understand, Sir."

All Don Armstrong heard was a "click" as the connection went dead. The President had slammed the receiver down so hard it broke into several pieces. The dent in the top of his desk would remain there as a reminder to him of the frustration he felt, knowing his lucrative source of illegal income had been cut off and the CIA had foiled his plans again.

You little bastard. I'll get your agent if it's the last thing I do. And you too, the President said to himself as he picked up the receiver of the second phone on his desk.

"Harriett, cancel my next appointment," he yelled through the door of the Oval Office to his secretary.

"Sir, it's with the Vice President, and he's on his way over."

"To hell with him. Turn him around when he gets here. Tell him I'm dead. Hell, tell him any damned thing you want. Just keep everyone out of here for the next ten minutes. Then cancel all my appointments for the rest of the day. I'm going out and won't be back until tomorrow morning. Tell the Secret Service to get the car ready."

President Hunt opened his desk drawer, retrieved his personal address book and dialed Henry Rothrock's phone number. His hand was sweating as he dialed his number in Georgetown. Rothrock picked up on the third ring. "Yes?"

"Rothrock, get the team together. I'll be over there within an hour. I want everyone there. You got that?"

"Yes, Mr. President, what's up?"

"I'll tell you when I get there. Just be sure everybody's there."

*   *   *

Holiday Inn Suites
Dulles, Virginia
Sunday, June 10 – Late Evening

Alec arrived at Dulles International on Sunday evening, took the hotel shuttle out to the Holiday Suites and after checking in, went down to the gym for a workout and a swim. He met Rob Downing for dinner two hours later at one of their favorite watering holes, the out-of-the-way Hanover Inn and Tavern, specializing in overpriced seafood and steaks where they could enjoy a degree of privacy without fear of anyone being able to hear their conversation.

"Great to have you back, old friend. Your debriefing on the kidnapping down in Mexico is scheduled for 8:30 tomorrow morning. And, the Director wants to see you as soon as the debriefing guys get through with you. By the way, how are Beth and my godchild?"

"They're fine, Rob. And I appreciate you and Don standing up for my son. You two will be good role models for him."

"I'm honored."

"It was great being able to spend a few days with my new family and just chill out in the mountains. But I'm not going to have any peace until we resolve this matter of Hunt giving me up down in Mexico. The bastard is going to pay for putting a higher value on his greed than on my life. I can't believe someone, especially the man occupying the highest office in the land, signed my death warrant to further his own self-interest."

"It's not the first time he's done that, Alec, and from what we know of him, he would do it again in a New York minute if he felt he could get away with it. But Don will give you all the details, and he does have details. His opinion of Hunt hasn't done anything but sink lower than before. As far as Don is concerned, when Hunt betrayed you, he betrayed the Company and everyone who works in the service. In Don's opinion, Hunt is a traitor, and traitors are usually executed by firing squad.

"We have a lot more dirt on Hunt than you can imagine, Alec. You and Don will just have to decide how you want to play this. In the meantime, let's have a meal to remember. I owe you one if I remember correctly."

*   *   *

CIA Headquarters
Langley, Virginia
Monday, June 11 – 9:45am

The early morning interviews by the three Internal Affairs agents assigned to debrief Alec on the recent events that took place on the Mexican Baja went smoothly and were over in less than an hour. Alec had periodically reported the happenings and his movements in Mexico as events developed, so much of what went down was already known to the Company and had been reviewed by the agents on a *need-to-know* only basis.

By 9:45am Alec was seated across the coffee table from Don Armstrong, the Director of Central Intelligence, in the small, secure conference room in the second level basement of the CIA Headquarters in Langley, Virginia. There were no other participants in the meeting.

"Coffee, Alec?" Armstrong had walked over to the sideboard and was pouring a cup of hot, steaming Columbia Narino Supremo coffee from the silver service, always placed there when he was using the room.

"Sure. Black, please."

"I've known you for more years than I care to remember, Alec. All the way back to our carefree days at William and Mary. By now, you would think I should know how you take your coffee," Don said, smiling at his close friend and handing the fine Oriental china cup and saucer to Alec. He poured a cup for himself and returned to his leather executive chair.

"So, I know you're still upset about what Hunt did to you. I know the anger you're feeling, Alec. I didn't expect this from Hunt; he blindsided me on this. What is the verse in the book of Mark: *For what shall it profit a man, if he shall gain the whole world, and lose his own soul?* What Jesus said in that verse is very apropos here. Hunt has lined his pockets during his political career, and in doing so he has lost his soul. Now it's time for him to lose his other precious possessions: his popularity, his legacy, his material wealth and ultimately, his life. By betraying you he also betrayed the Company, and me personally. For that, he's going to pay, and pay dearly, my friend."

"Good. I'm glad we're on the same page on this. Just what are we going to do to take this toad down?"

*　　*　　*

The President's Compound
Evergreen Avenue
Georgetown, District of Columbia
Monday, June 4 –11:45am

Hunt arrived at his secret compound on Evergreen Avenue in Georgetown within forty-five minutes. Cross-town traffic was light for late morning, and his Secret Service driver made good time without using lights or siren. When he assumed the office of President, Hunt ordered a plain brown Chevrolet Impala, which he used when not wanting to attract attention as his black Lincoln limousine and black Chevrolet chase SUVs did with flags flying, sirens blasting, and blue lights flashing.

The nondescript Chevrolet had been fitted with a supercharged V-8 engine, heavy duty transmission, heavily tinted bullet proof windows and Kevlar lining inside all of its side panels, its top and its doors. It was also fitted with self-sealing, run-flat tires. In effect, the car was a small fortress, but disguised to appear as a low-cost standard production Chevrolet. A state-of-the-art communications system and GPS transceiver with antennas hidden in the roof of the vehicle had been installed with direct links to the Secret Service's command posts at the White House and at the Capitol.

The three Secret Service agents accompanying the President on these clandestine outings, including the driver, were heavily armed with automatic weapons and 45 cal. side arms. The President was required to sit in the back seat, always on the right, giving the agent riding front seat shotgun direct access to a clear field of fire on the right side of the vehicle and the agent seated next to the President a clear shooting area to the left. If a fire fight took place, the driver would be free to initiate any one of several avoidance and escape maneuvers they had practiced so many times that they knew them by heart.

The Chevrolet rolled up to the ornate iron gate that controlled access into the compound. The Secret Service guard who was pulling gate duty had received a coded message from the agent who was riding shotgun in the President's car when it turned onto Evergreen Street, and had the gate open as the vehicle arrived. The security procedure allowed the President's car to continue through the gate at speed, without stopping on the street outside the compound, thus minimizing the risk of a terrorist attack on the President while sitting in a stopped vehicle in a vulnerable environment. Although the vehicle was heavily armored, a rocket-propelled grenade would do some serious damage to the vehicle, possibly injuring or killing the occupants, if it presented an easy target.

*   *   *

"Mr. President, good afternoon."

"Good afternoon, Mr. Rothrock. Are all of your Black Hawk team members here?"

"They are, Sir. They're back in the kitchen. I wasn't sure if you wanted to discuss anything with me in private before our meeting. If not, I'll call them in."

"Do that, Corky. I want every team member to tell me face-to-face that they're committed to the mission I want you and your people to undertake."

"Yes, Sir." Corky Rothrock, the Black Hawk team leader, excused himself and walked back down the wide ornate central hall, the hardwood floors covered with very expensive Persian rugs and walls hung with priceless works of art by such renowned European artists as Francisco Goya, Paul Cézanne, Pablo Picasso and Vincent van Gogh.

"OK, Guys, time to earn your keep. Be respectful. Remember, you'll be talking with the President."

*   *   *

The President's Black Hawk squad gathered in the living room on Rothrock's orders. Hunt was standing in front of the large fireplace facing the group of five expert assassins, smoking a Cuban Cohiba and looking every bit presidential.

"Gentlemen, I want you to kill a CIA agent, and it doesn't have to look like an accident. In fact, I want the world to know, especially his boss, that he got a bullet through the head. It will send a message, and only the DCI will know what that message is. Then I want you to arrange for Don Armstrong, my DCI, to have an accident. His death shouldn't look anything like a hit. I need to publicly grieve for him as a personal friend and colleague, although if the truth were known, he's no friend of mine. But, if it were known that both he and his agent were assassinated, someone could start pointing fingers, and I don't need that.

"I don't know this agent's real name or where he lives. But I do know one of the aliases he uses, at least the one he was using in Mexico recently. I also have access to some photographs that will give you a physical description. He was on an assignment on the Mexican Baja recently and disrupted a very lucrative business in which I have an interest. In doing so, he has eliminated a source of income for some of my associates and me. No one does that and gets away with it. My Director of Central Intelligence sent him down there to rescue the daughter of a friend of mine, and he stumbled onto an operation in which I have an interest. Instead of being a good CIA agent and bringing the girl home, he sent her back and decided to stay down there to look into my business. Neither he, nor his boss, knows I'm involved, so they have no reason to suspect that I've put a contract out on this guy."

"Sir, do you have any other information we could use? I'm not sure how we can locate someone we don't know anything about, unless we set up a stakeout outside CIA headquarters and hope we recognize him when he leaves work."

"That's your problem, Rothrock, not mine, but that won't work. First, there are too many cameras around the perimeter of their property, all the way out to the main highway, so your people would be spotted and taken into custody. Plus, my DCI told me when we discussed the Mexican rescue mission that he was going to use someone who worked for his agency, off the books, so to speak. I doubt he works at Langley, and probably doesn't even go there unless he's being debriefed on a completed mission, maybe not even then.

"But that's why I pay you people so damned much money. Hell, if I knew who he was, I could have an independent contractor take him out for a lot less money than I pay you guys. So, you figure it out. Just get it done before he craps on my parade again.

"And, get the hell out of here. I'm expecting a very nice lady in a few minutes, and I don't want you guys around."

CHAPTER SIXTEEN

CIA Headquarters
Langley, Virginia
Tuesday, June 19 – 9:00am

"WE'RE ON, TIM! Did you get the documents?" Alec was talking with his Scottish friend, Sir Timothy Sutherland, with whom he had worked a couple of years before to stop an assassination attempt on the life of the Queen. They had become fast friends during those troubled days, and Alec and Beth had honeymooned at the ancestral home of the Sutherland Clan, Dunrobin Castle, on the North Sea Coast of Scotland. It had been a storybook honeymoon in one of the most beautiful areas of the Scottish Highlands.

"Indeed I did, Alec. We're ready here as well."

"Great. We would like for you to mail the envelope tomorrow so your editor friend at the *London Times* receives it before the weekend. He'll want to substantiate the story before he prints it, and we would like for it to hit the streets of London on Sunday, Monday at the latest. The London bureaus of the major U.S. papers won't pick it up until Monday morning and that will be too late to get it out over here before Tuesday. That little delay should stir one hell of a lot of rumors on Capitol Hill before the story breaks to the general public the next day."

"Done, my friend."

*   *   *

Dunrobin Castle—On the North Sea
Sutherland, Scotland
Thursday, June 21 – 10:43am

"It was posted last night, Geoffrey, around midnight out in the village of Abridge. A brown envelope addressed to the Senior Editor. Keep an eye open for it, Old Sod. I suspect it will arrive this morning."

"Will do, Timothy. Are you visiting London this evening?"

"No. In and out last night. I'm working from home this week. Mother isn't well, you know, so I'm here looking in on her from time to time. I had almost forgotten how drafty this old castle really is."

"Your ancestral home is a beautiful place, Timothy. I'm surprised you don't live there year around."

"I guess I would if I didn't have to be in Edinburgh every day. Running the largest bank in Scotland is a full-time job, Geoffrey. Just like your running the largest newspaper in the U.K. But I'm thinking about retiring soon and giving the reins to one of my sons, like Father did. Maybe remain as chairman, but give up the day-to-day operations."

"Well, when you are next down this way, ring me up. We'll meet at the club for an early tea. And give my best to your Mom."

*　　*　　*

The London Times
Senior Editor's Office
London, England
Friday, June 22 – 3:15pm

"Geoffrey, are you really going to publish this tripe? It's pretty incriminating stuff. And it's going to stir up . . . How do the Yanks say it . . . *a shit storm*, I think."

"Aye, I agree, Sean. Sweet isn't it?"

The 9" x 12" plain manila envelope had been mailed from a postal substation in the small village of Abridge out in rural Essex, a community some fourteen miles from the center of London. It was later reported that a witness, a homeless man, had seen a black Jaguar stop outside the post. The driver had lowered his side window and deposited an envelope into the night drop without getting out of the car. The witness also recalled seeing the image of someone sitting in the rear seat of the Jaguar, but couldn't provide any more details. No, he didn't get the license plate. The only reason he remembered the incident was that it was most unusual to see a shiny new Jaguar in this rural, middle class community, especially in the middle of the night.

The envelope was addressed to the senior editor of the *London Times*. There was no letter, just a typed three-page report, unsigned. But, there were pictures.

Normally, such a story would go into the trash before it got to the senior editor's desk. But this particular envelope was expected, actually anticipated by the senior editor, and the word was out that it was to be delivered to whom it was addressed when it arrived and was not to be opened by anyone before it reached his hands.

"When are you going to run it, Geoffrey?"

"When do you suggest, Sean? How about front page in the Sunday edition? It'll get considerably more coverage if we run it in the Sunday issue with all the home deliveries. Then, again on

Monday with a different slant on the story and a different audience. And placing it on the front page above the fold will throw it up to the Yanks, big time. The AP and the London bureaus of the four largest newspapers in the U.S. will run to hell and back with this, especially if it commands an above-the-fold, front-page position over here in the U.K."

"Why are you so down on President Hunt? I thought he was a personal friend of the Prime Minister. So, that should make him a friend of yours as well."

"That's just politics, Sean, nothing else. A gesture to create an image of unity between our two nations. That's the sum of it. Below the surface, the PM thinks the man is a goat, a disgrace to his country and to the game of politics."

"How do you know that?"

"The political connections I have are not unknown to you, Sean. If you really want to know the truth about Hunt, get one of your sources over at MI-6 drunk and see if you can pump him for information. They'll tell you that their counterpart across the pond, the Central Intelligence Agency, has more dirt on Hunt than anyone can imagine. You probably won't learn much about what they have, since the CIA keeps that information close to the vest. But I've been in a few private meetings with both the directors of the CIA and of MI-6, and I'm here to tell you, Son, the fireworks this will create will be well worth watching."

*   *   *

The article ran in the Sunday edition of the *London Times*, the U.K.'s most widely read newspaper. It was repeated in Monday's edition from a slightly different perspective to insure the businesses communities that receive regular daily deliveries had access to the story. An editorial by a senior staffer slammed President Hunt as a philanderer, a womanizer, and a fraud who professes one set of moral codes and practices another. The man was under attack like never before.

Before the first issue was in the can, the article had been through six revisions involving input from the paper's entire business editorial staff. The paper's review board, including their legal counsel, debated for hours the pros and cons of running the article before eventually signing on. The story had been verified and the accuser had been interviewed. The facts she had included had been checked and rechecked. Everything appeared legitimate. This was late Friday night, before the article hit the streets two days later. By Monday morning, the buzz was all about John Hunt, President of the United States.

The Monday edition of the *London Times* hit the streets at 7:00am. In thirty minutes, the wire services were transmitting the news around the world. The paper was in such demand that it sold out almost before the retailers could get their quotas on the stands, even before most businesses opened that morning.

By 10:00am Monday, every politician in London was reading the *London Times*. The headlines rocked the halls of Parliament:

UNITED STATES PRESIDENT, JOHN HUNT, NAMED IN PATERNITY SUIT

The headlines were sensational and the story equally compelling. A French actress, who goes by the stage name of Monique La Tour, was accusing President Hunt of fathering her daughter. The affair, as she related the story, was short-lived, and took place in Paris during the time Hunt was attending a North Atlantic Treaty Organization meeting there.

Pictures of the child, now seven years old, and her mother, were in the envelope and were printed along with the mother's story. Also accompanying the story was a DNA report on the young girl and a telephone number at which the mother could be reached. The editorial staff of the *London Times* interviewed the actress, and confirmed the fact that Hunt was actually in Paris at the time the alleged affair had occurred. They were working on attempting to get a DNA report on Hunt to confirm the allegations when they decided to break the story without it. They later confirmed a DNA match, substantiating the fact that John Hunt was indeed the young girl's father. This gave them the information they needed to do a follow-up story, which was also a sellout. A note in the second story confirmed that Hunt's wife was alive at the time.

The actress was suing Hunt for ten million dollars, and a well-known American attorney who specializes in high-profile celebrity cases had already agreed to take the case. No one, not even the plaintiff, knew that the CIA had paved the way for the suit to be filed in the U.S. court system, rather than in France. Nor did anyone outside a small circle of CIA insiders know that the attorney was regularly hired by them to handle such matters.

It was 2:00am in New York and in Washington when the revelations were entertaining Londoners and the English public in general. America slept peacefully for another four hours before the shit hit the fan at 1600 Pennsylvania Avenue.

The story was picked up by the London bureaus of the major newspapers in the U.S. and around the world when it hit the London streets. The *New York Times,* the *Washington Post,* and the *Chicago Tribune* received the news too late to pull their papers back and change their headlines. Their Monday morning issues were already on the streets. Because of the later time zone in Los Angeles, the *L.A. Times* decided to run a special issue devoted entirely to the story. They got it out Monday afternoon, beating all the Eastern and Central time zone papers to what many editors referred as the story of the century.

Although Capitol Hill was generally quiet at 6:00am, close to half the Senators and a majority of the members of the House of Representatives were at their homes, but on their phones, talking with their staff or the several news services about the story. They were jubilant, and they were ready to let the press know their true feelings about the current occupant of the White House. The story precipitated a feeding frenzy by the press.

Alec Caldwell and Don Armstrong sat back and smiled. The end game was on, and the first play had gone like clockwork. They would

GEORGE FEILD

give the story a week to work through the public. Then, they would launch a second volley. Hunt's popularity rating was already beginning to plummet.

*   *   *

The White House Oval Office
1600 Pennsylvania Avenue
Washington, DC
Sunday, June 24

As soon as Hunt was awakened with the news coming out of the U.K., he showered, shaved and dressed. Instead of having his usual breakfast in his quarters, he called a meeting of his friend and personal advisor, and his Chief of Staff in the Oval Office, and canceled his morning appointments.

It was 7:30am Eastern, 11:30 in London, and all of England was reading about President Hunt's indiscretions. Breakfast was sent over for Hunt and the two people whose advice he often sought, who had gathered for the crisis meeting to give him the benefit of their advice as how to handle the incriminating news about him, now spreading around the world like a wildfire.

"Deny it, John. Tell the press you never heard of the woman. Much less took her to bed. You've got to get out ahead of this. Deny, deny, deny. It'll go away with time. Do the Bill Clinton two step, John, just announce that . . . *I did not have sex with that woman.* Tell the press that's your story and you're sticking to it. We'll find a way to squash the woman's suit against you. We can pay her off and she'll just go away, like the story."

"So, what's your take on this situation, Fred?" The President had turned away from his personal advisor who had just given him his advice, and was looking at Fred Pendleton, his Chief of Staff and a personal friend for most of his adult life.

"Well, John, let me tell you what's going to happen if you deny this. First, some sleazebag writer will find your lady friend over in Paris and give her a few hundred Euros for the rights to write a book about her affair with you. Her name will be on the book's cover to make the public think it's an authentic account of the affair, but she won't get any of the book's sales royalties. And, if you think it will only be about a one-night-stand, you would be wrong. It will make the public think your short affair went on forever. In a word, John, you will be the one who gets screwed.

"So, let's think this thing through, John. First, you need to turn this little inconvenience around. Let it work for you rather than against you. If you're this child's father, that's one thing. But, I haven't seen any evidence that you are, so I wouldn't admit to that, but don't deny it either. If the question is asked, and you know it's going to be asked over and over, just deflect the question and change the subject. You're a politician, so you know how to do that.

"On the other hand, if you did sleep with the woman, you'll be ahead of the game to admit that you did. Say it was a one-night stand. Mrs. Hunt is gone now, so this won't be an embarrassment to her. Even though she was alive when this allegedly happened, the press won't pursue that point. It wouldn't add anything to the story, especially if you admit your indiscretion. After all, you're now a very eligible widower.

"So, John, my advice is, if you did bed this lady, admit it. Bill's right, get out in front of this. But do it by taking the high road, not the low road, as he suggests. Tell the press that if the child is yours, you'll step up to your responsibilities. Hell, John, you and the former first lady had no children, so that eliminates any complications you could have if you had legitimate children. You may even want to consider telling the press that if you are her father, you will personally go to France and ask her to come back to the U.S. with you for a visit at the White House. Just think how the press will play a story like that.

"But, before you do that, John, send a couple of your boys over there to check her out. If she has purple hair, a ring in her nose and tattoos all over her body, we'll need another plan. But if she's just a regular seven-year-old child, you'll be taking a Paris street urchin and making her into a royal princess. If there was ever a Cinderella story, that will be it. Every child's mother in the States will love you for what you're doing. Your personal approval rating will go through the roof.

"At the same time you'll be disarming the press. They won't have any reason to try to dig up more dirt, and it'll just go away. Instead of trying to cover you up in more damaging innuendoes, they'll run with the Cinderella story, praising you for stepping up to your responsibilities. Instead of being labeled a womanizer you'll be praised for your forthrightness as a caring father.

"John, this is an opportunity to build character. Take the high road, Mr. President. Do the right thing."

"Thank you, Gentlemen.

"Both of you need to know that I've called a press conference for 10:00 this morning. I'm sure the briefing room will be packed. Those bastards already smell blood in the water.

"Fred, I like your take on this issue. We should take the high road. I don't really want to admit to having been involved with this woman. Hell, I don't even remember her. But, I probably did take her to bed. So, I want you to put your spin on this into a statement that sounds like me. And get it on the Teleprompter so I can read it if I need to. But, I want a copy on my desk no later than 9:00."

"You'll have it, Mr. President."

*   *   *

The White House Press Briefing Room
1600 Pennsylvania Avenue
Washington, DC
Sunday, June 24 – 10:00am

As anticipated, the White House briefing room was filled with every reporter who possessed a press pass officially designating them as a member of the White House Press Corps. It was standing room only. The sharks were ready for a feeding frenzy.

The President's Press Secretary strode up to the dais, smiling and waving to reporters with whom she enjoyed a personal relationship. She was a former member of the White House press corps, and as such enjoyed a reputation for fairness and kinship with the members of the White House press corps that her predecessor had not. Hands were already in the air, vying for attention.

"Good morning, Ladies and Gentlemen. Before we open the floor to questions, President Hunt wishes to make a brief statement."

On cue, the President entered the briefing room through the rear hall, smiled as he stepped up on the elevated platform and walked to the dais. His Press Secretary stepped away from the microphones.

The members of the press had risen from their seats as courtesy and protocol dictated.

"Ladies and Gentlemen, please be seated," the President said, continuing to smile. "I would like to make a statement regarding the allegations contained in the news story which I understand originated in the U.K. this morning, and which, I know is the reason all of you are here this morning."

Every member sat breathlessly, waiting for the President to deny having an affair with the French actress. Every one of them had questions, and they were ready to pounce.

"I do not know if I am the father of the little girl whose picture accompanied the story in the *London Times*. But, everything else contained in the article is true. If it is determined that I am this young lady's father, I will honor my responsibilities as her father. In fact, I will go to France and personally ask her to visit me in the White House.

"As all of you know, Rebecca and I had no children. And although my wife is deceased now, it is exciting to realize that I really might have a daughter I can help raise. This is a wonderful day in my life. Just think, I may be a father!"

The President stepped to the side of the dais as his Press Secretary approached. "Are there any questions?"

Not a hand was raised nor a question asked. The White House Press Corps remained silent, not believing what they had just heard. They were stunned.

"Thank you, Ladies and Gentlemen. This concludes this press conference." The President's Press Secretary reached over and switched off the microphone, smiled and waved at the members of the press corps, still seated, but not yelling at her and the President as they usually did, clamoring for a response to a last-minute question. She joined the President as he left the room by the rear hall.

The President was smiling. As the Secret Service agent closed the door behind them he said, "Shortest damned press conference I ever attended."

"Me to. You handled that like a pro, Sir."

"I am a pro, Jennifer," the President said, winking at his Press Secretary and patting her firm buttocks. He had already made plans for her.

*   *   *

CIA Headquarters
Langley, Virginia Sunday,
June 24 – 10:09am

"What the hell was that?" Don Armstrong asked, turning to look at Alec who was frowning. He and Alec were sitting in the small conference room adjoining Armstrong's office, watching C-Span's coverage of the White House press conference.

"Damned if I know. I would have bet the farm that he would have followed Bill Clinton's infamous statement . . . *I did not have sex with that woman.*

"Damn, we just lost the first round, Don. I can't believe he took the high road and turned this story around so he would look like a caring father, which we know he isn't. When the press gets through with this, I'll bet his approval rating will be through the roof. I just knew he would deny the story and the press would crucify him. That toad isn't smart enough to have done this on his own. He must have one hell of a smart advisor."

"True, but the game's not over yet, Alec. We'll get the toad. Just wait until the next bomb explodes at the White House. This time we're going to sink his boat for good."

"I can hardly wait, Don. But right now, I think I'll call Beth. I haven't talked to her since yesterday."

"Give her and Alexander my best, Old Man."

*   *   *

The London Times
London, England
Thursday, June 28

The follow-up article on the President's affair with the French actress appeared in the Thursday edition of the *London Times* and hit the wire services the same morning. The major revelation in the follow-up was the child's DNA report, and a similar report from President Hunt's personal physician that left no doubt that he was the child's father. The story also announced that he was already making plans to visit the President of France, and while there he would also be visiting his young daughter and her mother. Because of the President's initial confession of his transgressions, the story didn't make the front page on any major U.S. newspaper. In less than a week, it was a dead issue, forgotten by a majority of the public.

*   *   *

The President's Compound
Thursday, June 28 – 11:15am

The President had arrived a few minutes earlier and wasn't in a good mood. He was pacing back and forth in front of the oversized fireplace in the living room when Corky Rothrock, the Black Hawk team leader, walked into the living room.

"Mr. President, excellent follow-up article in the *London Times* today. Congratulations, Sir. You played the press like a professional. You really took the steam out of anything they were going to try to pin on you. An excellent ploy, Sir."

John Hunt didn't believe in exchanging pleasantries with anyone unless it was essential to his political career. He considered it a waste of his time.

"Thank you, Corky. So you're sure we aren't being watched?"

"Yes, Sir. We staked out the compound for three days, and no one suspicious came anywhere close to the place. I don't know who the guys were I saw earlier, but they haven't been back. I think I was just seeing ghosts."

"Is your team here?"

"Three of us are. The men I sent down to Mexico are still checking on some leads there."

*   *   *

CIA Stakeout Apartment
Evergreen Street
Georgetown, District of Columbia
Thursday, June 28 – 11:10am

"Sir, three members of the President's hit squad are in the compound, and the President just arrived. According to the one named Rothrock, he sent two of his people down to Mexico. They found nothing, so Hunt told the Rothrock person to have them keep looking. They still don't know who Alec is or for whom he's working.

"We were lucky to spot Rothrock the other day and pulled the street surveillance off. Evidently he made our people. From what he told Hunt, he thinks it was a false alarm. So, we're back in business. He doesn't know we're up here."

*   *   *

The President's Compound
Evergreen Street
Georgetown, District of Columbia
Thursday, June 28 – 11:32am

"Corky, I have another job for you. I don't know the source of the recent article about my being the father of the little French girl, but I have my suspicions. From what I'm told, it originated in the U.K. with the *London Times*, but that could just be a false trail to keep us from learning the real source. I think it may have originated here, but planted over there.

"I want you to take one of your best interrogators with you to London. Initially, I want you to pose as FBI agents. Your first target will be the *London Times*. Find out which editor at the paper authorized publishing the article. If he won't reveal his source, my suggestion would be to determine who serves on his review board, then pick a member and talk with him, or her. You might be able to get the source information without creating any waves. But, if you have to lean on the guy, do whatever is necessary to find out how the paper got the information. You people are good at that. If the source is there in the U.K., follow your nose. I suspect it will lead back to the Virginia countryside."

"You think the CIA is behind this, Mr. President?"

"You bet I do. I would bet my life on it. Those bastards are out to get me."

"How would they get their hands on the information behind these allegations, Sir?"

"You tell me. How do they get their hands on anything? They're everywhere and they're nowhere. They've got a budget that's a hell of a lot larger than Congress realizes. I promised the DCI that I would support his budget recommendation this round, but I'm going to do everything in my power to cut it to the bone. Those people have more contacts than Carter has liver pills."

"Sir?"

"Just an old expression, Mr. Rothrock. You're too young to remember *Carter's Little Liver Pills*.

"On the other matter, have the people you sent down to Mexico found out anything about the CIA agent who wrecked my little source of income down there?"

"My two people are down in Cabo San Lucas now. They're talking with the police and have the pictures the cops developed of the guy when they set up the APB on him. They're talking to employees of several resort hotels he stayed in, but they aren't getting much information. We don't have a real name yet. I think he used several aliases when he was down there. And, it's not like you can just go over to Langley and look through their yearbook to match a picture with a name.

"Sir, you told me the DCI sent the agent down there at your request to find your friend's daughter. Did your Mr. McKenzie get his name? I understand he went down there to bring his daughter back once she was found, so he must have met this guy. What can he tell us?"

"Unfortunately, not much. I asked that question when he and his family stopped by the White House on their way back to Boston to thank me for the favor. McKenzie did meet the agent while he was in Mexico and asked his name, but was told that any name he could give him would be an alias. However, his daughter let the alias he was using and the hotel they were hiding in slip out, so I gave that information to my contact in Mexico City. He had one of his top interrogators take the agent down. We had him in our hands, at least for a while. The interrogator and his team were trying to find out how much the agent knew about the drug running organization there and who he may have told, before they made him disappear. But, the damned guy escaped. I don't know how, but he did, and took out the interrogator's five-man SWAT team at the same time. The interrogator wasn't there at the time, so he survived, but he lost every member of his team.

"The police recovered some automatic weapons, so we know this agent had professional help, but how the CIA found out where they were holding him is beyond me. My contact tells me he didn't have access to any means of communication so he couldn't have gotten a message out. The automatic weapons the police found were made in China so we figure it was a CIA job. They tend to leave things around to keep the scent from leading back to their house. They had some outside help, but we don't know from whom.

"Anyway, I think my DCI set me up. He called a few days after all this went down about some other matter, and casually let me know his agent was still down there and closing in on the drug organization he had uncovered. He told me the Drug Enforcement Agency didn't even know it existed. I think he suspected I had an interest in that enterprise and casually mentioned the new alias his agent was using and where he was staying, because he knew I would pass it on. The son-of-a-bitch played me like a well-tuned fiddle, and I fell for it like he knew I would.

"I had no reason then to suspect it might be a setup, and I called my contact with the information. I think the CIA has my telephones in the White House bugged.

"To make a long story short, the agent was waiting for my contact's man sent to kill him, and took him out with a bullet between his eyes. At least that's what I was told. I'm sure he enjoyed doing it since the man he killed was the interrogator who had captured and tortured him earlier. And, in doing so, the agent switched identities with the assassin. Nobody claimed the body so the authorities had it cremated. Based on the information they had, his identification and passport, they assumed he was the agent, so they didn't do fingerprints or DNA. We thought we had finally gotten rid of this pain-in-the-ass, but before we learned otherwise, he had eliminated the guys who were our conduit between the people down in Central America who process the drugs and our people who repackage the stuff and get it into the States. At least they disappeared. I assume he was involved. So, our little operation is shut down for the moment.

"My DCI called me a few days ago to tell me his agent was home and safe. The bastard was rubbing my nose in it.

"And I know damned well he's behind this story about me that's coming out of the U.K. He's trying to screw me over because I gave up his agent. Once we take care of his agent, he'll be next on your list of things to do."

*   *   *

CIA Headquarters
Langley, Virginia
Thursday, June 28 – 12:15pm

"Interesting conversation, Alec. Those miniature, high-Tec listening devices we hid in Hunt's little playpen over in Georgetown are proving to be an excellent source of information, worth every penny of the exorbitant rent we're paying on the apartment across the street to house our listening post.

"At least after your exalted position as his number one target, I'm second on his list. I'm rather proud of my standing with that toad." Don Armstrong, said after he and Alec were briefed on recent information coming out of the President's compound.

"So, he's sending a couple of his Black Hawks to the U.K. to try to determine who's responsible for the story about his fathering an illegitimate child over in France. Why don't I give Timothy Sutherland a heads-up so he can warn his editor friend at the *London Times*? Maybe we should help his people on this. Put them on Tim's trail, and when they get to the Scottish Highlands, feed them to the Loch Ness Monster."

"Now, that's a plan, Alec. Make the call, but warn Tim that these guys play for keeps. And you should go over there and run interference for him on this. Taking down bad guys isn't something your Mr. Sutherland is used to doing."

"I agree. We shouldn't get Tim into something that's over his head. But I want you to call your contact at MI-6. Tell him I'm going to need two of his best men, preferably expert shooters. Tell him we have a couple of low lifes coming over who need to disappear. I'll meet their men at the Glasgow airport and take it from there. I just want to be the supervisor on this. Too much killing can get in your blood."

CHAPTER SEVENTEEN

The White House – Oval Office
1600 Pennsylvania Avenue
Washington, D.C.
Sunday, July 1 – 3:18pm

"MR. PRESIDENT, THERE'S a call for you, Sir. It's a man, and he won't identify himself. But he says you will want to take the call. The operator routed it through the screening room, as protocol dictates. Their equipment confirmed the call is being made from a pay phone on "U" street, downtown. They have the location. They couldn't detect any recording devices or scramblers, so they think the voice on the phone is real-time, not a recording, and not disguised. The profile they got indicates he's a white male, probably between thirty-five and forty-five. Voice inflection indicates he's probably Southern, maybe Virginia or North Carolina, but not deep South. The Service wants to know if they should pick the guy up.

"Sir, he told the operator to mention the work *corky* to you. The screening room put him on hold and called me. They say the word means nothing to them. They put it through their database of key words and aliases. Nothing found, Sir. Is this someone you may wish to speak with?"

"Corky, you say. Yes, that's someone I need to speak to. Tell the Secret Service to stand down. But, have the guys in the screening room transfer it over to a secure line. No recordings, no listening devices. This is personal."

"Yes, Sir."

"Mr. Rothrock, you know better than to call me here. What the hell do you want?"

"Sir, I was over in Georgetown this morning, and I noticed some men sniffing around. Not on the property, but hanging around in cars parked on Evergreen. Just like before, so I wasn't seeing ghosts. Somebody's got the place staked out, Sir. I would bet my life on it. I think the compound may be compromised. My boys are holed up a few blocks away in a third-rate motel."

"And?"

"We know who he is, Sir!"

"The guy who has the compound staked out?"

"No, Sir. The CIA agent you told us to find. The guy you say is trying to sink your ship. They're the words you used, I believe, Sir."

"How did you find him, Mr. Rothrock?"

"I have my sources, Sir. It's better you don't know who they are.

"His name is Caldwell. Alexander Caldwell, Sir. He's ex-military, army intelligence, I think. Joined the CIA after he retired as a Bird Colonel. Worked for them for a number of years until his wife died. Then disappeared for a while. Surfaced again out in Montana. I think that's where he's from. He still works for the CIA, but off the books, so to speak, a free agent. Handles jobs when they need someone with his special skills. I understand his parents died when he was young, and an Indian who taught him how to live on his own in the mountains raised him. I don't believe the locals know he's a federal agent. He lived alone for a couple of years, away from the locals, then worked a case for the CIA where he saved the life of the wife of the Secretary of the Interior. The Secretary was killed in a helicopter crash, but she survived. Anyway, Caldwell married her and they now have a son. Neither had children from their first marriages."

"I remember the incident. The Secretary was a personal friend, and I knew his wife, Elizabeth, I think. Pretty lady, but I didn't know she married this guy. Can you get to him?"

"My source tells me he's spending some time now out at Langley. Doubt we could get anywhere close to him as long as he's on the Reservation."

"OK, can you get to his family?"

"Absolutely. They live out in Montana near a little wide spot in the road named Lennep, no one around for miles. It would be an easy hit, Sir. You just give me the word and I'll go out there and take them out personally."

"No, not you. And no killing. At least not yet. I just want them kidnapped. He's the target, not them. They should be put in a secure place where he can find them, if he's as good as I think he is. Have your people leave enough clues around so he can pick up their trail. We're going to use them as bait to bring him to us. He'll come after them, and that's when your people will take him out. Then they can do what they want with his wife and kid. That'll be the time to clean up loose ends."

"I'm on it, Sir."

"Good, but not you Mr. Rothrock. You can't do this one. I want you to take care of the matter we talked about last Thursday. Just get two of your best men on a flight out to wherever this man's family is, or to wherever a commercial flight out of DC can get them close. Have them leave tonight if possible. They should rent a car and check out the area so they can tell you where they're going to take them. Be sure they stay in touch with you, and you with me.

"In the meantime, take one of your men with you and fly to London to track down the source of the story about my affair with that French actress. I want to know where that information came from.

"When you get back you can leak the word to one of your snitches, someone you know who is working both sides of the street, that your boys have Caldwell's family. The word will get back to him, and we'll let him sweat a while before you feed him enough information to put him in harms way. Then your people can blow him away.

"You know, Mr. Rothrock, I'm really beginning to love running this country."

*   *   *

Saint Giles Hotel
Bedford Avenue
London, England
Friday, July 6 – 1:00pm

"Mr. President, We've been over here with these Limeys for a week now, and we're finally making some worthwhile progress. We first interviewed the editor of the *London Times* who authorized running the story about you. At first he didn't want to see us, but when we showed him our FBI credentials and the forged letter from the Director asking for cooperation, he seemed to be more than happy to answer our questions. He told us he had received an anonymous letter, which contained the story facts and the pictures. He also gave us a copy of a police report in which a witness saw someone deposit a similar envelope in a post office in a rural village outside London around midnight on the night before he received the information. So we went out to the location to look around. There was a bank with an ATM across the street. It's amazing what FBI credentials can do for you, even in a foreign country. We walked in, flashed our credentials and walked out with the videotape from the ATM camera. We watched a new Jaguar pull up to the post office's outside mail drop around midnight. A man reached out the driver's side window and inserted a manila envelope into the mail slot. We have the license number of the Jaguar. It's registered to a Timothy Sutherland, President and Chairman of the First Sutherland Bank and Trust headquartered in Edinburgh. We're on our way to Scotland tomorrow."

"Sutherland, Timothy Sutherland," The President mused. "I've heard that name before, but I can't place it just now. Good work, Mr. Rothrock. Stay with it, and keep me posted."

*   *   *

Glasgow International Airport
Glasgow, Scotland
Saturday, July 7 – 10:17am

"Hello, Tim. I've just arrived in Glasgow. How've you been? Not uneasy about all of this, I hope."

"Not in the least, Alec. Quite exciting, really! Just like old times when you and Mason were over here saving the Queen's life. And, it's good to hear your voice again so soon. Why didn't you fly into Edinburgh? I would have met you at the airport and taken you to dinner."

"I have to meet a couple of MI-6 types here in Glasgow, and it's best we aren't seen together until this is over. But, I will take you up on the dinner invitation as soon as we are done. Did you prime your editor friend?"

"I did, and he tells me the two impostors made a convincing argument that he should share what information he had about the source of the story with them. He did, of course, just as I had suggested. They had a letter supposedly from the Director of the FBI requesting his cooperation. They wanted it back, but he excused himself, slipped out of his office for a minute on the pretense of answering a private call, and made a copy. He sent it to me and it's on its way to your director. You may be able to use it if Director Armstrong ever wants your Congress to begin impeachment proceedings one of these days.

"We also got to the bank manager in time. We happen to have a branch in Abridge across the street from the Post where I mailed the envelope. My manager played his part like a pro. Gave them the videotape that had my Jaguar stopping across the street. We know they accessed the vehicle registration database and made an inquiry about the Jaguar's ownership. It's in my name, and they were spotted by the police on the M23 driving out of London towards Heathrow. We checked and they've booked a Lufthansa flight into Edinburgh and should be there in an hour or so. They've also rented a car there, so I expect them to come by the bank looking for me sometime later today."

"Excellent. They're right on schedule. Now you know why I couldn't meet you at Edinburgh. They already have my photograph from the Mexican police files, and even though Edinburgh is a very large airport, there's always the chance they would spot me. I'm sure they now have your photograph as well. If they spotted you there waiting for me, or with me, they would have the answers they're looking for. Since they're traveling as FBI agents, I would bet they have permits to carry their weapons on the flight over. They may even think it would be worth the risk to shoot us on the spot. They probably could make a case with the local police that we were criminals, wanted in the States, and were trying to escape when they shot us. They're professionals, and with FBI credentials, they wouldn't be jailed, but would be advised to remain in Edinburgh until the investigation is over. By the time the local police learned the truth, they would be winging their way back to the good old U.S. of A.

"So, it's best we play the game out rather than give them too many answers at one time. Plus, it's a lot more fun doing it my way. Now, does your bank receptionist know the routine?"

"Only to call my personal secretary when they arrive. She will tell her to send them up to my office, but I won't be there. Neither will she. We have a rather pretty MI-6 officer who will take her place temporarily. She is what they call a soft interrogator. She uses her charms and her physical appeal to disarm her suspects, but she is very professional and does her job well. She will tell them I am in a meeting, should be out in a few minutes, and will ask them to wait with her in the outer office. To put them at ease, she will have tea brought up for them. It will have a mild sedative in it, which will make their responses less guarded and more truthful. She will also use the time to flirt with them and ask some innocent sounding questions. When she feels she has the answers she wants, she will signal my real secretary who will enter the office and inform the MI-6 agent that I was called out to Dunrobin. Seems my mom has taken a turn for the worse and I have to be at her side. No idea when I will be able to return, but apologies all around to the two FBI agents for taking their valuable time.

"I suspect they will begin their trek through the Grampian Mountains immediately, most likely on the A9, right through Inverness. Since I doubt either of them is familiar with Scotland, they will take the A9 all the way out to Dunrobin Castle. There will be some great places along the route around the village of Golspie where it runs along the cliffs overlooking the North Sea to take them out. If the car goes over one of the cliffs, the local constable will never find it, or them. And, if it's done right, and they are later discovered, no one will ever know it was anything more than a motoring accident."

"Well, my learned friend. Looks like you've put all the pieces together for us. Well done. Go back to visit your mother. I'll call you there when it's over."

*   *   *

FBI Headquarters
935 Pennsylvania Avenue
Washington, DC
Tuesday, July 10 – 8:15am

The secure phone on the desk of the FBI's Executive Assistant Director for National Security had rung once. Helen DuPont, his executive secretary picked it up before it could ring a second time.

"Sir, I have the Deputy Director of MI-5 on the secure phone. Do you want to take it in your office?"

"Yes, thank you, Helen." William Hannah, the EADNS, had just returned from an intelligence briefing with the Director and was on his way to his private office.

"Deputy Director O'Connor, How are you, Sir. How may we be of service?"

"Good morning, William. I just need to have someone check out a situation over here that has just been brought to my attention. Since we've had some dealings in the past, I thought it would be in order to contact someone over there whom I know personally. You may wish to direct me to someone else.

"To be brief, a constable up in the small village of Golspie on the North Sea coast of Scotland received a report yesterday of a vehicle on the rocks at the bottom of a very high cliff just off the A9. Evidently a net fisherman was running his fishing boat up the coast and saw the vehicle on the rocks. The village's rescue team was the nearest about and was called in. They had to rappel down the cliff to get to the wreck. The surf was too heavy to go in by rescue boat. There were two chaps inside the vehicle, both dead, we assume from the impact. The auto was crushed to the extent that no one could have survived the impact, but one of our forensic teams out of Edinburgh is on its way there to determine the cause of death. So far there seems to be no evidence of foul play.

"William, both of the men were carrying FBI badges and identifications, and both were armed. This morning I first checked with your Legal Attaché office in your Consulate in Edinburgh when we learned their identities and recovered their FBI credentials, and they don't have any agents whose names match up with the identifications these chaps were carrying. I decided not to tell them why I was inquiring. I thought this could be an operation being conducted on a *need to know* basis. As you are aware, my friend, all of your agents on U.K. soil must be registered with Central Registry. These two agents are not registered, according to my people.

"Since you fellows don't generally use aliases either for domestic or international investigations, we assumed the names we have are genuine. Also, we checked their weapons' serial numbers, and they don't match up with any serial numbers for weapons your people have over here, at least those registered with us. So, I'm at a loss. Who are these chaps, and are they yours?"

"I have no idea, Nigel. I certainly don't know the names of everyone we have over there. Many of the technical and public relations people don't answer to my department, but I can check them out and get back to you. I'll also check out their weapons numbers to see if they're ours. Give me the names and numbers, please."

"The IDs we have are for a Samuel Jacobson and a Myron Davidson. They look genuine, so if they are forged, the work must have been by someone with considerable knowledge of the process of manufacturing the genuine articles. You may want to check out some of your people in your documents section. These IDs have all the trappings your people use when they are manufacturing genuine documents. And, I would doubt that anyone not involved in the process would know all of this."

"I'll check this out, Nigel. And I'll be back in touch before the day is out."

"I'll be waiting for your call, William. Thanks. Oh, one other thing. The vehicle these fellows were driving went off the highway in a construction zone. The guardrail between the highway and the cliff had been removed and the road was being repaired. I understand there were reduced speed signs and a system of barricades, like sawhorses, running down the open area. And, all of the barricades were in place, but they were spaced far enough apart so a car could go through without taking one of them down with it. If these chaps ran off the road and over the cliff during the very early morning, the fog off the North Sea would have been quite heavy in that area. They could have easily become disoriented. Right now, we just don't have any answers, but this seems a little suspicious since this is a very dangerous area and the barricades should have been much closer together than they were when we found them . It will be a good while before they can winch the car back up the cliff.

We won't know how this happened until my people can examine the automobile.

"But, because of the credentials these chaps were carrying, we have put our best forensic team on this. They should be on the scene shortly, and if they come up with anything interesting, you'll be the first to know."

*   *   *

CIA Headquarters
Langley, Virginia
Tuesday, July 10 – 4:45pm

"Are you on your way back, Alec?"

"Not at the moment. I'm still in Scotland with Tim and his mother at Dunrobin Castle. We'll be having dinner together this evening, and I'll fly back to Edinburgh with Tim in the bank's helicopter tomorrow morning. I've booked a flight out of there. My ETA at Dulles is just after noon. Have someone pick me up there. It's a British Airways direct flight. I'll see you tomorrow afternoon."

"Well, don't leave me hanging, Alec. How did it go?"

"Like clockwork, Don. Tim had everything set up before I got here, and the two targets did exactly what he predicted they would. It was a brilliant plan. They delayed the targets in Edinburgh for an hour or so on the pretense that the vehicle they had rented had not been returned when it was supposed to be. They turned them loose in time for them to drive to Inverness by nightfall. They stayed the night there, which gave my two MI-6 agents and me time to get up here. The two Black Hawk team members were driving and we were traveling in an army helicopter, so we had time on our hands.

"We set up near the village of Golspie, an hour before the targets arrived, so we were ready. We knew the car they were driving, and the helicopter pilot picked it up well before they got to us. One of their agents in Inverness planted a transmitter in their car just after they arrived there, so it was easy tracking. It was still dark when they arrived, but the two MI-6 sharp shooters were using high-powered night vision riflescopes and could see the vehicle well in advance of their arriving in the kill zone. The shooters took out one of their front tires in a very dangerous section of the A9 on the Scottish coast, a section of the highway where the guardrail had been removed and was being replaced. It was in an area where traffic was being controlled using temporary wooden barricades, which we had removed before they got to the construction site. When the car's left front tire blew out, the car careened left and the driver overcorrected, causing the car to go over the cliff before the driver could stop. The impact from the long fall onto the rocks below the cliff did both of them in. We replaced the temporary barricade, but left enough space between them for a car to pass through, so if the vehicle is ever found there is no evidence that the barricades had been moved. So, case closed!"

"Looks as though your friend, Timothy Sutherland, is an excellent planner. Are you sure he's just a banker?"

"I suspect he is a little more than that, Don."

"I'll see you when you get back, Alec. Be safe."

"Thanks. By the way, Don. I've been calling Beth all day and can't locate her."

"Did you call her cell phone?"

"She doesn't have one. We don't have cell service out at the house. No towers around."

"Could she have gone down to Idaho to her family's ranch?"

"No, I called her brother, and he hasn't seen her. And, she wouldn't leave on such a long trip without talking to me first."

"When did you talk with her last, Alec?"

"Yesterday, around noon, her time. She was at home and not planning any trips unless she drove into White Sulfur Springs for groceries or milk for the baby."

"You want me to send someone out to check on her?"

"Yes, but don't call the locals. They don't know who I am, and I want to keep it that way. Just have one of your agents from over in

Great Falls drive out to check on her, please. She's probably just fine, but I worry. See you tomorrow."

*   *   *

FBI Headquarters
935 Pennsylvania Avenue
Washington, DC
Tuesday, July 10 – 1:25pm

"Sorry Nigel, they aren't ours. And I can't find the names you gave me in our NCIC files over here, or in the agency rosters we have, and they are updated within twenty-four hours of any personnel changes.

"The weapons aren't ours either. I had the weapons' serial numbers run through our database and we came up empty. In fact, we even went outside the bureau, and nothing. If they were federal or state owned, I would have picked them up.

"If you're sure they're from over here, you may want to make a call to Don Armstrong over at Central Intelligence. They may be running something over there and didn't want you fellows to know about it. And we don't have access to their information. They sure as hell don't tell us anything about what they're doing. And, I'm sure they use forged FBI credentials if they want to avoid the heat if something goes wrong. But, no Nigel, they aren't ours. Sorry, my friend."

"Then I think you may have someone in your documents section who is selling forged FBI identifications, William. These are just too perfect to have been made on the street. And, they have your identification mark that no one would know about unless he or she is, or has been, an FBI employee involved in the printing process."

"That's my next little snooping job, my friend. Thanks for the heads-up on that. Let me know if there's anything else I can do. Sounds like you have an interesting problem, Nigel. Good luck, Old Friend."

"William. There's more."

"More?"

"Yes. They were finally able to winch the vehicle up the cliff, and our forensic team had an opportunity to go through it. There were two Saco high-powered rifles in 30-06 caliber in the trunk. And, they were fitted with suppressors and night vision scopes."

"Damn, sounds like you may have a couple of hit men in your morgue."

"Yes, it does look that way. And we found a roadmap in the front seat floorboard. It was of the North Seacoast of Scotland. That's where the accident occurred. The route they were on was highlighted, but the curious thing is, someone had circled Dunrobin Castle. It's located about thirty miles north of where these lads were found.

"If you don't know this, William, Dunrobin Castle is the ancestral home of the Sutherland Clan. But, the only family member living there, excluding the servants, is Dame Meredith Sutherland, the Clan's matriarch. Her husband is deceased, and her only son, Sir Timothy Sutherland, lives in Edinburgh and is chairman of First Sutherland Bank.

"Would you have any idea why two men, posing as FBI agents from the U.S. would be motoring to Dunrobin Castle, and carrying high-powered sniper rifles? Certainly they would not be after Dame Meredith."

"I have no idea, Nigel, but again, give my counterpart over at the Central Intelligence Agency a call. He may know about this."

"I will do that, William. My investigating team is on its way to Dunrobin Castle to look around and talk with Dame Meredith. She may be able to shed some light on this."

"You said this lady has a son living in Edinburgh. Would he happen to be visiting his mother now?"

"I don't know, but we shall determine that shortly."

*   *   *

CIA Headquarters
Langley, Virginia
Tuesday, July 10 – 6:30pm

"I'm afraid you have the wrong agency, Commander Dunsmore. The CIA doesn't have anything running over in the U.K. Even if we did, we would have alerted your people first. I'm very proud of the relationships we've developed with your MI-5 and MI-6 people. But maybe we can help. You say the two men were carrying FBI identifications, but the FBI denies any knowledge of these people and their activities. If Bill told you that, Nigel, you can take it to the bank. Bill Sampson is an honorable man, and he wouldn't deny any knowledge of an FBI sanctioned action unless, of course, someone over in the Hoover building is running a clandestine operation without his knowledge. That happens over at the Bureau a lot these days."

"And how about in the Central Intelligence Agency, Director Armstrong? Anyone running anything over here we should know about?"

"Not of which I am aware, Commander. And yes, it could happen here as well. But, I doubt if anyone in the CIA is involved. So, Commander, give me the aliases the two men were using and their physical descriptions, including characteristics such as scars, tattoos and that sort of thing. If your coroner finds any old bone breaks, we would like to know. We have a pretty extensive anatomical database, and we just may have some matching X-rays or statistics. We also have a rather extensive file on just about everyone known to be in the business, both here and international, even some people working in the business who don't have an agency to answer to. Freelancers, we call them. They work for the highest price. If they're known, we'll find out who they are and for whom they're working or with whom they're contracted. And, of course, we'll share that information with you."

*　　*　　*

"Think we should tell the Brits that the two bodies they have were members of the President's dirty tricks team, and the older guy was his team leader and his number one assassin, Alec? That would really create a rift between the U.K. and the U.S."

"It would indeed, Don. And it would expose the toad for what he really is. I think we should let the Brits chafe his butt with the news that they know he was running something over there he didn't want them to know about. Let's not tell them that Tim Sutherland was their target. If they figure that out on their own, so much the better. They'll want to know why, but Tim can have the director of MI-6 put the squash on any investigation MI-5 undertakes. And, if they get too close to us, Tim will have the PM step in and button this up."

"And what about the President, Don; will he find out we're involved?"

"He may be a toad, as you said, Alec, but he's not a stupid toad. He already knows. He just doesn't know what to do about it yet."

*　　*　　*

CIA Headquarters
Langley, Virginia
Wednesday, July 11 – 1:30pm

"Commander Dunsmore, Don Armstrong here. Sorry for the lateness of the hour, but I wanted to get back to you as soon as I could. First, thank you for sending over all the details on the two bodies you have in your morgue. We assume they gained entrance into the U.K. using the FBI credentials your people found on them."

"I suspect they did, Director Armstrong. The security detail at Heathrow reported that two FBI agents had entered the country several days ago, but they didn't report in at Central Registry as protocol dictates. But, we know now their credentials were bogus, so we know why they didn't. We just don't know what they were doing over here."

"Well, Sir, I have some good news and some not so good. The good news is that we have identified the older of the two men whose photos and statistics you sent to us, the one using the Samuel Jacobson alias. His name is, or was, Henry Rothrock. At least that's the name he uses over here. His fingerprints were on file with us, although they were not in our domestic files. They came to us from a security agency in Somalia. Seems he was involved with a group of mercenaries conducting raids on Ethiopian villages across the border, trying to inflame relationships between the two countries. The Somalian police had him in prison and the government was about to hang him when President Hunt stepped in, saved his hide, and put him to work as one of his dirty tricks team members. We were told that several years ago he was elevated to leader of this clandestine group know to us as the Black Hawks, so his demise is going to put a serious crimp in Hunt's plans unless he has someone in the wings who can take his place. As for the chap calling himself Myron Davidson, we don't seem to have anything on him.

"Anyway, the scars you found on Rothrock's abdomen and on his right arm confirmed our suspicions. The abdomen scar was received in a knife fight when he was a mercenary in Africa. There's a clinical record of the incident that we also have in our files. The scar on his arm was made by a sniper's bullet only a year ago. It was a through and through wound that wasn't cared for by any recognized physician or hospital. An off-the-books doctor took care of it. His license to practice medicine was revoked some years ago, and since that time he has set up shop in a shoddy, run-down part of the District. He operates a cash only illegal practice taking care of gang bangers and street punks who get shot or cut up in their drug related turf wars and can't chance going to a hospital for fear of being locked up by the cops.

"These kids have a lot of money from their drug trade, and this guy's getting rich illegally practicing medicine for a captive audience. We've had him under surveillance ever since he was defrocked and even have videotapes of his patients coming to his office. His office hours are mostly at night, but he makes out-of-office visits when his patients can't make it in, usually because they've lost too much blood.

"Commander, this Rothrock person was the leader of a small group of assassins. I'm sure the other guy was also a member of the group, but we can't identify him. They work out of a compound located in the Georgetown area of Washington, owned by their employer.

"The two men, whose bodies you have, were employed by the President of the United States, Commander. He put together this five-man assassination team when he was first elected to Congress to keep his detractors in line. We have evidence that this group has been involved in the demise of several prominent political and business leaders whose deaths were thought to be accidental or suicides, but in effect, were the result of actions taken by this group on orders from their employer."

The telephone line was silent, as though Armstrong had been talking, but no one was on the line with him. "Are you there, Commander Dunsmore?"

"Yes. I'm sorry Director Armstrong. What you just said caught me totally by surprise. I simply cannot fathom President Hunt being involved in such matters. It's just not civil. Are you quite sure your information is accurate?"

"I'm afraid so, Commander. We've been tracking this group for several years, and we are very familiar with their modus operandi."

"Then why haven't you stopped them? Why haven't you exposed what they have been doing? You could possibly have saved some lives! Your inaction is inexcusable, Sir!"

"Over here, it's not that easy, Commander. First, who would believe us? The President is enjoying a very high popularity rating at the moment with his admitting to being the little French girl's father.

He would just deny the allegations, and everyone would believe him. After all, he's the *man of the hour*. Plus, his assassination team would just fade into the woodwork, with no trace left of their existence.

"The Attorney General would throw out any evidence we may have to support a case against the President since our methods of gathering information aren't always sanctioned by our legal system. It's a very frustrating situation, Commander, but it is reality, nevertheless."

"I understand, Director. I'm sure my people bend the law from time to time to make their cases. But your laws, and ours, are on the books to protect the innocent. Unfortunately, they also protect the guilty. Do you have any suggestions as to how we should handle this information over here? This is quite a delicate matter, you know."

"Indeed it is, and I appreciate your asking, Commander. Yes, I do. I would suggest you keep this information to yourself if at all possible. However, should you decide to alert the Prime Minister of this because you are bound by law to do so, I would certainly understand. On the other hand, may I suggest you recommend that he not broach the issue with the President. We would recommend he attempt to maintain the status quo between our two nations for the moment by keeping this information to himself.

"If the President learns that we have his team under surveillance, he will disband them and they will just melt away. In order for us to eliminate this threat to our system of justice and to our political system, please let us handle it in our own way. We have launched a plan that we feel will bring the President down without his knowing who or what is behind it. And I can assure you, it will in no way damage the office, just the man. But, we need a little more time for it to come to fruition."

"Well, Director, I will certainly honor your request, but you know full well I do not speak for the PM. I suspect he will want to see proof of your allegations, so please be prepared to fly over and explain yourself if he should request your presence."

"It would be my pleasure, Commander."

*   *   *

The Oval Office
The White House,
1600 Pennsylvania Ave.
Washington, D.C.
Thursday, July 12 – 7:30am

"Sir, you may want to see this." Fred Pendleton, the President's Chief of Staff, had entered the Oval Office through the entrance leading from the President's private office, a copy of the *London Times* under his arm. He knew John Hunt was there alone, so he entered, not waiting for the President to acknowledge his soft knock.

"I was browsing the *London Times* this morning, Sir, and came on this account of two Yanks posing as FBI agents who were killed in an automobile crash up in Scotland. The article states that the FBI has disavowed any knowledge of these men or why they were there. It wouldn't have meant anything to me, but the name of one of the men they were able to identify, a Corky Rothrock, seemed familiar. Somewhere in the back of my mind I believe I recall your mentioning that name, but I don't remember in what context. Have you ever heard of this man, or is my memory playing tricks on me?"

"The name isn't familiar, Fred. But let me see the article anyway."

Pendleton handed the page to his boss and turned away to answer his cell phone. He couldn't see the expression of surprise on the President's face, which quickly turned to one of concern, then anger. *What the hell has happened now?*

Hunt scanned the article and couldn't believe his eyes. *No wonder Rothrock hasn't contacted me these last few days. He's been lying in a morgue in Edinburgh. At least the Brits don't know he worked for me and was over there to take out that Sutherland guy who gave the story to the London Times about that French woman who had my kid,* he thought, as he crumpled the newspaper into a ball and threw it into the trashcan beside his ornate desk.

Little did Hunt, the FBI, or MI-5, for that matter, know that the left front tire of the automobile Rothrock was driving had been shot out by an MI-6 sniper who, with Alec Caldwell, and another MI-6 agent, had been lying in wait for the vehicle to enter the highway construction zone which they had selected as their kill zone. The Director of MI-6 had been fully briefed on the action, and the reasons for it, and had sanctioned the hit, albeit reluctantly. It was difficult for him to accept the President's treachery, and although he had his doubts, the life of his friend, Sir Timothy Sutherland was in jeopardy, so he had no choice

The blowout caused the vehicle to suddenly veer left, and Rothrock's immediate reaction was to overcorrect, sending it to the right over the cliff in the unprotected construction zone before he or his passenger realized what had happened. They died on impact on the rocks below. There was no evidence that their deaths were anything but a tragic accident.

CHAPTER EIGHTEEN

Billy Hudson's flat
Rue Championnet
Paris, France
Thursday, July 26

B ILLY HUDSON, A reporter stationed in the Paris office of the *Chicago Sun-Times*, was handed an envelope at 12:09am by one of his several sources. He had taken the handoff after responding to a note slipped under the door of his flat earlier in the day, instructing him to be on the west bank of the River Seine across from the posh Relais Hotel Vieux in Paris' Latin Quarter at midnight. The contact was also a reporter, and a drinking buddy, but was employed by *Le Parisian*, a well-entrenched and highly respected French daily whose editorial staff had decided not to break the story because of its possible detrimental influence on the once frigid, but now much improved relations between the French and U.S. governments. There were very strong ties between the owners of *Le Parisian* and the French President.

The *Le Parisian* reporter felt the story was much too important to languish in his employer's dead files, and since he had no say in the editorial decisions of his newspaper, he decided to cash in on what had been mailed to him from an unknown source, by giving it to his friend from Chicago, whom he knew worked for a daily with far fewer scruples than *Le Parisian* and which had no political ties to the current Washington administration. Plus, he knew his friend would pay handsomely for such a sensational piece of news, and would give him some degree of credit if the story was factual. After all, if the information could be confirmed, it could rate up there as Pulitzer material. He wasn't interested in fame, but money-now that was a motivator he understood.

Both reporters were seasoned newsmen with years of experience under their belts at getting at the truth by whatever means it took. So, they decided to work together on the story as they attempted to ferret out the truth.

Their first calls were to an offshore financial institution headquartered on Grand Cayman Island. The name of the bank was contained in the documents that they had spent the previous day reviewing together. Both had worked this particular angle several times, and in a matter of minutes had established the authenticity of the banking connection. Confirming the several account numbers was a little more difficult, but persistent questions finally established their relationship to the owner of the accounts. The target bank couldn't confirm the final question; they just didn't have the answers. But, the reporters had more information than they had needed to use, and were ready to press their search. The question was simple, yet complex: *what are the sources of the funds flowing into the owner's offshore accounts?* The amounts were nominal, all less than five thousand dollars a pop as meticulously recorded by date, time and amount on the many pages of the document reviewed by the reporters. The number of transfers recorded was staggering.

"That's over ten million dollars, if my math's correct."

"Your math is correct, my friend, and yes, it's a hell of a lot of dough to accumulate in a tax-free account in a little under eight months. I wonder for just how long these transactions have been flowing into this guy's account?" the American reporter, Billy Hudson, questioned.

By the end of the day, the two reporters had all the information they needed to confirm the owner's name and his current employment, if you could call it that. They also had the account numbers of his several accounts, and most important, they had the sources of the multiple funds transfers and the route used to funnel the money into the U.S.

"I don't believe any of this. It's just too un-American for the President of the United States to be involved is drug trafficking and taking kickbacks from Mexican whorehouses. And Hunt and the President of Mexico are both up to their butts in all of this.

"This has all the markings of a laundering scam if I've ever seen one. The guy brings the funds into the U.S. through a philanthropic trust he calls The Spartan Foundation, and then he moves the funds out as operating grants for another front he calls the Georgetown Community Medical Center, which is supposedly operated by The Black Hawks Group, another not-for-profit shell corporation. I know the Washington area, my friend, and there is no such organization called the Georgetown Community Medical Center. This is, without a doubt, a sophisticated money-laundering scheme to get his illegal funds into the U.S. without arousing regulatory suspicions.

"You're talking about a shit storm-just wait til this hits the streets. I'm not wiring this back to the States, not on your life. I'm taking this back with me personally and I'm going to walk right into the senior editor's office and deliver it personally to that fat old man. He'll be kissing my butt for months to come. Not only that, I'll be reassigned back to good old Chicago where I belong. And, if old man McFarland plays it right, this could be the story of the century. Pulitzer, here I come!

"I love you like a brother, Maurice, I really do. But I get a little tired of all these frog brothers of yours over here putting down the

U.S. I guess the next time France needs liberating, probably from all the radical Muslim Arabs moving into your country, your leaders can call someone else. We spilled too much American blood over here to be so stupid as to do it again. Tell your government leaders to call the Spanish if you need help. They just may send both of their soldiers over to help you guys out," Billy Hudson snickered, as he winked at his French friend and headed for the door.

"Glad you're enjoying this so much, Mon Ami. But before you go flying off to fame and fortune, let's be sure you wire the thirty-six thousand, eight hundred and seventy Euros into my account. I think your Chicago gangster friends refer to it as *fifty large*."

"Already there, my friend. Give your banker a call. The fifty thousand dollars is already resting in your account. See ya!"

*   *   *

Chicago Sun Times
350 North Orleans
Chicago, Illinois
Monday, July 30 – 7:45am

"Those turkeys over at the *Tribune,* we're going to blow them out of the water with this!"

J. Donavan McFarland, publisher of the *Chicago Sun Times*, had no idea how true his off-handed remark was, or how the revelations would reverberate around the world and send the current occupant of the White House into a tailspin.

The U.S. based news services are usually not slow to pick up on stories, especially if they smell blood in the water. And, the story that hit the wire services early on the morning of July 30 had all the trappings of a sensational exposé. That is, if there was any truth to it. Of course, before releasing the story to the wire services, the *Chicago Sum-Times* had it on their front page, and on the streets of Chicago and around the nation. America would be waking up to one of the most sensational stories of the decade.

*   *   *

The White House – Oval Office
1600 Pennsylvania Avenue
Washington, DC
Tuesday, July 31 – 9:45am

"Sir, there's a federal agent here. He has a warrant and is insisting that he is required to deliver it to you in person."

"What are you talking about, Fred? A federal agent! What agency?"

"Yes, Sir, a Federal Marshal. He says it's a subpoena requesting your appearance before a grand jury. I suspect it's been convened in relation to the fabricated story about your laundering money out of Mexico through the Cayman Islands."

"Screw him! Tell him I'm not here. And get that bitch I appointed as attorney general over here. I'll stop this right now."

"He knows you are here Sir. Keep in mind that the US Marshals Service answers directly to the Attorney General, so let's think this through before you react. And let's not get in a tiff with the attorney general just now. She doesn't have a choice in this. And you don't need to give her any cause to think you may be guilty."

"Just like the story about the French lady who bore your child, let's take the high road. Invite the agent into the Oval Office, and accept the warrant graciously. Pour him a cup of coffee and show him that you're visibly upset about this. This guy is just the messenger, but he'll be impressed by your allowing him into the Oval Office and taking the time to talk with him. He'll go back to his bosses and tell them how genuinely upset you are to think anyone would believe such a fabrication designed solely to destroy your integrity. He'll tell them that you think someone is trying to ruin your reputation, and you have no idea who would want to do such a dastardly thing. The word will get back to the attorney general and her grand jury and although you won't convert all of them, you will gain some points with some, and you need all the friends you can get if this goes the way I think it will."

"What do you mean? Do you think this story has any merit?"

"Of course not, Mr. President. But let's be realistic for the moment. Somebody is out to get you, Sir, and they've put together a pretty convincing story. Convincing enough for the Attorney General to appoint a special prosecutor to look into the allegations in that story the *Chicago Sun Times* first published. Evidently the prosecutor has convinced a grand jury that there is some merit to the story. You really don't have a choice, Sir. You will be required to testify before the grand jury, or at least give them a deposition."

CHAPTER NINETEEN

As Charles Dickens wrote in **A Tale of Two Cities**, *It was the best of times; it was the worst of times*. For President Hunt, it was the latter.

The Chicago Sun Times
Front Page Headlines

President Accused of Laundering Drug Money

T HE STORY, A full front page spread in the *Chicago Sun Times*, and later repeated in all of the major newspapers, nationwide, rocked the White House to its core. It had a similar effect on the members of Congress. By 6:00am, a herd of print and electronic media reporters were camped out in the halls of the Capitol, buttonholing every Senator, Congressman and congressional aide who dared to enter the Capitol building by the public entrances. Most scurried into the building by way of the private elevators in the basement and into their offices before the reporters could catch them. That is, except the

Republican members of the House and Senate who were eager to repeat what the story had already said. No one in the press learned anything new that morning. They could only repeat what was printed initially in the *Chicago Sun Times*.

The White House briefing room was again filled to capacity when the President's press secretary called an impromptu press conference at 9:00am in which she denied the allocations of any wrongdoing on the President's part, telling the reporters that it was all a fabrication designed to smear the good name of John Hunt.

*   *   *

Janice Hawkins, the U.S. Attorney General, was having coffee and toast with her husband, a prominent corporate law attorney practicing in the District, when her cell phone rang. The couple was seated at the breakfast table in their home in Georgetown. The hour was 6:30am, quite early to be receiving a call, especially on her cell phone. Only a limited number of associates had access to the number.

Mrs. Hawkins looked at the name of the caller before answering, and frowned. "This had better be good, Jeremy. You know this is our quiet time, when my husband and I do not want to be disturbed unless it is a dire emergency."

"Yes, Mrs. Hawkins, I know, and I apologize. But you need to read the story on the front page of the *Chicago Sun Times*. It hits President Hunt pretty hard, and if it's true, you should get out in front of it as quickly as possible. I hear every reporter in Washington has descended on either the White House or the Capitol. I have a car on its way over to your residence. The driver has a copy of the story. You can read it on the way in."

"What's the *down and dirty,* Jeremy?"

"President Hunt is accused of being involved in drug running and prostitution in Mexico. The President of Mexico is also being accused. The story names names, places and dates, and tells about secret bank accounts in the Cayman Islands owned by Hunt, and laundering schemes set up to bring the money into the States without paying taxes. It's a hell of a story!"

"Jeremy, don't use foul language in my presence. You know better."

*   *   *

Janice Hawkins kissed her husband good-by and walked down the brick walk to the black Lincoln Town Car waiting at the driveway curb. The driver was standing beside the vehicle with the rear door open for her, a copy of the morning's issue of the *Chicago Sun Times* in his hand.

"Good morning, Madam," the driver said with a slight English accent.

"Good morning, Mr. Thomas." Janice Hawkins was always polite, but formal with the employees of the Justice Department, regardless of their position in the agency.

*   *   *

British Airways Terminal
Dulles International Airport
Washington, DC
Tuesday, July 17 – 12:23pm

When the crew on the flight deck of the British Airways giant Airbus began shutting down its four huge engines, a black Lincoln Town Car, with blue strobe lights flashing, pulled alongside the aircraft. Two young, clean shaven men, dressed in business suits, sprinted from the automobile and approached the stairs that had been pushed up to the left side of the aircraft to offload the passengers. They rapidly ascended the steps and entered the aircraft as soon as the crew opened the forward passenger hatch. Passengers were already beginning to leave their seats, gather their carry-on luggage from the overhead compartments, and assembled in the aisles. Standing at the door, Alec saw the two men enter and held up his CIA credentials to identify himself. He didn't know either of the two men, but recognized their dress and demeanor.

After receiving the call from Ground Control, one of the senior crew members had gone back to the business class section of the aircraft and asked Alec to come with him so he could leave the aircraft before the other passengers were allowed to disembark.

The trio exited the aircraft quickly. One of the agents opened the back door of the Lincoln for Alec. The two agents got in the front seat and the automobile quickly departed for a remote and well-guarded section of the airport.

"I didn't expect to see you here, Don." Alec was sitting beside his old college chum who happened to be the Director of the Central Intelligence Agency, and his boss. "What brings you out of your cocoon out at Langley?"

"Alec, I have some news, and it isn't good. We think Beth and your son have been kidnapped."

"Kidnapped?"

"It looks that way. After talking with you yesterday, I dispatched a couple of agents out of the Great Falls field office to your home to see if everything was OK. Unfortunately, it wasn't. Beth and your son were gone. The front door was open and the door to your and Beth's bedroom had been kicked in. And, we found a blood trail from the bedroom to the front door and out on the porch."

Alec sat motionless, staring at his close friend. It was as though he was in a dream world, not really hearing what Don Armstrong was saying to him.

"The agents didn't have any forensic tools with them, but they found some Ziploc bags in the kitchen and got samples of the blood to take back to the lab in Great Falls for DNA identification. They also took some hair samples from what they think was Beth's hairbrush and a small baby brush they found in the nursery. One of the agents left immediately to get the samples back to the lab as quickly as possible to see if the blood matched Beth's or your child's DNA. They would get their DNA from the hair samples.

"Alec, events are unfolding very fast now, as we speak. The entire agent staff of the Great Falls field office is out at your place. We flew them in last night after I got the first report from the agents who went out to check on Beth. I'll give you all the details on our flight out to White Sulfur Springs. That's the closest airport that can handle the Citation. We are fueled and have a priority clearance out of here, and your luggage is being taken off the plane now. Our plane is waiting for us now, so we will be out of here in a matter of minutes, as soon as my people load your luggage."

"Who did this, Don? Who would want to harm my family?"

"You know as well as I who's behind this. The bastard thinks it's payback time."

"If that son-of-a-bitch harms a hair on Beth's or Alexander's head, I will personally walk into that big white house he lives in and put a bullet through his brain!"

"Calm down, Alec. Let me tell you what we know so far. Or at least what we think we know. First, we don't think the blood the agents found in your house is Beth's, but we won't know until we have the DNA results later this evening. The first trace of blood they found was spatter on the bedroom's doorframe, some eight feet from the bottom of the bed. We're guessing now, but it looks like Beth heard someone in the house and had time to get a weapon out before they burst through the bedroom door. We think she shot one of the assailants as he entered the bedroom, but wasn't fast enough to shoot the other one before he subdued her. The agents told me they could smell pepper spray in the bedroom, so they probably sprayed her with that before she could get off a second shot."

"Pepper spray? That doesn't make sense."

"It does if they had been told to take Beth alive. What better way to subdue someone than to spray Mace in their eyes? Otherwise, they would have just broken down the door and shot her.

"Also, we know it was a professional job. It was very methodical. If it had been a crime of passion, someone bent on rape or worse, the house would have been in disarray. It wasn't. Everything was in its place. No overturned chairs or tables, no broken mirrors, everything still in its place. Whoever did this was under strict orders not to harm Beth or your child. So, we feel good about that."

"What about the blood trail?"

"It started with blood splatter on the bedroom door frame but wasn't anywhere around the bed. This is speculation, of course, but our agent thinks she shot one of the perpetrators, and the guy fell at the door, but was only wounded. There is blood smear down a part of the doorframe as though the force of the bullet knocked him back into the frame. He thinks he slumped to the floor there, so the other guy must have been quick enough to get to Beth before she could shoot again. The agent found a weapon under the edge of the bed, but he didn't touch it. He also found the slug in the doorframe, so we suspect her shot was a through and through. We are waiting now for the forensic team to get me their preliminary report. Evidently the guy Beth shot, if our speculation is correct, was able to walk out of the house. At least the blood trail suggests that. As for whose blood was in your house, we should get the DNA report from the lab before we get there this evening. The lab will run it through the database, so we may have the name of one of the perpetrators before we set down in Montana."

"More than one?"

"We think at least two. Someone wearing boots stepped in the blood trail out the front door. That tells us there were at least two people involved. The bleeder wouldn't have left footprints in his own blood. Maybe blood on the top of his shoes, but not on the soles. There had to be a second person. That is, if it's not Beth's blood. And Alec, we're pretty sure it isn't hers."

*   *   *

Hangar 307
CIA Operations High Security Area
Dulles International Airport
Dulles, Virginia
Tuesday, July 17 – 1:05pm

Alec slumped back in the Cessna Citation's soft leather seat, buckled his seatbelt and closed his eyes. He was usually good at hiding his emotions, but the tears began to swell in his eyes, running down his unshaven cheeks. He had worried about Beth since trying to reach her from Scotland, but he wasn't prepared for anything like this. He hadn't been able to reach her on his long trip back to the States, nor had Don answered the several calls Alec had made to his cell phone. Caller identification had alerted him that Alec was calling, and he didn't want to break the news he had for him while he was over the Atlantic. They were close friends and college roommates, and he felt that bond required him to tell Alec, face to face. Plus, he was concerned that Alec would try to commandeer the aircraft and attempt to fly it directly to Montana. He didn't need an international incident to explain to the FAA and to the British right now.

At first, Alec's emotions were mostly worry about the safety of Beth and his son. But as the Citation climbed through the thin cloud cover blanketing the mid-Atlantic coastal region into the bright sunshine of another fall day, his concern for his family's safety turned into anger, then into rage. He had not anticipated anyone going after his wife and newborn child as a means of extracting revenge for what he had done to the personal plans of the corrupt President of the United States. Although there had not been a link established between the kidnapping incident and the White House, Alec knew in his heart that John Hunt was behind this. His resolve to finish the President's political career and shorten his life was deeper now than ever before.

"Alec, calm down. Try to relax. You're sitting there with your eyes shut, but your face is so contorted, I know you're planning what you will do when this incident plays out. You're about to punch your fingers through the leather on the seat's armrests. Look at your knuckles, they're bone white, and your tension is evident, just by the way you're sitting, so erect. You need to regain your control, my friend. There's nothing you can do right now, but think rationally about what you will do when we get to Montana, and what we will do after this thing is over."

"I know, but I've never been in a situation like this before. I feel so damned helpless. I've had enough sadness in my life for several lifetimes, and now the two people I love the most are in danger, and it's because of me."

"Well, keep your chin up. We have some good people on your side, and we should be getting reports every few minutes during our flight. The agent who remained at the scene immediately called our forensic lab in Great Falls, and they got there last night with the agents from that office."

*   *   *

White Sulfur Springs Airport
White Sulfur Springs, Montana
Tuesday, July 17 – 6:37am

The silver Learjet was sitting on the far side of the airfield at the end of one of the two runways as the sun rose over the hills to the East. The wheels were blocked and the aircraft was tied down, as though it had arrived with a purpose. An armed guard in black uniform with an M-16 and sidearm was standing at attention, guarding the aircraft. The area had been declared "off limits" to all civilian personnel, including local law officers, but it was early morning and no one in the local sheriff's office had arrived for work.

The first local resident to notice the aircraft that wasn't there the day before, but had landed undetected late the previous night, with the aid of the field's pilot activated runway lights, was a local crop duster who came out early to get his aircraft ready for another day of low flying over the crop fields in the expansive valley to the east.

He was about to drive his truck out to the jet when he spotted the guard, and decided against the idea. Instead he turned his old battered Ford truck around and headed for town. He first stopped at the Meagher County Sheriff's office, but the old man wasn't in, and he wasn't about to mention the mysterious aircraft to the two deputies, who were hanging around and drinking coffee when they should have been out on patrol.

Why would someone park an aircraft that far away from the hangar that serves as a terminal should any out-of-towners land there and need fuel? He wondered.

The second stop he made was at the coffee shop, the hangout of most of the locals for morning coffee and up-to-date gossip. As he suspected, the sheriff was having coffee, biscuits, eggs and sausage with white gravy, his usual fare, since his wife had passed away two years ago. Since developing the habit, he had gained forty-five pounds and his doctor had put him on cholesterol and blood pressure medicines. He had developed into a walking heart attack.

"Sheriff, you been out to the airport lately?"

"Why do you want to know, Kermit?"

"Cause there's a jet airplane out there parked down near the pines, and there's a guard with all kinds of firepower handing off him."

"You been into your shine this early in the morning, Kermit?"

"I ain't been drinking, Sheriff. Honestly. I just went down there to get the duster ready and there it was, all shiny in the sun, like a new dime."

"Kermit, you do have a way of expressing yourself, don't you, Boy? Where did you say this shiny new dime is parked?"

"Down by that grove of pines at the edge of runway 28, Sheriff."

"I'll check it out, Kermit. Thanks for the information."

"You bet, Chief. Can I go with you?"

"Nope."

*   *   *

White Sulfur Springs Airport
White Sulfur Springs, Montana
Tuesday, July 17 – 8:35am

Sheriff Buford Baxter drove his four-year old Ford patrol cruiser out to the airfield as soon as he left the greasy spoon, his favorite descriptive term for the Columbine Grill. He didn't bother to stop at the hangar, since there was no one there anyway, but continued on across the grassy infield between the two runways.

"Damned grass out here always needs cutting," he said out loud to no one. He had grown accustomed to talking to himself since there was very little for him to do in Meagher County except write a few traffic tickets and occasionally deliver a court summons to a wayward ex-husband late on his child support. As he approached the Lear, he flicked on his blue lights so the guard, who had seen the car approaching and had leveled his M-16 into ready alert position, pointing the muzzle towards the oncoming vehicle with his finger just above the trigger guard and the safety off, would know he was approaching the aircraft on official business.

"After all, I'm the law around here," he said to himself as he approached the aircraft.

"What you doing here, Son?"

"That's close enough, Sheriff. What can I do for you?"

"Like I asked, politely I might add, what are you doing out here?"

"I'm keeping sightseers away from this aircraft, Sheriff."

"Whose is it?"

"The Federal Government's."

"I don't see no markings, Boy. What part of the Federal Govment you with, Agriculture? Maybe the Park Service or BLM?"

"You'll have to ask my boss, Sheriff."

"You're just full of information this morning, ain't you, Boy? The sheriff could feel his blood pressure rising. "So, where could I find this boss of yours if I wanted to pursue the question you don't seem to be able to answer?"

"Couldn't say, Sheriff. But as you folks around here would say, he ain't here. You really should move on now. This airstrip was declared off-limits to all civilians, as well as to all civilian aircraft as of 0730 this morning. There should be a fax on your desk with the proper authorization. And, the off limits mandate includes you and your people, Sheriff, and any other local and state law enforcement officers."

"You have a nice day, Boy," the sheriff said between clinched teeth.

"You bet, Sheriff."

Sheriff Buford Baxter got back in his patrol car, slammed the door and pushed the accelerator to the floor, cutting the steering wheel hard to the right to throw grass and dirt all over the guard who had just stood him down. Fortunately, his vehicle was too far away to accomplish his mission, which added to his quickly rising level of frustration.

"Nobody talks down to me like that. I'm the damned law around here, and what I say, goes. These people haven't seen the last of me yet, damn it," Sheriff Baxter mumbled to himself as he hit Highway 89, tires spinning and laying down rubber as he sped away towards White Sulfur Springs.

*   *   *

"Hey Buford, Jonesy wants to talk to you. He's out on patrol. I'm going to patch him through to you. You hang on, now." The sheriff's dispatcher was calling Sheriff Baxter on his mobile equipment.

"What do you want, Deputy? Don't ask for any time off, Son. I ain't in the mood."

"No, Sir, Sheriff. I'm over here on Route 294 out past Lennep, almost to Groveland. I'm out at that dirt road that goes off towards the Castles. There are a couple of fellows here in some type of military uniforms. Looks like a SWAT team if you ask me. Like you see on TV. They got the road blocked and won't let me through. What do you want me to do, Buford?"

"What in hell are you doing way over there, anyway? And, why did you want to go down that dirt road? It's a dead-end, and there's only one house down there that some old weirdo lives in."

"Cause they have it blocked."

"Why?"

"How the hell should I know, Sheriff? They won't talk to me."

"Damn it! You just stay there, Jonesy. I'll get there as quick as I can. I just got a rash of shit from a guy out at the airport who was wearing the same kind of uniform. Just don't get your mouth in gear and get yourself shot, you hear."

"Yes Sir, Buford."

"And stop calling me Buford.. I'm Sheriff to you, Deputy."

"Yes Sir, Buford."

*　　*　　*

CIA Roadblock
State Road 295
Meagher County, Montana
Tuesday, July 17 – 9:05am

"Hey, guys. The High Sheriff just left the airfield over here in White Sulfur Springs, and he was pissed. Headed towards town, but a few minutes later I saw his cruiser, lights and siren on, heading back east towards Lennep. Looks like he's heading in your direction, guys. Just thought I would give you a heads up."

"Thanks Jimbo. We're looking forward to the meeting."

Forty-five minutes later, the Sheriff, siren wailing and blue lights flashing, powered up to the roadblock, skidded to a stop inches from the two agents who stood their ground, put on his dark sunglasses, adjusted his cowboy hat and stepped out of his patrol car, his sidearm hanging low on his hip, and his thumbs in his belt.

"Here comes another one," one of the agents whispered to his companion guarding the roadblock made by pulling two black Chevrolet Tahoes across the narrow road to block access. "This must be the High Sheriff who Jimbo said was on his way out here. It's your turn. Remember, the boss said to be nice, but be firm and stand your ground."

To balance the equation, both agents took their sunglasses from the breast pockets of their black SWAT uniforms and put them on. "Now, that should piss him off," the first agent whispered with a smile, as Sheriff Buford Baxter strutted up to the two agents.

"Good morning, Sheriff. Nice weather you folks are having up here."

"Who's in charge of this shit?" the Sheriff asked, not acknowledging the agent's pleasant greeting, but hooking his thumbs in his holster belt, feet wide apart, and striking a pose he thought would intimidate the two men he was confronting. He was wrong.

"Who wants to know, Sheriff?"

"Me. Sheriff Buford Baxter. I'm the law in Meagher County and you're in my jurisdiction."

"Glad you brought that up, Sheriff. Let me clarify this for you. This used to be your jurisdiction. It's not anymore. All the land around this road for five hundred yards out on both sides has been temporarily nationalized. At the moment, all of this belongs to the Federal Government, and that's me, Sheriff! There should be a fax back at your office that will explain the laws under which we have usurped your authority. It's called national security, Sheriff. That includes the airport over at White Sulfur Springs as well. Understand?"

The agent put his arm around the sheriff's stooped shoulders before he could answer, and walked him a few yards away from his deputy.

"Let me put this another way, Sheriff. We don't want this to turn into a pissing contest between you and me, but if that's the way you want to play it, I'll roll over you like a frigging steamroller. I have the law on my side, and the balls to make it happen. Do you understand me, Sheriff?"

"Uh, yes, Sir."

"We're going to turn around now and stroll back to the roadblock nonchalantly, just like we're old friends. You're going to smile and we're going to shake hands. You'll get into your cruiser and tell your deputy to do the same. Then, both of you will go back to your office where you can read the fax sent to you by the Secretary of Homeland Security."

"Is that who you fellows work for?" The sheriff's tone had softened considerably.

"What do these badges say, Sheriff. Don't they say Homeland Security?"

"Yes, Sir."

"Good bye, Sheriff. Don't come out here again unless we ask you to. Do you understand?"

"Yes, Sir. Thank you, Sir."

Sheriff Buford Baxter got back into his vehicle after telling his deputy to do the same, and both drove slowly away from the roadblock

*　　*　　*

"Damn, you're good," the second agent commented to his partner after the sheriff and his deputy had driven away. "What did you tell him?"

"Just that I would screw him up royally if he got in our way. And, I was nice. Couldn't you tell?"

*　　*　　*

Sheriff Buford Baxter's office
White Sulfur Springs, Montana
Tuesday, July 17 – 2:08pm

"What's this all about, Buford? What did they tell you? Who are those people? And what's Homeland Security doing out here?" The mayor of White Sulfur Springs was sitting behind the sheriff's desk reading the fax when Sheriff Baxter walked in.

Rosie Jemez, the dispatcher, had called him when she patched the deputy's radio message over to the sheriff. She just happened to listen in on the conversation and felt the mayor should know.

"Not a God-damned thing, Leonard. They just said it was a national security issue, and wouldn't say anything else."

"National security? What do you think it is?"

"How the hell do I know, Leonard. Hell, a UFO may have landed out there for all I know. How did you know it was Homeland Security?"

"Cause the fax lying here is signed by the Secretary of Homeland Security, Dimwit."

* * *

"What the hell was that?" Rosie screamed as the UH-60 Black Hawk helicopter flew low over the town of White Sulfur Springs on its way to the airfield on U.S. 89 just south of town. The windows in the sheriff's office rattled as it passed overhead.

"Look at that thing, Leonard," the sheriff said craning his head out of his office window as the aircraft's pilot began to decrease its speed in preparation to land.

"Damn, that's a big sucker, Buford. And painted all black. Did you see that seal on the side? I think it said Homeland Security but I can't be sure. It was going too fast. Must be a lot going on over there in Lennep. What say we take my car and drive by the airport again and then go over to Lennep to see what's happening with your SWAT people?"

* * *

It took all of thirty minutes for the rumor to spread around town like wildfire. According to Rosie, a flying saucer had crash-landed north of the village of Lennep just off Montana Route 294, and the Feds were out there rounding up the Martians. Rosie was a great rumormonger, but all the locals knew that! That didn't stop half the town from following the mayor and sheriff out to the airport and on to Lennep.

*   *   *

Cessna Citation N4768 N
Somewhere over West Virginia
Tuesday, July 17 – 3:15pm

The first message relayed to Don Armstrong, flying from Dulles International to White Sulfur Springs, Montana, in the Company's sleek Cessna Citation X confirmed that the forensic team had arrived and had assumed control of the crime scene. They had set up an initial perimeter some fifty yards out from Alec's house, but expanded it to encompass the entire length of the dirt road leading from Route 294 to Alec's home at the foot of the Castle Mountains and up to five hundred yards on either side. Traffic on Route 294 was stopped and checked before being allowed to pass through the quarantined area, but there were very few vehicles on this stretch between Lennep and Groveland until the mayor and sheriff arrived. The area was in virtual lockdown.

The second message was even better news. The blood found at the scene was not Beth's, nor was it Alexander's. The CIA could not match the DNA with anyone in their secure database that they did not share with other federal agencies or in the interagency database maintained by Homeland Security. That method of identifying the perpetrator seemed to be a dead end.

Alec turned to Don Armstrong, "What cover are we using this time?"

"Homeland Security. The team out of Great Falls flew into White Sulfur Springs in a leased Lear with just the *N* number, no other markings. We have a Black Hawk with a Homeland Security emblem embossed on each side standing by in White Sulfur to take us over to your house to meet with the forensic people, and the two vehicles they are using have like markings. I think we're pretty well covered. But just in case, we faxed a memo to the Meagher County Sheriff on Homeland Security official stationery citing a number of laws that give us authority to temporarily nationalize whatever assets we need out here, including land. It's signed by the Secretary, and it looks authentic. Unless a smart lawyer gets hold of it, it should be all we need to keep the locals out of this until we wrap it up and get out of here."

*   *   *

White Sulfur Springs Airport
White Sulfur Springs, Montana
Tuesday, July 17 – 2:35pm

Sheriff Buford Baxter and Mayor Leonard Hamilton sat in the mayor's Lincoln on the shoulder of U.S. 89, watching the activity at the airport through their binoculars. The Blackhawk had set down close to the Lear, and the two helicopter pilots were outside talking with the plane's uniformed guard whom the sheriff had confronted earlier in the day. They couldn't hear what was being said, but they heard the roar of the second aircraft overhead at the same time the guard and the pilots looked up. The Black Hawk pilots sprinted over to their helicopter and began spinning up the turbines.

The Cessna Citation X screamed across the field at a thousand feet, made a wide counter clockwise turn about a mile out and set up for an upwind landing on runway 29, the longer of the two paved runways.

"God damned, Leonard, look at that sucker! They're bringing in reinforcements. There's a lot more to this than we thought. You better start making some calls to find out just what the hell is going on before Rosie has the whole county thinking we're being invaded by a bunch of Martians."

"Hell, Buford, the word's already out. Have you noticed that line of pickups behind us?"

* * *

When the Citation had been parked, wheels blocked and tied down, they watched the passenger door open and two men leave the aircraft. They walked quickly over to the Black Hawk, which was already fired up and ready to go. It took off immediately and headed southeast.

"They're heading towards Lennep, Leonard. Get this piece of junk in gear. It's time for us to take a ride over there."

"Yeah. Go back there Buford and tell them other people to go back home."

"Yeah, good luck, Mayor."

CHAPTER TWENTY

Chicago Sun Times
350 North Orleans
Chicago, Illinois
Monday, July 30 – 8:15am

J. DONAVAN MCFARLAND arrived at his office on the seventeenth floor of the *Sun Times* building in downtown Chicago at 5:15 am. He knew his phone would begin ringing a good hour before he arrived. He was right.

"Donnie, this is Janice Hawkins. I hope you are well, My Dear."

"I am indeed, Janice. How are you and Stephen holding up under all the political pressures in DC? I was wondering if you would call today."

"Piece of cake, My Friend. At least until I read your front-page exposé earlier this morning. I've known you for most of your life, Donnie. Long enough to know you wouldn't publish anything you had not checked out thoroughly before you started the presses. Tell me about these allegations. You know I'm going to have to act on this."

"I knew that. That's why I was waiting for your call. And, I'm flattered you read my rag."

"Donnie, I suspect all of Washington is reading your rag, as you call it, this morning. So, tell me."

"Basically the story came to us out of France. It was delivered to Le Parisien but they refused to print it, thinking it could cause a rift between the U.S. and France, and hurt the current efforts to bring our countries together. One of their reporters sold the story to one of our men over there, and he brought it to me. It's been checked and rechecked, Janice, and it's real. You have a real problem beginning to develop down on Pennsylvania Avenue, Love."

"Donnie, I have a couple of FBI agents from our Chicago district office on their way over to your office with a a federal writ to pick up all the information you have on this. It's a national security issue, My Friend, so please don't try to hide behind the constitution, citing the First Amendment. Anyway, I'm not interested in your sources so much as I'm interested in getting to the truth. And, the only way I can be sure of that is to see what you have and have our people analyze the information."

"What we printed is the truth, Janice, but I understand the box you're in. You serve at the pleasure of the President and it's his butt that's on the line. You don't have a choice, Old Girl, you have to go after him or Congress will impeach you before they impeach him. I don't envy you on this, Love. You're between a rock and a hard place. Makes no difference which way this goes down, you're going to be right in the middle."

"Well, Donnie. What you say is so true. I don't mean to sound crass or vulgar, but the good old boys in the Department of Justice are about to find out just how big my cahonies really are."

"Good for you, Old Girl. By the way, we've verified everything in the story and everything checks out. In fact, if your agents are going to fly the information back to DC, I'll send my reporter along with them so he can brief you first hand."

"You're a true friend, Donnie, and a true patriot. I wish the press had more people with your level of integrity. Give my love to Barb, and you guys hop a flight over here to DC soon. Stephen and I will treat you to an evening on the town."

"I'll give Barbara your love and your invitation. I'm sure she would love to get away from Chicago for a few days, and Washington would be fun, especially if you and Stephen are involved."

*   *   *

Alec Caldwell's Home
Lennep, Montana
Tuesday, July 17 – 3:21pm

The Black Hawk helicopter carrying Alec and Don Armstrong settled gently onto the roadbed in front of Alec's house at the foot of the Castle Mountains outside Lennep. The pilots cut the engines and the rotors began to slowly lose speed. Alec and Don stepped out and walked directly towards the house.

"Where are your people staying, Don?"

"There's only one motel within fifty miles of this God-forsaken place, the Super 8 in White Sulfur. We have all the rooms rented. You want to stay there with us?"

"Don't think so, Don. I'd rather stay here by myself if the forensic team doesn't object. I've got some serious thinking to do, and I can't do it with other people around. But, why don't you get your special agent in charge to meet us in the house so we can talk this thing out? I have a few questions to ask."

*   *   *

"Sir, the forensic team finished up inside the house about an hour ago, and they've lifted the quarantine. We can go in now." Special Agent Bryan DeWitt opened the front door for Alec and Don to come in.

"Bryan, you remember Alec Caldwell, don't you?"

"I do, Sir. I'm very sorry to be seeing you again under such circumstances. This has to be very hard on you, Alec. But we've developed a good bit of information since my last communiqué with

Don when you were flying out. We're much closer to getting to the bottom of this than we were a couple of days ago."

"Good. Sit down and tell us all you know, Bryan."

*   *   *

Office of Attorney General Janice Hawkins
Department of Justice
Robert F. Kennedy Building
Washington, DC
Monday, July 30 – 10:45am

"Hello Janice. I'm delighted you called. It's not very often a poor working class lawyer is granted an audience with the Attorney General of the United States. I'm flattered. And, you were mighty mysterious on the phone. I can hardly wait to find out what you want from me."

"George, stop trying to blow smoke up my butt and take a seat. I haven't seen you since you left Justice six years ago. But, I have followed your career with a great deal of interest, thanks to your public relations people. You always seem to be out there in front of the public, saying something important or defending a high-profile client. How do you like being on the other side of the law?

"In a word, it pays a hell of a lot better than the meager salary you paid me when I worked for you over here."

"True, but you wouldn't be where you are today if we hadn't groomed you so well, George. A good lawyer must always work both sides of the street before he begins building his career. Otherwise, how would he know what the other side is thinking?"

"Good point. See, we do agree on something, although that wasn't the case when I worked at Justice. Now, what's on your mind, Janice? I presume you will permit me to use your first name since I don't work for you any more."

"If you take the bait I'm going to offer you, we will be working together again, but this time as equals. So, yes, Janice is fine."

"Sounds interesting, tell me more."

*   *   *

George Connors had been practicing law for some sixteen years. He was only thirty-eight and had begun his career in the Department of Justice right out of Harvard Law. Since he had not taken the DC bar exam, he signed on as a research assistant, passed the DC bar on his first try that year and went on to pass the Virginia and Maryland Bar Associations examinations as well. At the end of his first year, he was brought out of the research department and elevated to the position of junior attorney, assigned to the Criminal Division where he remained for the ten years he was with the Department of Justice. On several occasions, he had provided advice and counsel to the Attorney General and had been called as an expert witness before several Congressional committees. Although Janice Hawkins had not agreed with some of his findings in several cases prosecuted by Justice, she had been impressed with his thoroughness and his tenacity. It was those attributes that convinced her to call George Connors and ask him to meet with her in her office.

*   *   *

"George, I know you've read the *Chicago Sun Times* account of the corruption that seems to exist in the White House, or at least in the Oval Office. What is your take on all of this?"

"I only know what I've read."

"I know better than that, George. You're too inquisitive not to have already stuck your nose into this deeper than most of your peers. And I know your political affiliation. Don't tell me you didn't smile when you first read the story."

"Well, a little, maybe. I do know you've been put in an untenable position on this. Congress and the public are going to want answers, and since you serve at the pleasure of the President, you don't have anywhere to turn."

"That is so true, George. My only out is to appoint an independent counsel to look into this matter and determine its validity. And you, My Friend, have been chosen. It's you who will be on the hot seat, not me."

"Why me, Janice? There are lawyers here in DC with far more experience than I, and whose opinions are looked upon as gospel. I'm just a nobody."

"Why? Well first, because I respect you as a person and as a lawyer. I had a very high regard for your opinions when you were with Justice. I may not have agreed with you all the time, but your opinions were always based on sound logic and a deep sense of conviction that what you were doing or saying was right in the eyes of the law. I'm not so sure I can say that about most of the blowhards in this town you think are more qualified than you.

"And, secondly, I know you will look into this matter thoroughly, and with conviction. Even though your political convictions run contrary to the President's, and to mine, you will put them aside and judge this matter on its merit, not on the basis that it can take your career to new heights.

"And, before you decide, please remember that I have the authority to appoint anyone I want, and whomever I appoint is required by law to serve, end of discussion.

"So, what say you my young learned friend?"

"You really don't mince words, do you Madam Attorney General?"

"No, not when I have two FBI agents flying in from Chicago this afternoon with all the information the *Sun Times* has, plus bringing with them the reporter who found the story.

"I've known the publisher of the *Sun Times* for years, George. He's a very old and dear friend. He could hold us up by hiding behind the First Amendment, but ultimately we would have the information he has, so he is willing to give it to us now, today. Your new job starts immediately. You can work from your office or from an office here, but I would suggest you work here. It is a much more secure environment and I will have a staff of attorneys, paralegals, research analyst, and secretaries at your disposal. And you are going to need a rather large staff, because this is very, very serious, George, and of all people, it involves the President.

"Now, go back to your office and put your affairs in order. The agents and the reporter will be here around three this afternoon and I want you to be here when they arrive. Capiche?"

*   *   *

Alec Caldwell's Home
Lennep, Montana
Tuesday, July 17 – 3:30pm

Bryan DeWitt, Special Agent in charge of the investigation of the suspicious disappearance of Beth Caldwell and her son, was briefing Alec and Don Armstrong who had arrived at the scene of the kidnapping only minutes earlier.

"As you suggested, Director, we began our search with the nearest commercial airports. There are no direct flights out of National or Dulles to Montana. The most logical transfer point is Denver because you can catch a direct flight to Denver out of DC from Regan National or Dulles, and transfer to a flight to Great Falls without having to change airlines if you fly American or Delta. Both have a number of flights connecting in Denver each day, so we thought we should try Great Falls International first. It is fairly close to Lennep.

"There are, however, four other airports in the vicinity of Lennep with flights from Denver, but all require carrier changes, and most of the majors use smaller regional commuters for that leg. But, to be on the safe side I sent agents to Billings, Bozeman, Butte, and Helen, but concentrated primarily on Great Falls. There are other airports, but all are further away from the target area. And, there are a good number of smaller airports scattered around Montana, but most of them handle short hauls, mostly second and third level commuters out of regional hubs in surrounding states. So, if they took a direct flight to Denver and on to Montana, they probably landed at one of the five hubs I mentioned. All of our agents have the photos of the five men you sent us, but if we believe the tapes, we know the leader of the group, the Rothrock guy, wouldn't be one of them, since Hunt told him he was needed elsewhere. But, we couldn't find anyone who could recognize any of them anyway.

"On the four days preceding the night Agent Caldwell's wife was taken, there were three direct flights out of Washington National to Denver and four out of Dulles. They were all Delta and American with minimum wait connections in Denver to Great Falls. In fact, four of the seven didn't require changing flights, so passengers going on to Great Falls didn't have to disembark.

"Our specialists are analyzing the film from all of the security cameras at every point of entry in the five airport terminals we targeted, but they haven't come up with anything there yet. But, as you know, that's a slow, laborious process, and we've only had some of the tapes for a few hours. Others are still coming in, but that information may not be needed anyway."

"What do you mean, not needed, and why just a four-day window, Bryan?"

"The tapes of the conversation between President Hunt and the one who calls himself Corky Rothrock took place six days ago. The President told Rothrock to get two of his men on a direct flight to Montana as soon as possible. If he did what Hunt said, his men would have arrived late that night. But since there are no direct flights from DC to Montana, the fastest way to get there is through Denver to Great Falls. That was day one.

"They would have rented a vehicle in Great Falls, spent the night there since their arrival time would have been late, then they would have taken at least one day to drive to Alec's and case the house and neighborhood. They would have been looking for close neighbors, a primary route in, and at least a primary, and a secondary escape route. With no close neighbors and only one way in and the same way out, their options were decreased considerably. They couldn't be sure that some of Mrs. Caldwell's friends wouldn't be visiting during the day, so they would most likely execute their takedown at night to avoid the possibility of another vehicle being on the only road in and out. They couldn't afford to be seen. That's their first full day in Montana, but it's day two in the four-day window of opportunity.

"Then they were faced with the problem of what they were going to do with the woman and her child. They had to find a place, a cabin, or a house where they could keep them without fear of their escaping, or being seen. And they had an even bigger problem, the child. Children, especially very young children, present special problems-feeding, sleeping habits, crying, and a multitude of other problems you don't concern yourself with if you are just holding an adult. They had to select a special hiding place, and it couldn't be where someone would come upon them unexpectedly. How long would that take in an area totally unfamiliar to them? I would say two days at a minimum. That's days three and four in the four-day window. Our evidence tells us Mrs. Caldwell and her child were taken two night ago, the evening of the fourth day, more probably late that night. Counting yesterday and today, that's a four day window in a six day count, Sir."

"Good analysis, Bryan. What else?"

"We got lucky, Sir. One of my agents found tire tracks in the front yard that didn't match Mrs. Caldwell's vehicle. Too wide and the wrong tread pattern. They appeared fresh since it had rained several days before we arrived, so any old tracks would have been washed away. They could have been made by someone visiting Mrs. Caldwell, but we took a plaster cast of the print anyway. The lab rats told us the tire track matches a twenty inch Bridgestone tire that's original equipment on '07 and newer heavy duty Chevrolet vehicles like Silverado 4 x 4 trucks and certain heavy duty Chevrolet vans.

"We believed the tread print belonged to the vehicle the perpetrators leased when they arrived in Montana. This was the best break we could get, because it led us to the Budget Rental counter at Great Falls International.

"Just before you arrived, we got a call from the agent making inquiries at Great Falls. During the four-day window, only two vehicles equipped with twenty-inch tires were rented at Budget, but none at the other three rental agencies. One was by four ladies on a "no husbands" sightseeing trip around Montana. The other was rented by a guy matching the description of one of the four remaining team members, excluding Rothrock. The rental agent couldn't be sure, but he believes the person renting the van was one of the team members he recognized from the photos our agent showed him.

"The vehicle is a Chevrolet heavy duty panel van, series 3500, with twenty inch wheels, and, can you believe it, an On Star system. That little system has a built in Global Positioning System so the On Star operators can access the vehicle's position at any time without alerting the driver. They have access to overlay maps from Google Earth so they can pinpoint the vehicle's position on or near an established road using the vehicle's Latitude and Longitude coordinates.

"And, there is no way a jackleg could disable the system. Of course the rental contract is bogus, and it was paid for with a bogus credit card, but we know who they are now. But, there was only one man, not two. The clerk didn't see a second person. The guy who leased the van was alone."

Don turned to Alec. "What do you make of that?"

"Odd. Possibly they wanted to minimize their exposure if a BOLO had been issued."

"Sir, before the day is out, we'll know exactly where the van is located. The agent there is having the On Star people locate the vehicle and give us the coordinates when they come in."

*   *   *

Department of Justice
Robert F. Kennedy Building
Washington, DC
Monday, July 30 – 2:30pm

"Gentlemen, this is George Connors. I have asked him to serve as Independent Counsel in this matter. As such, he has the full resources of the Department of Justice, the FBI, the CIA and all other federal agencies, including Homeland Security at his disposal. In effect, Gentlemen, he is next to God in this matter!

"He is free, within the bounds of the law, to pursue this matter to its fullest extent. It will be his responsibility to look into the allegations of wrong-doing by President Hunt, as outlined in the materials you brought with you from Chicago. He can request an expansion of the scope of the investigation, should he feel it is pertinent to the outcome of his work."

Janice Hawkins turned to the two FBI agents. "You, Gentlemen, will be free to return to your office in Chicago after Mr. Connors has a chance to interview each of you. But, should Mr. Connors wish to speak with you at any time during this inquiry, you will make yourselves available, in person, if requested. You may even be required to testify before the grand jury, but a subpoena will be issued if your testimony is required."

"And you, Mr. Hudson, you are the reporter who was assigned to the *Sun Times'* Paris office who broke this story that has all of Washington wondering just what is going on over on Pennsylvania Avenue. You will remain here in Washington until Mr. Connors releases you. He has a federal warrant which commands you to cooperate with him in this investigation to the fullest extent, under penalty of imprisonment. And, I have cleared your absence with your boss. Do you understand this, Mr. Hudson?"

"Yes, ma'am."

"Then I'll leave you, Gentlemen. George, stop by my office before you leave, please."

*　　*　　*

The press had a field day with the story, and rumors spread like wildfire. The public, which had stood firmly behind John Hunt when he admitted fathering a child by a French actress, began to fall away as more and more information was leaked to the press. It was as if there were a Deep Throat within the Independent Counselor's team, but, in reality, the source was within the CIA, which had initially gathered the information and passed it along to the French reporter who sold the story to the *Sun Times* reporter.

Director Armstrong had selected a reporter he knew he could trust, and arranged the first of several meetings between the reporter and Alec Caldwell.

The FBI even questioned the reporter for *Le Parisien* at length, but he had no clue as to where the information originated or who had put it together. It was slipped under the door to his flat one night, and that was all he knew.

The case against President Hunt was thought to be solid. All indications pointed to his having received large sums of money from a drug operation on Mexico's Baja Peninsula, as well as equally large sums of money from the thriving prostitution trade there that catered to the booming tourist trade. At first, witnesses were hard to find, but as the team, assisted by the FBI and the Mexican authorities, dug deeper, people began to talk, especially when offered immunity from prosecution.

The convoluted money trail was hard to follow initially, but when the CIA was asked to assist, most of the unknowns fell into place. They had ways of learning the truth that the FBI could not use. In fact, they already had the information the investigation needed, but gave it to the Independent Counsel's team piece-by-piece over a matter of months as though it were just being discovered.

CHAPTER TWENTY-ONE

Alec Caldwell's Home
Lennep, Montana Tuesday, July 17 – 3:45pm

"WHAT DO YOU mean, another wrinkle?"
Alec had picked up his phone on the first ring. He had hoped it would be one of the kidnappers, but it was Bryan DeWitt, the CIA senior agent whom Don Armstrong had placed in charge of the investigation of Beth and Alexander's kidnapping.

"Our agent out at the Great Falls airport found a second car."

"Another car?"

"That's right. After he left the Budget counter, he decided to check the off-airport rental agencies in Great Falls to be sure there wasn't anything he had overlooked. Damned glad he did, because a clerk at the Rent-A-Wreck agency there recognized one of the photos he had. It was the same guy who rented the van out at the airport. They have a video camera trained on their rental counter, and the agent confirmed that the person who signed the lease is one of Hunt's people.

He rented a 2004 non-descript Ford, blue, four-door sedan. The plates are Idaho, ZX-2099. Evidently it was assigned to an agency in Idaho, but had been left in Great Falls on a one-way rental contract.

"So, these guys are driving two vehicles, or, at least they have access to two. We've been able to locate the van through its GPS, but the only way to find the Ford is *eyes-on* only."

"Humor me, Agent DeWitt, what are the location coordinates of the van?"

* * *

"OK, thanks for the update. Do you know if Director Armstrong is coming out tomorrow morning?"

"Yes, Sir. But, I believe he has to get back to Washington tomorrow. He plans to leave no later than 10:00 in the morning. He told me Hunt has called all the heads of the security agencies to a special meeting at the White House.

"Get some rest, Alec. You need it. We'll see you tomorrow morning."

"Year, right," Alec said in a very low voice as he hung up the receiver and picked up the old topo map he had retrieved from his basement where he stored all of his hunting equipment and weapons.

* * *

OK, the GPS coordinates put the van's location southwest of the village of Twodot, some twenty-eight miles out, as the crow flies. Alec was plotting the coordinates on his topography map. *That puts the van at the edge of the Lewis and Clark National Forest. There's no place out there to house a couple of hostages, no cabins, and no campsites. I've hunted and fished that area and I know there isn't any habitation on the road where the van's stashed. It's got to be a decoy. These people are a lot smarter than the CIA thinks they are. They knew damned well we would learn what they were driving and could find their location through the On Star system. They didn't try to hide the fact that they used Budget to lease their van. I suspect they selected their vehicle just for that purpose, to be sure we found it. The van is the bait, not my family. If their little ambush plan goes south, they still have Beth as a hostage, very clever. So, they stashed the van, transferred to the Ford, and drove out to where they were planning to keep Beth and our son.*

Number two, I don't think they'll be very far from their van because they don't know I know they are using two vehicles and they think I'll go after the van. They'll set up there to take me out. But if there are only two perpetrators, one will have to stay with Beth while the other sets the trap. That's good, because I only have to worry about one gun, not two. I'm their prime target, and they won't do anything to my family until they've taken me out. So they're safe for awhile. Now, the question is, just how good is this guy going to be in a mountain environment? I suspect he's a city boy, and this is going to be a turkey shoot, with me doing the shooting.

Number three, the only cabin within a three mile radius of the van's location is an old hunting and fishing camp up in the mountain a ways up on Sweet Grass Creek. Unless, of course, someone has built up there since I was there. But, that's National Forest and the only private land up there is that old cabin site.

*   *   *

Alec placed a call to an old friend who had retired to the beautiful town of Big Timber several years earlier. Bill Hawks had opened a small real estate firm specializing in the sales and rentals of up-scaled condominiums in Sweet Grass County. He had spent most of his life as a loyal agent of the Drug Enforcement Administration until he was shot in the leg by a drug dealer in a downtown Newport News, Virginia drug bust. The incident left him with a pronounced limp, and he was forced out of the DEA after twenty-eight years of service on a small partial pension at the young age of fifty.

Hawks' bitterness over the fact that the DEA had abandoned him in his hour of need left him in a severe state of depression. But, a friendship forged with Alec, years earlier when the two worked together on a number of related cases, helped him claw his way out of the pit this debilitating disease had dug for him. Alec had invited him out to Montana to fish and hunt on several occasions. Hawks fell in love with Big Sky Country and decided to move to Montana to redefine his remaining years. He settled in Big Timber after fishing the trout-filled creeks, lakes and rivers throughout Sweet Grass County, and hunting the elk and mule deer that roam the wooded slopes of the Gallatin National Forest in the Crazy Mountains.

When Bill Hawks arrived, Big Timber was a small, picturesque town on Interstate 90 some eighty miles west of Billings. The building boom had not yet begun to overflow Montana with new citizens wanting to get away from it all. And condominium complexes were generally found only associated with the ski slopes that had made the state famous with the weekend crowd.

But Hawks knew it was just a matter of time. He had seen it happening elsewhere, and with his meager savings he began to buy up *land with a view*, as he called it, and waited. During these formative years, he concentrated on building up the clientele of his small real estate business, selling the properties of others as he continued to warehouse inexpensive properties with potential not yet recognized by others in the real estate business in Sweet Grass County, Montana.

*   *   *

"Bill, hope you're faring well out there in Big Timber. We've got to get together and go after a few cutthroats soon." Although Alec was hurting, he was able to mask his true feelings when the situation called for him to put on a different face.

"I am, thank you, Old Friend. How is your new family doing?"

"Wonderful, thank you." Although Bill was a close and trusted friend, Alec wasn't ready to trust with anyone the information that his wife and son had been kidnapped.

"I have a question. Do you remember that old cabin we used to use when we were camping up on Sweet Grass Creek hunting elk in the Gallatin?"

"Strange you should ask me about that cabin today of all times. Yes, I do. I bought it a couple of years ago and rent it from time to time to hunting and fishing parties. In fact, I just rented it a couple of days ago to two guys who said they wanted to fish up there on the creek. Funny though, they said they were from Chicago, but I can recognize a Virginia accent when I hear it."

"Why do you think they were from Virginia, and not from the Chicago area?"

"You remember that I lived in Virginia for years when I was with the DEA. Folks from around Richmond have an accent all their own. They really sound like Canadians when they say *out* or *about*. It just stands out. And these guys were from the Richmond area, or maybe north of there. I would bet my life on it, Partner. I just can't figure out why they didn't want me to know they were from Virginia."

"I have no idea, Bill. I have a friend who wanted to fish that area, and I remembered the cabin, but I didn't know you were the owner. Let me know when it's back on the rental market, My Friend. I'll be back in touch."

Alec replaced the receiver and smiled. "*OK. Now I know where you guys are keeping my family. It's just a matter of time, Boys.*"

*   *   *

"Yeah, what?" Again, Alec had answered his phone on the first ring. He was hoping it was the kidnappers calling.

"Is this Alexander Caldwell?"

"Who wants to know?" Alec knew it was one of the kidnappers, and reached for his tape recorder.

"It must be. No one else would answer your phone with such an attitude."

"Who are you?"

"No matter, Mr. Caldwell, just take my message to heart. Back off, Sir, and do it now."

"What?"

"Mr. Caldwell, listen carefully. We have your wife and your son. She's a very pretty lady and your young son should grow up to be a very handsome man. You really don't want anything to happen to them, now do you? So, be smart, Mr. Caldwell, back off of your campaign to unseat the President. Go back to Washington and tell your boss to cease and desist. Back off this vendetta of yours, Sir. You can't win. If you don't, you won't see your wife and your little boy again. Do you understand me, Mr. Caldwell?"

"Listen to me, Dickhead. I'm coming to put your ass in a sling." Alec slammed the receiver down and sat back in his chair, folding his hands behind his head and stretching his legs. "That should convince them I've gone off the deep end. Now they'll think that not only am I distraught over the kidnapping of my family, but I'm also pissed off because of their threat. They think they've got me rattled. I bet they're congratulating themselves, thinking I'll be coming at them like a bull in a china shop. Not so, boys. Now it's my turn to make the rules."

*   *   *

When Don Armstrong arrived at Alec's house early the next morning, his Special Agent in Charge was already there. He handed him a white business-size envelope as he entered the house.

"What's this, Bryan?"

"I suspect it's from Caldwell. It was on the coffee table when I came in. It's addressed to you, Sir."

"Where is Alec?"

"He's gone, Sir. The old jeep he had in the shed out back is also missing."

"Son of a bitch," he exclaimed, tearing the envelope open and unfolding the piece of white paper that was inside. "I knew he would do this."

Good morning, Don,

I know you're pissed, and you have a right to be, but you also know I don't let others fight my battles. These people have my wife and my son. That makes this my fight, not anyone else's. They called last night and I recorded the conversation. The recorder is in the left side table next to the sofa. Unfortunately, it's not going to tell you where they are. Only I know that, because I'm the only person involved who knows this country.

By the time you read this I will already be in the mountains, probably close enough to these degenerates to smell their breath. They think they have me riled, and my emotions will cause me to overreact. Acting irrationally would be last thing I would do. You know me better than that. I've been setting this up ever since you and I arrived yesterday. Now it's game time, my game and my time, not theirs!

Don, I want you to promise me you will not send your storm troopers out to the location of the van. I'm sure your people have figured out where it is from the GPS signal. I can assure you that Beth and Alexander aren't there, but I know where these people are keeping them, and none of your other people do.

My family is my first priority and I will be sure they are safe before I do my thing on these degenerates. They think I will go to the van, thinking Beth is there. They're using the van as bait. It's a trap. They will be set up to take me out when I arrive, but they won't expect me to already be there before dawn. And I won't be arriving by the road where the van is parked. In fact, by the time you read this I will have been there for a couple of hours.

By the way, these guys purchased a shit pot full of dynamite yesterday in Big Timber, along with an electronic detonator. So, my friend, the van is probably loaded with the stuff. I had thought I would be up against someone with a gun, and maybe that's their backup plan, but as I see it, they plan to detonate the dynamite when they see me approach the van. But, that ain't gonna happen, My Friend. By the way, there will be only one of the kidnappers watching the van. The other will be with my family. I'll take care of him first, then the watcher.

Don, contrary to what some of your agents believe, these guys aren't stupid. They're counting on our locating their van. They're both ex-military killing machines and probably know explosives better than any of us. They're used to planning missions that succeed. That's why they're still alive. If your boys storm the van, they could break a trip wire and set off the dynamite before I can execute, and that could spell the end of my family if word gets back to the guy holding them. I don't know, but there is the possibility that the sound of the van exploding could be the signal for the other guy to kill my family. I just can't take a chance that someone unfamiliar with these mountains could do something stupid and end up causing my family to be taken away from me.

I'm sure these guys have two-way radios, so please heed my warning. Keep the troops back and let me handle this.

And, if you decide to skip the meeting with the President and hang around, Beth and I, including Alexander, should be back before lunch to welcome you to our home.

You take care, my good friend,
Alec

*   *   *

"Well, shit! That settles that. You would think he's running this damned agency, not me. Bryan, call my pilot and cancel my flight to DC. I'm staying here until this is over. And, read this." Armstrong handed Bryan DeWitt the letter.

*   *   *

Destination: Gallatin National Forest
The Crazy Mountains
Sweet Grass County, Montana
Tuesday, July 17 – 11:35pm

Alec backed the old CJ-7 Jeep out of the shed, loaded his backpack and rifle and topped off the gas tank before driving out to Montana Route 294 and heading east towards Martinsdale. The barricade preventing traffic in and out of the side road leading to his house had been removed. Because of the lateness of the hour, no one saw him leave. It was just past midnight

Beyond Martinsdale, Alec turned right onto U.S. 12 towards Harlowton, but some twelve miles out, he slowed the Jeep and turned right again onto the two lane paved road leading through the old cow town of Twodot, now little more than a wide spot in the road, and named for the two dots brand a local rancher used to distinguish his cattle and horses from others grazing the open range here in the early part of the last century. Beyond the sleeping village he stayed on Wilson Street, now a gravel road, until it ended at a "T" intersection. He knew to take the road to the right, which was dirt now, hardly wide enough to pass two vehicles going in opposite directions. But then again, the only traffic out here were the ranchers whose spreads were widely scattered across this fertile plain.

The land here was relatively flat with many dry streambeds and low buttes. Corn and wheat fields dotted the surroundings until Alec turned again towards the distant Crazy Mountains, now visible in the moonlight. As the land began to rise to meet the mountains, the air began to cool. The road was now little more than a one-lane dirt path.

In another thirty minutes of twists and turns, the path vanished into a grove of aspens, their green, heart-shaped leaves shimmering in the moonlight. Alec drove his Jeep down into a gully that hid it from anyone who might come through the area on the ridge above. He shouldered his backpack and rifle and checked his watch. *Plenty of time*, he thought as he moved out.

*   *   *

Gallatin National Forest
Sweet Grass County, Montana
Wednesday, July 18 – 1:45am

One forty-five. Using his Lowrance (i) Finder hand-held GPS, he began to trace the route he planned to take over the mountain looming in front of him. It was only a little over nine thousand feet, but because of the bitter winter winds that blew across these mountains, the vegetation ended well before the summit, exposing its rock face, bathed in moonlight. From a distance, the tops of the Crazy Mountains appeared almost white.

Sitting in his living room the previous evening, and using both his GPS and his topo map of the Gallatin National Forest, he had plotted the coordinates of his route in the GPS memory, taking advantage of the contours that provided the easiest and safest route over the mountain and down to the cabin beside Sweet Grass Creek some five hundred yards back in the surrounding timber, where he felt his wife and child were being held. His plan was first to check on his family to be sure they were safe. Then, all hell was going to break loose.

Alec's approach to the Gallatin National Forest was well north of the road the kidnappers had used to stash the van. The vehicle was hidden in a grove of evergreens, but not so well concealed as to make it invisible from the road. The kidnappers wanted to be sure Alec would see it as he approached. What they didn't know was that Alec had already figured out what they were planning and was changing the rules of the game in his favor.

Bait, Alec thought, as he stood on a rock outcropping high above the road, using the moonlight to glass the set-up the kidnappers had devised for him. He lingered for only a moment. Then he moved on, giving the set-up a wide birth as he climbed higher into the mountains, angling constantly south and steadily gaining altitude. The timber here was sparse, but the downfalls slowed his progress. He occasionally crossed an isolated burn, creating by long-ago lightning strikes, and now filled with young evergreens struggling to renew nature's promise. The timber, as he moved steadily upward, was laced with grassy meadows and an occasional crystal-clear brook cascading over huge boulders scattered about the landscape like giant pebbles. A series of advancing Ice Age glaciers had once spread across the area, carving deep gorges in the barren moonscape that was North America, millions of year ago.

Perfect habitat for elk, he thought as he continued to climb. It was too early for the rut, and the big bulls were still herded up in small groups, mostly in the low country, gorging themselves on the meadow grasses and preparing themselves for the bloody sparring that would begin as soon as the cows came into estrus. The first frost had not yet arrived and the grass was still tender, now the favorite food of the elk and mule deer that roam these timbered slopes.

Alec had hunted these meadows and burns in years past with his friend, Bill Hawks from Big Timber. It was these outings that had brought Hawks back from the state of depression his life had led him into. He smiled at how successful Hawks had become by focusing on his real estate business and not on the fact that his former employer, the DEA, had forsaken him.

The moon, now almost full, provided sufficient light that he could stay on his trek up the mountain without having to use his night vision equipment, still in his backpack.

When he reached the summit he stopped to rest, but only momentarily. He had covered three thousand vertical feet in less than two hours and it was beginning to show. The thin air at this altitude required an extra effort to keep moving upward. But Alec had worked out every day to build his lung capacity and to repair the damage to his lungs a bullet had caused months earlier as a rogue FBI agent almost made good on his promise to kill him.

It was three-thirty in the morning as Alec crossed the headwaters of Sweet Grass Creek and worked his way down through the boulders on the far side. The sound of the water cascading over the rocks was the only sound he heard except the mournful howls of an occasional pack of coyotes, baying at the moon. He knew the cabin was ahead of him, about a mile distant, and he now began to stop occasionally to listen for any noise not a part of the natural habitat. There was nothing that aroused his suspicion. He was almost on the cabin when he heard the door open and then close. Alec stopped, crouched low, and listened. All was quiet. He had taken his night-vision binoculars from his pack and was wearing them around his neck, but inside his jacket, to keep them from getting tangled as he worked his way through the brush. As he focused them on the cabin in the distance, he could make out the image of a man standing on the porch, urinating on the ground.

"If I had the time to get in position, I swear to God, I would shoot his dick off," Alec said to himself in a barely audible voice. "And, that's a damned tiny target at this distance, hell, at any distance."

When the man went back into the cabin, Alec waited a few minutes before approaching. The moon had moved across the sky in its westerly trek towards the distant horizon, so he moved carefully around the rear of the cabin to take advantage of the moonlight streaming into the windows on the cabin's west side. As he peered into the rear window of the one-room cabin, he saw Beth, rocking his child. He could tell Alexander was awake, staring at his mother's smiling face.

Tears welled up in his eyes and he wanted to rush into the cabin, take out the kidnapper and hold his wife and his son in his arms. But he waited. Discipline, *patience is a virtue,* he remembered.

*   *   *

If there was one attribute of Alec's character that stood out above all others, it was his discipline. Early in life, as he wandered through the mountains surrounding Cut Bank with his Black Foot Indian mentor, he had been taught the mountain-man skills that distinguished him from his childhood friends and later his military and agency peers. And the one skill his mentor constantly harped upon was discipline. The old Indian, a close friend and hunting partner of his father, had told him that patience was the one virtue he had to master. And he could do that only if he first learned that discipline was absolutely essential to being successful, regardless of the task or the goal.

*   *   *

Gallatin National Forest
Sweet Grass County, Montana
Wednesday, July 18—4:17am

Four-seventeen, and dawn was just under two and a half hours away. Only one of the kidnappers was in the cabin with Beth. He was sitting at the old wooden table that had been placed as a divider between the kitchen and living area of the one-room cabin, his automatic lying on its top only inches from his right hand. His back was to Alec so he was unable to read the man's age or get an idea of his level of strength. Alec knew his background, ex-military and trained as a killer. He also knew that he could not afford to underestimate this man's skills and cunning. It could turn the game against him.

Alec knew he wouldn't be fast enough to break down the cabin door and rush the man before he would grab his pistol and get off several shots. That would be suicide. He had to get the man away from the table and his weapon to stand any chance at all. He had to be distracted.

* * *

As if she knew he was there, Beth slowly lifted her eyes from her child and looked over at the window where Alec was standing outside. She smiled, only slightly, acknowledging his presence. He knew she had seen his face in the window. Beth glanced over at the kidnapper who was still looking in the opposite direction, and back at Alec. He made a gesture to Beth by putting his thumb in his mouth while taking his eyes off Beth's face and moving them down to his child lying in her arms, then elevating his head slightly as though he were drinking a beer. Beth nodded slightly as Alec's image faded into the darkness outside. She knew exactly what he wanted her to do.

Beth stood and laid the child down in his makeshift bed. He stirred slightly and began sucking his thumb. The kidnapper heard her chair scrape the floor as she stood. He shifted his gaze to her as she unbuttoned her blouse and removed it, then her bra, exposing her well-formed breast, swollen from the milk she was producing for her child. The man's eyes widened as Beth bent over and picked the child up. "Feeding time," she said, smiling first at her son, then at the man.

"Me first," he replied, getting out of his chair and walking over to Beth, who was now seated with her son in her arms. "Put the baby down, Mrs. Caldwell. I've been wanting to do this since we took you."

* * *

The kidnapper's slacks were below his knees when the door was knocked off its hinges and crashed onto the cabin's floor with such force that the man, planning to have his way with Beth, didn't understand what was happening until he saw Alec's imposing hulk standing in the threshold. Alec was on him before he could turn back towards the wooden table to get his weapon. He tried to take a step, but his pants, now around his ankles tripped him, sending him to the floor with Alec on top of him.

When the kidnapper awoke, he was hog-tied, gagged and lying on the cabin's floor, face down. The first image he saw was Alec embracing his wife who was now fully dressed, and his young son, both safe from the nightmare they had been forced to live the last two days.

"I knew you would come tonight," Beth said, still in Alec's arms. "Something told me. I just knew it."

"Sweetheart, I'm so sorry you had to go through this. I never expected this to happen. If I had, I wouldn't have gone to Scotland to help Tim Sutherland. I didn't think these people knew who I was. I thought we were safe, but someone in the company ratted me out. There was no way they could have learned my true identity or where we lived unless someone at Langley was paid off. Whoever it was will regret the day he decided to do this."

"Who are these people, Alec? They kept talking as though they work for the government. That couldn't be. Government employees don't kidnap innocent wives and children. They don't kill people."

"They work for the President, Beth. They're members of a very secret and highly specialized hit team we've been tracking for several years. They do the dirty work for the President to keep his enemies in line. They do things that he can't be associated with. In effect, they're criminals and they deal mostly in murder and extortion."

"That's impossible, Alec."

"We have the evidence, Sweetheart. And, we're going to bring it to the public's attention. But, timing is critical.

"Honey, I really have to go. The other man is still out there, and I have to get him before he gets us. I want you to stay here with Alexander and that toad." He handed her the automatic the kidnapper had placed on the table. "You know how to use this, Sweetheart, so if he tries to get away, shoot him. But shoot him in the knee. Then he can't run, but he can still talk. He and I are going to have a little session before we leave here in the morning. If he's willing to cut a deal-his life for a complete confession of what he and his buddies have been doing for the President-I'll be sure he's given immunity from prosecution. We may even ship him over to some third-world Moslem country just so he can raise a little hell over there. Either way, I'm going to drag him back to DC when this thing is done and parade him before a grand jury. Or, I'll leave his sorry ass here for the coyotes to feed on. It's gonna be his choice."

"Alec. The other man left late yesterday evening. I heard them talking about his going to where they left the van to get ready for you. They're going to ambush you, Sweetheart. You've got to be careful. From what they said, I think they have the van full of some sort of explosive. They think you'll go there to rescue me, and they're planning to blow it up when you get there, you included."

"I suspected as much. Don't worry about me. I've already seen their set-up. I know what they're up to and where they plan to take me down. The advantage I have is that they don't know I know. By the way, this fellow isn't gunshot, so did you shoot the other one?"

"Yes, but only in the shoulder. This one must have bought some medical supplies after I shot his buddy, because he cleaned the wound and patched the other guy up. He knew what he was doing because he gave him a shot of penicillin and a fist full of antibiotics.

"This is the shithead who hit me with a face full of pepper spray before I could clear my automatic's chamber. The second round jammed and he was on me before I could get off another shot. If the damned gun hadn't jammed, both of them would be dead."

"You did just great, Sweetheart. Like I said, these guys are ex-military. They've been trained in how to take care of themselves. Dressing a gunshot wound isn't rocket science for them. I suspect they've done this more than once.

"Now, try to get a few winks while I go find the other toad. I'll be back for you around daylight. And, don't be alarmed if you hear a pretty loud explosion."

*   *   *

Gallatin National Forest
Wednesday, July 18—5:31am

Five thirty-one. Alec had just under an hour before the first evidence of the approaching dawn would begin to lighten the eastern rims of the Crazy Mountains. *More than enough time*, he thought, as he set out towards the kill zone the kidnappers had set up for him. He wanted to be in position when it was light enough to see his adversary.

The trees were larger and grew closer together here on the mountain's lower slopes, preventing the waning moon's light from penetrating the overhead canopy. Alec had just over a mile to travel, but the going was more difficult than if he had been on the higher slopes where the timber was sparse and the footing easier to negotiate. He picked up a well-worn game trail just above his trek that followed the ridge through the heavy timber. It made his travel easier, and he followed it for over a half-mile until it turned right and led down the mountain to a large meadow a hundred yards below him. In another fifteen minutes he stopped, knelt in the soft leaves, and began scanning the timber in front of him for any movement or sign of the man he knew was waiting somewhere out there. It was still dark, so he felt he could continue to move towards the target area without being seen.

Alec reasoned that the man would want to command the high ground above the kill zone in order to maximize his visibility and to be able to control the situation should a firefight break out. He would also want to be able to cover his flanks, so his set-up would be in cover with good visibility both left and right. *If he's smart, he'll select a site back against a rock outcropping so he wouldn't have to worry about being surprised from behind,* Alec thought.

There was also another factor influencing his selection of a site. *If this guy is planning to detonate the dynamite with the electronic switch he and his partner purchased in Big Timber*, Alec reasoned, *he will have to be within three hundred yards of the charge. Beyond that distance, the signal could be too weak to activate the detonator.* He knew the man wouldn't take that chance. He was too smart for that.

Alec knew he wasn't dealing with an amateur. His adversary was a seasoned executioner with years of military experience under his belt before joining the President's Black Hawks hit squad, where he and his fellow team members carried out the President's orders when he wanted someone brought in line or eliminated. But, Alec wasn't an amateur either. And, these were his mountains.

*   *   *

The eastern sky was beginning to brighten when Alec found the man. A slight breeze had freshened as dawn approached, blowing left to right across the ridge on which he was sitting. At first he saw no movement, but the slight smell of cigarette smoke told him the man was close, but where? Alec had put away his night vision binoculars as the sky continued to brighten. He pulled his Steiner monocular range finder from his pack and systematically scanned the area in front of him. Still no movement, but a patch of white behind some low growing bushes a hundred yards in front and below his position, caught his eye. *That's him*, Alec thought. *Good set-up, just not good enough.*

The man was somewhat lower on the mountain than he had expected, only three hundred yards from the van, and a hundred yards below Alec's position. *He's not taking any chances that he wouldn't be able to blow up the van,* Alec thought.

As dawn crept across the ridges, leaving the hollows in deep shadow, the man's outline became more visible. Dawn, and a freshening breeze, had brought a slight chill to the mountains. The man had shifted his position twice since Alec had spotted him. *He's getting chilled,* Alec thought.

The man's rifle was propped on a collapsible bipod to steady his shot, should he be forced to use it. He was glassing the road beyond the van, looking for movement that would tell him Alec was approaching the van from the road. He wasn't.

Alec had dropped to a prone position, and laid his rifle on his coat, which he had rolled into a cushion to steady his shot. The leaves and moss were damp to the touch, but softened his position. He could feel the cold inching its way into his bones. *Damn, I'm getting old. Too old for this kind of young man's game,* he thought, as he glassed the man through the rifle's high-powered scope, looking for any twig or leaf that would deflect his bullet from its intended target. Alec had wondered what the white color was that gave the man's position away. *So, his left arm is in a sling. If he's forced to use the rifle to shoot me, he can use his right arm to shoulder the weapon and the bi-pod to steady the shot. I think I'll play this man's little game and see what he does.*

Alec centered the scope's crosshairs on the man's right shoulder and applied slight pressure to the rifle's custom-made trigger. When the trigger pressure broke two pounds, the weapon fired, sending a 120-grain, ballistic tip boattail projectile into the man's shoulder, shattering his collarbone as it blew out through the back of his shirt and coat in a mist of blood, flesh, and bone fragments. The force of the bullet spun the man around and sent him tumbling down the ridge and over a shallow rock outcropping onto the hard ground some ten feet below. When he landed, the detonation switch in his coat pocket was activated. The violent explosion sent the van twenty feet into the air in a fireball that lit up the sky and surrounding woods, like a giant Roman candle.

"Son-of-a-bitch," Alec exclaimed, as he watched the van disintegrate into small projectiles of burning metal that were hurled at supersonic speeds away from the point of the explosion. Although he was more than three hundred yards away from the detonation site, he instinctively ducked, burying his face in the leaves, as the concussion wave blew by and pieces of hot metal fell around him.

He stood up and used his range finder to search the area where the man had been hiding. His rifle was still there, lying on the ground, but the man wasn't. Alec was close enough to see a heavy blood trail leading down the slope from his hide for about ten yards where it ended at a small outcropping of rock. Alec crept down the slope and peered over the outcrop. The man was sitting upright, his back to the rock on which Alec was standing; his head slumped on his chest. Blood had stopped draining through a large hole in the rear of his coat, just behind where his right shoulder used to be. But what Alec noticed first was a large piece of metal, part of the van's steering column, protruding from the man's chest. *When the dynamite he packed in the van exploded, the steering column must have been hurled through the air like a javelin,* Alec thought, looking at the lifeless body of the man, sitting there in a pool of his own blood, who had waited all night for a chance to assassinate him. "Serves you right, you son-of-a-bitch. Kidnap my wife and son, will you. You'll make a good meal for a bear or a pack of wolves or coyotes," he yelled, holding his rifle with both hands high above his head as his Black Foot mentor had taught him to do when he made a successful kill, either food or enemy.

*   *   *

Alec found the keys to the Ford the two kidnappers had rented, and holding his young son in his arms and his rifle over his shoulder, walked with Beth down the mountain to where the men had parked the car. The kidnapper, whose life Alec had spared, stumbled behind them, his hands tied behind his back, blindfolded and a rope around his neck, which Beth held in her hand. When they reached the car, the man was cut and bruised, but alive. Alec opened the car's trunk and dumped him inside.

"Now don't you suck up too much carbon monoxide back there, and die on me, Boy. I need you to honor your commitment to tell a grand jury everything you know about a number of suicides and disappearances around DC that we know the President orchestrated." Alec slammed the trunk as the man stared up at him, hate evident in the strained look on his bruised face. He started the Ford and drove to where he had left the jeep, some six miles away. Together, he and Beth headed back to their home outside Lennep, he driving the Jeep and she, the Ford, with her young son lying on the seat beside her.

*   *   *

Alec and Beth's Home
North of Lennep, Montana
Wednesday, July 18 – 10:15am

"So, you decided to stick around to see the end of this, Don," Alec said, as he stepped out of the Jeep, shutting down the engine. Before Don Armstrong could answer, Alec turned and walked over to the Ford, opened the door and picked up his son who was in the process of wetting his diaper.

"Don, meet the next Alex Caldwell, Mountain Man to be! Alec, this is my college roommate and very good friend, now my boss, Director Donald M. Armstrong, your Godfather. Just don't ever, ever, ask him what the "M" stands for." Alec held his son out for Armstrong to take into his arms, wet diaper and all.

Beth walked around the Ford and took the baby from Don Armstrong, kissing him on the cheek.

"You've been through a hell of a lot, Beth. I'm just glad this old boy got to you before they did something they would regret. How are you coping? Don asked, embracing Beth whose wedding he had attended just months earlier.

"I knew this guy was a long shot, Don, but I fell for him anyway," she said, taking Alec by the arm. "This has just been another surprise that I guess keeps our marriage together. I'm not sure I could stand having him around all the time, so you keep him busy, but please give him something to do that isn't quite as strenuous, especially on Alexander and me." She smiled at Don and winked at her adoring husband, who was smiling and looking down on her pretty face. "I need a bath, Gentlemen, and my son needs a change of diapers. You all come on in. I'll get some coffee going first."

"By the way, Don. I have a little present for you," Alec said, as he walked to the rear of the Ford, popped the trunk lid, and dragged the bruised and bloody man out. "This is one of the two mutts who were holding my family up in the Gallatin." Alec pushed the man towards Don. His hands were tied behind his back, and he stumbled and fell just beyond the car.

"Doesn't look like he's the worse for wear. A little bloody on the outside, but I think he'll live, at least for a while. Who is he anyway? Did he tell you anything?"

"Not really." Alec reached in his jacket pocket, pulled out the man's wallet and identification, and handed them to Armstrong. "He's using an FBI identification, but it's just a cover. It says his name is Lawrence Madre, but he confirmed that his true name is Joshua Bowen. You can check all that out when you get him back to DC. I'm sure he'll be more than willing to tell you everything about the work he and his fellow conspirators have been doing for Hunt, once your people have explained his precarious situation to him.

"His friend is sitting out in the mountains with a piece of metal sticking out of his chest. I left his body there for the bears, but here's his FBI identification. I probably would have dragged him out, but I needed to get back to Beth before she shot this mutt just out of spite, and I knew you would need his testimony. He's agreed to talk to you and to a grand jury, if necessary, but he wants immunity from prosecution and wants to disappear after he testifies. I told him we would arrange for his disappearance, but once he was out of the country, he would be on his own. I also told him the immunity he wants is out. He's going to have to take his chances wherever he goes. I did tell him that as long as he never comes back to the States we will leave him alone. He knows if he comes back to our shores, and I find out, he'll be dead meat."

*   *   *

"You need to spend some more time with that lady, Alec. And with your son. I'm sure he hardly knows you. We can put this thing on hold for a while. Why don't you take a couple of weeks off and go somewhere, Hawaii, maybe? How about the Italian Riviera, maybe Monaco?"

"No thanks. We talked about this earlier this morning. We're going down to Idaho Springs to her family's ranch. She says she just wants to chill out, just sit on the front porch in her mother's old rocker. And that suits me just fine. I can use the rest.

"She loves the mountains down there, Don, and she wants to watch the Aspen leaves turn golden yellow in the hollows, watch the sun set like she used to do when she was just a child. And, of course, spoil Alexander.

"I'm going to stay with her as long as she wants me there. She's got some healing to do and that's the place that will make her well. We'll fish a little. Maybe go after a bull elk in the early season. Just relax and find ourselves again."

CHAPTER TWENTY-TWO

4516 Evergreen Avenue
Georgetown
District of Columbia
Tuesday, August 7 – 2:30am

T HE DRIVER OF the black Chevrolet van pulled up to the curb, cut its lights and engine, but did not get out. He waited for a good fifteen minutes, listening to the night sounds of the neighborhood, while the man beside him scanned the street and sidewalks ahead through night vision binoculars. One of the two men in the rear of the van did likewise along the route the van had taken, while the other passenger checked the President's compound across the street, all through binoculars. Anyone passing by the van on the street or sidewalk would not have been able to see the four men inside. The windows were heavily tinted, and the bulletproof glass was much thicker than regular vehicle window glass.

It was 2:30am and the street was deathly quiet. No one was stirring in the neighborhood; only a stray cat passed the van. The gaslights, evenly spaced along the sidewalks on both sides of Evergreen, were somehow mysteriously dark in this block. It was a total blackout, just as the driver had been told it would be.

Three of the four men, all dressed in black, quickly exited the van and hurried up the concrete steps and into the old three story apartment building across from the President's compound, mounted the interior steps, two at a time, and entered the third floor apartment that faced onto the street. With curtains closed, they quickly loaded all of the electronic surveillance equipment there into foam-padded boxes. When they were ready to leave, they signaled the driver, who, after giving the area another sweep through his night vision glasses, gave them the "all clear" signal. The boxes of equipment were carefully loaded into the back of the van, and when the apartment was cleared, the van pulled slowly away from the curb and headed out of the District towards the Virginia countryside. Their destination was Langley, Virginia

The previous night, the same van had turned into the President's compound on Evergreen. Earlier that evening, the driver determined that no one was at the residence, and their log showed that no one was expected, based on past history. The passenger sitting next to the driver stepped out and unlocked the heavy iron gates and swung them open as the van passed through and up to the front steps of the main house. The team quickly gained access to the house and meticulously removed the state-of-the-art listening devices and video cameras they had hidden in every room of the residence years ago when the President first purchased the residence. They replaced their equipment with generic equipment that could be purchased on the open market by anyone wishing to conduct a low tech surveillance of the premises and its inhabitants. Even though the President's men had swept the residence for electronic devices countless time, none had been found With their shielded devices removed, the new equipment would be found when the FBI searched the premises after learning it was owned by a non-existent shell company created by the law firm that represented the President on personal matters. Their information had come from an undisclosed source.

*   *   *

CIA Headquarters
Langley, Virginia

Alec had been away for the better part of three weeks. He arrived at CIA headquarters after a sleepless night at the Hyatt, and took one of the elevators up to Don Armstrong's office on the sixth floor of the new headquarters building. He was sitting in the conference room adjacent to his office when Don entered.

He had spent the last three weeks with Beth and their son at her family's ranch, north of Idaho Falls. He knew they would be safe there, and she would be with family.

She could tell he was getting restless. He had that far-off look in his eyes, and his having to apologize constantly for not listening to what she was saying wasn't like him. He wasn't losing his hearing. She knew his mind was miles away, possibly up in the Bob Marshals, hunting elk, or trout fishing on the Madison in southwest Montana. He was somewhere, but he wasn't with her in Idaho. So, as gently as she could, without hurting his feelings, she sent him away. "Go back to DC and get this over with," she told him. "Then come back to me and to Alexander. We'll be here, and we'll be waiting."

*   *   *

Beth's kidnapping had been a traumatic experience for her-not so much that she and her son had been kidnapped and held hostage-but that the two perpetrators had taken her by surprise before she could shoot them both. She had wounded one, but her automatic had jammed as the second round was fed into the chamber, leaving her defenseless.

Two of the President's hit team had been eliminated in Scotland, weeks earlier, as they were on their way to assassinate Timothy Sutherland, and Alec had just eliminated one of the two other members of the President's five-member Black Hawks team who had been holding Beth and his son hostage. The CIA was holding the survivor of Beth's kidnapping incognito, and the remaining member of the hit team had gone to ground.

*   *   *

"You should have stayed longer out at the ranch with Beth, Alec. She's been through a hell of a lot, and probably needs you there to give her some support."

"Are you kidding? She had me babysitting while she joined the ranch hands in their annual cattle roundup. It's like nothing happened to her. She's a tough lady, Don. She was raised to be independent. Ranch life grows you up in a hurry. That's one of the reasons her marriage to the Secretary of the Interior fell apart. He wanted a trophy wife on his arm as he manipulated his way around the Washington social scene. That wasn't what she felt her role was supposed to be. She had been a successful lawyer in her own right and wasn't comfortable playing second fiddle to someone who couldn't measure up to her mettel. It was just good luck that we found each other after his death. Especially since she had been slated to join her husband after the assassin got through with her."

*   *   *

"So, Don, back to business. I think we're on the right track now. I thought the story about the President and his illegal laundering of drug money would break in France, but having it originate in the U.S. is even better. I suspect the Attorney General is all over it by now. Doesn't look like old John is going to be able to squirm out of this one. I believe we've got him by the short hairs, Don."

"Amen. I suspect the Attorney General will be pursuing this in the name of the American people, if for no other reason just to cover her ass. But to keep the investigation aboveboard and out of the political arena, she will probably appoint an Independent Counsel to head it up. If he's smart, he'll convene a grand jury so the people can decide the guilt or innocence of the President. That's where we introduce our surprise *tell all* witness. If Congress follows the grand jury's lead, assuming they hand down a guilty verdict, it will add some credibility to whatever Congress does with it."

"So, what role do we play in this so-called developing and deepening story of greed and deceit?" asked Alec with a smile on his beard stubbled face.

"We're going to lie low for a few days and see where it goes, Alec. If the story seems to be slipping in the press, I'll want you to develop a *deep throat* relationship with Sam Davidson over at the *Washington Post*. We've used him before to feed information to the public when we wanted to push a particular agenda. He's a good investigative reporter, and he'll check out whatever you give him before he takes it to his editors. But, if it's solid, he will run with it.

"But, he's going to try to find out who you arc and for whom you work. You can't let that happen. He'll tell you he can't use anything you give him unless he knows the source. That's bullshit, and you tell him that. He'll steam about it for a while, but he'll come around and be damned glad to get your phone calls. Everything you give him, he will be able to verify, except he won't know who you are or where you're getting the information.

"Always call him at night. Preferably late, after he has been sleeping for a while. Never before 2:00am. He'll be groggy from sleep and won't be able to focus as he would if he was wide-awake and waiting for your call. Always vary the nights you call him. Don't establish a routine of time of your calls or the nights you call.

"And, you'll always meet him at night, after dark, and in a dark place so he can't see your face. Wherever you meet him, a parking garage for example, always arrive before he does and always leave after you can verify he has left. If he waits in hiding and tries to follow you, keep him off guard by always taking a different route. If you suspect you're being followed, always go to a location away from your hotel.

"Tell him if he uses a flashlight to find out who you are, you will have him killed. We told him that once, so he will know you are a messenger from the same source of other information we have given him. He knows the rules we have established for the exchanges, so once you tell him you will have him killed, not that you will kill him, he will understand and no further warnings should be necessary."

*   *   *

Department of Justice
Robert F. Kennedy Building
Washington, DC
Thursday, August 2 – 10:26am

"Janice, I want to ask a DC Superior court justice to convene a grand jury on this. The evidence in these documents deserves nothing less. And I'm going to subpoena the President to testify. These are crimes against the laws of the United States, and I know the 23 jurors will return a true bill against him."

"He won't do it, George, because he doesn't have to. Remember, innocent until proven guilty, and a person can't be compelled to testify against himself, even the President. And, Presidents don't testify in person, ever. You may get him to testify from the White House using a television hookup, if he feels he has evidence to refute what you have and can get a no bill verdict from the grand jury. But, I really think the best you can hope for is to depose him and let the grand jury hear what he has to say on tape. Regardless of whether he gives you a deposition or testifies before your grand jury, he'll be under oath, and that's what really matters. All we want is the truth."

*   *   *

Underground Parking Garage
Watergate Complex
2650 Virginia Avenue NW
Washington, DC
Sunday, August 12 – 1:30am

Alec arrived at the Watergate Hotel underground garage at one-thirty in the morning, an hour before his scheduled meeting with Samuel Davidson, the investigative reporter with the *Washington Post* to whom the CIA had fed information during the Nixon investigations and several times during the Kennedy and Clinton years. He parked on the level above the rendezvous location and walked down the ramp to level six, carefully observing his surroundings. Although there were very few parking spaces remaining unfilled, there was no one around. At 2:00am, he used his cell phone to call the reporter.

"You have thirty minutes to get to the Watergate Hotel underground parking garage. There is no one on duty in the entrance gate. Drive up to level six and around to the far side to parking space 698. It will be vacant. Park in that space and remain in your car with the windows up until I tell you to get out. You have thirty minutes, so if I were you, I would hurry on down."

The quick turn-around time prevented Davidson from staking out the parking garage before the rendezvous or from contacting a friend to set up a stakeout and identify Alec as he entered or left the complex. Alec knew the location of the reporter's apartment and had timed the drive time at the designated time of night when traffic was almost non-existent in that part of town. The CIA had also bugged his home phone, but had no access to his cell phone.

At 2:25am Alec removed the orange highway cone he had placed in parking space 698 earlier in the day to keep anyone else from parking there, and waited behind a concrete pillar some fifty feet from the rendezvous point. At 2:37 the reporter arrived, but as instructed, remained in his car, his windows closed.

Alec watched the reporter's car for another five minutes. No one drove up the ramp onto level six, and no one, other than the reporter and Alec, seemed to be there. At 2:42, Alec dialed Davidson's cell phone.

"Hello?"

"You were late."

"Not by that much. Who are you?"

"It really doesn't matter who I am. Get out of your car, close the door, and stand facing the car until I tell you otherwise."

"Why the hell should I do what you say? I don't know you or what you want."

"Let me put it another way, Mr. Davidson. If you don't, I will have you killed."

There was no smart-ass response to Alec's threatening statement, just quiet for a few seconds as the reporter thought about what Alec had just said.

"Why do I have the distinct feeling I've heard that before," the reporter finally said.

"Because you have, Mr. Davidson. Just a different messenger this time."

"What are you talking about?"

"You know what I'm talking about, but it's not important at this moment."

Davidson got out of his car as he was told.

"Please turn around, Mr. Davidson. You are now facing a concrete column. At its base is a brown envelope taped to the column. Pick it up and get back in your car. Then open the envelope and read the several pages inside. You have ten minutes. After you've finished reading the document, flash your car lights once. I will call you on your cell phone and answer any questions you have. That is, if I feel answers are necessary. Do you understand?"

"Yes, I have the envelope. How did you get my cell phone number?"

"Another unimportant question. Just know, Mr. Davidson, that I know more about you than your mother ever knew."

Without saying anything else, the reporter got back in his car and slammed the door.

Alec smiled. He knew the reporter had recognized the code words *I'll have you killed*, that the CIA had used on several previous investigations in which they had used Sam Davidson to get information to the public without revealing the source.

Ten minutes later, Alec saw the reporter's car lights come on, then go off. He dialed the reporter's cell phone number. It was answered immediately.

"Who are you?

"It really doesn't matter who I am. The question is this: have you read the document?"

"Yes. Where did you get this information?"

"That doesn't matter either. What matters is that you can verify all of the information you have."

"How?"

"You're the reporter, you figure it out. Do you have any other questions, Mr. Davidson?"

"Not now. But you know I can't use this information unless you tell me who you are and how you got this information."

"You and I both know that isn't so. If you aren't interested, put the envelope and its contents back where you found them, and drive away."

"May I go now?"

"Yes. But know that we have this complex under surveillance. When you leave here you will be followed. When you arrive at your apartment complex I will be notified, and I will then leave. And, don't attempt to learn my identity. That would be unhealthy."

Alec heard the reporter's car start, watched him back out of the parking space, and drive back down the ramp to the exit. He walked over to the concrete column adjacent to the space where the reporter had parked. The envelope wasn't there.

*　　*　　*

FBI Headquarters
J. Edgar Hoover Building
District of Columbia
Monday, August 13 – 10:45am

"This is interesting information you have, Mr. Davidson. Your front page exposé of the President's hit team, what did you call them, the *Black Hawks*, I think, really shook up Washington. I was truly amused."

Special Agent Leroy Bazemore, to whom the investigation into the allegations against the President had been assigned, had read Sam Davidson's article in the *Washington Post* that had appeared in this morning's issue, and had sent a junior agent over to the *Post* to bring the reporter to his office, in handcuffs, if necessary.

"I just had a little chat with your editor and your publisher. They just left, Mr. Davidson, and I can tell you, the *Washington Post* could be in for a serious lawsuit if you can't prove all the allegations you've made in your little article this morning. You want to comment on this, Sir?"

"Yes, but only to say that I've been on this beat for a good number of years, and my reputation as a fair and balanced investigative reporter precedes me, and you know that. I always do my homework, Agent Bazemore, and you know that as well. I verified every detail of my story and have the evidence to back it up. I'm surprised you found my story amusing. It certainly wasn't meant to be. This is damned serious business, Sir.

"And will I turn these documents over to you and your agents? Absolutely not! The First Amendment to the Constitution protects my right not to reveal my sources or to give up the information my sources gave me.

"Sorry, but check out the story for yourself. Get your warrant and check out the address in Georgetown. I couldn't do that legally, but you can. And have your legal eagles look into the ownership of the property. The paper trail will be hard to follow, but it was meant to be. I guarantee you can trace it back to the President if your legal people are any good. I did.

"And, Special Agent Bazemore, I know your people have been working with the Independent Counsel on the grand jury investigation of the President, so I don't understand why these revelations would surprise you. The son-of-a-bitch is dirty, and you know it as well as I."

* * *

Department of Justice
Robert F. Kennedy Building
Washington, DC
Monday, August 13 – 3:45pm

Independent Counsel George Connors had asked FBI Special Agent Leroy Bazemore to meet him at the Robert Kennedy building to pay a visit to Attorney General Janice Hawkins. They had been ushered into the small conference room three doors down from the Attorney General's spacious office complex.

"Special Agent Bazemore, this is Janice Hawkins."

"A pleasure, Madam Attorney General."

"The pleasure is mine, Special Agent. I've been reading your report on what you accomplished in searching the Georgetown residence that allegedly belongs to the President. It seems you and your fellow agents struck pay dirt. You gentlemen please be seated. Robert will bring coffee and shortbreads in a few minutes.

"Now, Special Agent, please give us an account of your findings. Reports just don't tell the whole story."

"Of course, Madam Attorney General. Although the Georgetown compound wasn't specifically mentioned in the *Post* article, the reporter did give us the address and suggested we search the premises to substantiate his story. We couldn't get a warrant to do that until we could convince a judge that the President owns the property. Seems it was purchased by a small law firm a number of years ago for a corporate client using the name Black Hawk Corporation. We found out the corporation was only a shell, and their business address was bogus. But, the corporate charter, on file with the Delaware State Corporation Commission, listed one of the firm's former attorneys as the sole owner. So, we brought him in to be interviewed, and he finally confessed that President Hunt had purchased the property in the name of the shell corporation to eliminate any connection to himself, personally. He's willing to testify to that, and we've already turned the information over to your Independent Counselor.

"With the lawyer's sworn statement, we were able to secure the warrant we needed to search the premises. As you know, we are required to serve a warrant before we can enter and search a property, so we served it on the attorney named in the corporate documents, and conducted our search. I'm sure the President knew within a matter of minutes that we had found his little sugar shack."

"Sugar shack? What is a sugar shack, Sir?" the Attorney General asked.

Somewhat red faced, the FBI agent explained that the President used the Georgetown property to entertain his lady friends.

"What else?" the Attorney General asked, a look of concern on her face.

"One of the first things we did was to sweep the property electronically, both outside the residence and inside. What we found was quite interesting. Someone had installed a series of listening devices and miniature video cameras throughout the residence, and strategically along the driveway leading to the house. Although they were fairly sophisticated, they weren't as high tec as those we use, or are used by Homeland Security, the CIA or DEA. So, we have eliminated those three agencies from our list of suspects. Our take is that some outside group was conducting the surveillance, not a Federal agency. The listening devices and the miniature video cameras can all be purchased on the open market, and they aren't that expensive."

"Have you considered that whoever was conducting the surveillance may have known you would be searching the premises, and had removed their more sophisticated devices, replacing them with less expensive generic gear to make you think the surveillance was a civilian job, thus throwing you off their trail?"

"No, Ma'am. That never occurred to us."

"Then consider this, Special Agent Bazemore," the Attorney General's tone somewhat more hardened now. "If you were using the property for your indiscretions, acts quite unbecoming the high office of President of the United States, and if you had a cadre of specially trained Secret Service agents at your beck and call, wouldn't you have had the place electronically swept every so often, just to be sure no one was watching or listening?"

"Of course I would," responded Agent Bazemore.

"Then why had the President's Secret Service agents not found the bugs and cameras that you so easily found?

Special Agent Bazemore didn't respond.

The Attorney General continued "Let me ask you another question, Agent Bazemore. Is the equipment the FBI uses to conduct surveillances fitted with electronic shields that prevent their detection?

"Yes, Ma'am, they are."

"And, do the CIA and the DEA also use electronic shields on their bugs?"

"Yes, Ma'am."

"Then if you're looking for whoever planted the bugs, let me suggest you widen your search to include the spooks in our other clandestine agencies, especially the CIA and the DEA, maybe even the ghosts over at military intelligence. You know if the property was bugged and the Secret Service didn't find the surveillance devices, they had to be shielded, and whoever was conducting the surveillance had to be someone in the Government, not some bungling outsider.

"Next question. I assume that if the bugs are available to the public and aren't too costly, their transmission ranges are limited, considerably more so than if they were the more sophisticated equipment you folks use. Did you have your people plot the limits of their ranges and do a house-to-house search within the established perimeters to see if you could find where the eavesdroppers had set up their listening post?"

"Yes, Ma'am, we did. And we found a third floor apartment in a building across the street that had been leased on a year-to-year basis for several years. But, when we searched it, it was empty. I mean every chair, table and coffee cup. All gone. And wiped clean. Not a single print, not even under the toilet seat. It was a professional sanitizing, Ma'am."

"Who was on the lease, Special Agent?"

"No one we could identify, a bogus name."

"Was the rent paid by check?"

"Yes, personal checks drawn on an account at Riggs. Same bogus name, and the account had been closed when we got there. Just after the last check was written. We have the account's activity. Funds always transferred into the account the day before the rent checks were drawn. The funds came from offshore and we lost the electronic trail among a maze of banking houses in the Caymans and elsewhere."

"Could the apartment house manager identify the person paying the rent?"

"The checks always arrived by mail. And they were mailed from various posts around the District. That, in itself, is suspicious. The manager didn't have any of the envelopes, so no prints. And the man who was the manager when the apartment was initially leased is deceased."

"Anything else?"

"Yes, Ma'am. We found an office in the attic, behind a false wall in the President's digs. My people are working on a computer's hard drive we found there. There are two phones there that aren't extensions of the house phone, separate lines, and a scrambler. No numbers listed on the instruments, so I asked your George Connors if he had any phone records from the information he has in the case he is prosecuting against the President. He emailed me several pages of phone records from one of the banks on Grand Cayman.

"We began dialing the numbers listed in the records as originating numbers, and low and behold, the office phone rang on the second try. There were six pages of numbers, and most of the originating numbers were for the two phones in the office. It looks like transfers were being made just about every day, and the transfer instructions were coming from that office. Unfortunately, no one at the bank could remember any of the conversations. The calls from the office to the depository banks in the Caymans were probably confirmed by electronic mail, and we hope to prove this by breaking down the data in the computer's hard drive."

"What makes you think so, Special Agent?"

"Because the timing of the bank's funds transfers out of all of the President's accounts always occurred moments after the consummation of the calls. It just fits that they are related."

"Looks like you may be on to something, Special Agent Bazemore. Good work, Sir."

*　　*　　*

Underground Parking Garage
Watergate Complex
2650 Virginia Avenue NW
Washington, DC
Sunday, August 19 – 2:30am

"Back so soon! You must be brimming over with revelations about the President."

"You do have a mouth on you, Mr. Davidson. If you want to continue to be the darling of the Washington press, I would suggest you button it up and pay attention. I don't like to repeat myself. So, be a good boy and play the game by my rules. *Lei capisce?*"

"Yes, Sir, I understand."

"Good. Same drill. Pick up the envelope, read the material and signal when you have completed this little task. I'll call you."

Alec dialed the reporter's cell phone number. "Questions?"

"Not a question, but an observation. To get all of this stuff, you had to have bugged the President's compound. To do that, and not get caught, you have to be a Fed. My question is: what agency do you work for?"

"And my answer is, Smart Ass, you know the rules, direct your questions to the material at hand. End of session. Go home." Alec closed his cell phone and waited to see what the reporter would do. Five minutes passed, and the reporter didn't move. Alec heard the reporter's car window come down.

"Hey! Call me, Deep Throat. I need to talk to you."

Alec dialed the reporter's phone again. "This is our last meeting, Mr. Davidson. I can't trust you. You yell out your car window as though there couldn't be anyone else listening. There could. This isn't a game, young man, it's life and death. It's real! Now what do you want?"

"Sorry, Sir. I just didn't know how to reach you. I knew you were close by but I didn't know where."

"OK, what questions do you have about the materials you've just read?"

"Only that someone had a great sense of humor naming their escort service after Ira Levin's book, *The Stepford Wives;* perfect wives programmed to do everything you could ever wish for. Perfect prostitutes, also trained to please. Great analogy.

"But, I do have a question. Why no names of the prostitutes who work for the Stepford Escort Agency? It would make a much better story if we could name some of the ladies of the night whose services he uses."

"Sorry, no names. What else?"

"Nothing else."

"Then go home."

*   *   *

Washington, DC

The story in the *Washington Post* was another sensation. No names of the ladies who practiced their trade in the highest social circles of Washington's political elite were mentioned, but names of Senators and Representatives, aids and lobbyists, who had used the services of the Stepford Escort Service were set in bold type on the front page of the *Post*, right beside the President's. The White House was in meltdown mode, and the dome was about to blow off the Capitol!

All over Washington, politicians were calling press conferences, exclaiming their innocence, denying the allegations, and threatening lawsuits against the paper, the reporter, and anyone else they could think of. But the people weren't buying it. The telephones in the posh offices of the high priced downtown DC lawyers were ringing off their hooks. The first question the attorneys asked was, *Are you innocent?* The answer was always, *no.* The next statement was always the same, *Don't call me, I'll call you,* or something to that effect.

The expose' catapulted the paper's number of readers to new heights, as people waited for the next shoe to drop. The President's popularity was at an all time low, and friends he once counted on in Congress were now calling for him to step down gracefully. No one had mentioned impeachment to him, but he knew it was just a matter of time. The party was slowly, but surely, abandoning the man who had been its leader for the past seven years.

*   *   *

The White House – Oval Office
1600 Pennsylvania Avenue
Washington, DC
Wednesday, August 22 – 8:45am

"Where the hell is all this garbage coming from?"

President Hunt was pacing around the Oval Office, talking to himself. His Press Secretary had just brought the *Washington Post* to him, and quietly backed out of the Oval Office. She knew if she stayed, he would soon be yelling at her, and she had enough problems keeping the press at bay to have to listen to his ranting and raving. Things were rapidly unraveling around the President, and she wanted to stay as far away as possible and still hold on to her job.

"Who's feeding this damned reporter all this crap about me? This guy is ruining my life. First, someone finds all of my accounts in the Caymans and exposes my laundry operations. Then, that bitch I set up as the Attorney General turns on me and appoints an Independent Counsel to stick his nose in my business. Then he gets a judge to convene a Grand Jury to hear all the so-called evidence they think they have against me. And to top it all off, they freeze my accounts. All the money I've been accumulating over the years is locked up. Those bastards aren't going to get away with this."

He walked over to his desk, picked up one of the phones and dialed the number he used to contact members of his Black Hawks team. The phone in the secret office in his Georgetown compound rang several times before it was answered.

"Who is this?" the President yelled.

"Special Agent Leroy Bazemore, FBI. Who is this?"

The President slammed the phone down and collapsed in his chair. He was beginning to sweat, and he could feel the beautiful office closing in around him. He needed to get out, get free of all this, breath some fresh air, and get his thoughts together. "Shit! Shit! Shit!"

In less than forty-five seconds, a call coming into the White House switchboard was automatically routed to a phone on the desk of the President's secretary. The phone number was known only to a select few of the President's closest advisors who had direct access to him, and had been programmed into the system to go to the automatic router without being handled by the battery of Secret Service Agents who man the screening room.

"Oval Office, this is Barbara Mansfield, may I help you?"

Special Agent Bazemore quietly replaced the receiver without speaking. He was smiling. "Gotcha, you scumbag!"

*   *   *

"You saw the *Washington Post* this morning, Fred. I've given up trying to figure out how this reporter gets his information. Bill told me this might happen. It happened to him, and his people could never figure out who the deep throat was. Somebody's had my every move bugged for I don't know how many years. It has to be the CIA, and I guess that Armstrong person thinks it's pay back time. He knows I ratted out his agent down in Mexico. Shit, we had him too, at least for a while.

"With this damned story in the *Post*, what's the Independent Counsel's next move, Fred?"

"Well, Mr. President. Since the Grand Jury has handed down a multi-count indictment against you, I suspect the Independent Counsel will take his findings to Congress, and try to make a case for the House of Representatives to begin impeachment proceedings to have you removed from office. He's convinced you lied under oath to the Grand Jury, and he's got a pretty strong case against you, Sir. I suspect with popular opinions running against you as they have been since this mess surfaced, they're going to feel the pressure from their constituents to take this to the next level. If they are successful, it will be an embarrassment for the party, and with this being an election year, your impeachment would give their candidate a leg-up on taking back the White House.

"And, I'm not so sure the party doesn't consider you expendable this late in the election game. Regardless of how this goes down, you have just become a liability to the party, and I think we will see their support melt away quickly as they attempt to distance themselves from you and your problems. It's just a fact of life, Sir. Political friends are fair weather friends. As long as you are an asset, they are always at hand. But, be perceived as a liability, and you can't find them.

"The Republicans are going to want to impeach you, Mr. President. I'm certain of that. The word is out on the street. They want the House to indict on charges of high crimes and misdemeanors."

"High crimes and misdemeanors! They don't stand a snowball's chance in hell. They can't impeach me. I'm the President of the United States. They don't have any jurisdiction over me or over this office."

"Not so, Mr. President. They have the votes in the House to impeach you, and the law is quite clear on the matter. They do have jurisdiction. They just need a simple majority, and they have that if they vote in block, and you know they will vote along party lines.

"But the articles of impeachment have to get out of the Judiciary Committee, and it's made up of an equal number of Congressmen from both sides of the aisle, regardless of which party is in power. Again, if the committee members vote their allegiance, it won't get to the floor, but you know public opinion is going to force some of your colleagues on the committee to vote it out. After all, John, it's an election year and the public sentiment is running against you right now. And half the House members are up for reelection. That's just the nature of the political game, but you know that, Sir.

"But, the Republicans don't have the votes in the Senate to vote you out of office. Kicking the President out of the White House is a totally different matter all together. A super majority is needed to vote you out, and the Republicans can't muster that many votes against you in the Senate. But, John, if it goes that far, your career is down the toilet anyway, so you should consider resigning before the situation gets to that point.

"However, if you decide to try to beat this, the best way to do that is to keep it on the front burner for as long as possible. Fortunately, the American public has a short attention span and will quickly tire of hearing all the allegations against you over and over again. And you know the press will play this to the hilt. The public will get tired of it all, and the longer it goes, the more public sentiment will turn in your favor. You'll tell the people that the press is out to get you, and they'll start believing it. You know how gullible the public is. Keep it going long enough and they will be praising you as an innocent scapegoat, and calling for the heads of the Senators trying to take you down.

"If you don't believe me, call your friend Bill Clinton, who told you this could happen. He was impeached by the House, but the Senate couldn't muster enough votes to kick him out of office. It was a party line block vote and the opposition didn't have enough converts from our side to get it done. They needed a two-thirds majority, but couldn't get the 67 votes they had to have. And they knew it going in. On the Hill, guilt or innocence really doesn't matter. It's what the party leaders tell their followers to do that they do. There is a little integrity left in the House, but little to none in the Senate. It's the simple fact that the party controls the purse strings. You know as well as I that over there, money talks and integrity walks.

"Clinton lied under oath, and had he been a Republican, he would have been crucified by the press, and Congress would have tarred and feathered him and run him out of Washington on a rail. And the public would have thought it was wonderful. Lying under oath just isn't something a man of character would do. But Clinton did. Then when the evidence proved he did, he just said, *Oh well, so I didn't tell the truth. So what. I'm sorry, so let's get on with healing the nation.* And, the public forgave him because the proceedings had gone on for so long that they were tired of it, and although the evidence against him was irrefutable, it really didn't matter. The public just wanted to get on with their lives. After all, the President was only human.

"And the Senate, well, they looked at who would be running the nation if they found Clinton guilty and kicked him out of the White House. They couldn't abide the idea of Gore sitting on the throne, so they let Clinton finish out his second term.

"Of course, Clinton should have resigned before the impeachment vote by the House, but he didn't. It would have saved him a great deal of embarrassment, but as it worked out, he was too self-absorbed to be embarrassed, which reflected his true lack of character and moral fiber. He now has to carry the burden of being only the second president in the history of our nation to be impeached, and the first elected president to carry that dubious honor. Andrew Johnson was the first, back in 1868, but he wasn't elected. He succeeded Lincoln by default, after his assassination.

"Nixon, on the other hand, was smart. Or, at least he had some smart advisors. After Watergate was exposed, he resigned before Congress could act, eliminating the stigma impeachment carries with it. As I said, that's something you should seriously consider, John."

*   *   *

DC Superior Court
500 Indiana Avenue, NW
Washington, DC

The inquiry lasted the better part of two months. During that time, George Connor, Independent Counsel, and his team dove into the allegations against the President with such zeal that no stone was left unturned. Attorney General Janice Hawkins knew he would.

*   *   *

Office of Attorney General Janice Hawkins
Department of Justice
Robert F. Kennedy Building
Washington, DC
Friday, September 28 – 7:00am

Connors arrived early at the Robert F. Kennedy building for his 7:00am appointment with Janice Hawkins. She was waiting for him when her secretary ushered him into her spacious office.

"It's done, Madam Attorney General. The Grand Jury returned a True Bill against the President late last night. In fact, it was early this morning, around two-thirty. Three indictments, one count for lying under oath and two counts for obstruction of justice.

"And you were right; he refused to testify in person. Instead, he elected to do it by televised deposition. And he immediately began to lie by insisting he had no knowledge of his offshore accounts in the Caymans. In total, we caught him in seven lies, but the Grand Jury wanted to combine all of them in one indictment instead of seven separate indictments. I think they were feeling sorry for him about that time of the morning."

"Was the President's name on any of the off-shore accounts?"

"No, but we know the accounts were his."

"Sounds circumstantial, George. You sure you can make the charges stick?"

"Absolutely. Some of the witnesses we brought up from Mexico told us they had been leaned on by some strong-arm people who they say are connected to President Montoya. They were told not to cooperate or they and their families would disappear. And some of them did, unfortunately. We're not sure if they just ran, or were made to disappear.

"But, others decided to come clean under our *Freedom From Prosecution* offer. We couldn't have made our case without the assistance of the Mexican Judiciary. They're looking into President Montoya's role in all of this now. He's in a lot of trouble down there, and we will be cooperating with them to help with their case. Our witnesses from down there were little players in this whole mess, so we offered them immunity from prosecution both here and in Mexico for their testimony. We figured it would be worth it if we caught the big fish. And it looks like we did."

"I don't know, George. If you take this to a district judge and he decides to let you take it to trial, his battery of lawyers will have a go at your witnesses, and you know how brutal they can be in their cross examination."

"We have a surprise witness, Janice. One we didn't know existed until the CIA produced him."

"The CIA! What is Don Armstrong up to now? Are you sure this witness is legit?"

"Yes, Ma'am. I interviewed him at length personally before the grand jury heard him. What he told me, what he told them, put a lid on this case."

"And what was that, George?"

"Well, his name is Lawrence Madre. He works for the President as one of the five members of a group they call the Black Hawks. A CIA agent sat in on my interview. He had a complete dossier on this Madre person, and whenever I asked for proof, he supplied it. It was like he knew what questions I would ask, and he had the proof to back up the answers this guy gave me."

"Who was the agent, George?"

"A Robert Downing. Your Mr. Armstrong called before Downing arrived with the witness and assured me he knew as much about the guy as anyone else in the Company. For some reason, he knew I would be talking to you, and he said for you to call him on his secure number if you needed any verification. You have his secure telephone number?"

"Yes, he and I go back a long way. We both grew up in the service. I was a young lawyer, just recruited out of school and Don was an up-and-coming field agent. We worked a number of cases together, then he was assigned to a post in the Middle East and we got separated. After that, we corresponded occasionally, but absence doesn't make the heart grow fonder. He found someone else, and I did also. Probably good we did. We both are pretty strong willed, and probably would have divorced before we really got to know each other.

"But, that's another story. Now, tell me about this Lawrence Madre person."

"The CIA gave me his military record. Lots of experience in covert military operations. Sniper training, as well as explosives, sort of a hands-on type. He tells us he worked for the President, and had done so even before Hunt took his oath of office seven years ago. Downing confirmed that. The CIA has been monitoring this guy and his associates for almost the entire time they've been active."

"Associates? What associates?"

"There were five members of the team he worked with. Called them *The Black Hawks*."

"Five. Where are the others? Do Director Armstrong's people have them in custody?"

"No, Ma'am. Agent Downing confirmed that two of the team members were killed in Scotland recently. One of his operatives was there and saw their vehicle go over a cliff into the North Sea. This Madre person and another member of his team, kidnapped an agent's family several weeks ago out in Montana. The agent went after them and took this one captive. He left the other guy back in the mountains with a piece of steel sticking out of his chest."

"Good God, how gruesome! Is the agent's family safe?"

"His words, Ma'am, not mine. And, yes, they are alive and well, so Agent Downing says."

"Where are you keeping this guy, George?"

"A four-agent FBI team has him. They're a part of the Agency's Witness Protection Plan. I don't even know where he is. I suspect he's safe."

"Don't be so sure. Everybody who works in this town has a price, George. Not just the politicians and the lobbyist, but everyone, the aides and the bureaucrats and even the janitors and cab drivers. And that includes the security agencies, the CIA, the FBI, Homeland Security, DEA, Secret Service, everyone, including Justice. So, you find out where this guy is being kept and you personally check on him daily.

"What else did he tell you? Do you have anything concrete?"

"Yes, Janice. Do you remember when Senator Longstreet died in 2003?"

"Sure. They found him in his car somewhere in Virginia. He had a heart attack."

"Well, yes and no. He did have a heart attack, but it wasn't from natural causes. According to Madre, he and two other members of the Black Hawks, the two who were killed in Scotland, took down Senator Beauregard Longstreet when he was about to enter the front door of his home on the Potomac out in the Virginia countryside. They hid in the boxwoods that lined his sidewalk and used chloroform to subdue him. Quick and cheap.

"They gave him a hot cocktail in the vein behind his left knee while he was out, a lethal dose of potassium chloride. It didn't take much, and it stopped his heart almost instantly. They reasoned that if they gave him the injection behind his knee, it wouldn't be discovered, and they were right. Madre told me he had used that injection spot several times before while working for the President."

"So he actually admitted to other murders sanctioned by Hunt?"

"Yes, but he didn't say how many. They dumped the Senator in his car and one of the other team members drove him down into Caroline County, Virginia on I-95, while the other two followed. They cut over to U.S. 1 south of Fredericksburg, and he drove the Senator's car into a turn-off just north of the North Anna River Bridge, and wedged it against the guardrail so it wouldn't move. They had to keep the car in gear and the engine running to support their cover that he probably felt sick, decided to stop, and died before he could stop the car and turn off the ignition.

"The car, still in gear and the engine running, was supposed to look as if it drifted forward until it wedged against the guardrail. He says they put him behind the wheel around four in the morning, knowing no one would be on U.S. 1 at that time of night and he wouldn't be discovered until the next morning. All the tourist traffic uses I-95 in that area so U.S. 1 is deserted at night.

"They had killed him around midnight and needed at least five to seven hours after death for the body's cells to break down enough to produce sufficient potassium to mask the potassium chloride cocktail they had given him.

"The Senator's body was discovered by a long haul driver who pulled off to catch a little sleep around dawn, and noticed the car's engine was still running. The truck driver called 911 when he saw the Senator slumped over the steering wheel, and the Bowling Green Rescue Squad responded. They took the body to Mary Washington Hospital in Fredericksburg. The CIA had a copy of the medical examiner's report indicating he died of natural causes, a heart attack. No evidence of foul play, just a simple heart attack. Now that's just about a perfect murder, Janice."

"Why Senator Longstreet? He was over eighty and about to retire anyway."

"According to Madre, President Hunt wanted him out of the way, and he wanted it done fast. He was the senior Senator from Mississippi, and a very powerful and outspoken Republican who chaired the Senate Appropriations Committee. Seems Longstreet was holding up a good number of the President's legislative initiatives by not letting them be reported out of his committee. With Longstreet out of the way, the new chairman wasn't powerful enough to stop the President's legislative agenda from moving through the approval process. Hunt knew who would be appointed to succeed Longstreet and he knew he could control him.

"So, you may want to ask the Virginia Commonwealth's Attorney to have the Senator's body exhumed to see if there is any residual evidence of the potassium chloride remaining. It's been almost seven years, so the chances of that are nil. But, with Madre's confession, we can give the Senator's family closure and nail the President on this charge through a different jurisdiction."

"You have anything else?"

"Yes. This guy was screaming for immunity from persecution if he told his story to the Grand Jury. I agreed to that, at least from a Federal perspective. But, if Virginia gets involved in the Longstreet murder, there would be no freedom from prosecution from any state action by the Commonwealth. They can nail his ass along with the President where we can't."

"Good thinking, George. You have anything else?"

"Yep, Madre told the Grand Jury that he and the mutt who died out in Montana also arranged the death of your predecessor."

"William Greystone? No way. He committed suicide. The FBI even found some photographs of Bill and a young prostitute he was seeing. The word was that someone had taken the photographs without his knowing it and was blackmailing the Attorney General. His friends surmised that he just couldn't stand the public humiliation if word of his affair got out."

"Yes, the CIA gave me copies of all the press releases of his death and his affair, plus copies of the photographs. The press really had a field day with that one. But, it was all a lie, a fabricated story to justify the suicide. According to our witness, the photographs were fake. Someone on the President's payroll doctored the photographs to make them look like the Attorney General was in the arms of the woman. It was a matter of superimposing one photograph over another. It's amazing what you can create with all the computer software available on the market today.

"Our witness admitted to using chloroform to subdue Mr. Greystone, as they did with the Senator, but instead of using potassium chloride to induce death, they garroted him. They took him down to the basement of his house through the outside entrance and strung him up from a floor joist while his wife slept upstairs. They also turned over a chair next to where he was hanged so it would look like he had gotten on the chair, then kicked it over to hang himself. Since the rope was fitted around his neck, over the ligature marks left by the wire they used to strangle him, there was no evidence that foul play was involved. And with all the fabricated evidence indicating an extramarital relationship, the autopsy the medical examiner at Bethesda Naval Hospital performed was just routine. With no evidence of foul play, he was put to rest with no real investigation.

"Hell, it was two days before they found him. His wife thought he was probably on a trip or something. The maid found him when she took soiled clothes down to put them in the washing machine. I think Greystone's wife may have a little dementia."

"Why Bill Greystone? He was a good guy, loyal to the party, and to the President. He wasn't a threat to Hunt. He appointed him to the position of Attorney General. I don't understand the rationale."

"Our witness doesn't know either. He says the *Black Hawks* knew not to ask questions. They got their orders directly from the President. What he told them to do, they did. They were paid a lot of money to take care of Hunt's problems and not to question his motives. So, that's what they did. He told them that if any of the team members were caught and convicted of a crime, he would give them a Presidential pardon. In effect, they felt they were conviction proof, or if convicted, wouldn't do any jail time.

"Anyway, the Greystones lived in Chevy Chase, Maryland, so you can involve their Attorney General, just like Virginia, if you want another party in this."

"God, George, this is beyond reason. You've got a hell of a case built around this one witness. I still think some of your other evidence is a little shaky, and a jury just may let him walk if that was all you had. Remember, reasonable doubt has put a lot of criminals back on the street. So, keep this guy safe. He'll blow the roof off the White House before you're finished with him if he lives long enough to testify in court."

"I agree, Janice. Since these proceedings weren't open to the public, I know the press is camped out at the federal building, but I still have the jurors sequestered. I wanted to discuss this with you before I let the press get hold of these folks. They'll be released from their responsibilities around 10:00 this morning, and the press will be all over them as soon as they walk out the door. Although they aren't supposed to talk about the verdict, we both know they will. Since they've already reached a verdict, whatever any of the jurors say to the press can't unduly influence the proceedings. We're beyond that now."

"George, you have one major concern now. If the members of the Grand Jury begin talking, you know they're going to name your star witness, especially since your evidence against the President is mostly tied to him. What happens to your case if he goes missing? You know he could have second thoughts and try to escape. Or, the agents could be bought off. That's happened before, and in your case, it would spell disaster. We've got to put Hunt away, and you can't do that if your star witness flies the coop."

"How well I know. But, this is too far reaching to just take to the Federal District Court, Janice. I wanted you to know that I plan to take these findings to Congress and ask them to convene the House Committee of the Judiciary to begin impeachment hearings. The committee needs to hear our evidence and determine if they feel the President should be impeached or not. But, I wanted you to go through this testimony as *a friend of the court* to tell me if I've missed anything. I know your staff has kept you in the loop on what has been revealed during these proceedings; so, going through this shouldn't be an arduous task."

"I agree with your decision, George. I'll get you an appointment with the Speaker of the House this afternoon. I know Herman well. In fact, I'll join you if he balks at the idea of a meeting. You may need what influence I can lend to get him to agree to this. I'll also contact Doug Chapman, Chairman of the House Judiciary Committee, and ask him to join you."

CHAPTER TWENTY-THREE

F RED PENDLETON, THE President's Chief of Staff and persona friend since childhood, answered the President's summons immediately. He had been at his desk looking over the briefing from the Secretary of State when the red light began to flash.

"I'll be with the President," he told his secretary as he left his office and walked the few yards down the back hall to the Oval Office.

"Good morning, Mr. President. You called?"

"Yes, Fred. Since my quarters over in Georgetown have been compromised, I need a favor. There's a lady friend of mine who lives over in the university area of Georgetown whom I would like to see tonight. I want you to arrange for her to drive over and not be detained at the gate. Clear her through the front gate on Pennsylvania, but have one of the guards take the golf cart and lead her around to the side entrance to my living quarters. I'll have her arrive around eight for dinner. The press should be gone by then. Tell the Secret Service guards at the entrance to my personal quarters to let her park there and to let her through without questions. Get her a pass to identify her. The name I know her by is Patricia Simpson. I doubt it's genuine, but what the hell, as long as she does what I tell her to do, she can be anyone she wants to be."

"Sir, has she been vetted?"

"No, I'm not in the habit of asking the Secret Service to check out my whores, Fred.

"And Fred, you be sure everyone she comes in contact with knows she is not to be questioned. Use this picture on her ID. She will be my personal guest for the night, but she will leave before morning.

"I want you to personally deliver her identification badge to her, Fred."

"Mr. President, my job is to run the White House, not be your errand boy. I'll have one of my staff deliver it to her."

"Fred, I don't usually ask you to step outside your assigned duties here, but I'm asking now. No, I'm telling you to do so this time. I want to keep my personal life personal. If someone else delivers the ID, it will be all over the White House before the day is out that I'm seeing someone. And someone will dig a little deeper and find out she's a call girl. I don't mind you knowing that, because you already do, but I don't want it on the front page of the *Washington Post*, so you have to do this for me.

"I'll call her and she'll be expecting you. And I don't want another lesson on morality from you this morning. I may be the President, but I'm still a man with normal sexual needs. And it's not as if Rebecca is still with us. She's been deceased for a long time now, and I'm moving on, as they say. And, its not as if this is going to be picked up by the press. Those bastards have too much to do smearing my good name to be interested in anything as mundane as sex for money. Hell, that's what keeps this damned town going anyway. So, Fred, just keep your mouth shut and do as you're told. You need to get out more anyway."

"A little testy today, aren't we, Mr. President?"

"I'm sorry, Fred. This damned Grand Jury thing is getting me down. I can't find out a damned thing about what they're doing. I know the Attorney General is in the loop. Hell, that special prosecutor, George whatever his name is, is working out of Justice, so she has to know, but when I ask her how it's going, she avoids the questions and changes the subject.

"Damn it, that business about my accounts in the Cayman, how did that reporter get that information? Now they have the accounts frozen so I can't get to the money. I'm not sure denying the money is mine was the right thing to do. But that's what the lawyers told me to say, and I pay them enough so they had better be right. I should have taken the fifth, and let them try to figure it out themselves. If they are ever able to trace those accounts to me, I'm screwed. Lying to a Grand Jury under oath is an impeachable offense. But my name isn't on any of those accounts so they can't absolutely prove they're mine, so I'm covered there. But, God damn it, I can't get my hands on that money now.

"Get out of here, Fred. Go back to your office and get the presses rolling on that ID for Patricia. I'm going to call her in a few minutes and what we talk about is none of your damned business. Let me know when her ID is ready. I'll tell you then how to contact her. So, take off."

"Yes, Mr. President."

*   *   *

Apartment 301, Fairgate
209 Hamilton Boulevard
Georgetown, District of Columbia
Sunday, October 7 – 11:45am

Fred Pendleton didn't like being relegated to delivering messages for anyone, even his long time friend, John Hunt. He had worked hard making a career for himself, and being named White House Chief of Staff by Hunt in the weeks preceding Hunt's inauguration over six years ago was his crowning achievement. His position of access and the fact that he knew where the bodies were buried in Washington, so to speak, put him at the top of just about every short list for executive positions where political influence was one of the unspoken questions on the resumes.

And here he was, personally delivering an identification badge to a prostitute so she could gain access to the White House and screw the President. *I'm too damned busy to be doing this kind of crap,* he thought as he walked up the wide tiled steps leading to the enclosed foyer of the old brownstone. As he was about to open the outer door, it was opened for him from within. "May I be of service, Sir?"

"Yes, thank you. I have an appointment with Miss Patricia Simpson, please," he said, somewhat condescendingly, to the uniformed doorman.

"Very good, Sir. May I tell Mrs. Simpson who is calling? You may have a seat if you wish. It should only be a moment."

"Thank you, I'll stand. My name is Fred Pendleton. Did you say Mrs. Simpson?"

"I did, Sir." The doorman picked up the house phone and dialed the number of the Simpson apartment.

"Very good, Madam." The doorman replaced the phone's receiver and turned back to Pendleton.

"Sir, you may go up. Mrs. Simpson will see you." The doorman turned towards the single elevator. "Charles, please take Mr. Pendleton to Mrs. Simpson's floor."

"Yes, Sir." Fred stepped into the elevator and was whisked up to the third floor of the Georgetown Fairgate Apartments. Charles stepped out of the elevator with Fred Pendleton and pointed down the hall to the left. "Mrs. Simpson's apartment is at the end of the hall there. There are no apartment numbers but the main entrance is the door you can see directly ahead of you, the one with the gold door frame."

Damn nice digs for a prostitute. I wonder how much John is paying to keep this whore in such a grand style, he thought, as he approached the very large and ornately carved walnut door. He raised the knocker, designed as a gilded cherub, and let it fall softly.

He waited for what seemed an eternity, and was ready to leave when the door opened slightly.

"Are you Fred Pendleton?" the voice asked.

"Yes."

"Please come in, Mr. Pendleton." The door was opened by a beautiful young lady who appeared to be in her early twenties. She was dressed in a stylish dress, which accentuated her slim but well proportioned body. And, she was cradling a child in her arms.

"I'm sorry. I must have the wrong apartment. I was looking for a Patricia Simpson."

"I am Patricia Simpson, Mr. Pendleton. I believe you have something for me. But, please come in. You're embarrassing yourself and me, standing out here in the hall."

"I'm sorry. The doorman referred to you as Mrs. Simpson. I didn't know you were married. And you have a child."

"Guilty on both counts, Mr. Pendleton. Unfortunately, I lost my husband in Afghanistan two years ago. He was a Marine on his first tour of duty when his Humvee ran over an IUD. He and two of his men were killed. He never had the chance to get to know his daughter."

"I can tell from your expression that you're having a hard time rationalizing my decision to *get in the life*, so to speak. Well, it wasn't a decision I made lightly, Sir. The death benefits paid to a second lieutenant's widow leave much to be desired, and we were still paying off student loans when his National Guard unit was called up to active duty. And on top of that, I was three months pregnant when he shipped out. Christy was born while he was in Afghanistan, and he was killed before he could get home to see her." She looked down at the child, smiling and tickling her tiny chin. The child smiled back at her.

"I'm sorry, Mrs. Simpson. I didn't know."

"How could you have known, Mr. Pendleton?" The President doesn't even know I was married or, for that matter, that I have a child. So, although I have a nursing degree, I needed a job that paid much more than what a nurse makes to pay off our obligations and continue to raise my daughter the way I wanted to.

"As a wife I had plenty of experience in pleasing my husband, sexually that is, and I decided to put that knowledge to good use. I am relatively intelligent, and with a finishing school background, I can pretty much hold my own in just about every level of social intercourse in Washington, so why not? After all, I can spend my days with my daughter, and hire a baby sitter to do so when I'm on call, so to speak. The hours are great, I choose with whom I am going to have sex, and the money is many times more than I could make sticking thermometers into sick peoples' mouths. It really doesn't take a mental giant to figure that out. So, here I am, the President's girl friend. How many women can say that?"

Patricia stood, continuing to cradle the child in her arms. "You'll have to excuse me a minute, Mr. Pendleton. Christy seems to have had an accident. I'll only be a moment."

She walked out of the living room and down the hall to one of the bedrooms. As soon as she had left the room, Frank Pendleton walked over to the antique roll-top desk standing in a corner. The top was open and on the writing surface stood a single picture of a young man in a Marine Uniform. Fred noticed the single gold bars on his shoulder boards. His nametag read *Simpson*. *That checks*, he said to himself.

He was about to open one of several letters held together by a red ribbon he found in a pigeonhole in the desk, when he heard her returning. Instead, he stuffed it in the breast pocket of his jacket and picked up the picture.

"My husband," she said. "He had just completed OCS and received his second lieutenant's gold bars. Were you in the service, Mr. Pendleton?"

"No, Ma'am, I wasn't. If I may be so bold, Mrs. Simpson, where do you see this affair with the President going? You have been accompanying John around town socially ever since his wife passed away. This may sound cruel, Mrs. Simpson, and I don't mean this to be degrading in any way, but you are a prostitute, and you know nothing can really come of this affair."

"I understand your concern, Mr. Pendleton. One of your duties is to keep the President's reputation safe, and our affair is making your job much more difficult. I know nothing will come of this, but you must understand that we are very fond of each other. He has even mentioned the possibility of marriage after he leaves office, but I suspect that will be a topic that will require considerable conversation, and thought, before any decision is made. In the meantime, I will try to measure up to your expectations of me, Mr. Pendleton."

"Thank you, Mrs. Simpson. I really must run. And thank you for your hospitality and your frankness. You are a brave young lady, and I must admit, I had misjudged you terribly. I sincerely apologize, and I wish you much success and happyness."

"Thank you, Mr. Pendleton. I can assure you I will be successful. You can count on that," she said with a smile, as she opened the door for him, cradling the child in one arm.

*   *   *

Office of Attorney General Janice Hawkins
Department of Justice
Robert F. Kennedy Building
Washington, DC
Tuesday, October 2 – 8:30am

"How did your meeting with the Speaker of the House go this morning, George?"

"Very well, Janice. I had not met Congressman Parsons until our meeting. He seems to be a very learned individual, and quite the gentleman. I was a little nervous about broaching this problem about the President with him, but he was quick to put me at ease. I really like him."

"He's quite the politician, George, and quite the gentleman, as well. And very intelligent, I might add. That's why he's the Speaker of the House. He wields a lot of power over there on the hill. What was his reaction to your news?"

"Shock. At least that was his first reaction. But he quickly regained his composure. As you suggested, Congressman Chapman was also there, so I had the opportunity to speak with both the Speaker and the Chairman of the House Judiciary Committee."

"And?"

"And they agreed with the Grand Jury's findings. At least I think they did. They really didn't say as much, but they seemed to be interested from the questions they asked. We met for about four hours, and I think I accurately answered all of their questions. I gave both of them the list of charges against the President and the volumes of witness testimony supporting the charges. And I indicated that we had planned to take the charges to the Circuit Court, but told them you had suggested I meet with them first, since you felt the charges warranted their review, should they wish to take them to the House to consider impeachment.

"The Speaker indicated he and the Chairman would review the material, and if they felt the charges could be prosecuted successfully, the Chairman would call the Judiciary Committee together to discuss the allegations. I understand they will call some of the witnesses the grand jury heard, and if the full committee is convinced the charges are legitimate, they will draw up the impeachment proceedings and refer the case to the full House.

"I also understand that even if only one of the three articles of impeachment recommended by the Grand Jury is approved by the full House of Representatives, the President is impeached."

"That's true, George. But it's up to the Senate to conduct the formal trial to remove him from office, or declare him innocent of the charges brought against him. Unfortunately, a super majority of the Senate has to vote against the President for him to be removed from office, and that's where politics usually raises its ugly head."

* * *

CIA Headquarters
Langley, Virginia
Sunday, October 7 – 10:30am

Bill Elmore picked up his phone on the first ring. "Sir, my name is Sarah Jacobson. You know me by my street name, Patricia. The President just called me. He wants me to come to the White House tonight. He wants me there at eight for dinner. That's a first, Sir. We usually rendezvous over here in Georgetown.

"And, he's sending his Chief of Staff over here this afternoon to personally deliver an ID for me to use to get through the front gate. Something's wrong, Sir. Why isn't he using his quarters over here?"

"It's a long story Miss Jacobson, or should I call you by your street name, Patricia? To answer your question, one of his men suspected the compound was under surveillance, and he abandoned its use as a rendezvous point. Then the stories of his sleeping around, the child he fathered in France several years ago, and his money laundering activities began to break and the FBI raided the compound. We don't know how they learned about the Georgetown property, but they did."

Bill knew exactly what he was going to tell Sarah Jacobson. She had no need to know any of the details, or the truth, for that matter. She had willingly accepted employment with the Stepford Escort Service when approached by one of their recruiters, and as one of their higher priced prostitutes, she had been the source of some excellent information, valuable to the CIA in their quest to bring down the President. And, she had been paid well for both her services and her information, considerably more than she could make as a young Washington based lawyer.

The work was rewarding as long as the players retained their looks and their charms, but careers in the *life* were short lived, and retirement benefits were non-existent unless the girls set up their own Individual Retirement Accounts. Sarah Jacobson knew this, and was ready to walk away and pick up where she had left off in her pursuit of the law.

"Patricia, the compound was empty when the FBI arrived, but they found a hidden office from which his money laundering activities were coordinated. So, he can't go back there any more for fear of being linked to these criminal activities. We assume that's why he wants you to meet him in the residence at the White House.

"I suspect your duties as a high priced call girl named Patricia are coming to a close, my dear. That is, unless you enjoy the work and want to continue your employment with the Stepford Escort Service. I understand you got rave reviews. We could certainly use you, if you're interested.

"We're going to keep the escort service up and running, Patricia. We have too many politicians from both parties as regular clients to close it down. It's one of the best sources of information we have on what's going on behind the political scenes on Capital Hill, and up to now, in the White House."

"Thanks, but no thanks, Bill. I really want to get back to my law studies, full time. The next semester enrollment will begin soon, and I want to finish up, get my law degree and then come to work for the Company full time as an agent, not just a well-paid informant and one of your ladies of the night. You guys need some female direction over there at Langley."

"Well, you're always welcome, Patricia. Stay on the line a minute and let me buzz the section chief. You have one more assignment before we say good-by, and he needs to be the one to talk with you about it."

Rob Downing picked up his phone and listened. "The young woman we know as Patricia is on the line, Sir. She says the President just called to tell her to come to the White House and meet him in the residence tonight around eight. She says he's sending his Chief of Staff in person over to her apartment to deliver a photo ID this afternoon that will get her into the grounds through the Pennsylvania Avenue main gates. It's time, Rob. I think she's ready to do this."

"Transfer her call up here, Bill. But have someone check out the security cameras in front of her apartment building, and in the vestibule. Also check the cameras you have inside her apartment. I want to have some evidence that he was there today visiting her. It would be good if we could get some footage of him talking with her inside her apartment."

"I'll see to it immediately, Sir."

"Oh, get this woman a car. Something simple we can dispose of without arousing suspicions. Check with the garage and pick out one that the Secret Service or the FBI can trace back to her when they find it. Be sure it's a GM and is equipped with *On Star*. I'm going to have her rendezvous with the pilots at Andrews, but I want one of your men to drive her car out into the marshes near the Susquehanna Flats north of Baltimore and leave it beside the road. Just be sure it's in a desolate area, preferably on a dirt road with little to no traffic. There are a good number of duck hunting shacks out that way, so finding a place shouldn't be difficult and someone will report it soon enough. Register the car in her name, and backdate the registration to a date close to when she arrived in DC. And, be sure there is plenty of trace evidence the Bureau's forensic people can link to her. Strands of this woman's hair are great DNA code identifiers they can match up quickly."

"Is her DNA in the system anywhere?"

"Yes. When she entered American University she had to give them a blood sample for her entrance physical. They always do a DNA identification for future reference, if needed. It remains on record just about forever. Also, be sure there's something in the car that links her to the university so they can follow that lead."

"One more thing, Bill. I want you to get a message to Caldwell. Tell him I want him on a flight to Rio de Janeiro no later than tomorrow. Send it coded."

"Got it covered, Sir."

"Good, now put her on."

*   *   *

"Hello, Patricia. Or, can I use your real name now?"

"Whatever turns you on, Sir. Bill says you have another job for me. If it's more money, I'm up for it. I'm a little short right now."

"It's quite a bit more money, Sarah. That is, if you pull this off. Twenty thousand dollars to be exact, and it's untraceable. Ten on the front end and the balance when you finish. And a nice long vacation in Rio. You'll love Brazil. That's the bonus that goes with it. This is when all that training we've given you at the medical clinic pays off."

"You mean how to use a hypodermic? I can do that in my sleep, Sir."

"Good, because you're going to give the President of the United States a little tonic tonight. It's no big deal. You'll knock him out first with a little Zolpidem in the cup of coffee he always has after dinner. Get him into bed as soon after he drinks his coffee as possible. The Zolpidem will hit him all at once. When he passes out, apply a tourniquet to his arm above the elbow and then inject all of the liquid from one of the syringes into a vein below the tourniquet. You've been practicing this for a long time now, so it should be a piece of cake, Sarah. Shouldn't take you more than a couple of minutes, then you're out of there and on your way to a new life."

"What will I be injecting?

"Does it matter, Sarah? We've talked about this a number of times and it's never concerned you before."

"No, it really doesn't. I was just curious, Sir. I'm in this for the money, and you guys have already done what you said you would do. So, I'll do it. I'm ready to get away from this life anyway, and get back to my studies. How are you going to set this up?"

"It's going to be easy, Sarah. I'll walk you through it.

"First, the guards at the Pennsylvania Avenue Main Gates are DC cops, and they'll have been told to let you through when you show them your picture ID without asking any questions. They're old hands at this game. Kennedy and Clinton had so many women coming and going through those gates that the guards couldn't keep up with them. Plus, the boys in blue sell us information on a regular basis, so we pretty much know who has been asked to visit the White House, and whom they are visiting. We'll call them just to be sure you aren't stopped and searched.

"The cops will let you through without asking you any questions, but you'll have to sign in. It's very important that you use your street name, and not your real name. By the way, does the President know your real identity?

"No, Sir. If he does, he's never used it in my presence. And, unless he had some way of finding out, the only name he knows is my street name, Patricia Simpson."

"Good. No one needs to know your real name, especially now.

"As usual, Bill Elmore will be your contact. He'll give you the keys to a car we want you to drive to the White House. When you are ready to leave, it will be parked outside your apartment. I don't know anything about the car, but Bill will give you a description when he sees you after the President's man leaves.

"Also, Bill will give you two syringes filled with a clear liquid, and a small vial of the Zolpidem. You can easily break the top off the vial and pour the liquid into his coffee cup. When you have him sedated, use only one of the syringes. The other is a back up in case something happen to the first. Bill will tape them to the small of your back because the agents guarding the residence will search your handbag, even if the President tells them not to. It's standard operating procedure, and although they guard the President, they don't answer to him. They have their instructions and know their routines, so go along with whatever they say. Get rid of the needles and the balance of the liquid in the extra syringe and the vial before you leave. Each of the syringes contains

5ccs of the liquid. It is very important that you inject all of the liquid from one of the syringes into his arm. But remember to use only one syringe."

"How am I supposed to get rid of the syringes and the vial?"

"Flush the vial, but tape the syringes to your body under your arms.

Remove the needles and flush them down the toilet also. Be sure they don't remain in the bowl. That's critical.

"What you're going to inject into his arm will keep him out for an hour or so. He'll go into a very deep sleep, hardly breathing. He'll be fine in the morning, but he won't remember your being there. The drug erases short-term memory."

Rob Downing was lying very convincingly, and Sarah seemed to have no idea what she was being asked to do. Had she known the truth, it would have stopped Sarah Jacobson cold, Rob reasoned. She was a law student first, a prostitute second, but certainly not a killer. At least that was the opinion shared by those in the CIA who had any knowledge of Sarah Jacobson. What they didn't know was that Sarah had her own agenda.

The 5ccs of potassium chloride injected into a vein of a 185-pound man will induce cardiac arrest as soon as the liquid reaches the person's heart. Cerebral hypoxia results, causing a loss of consciousness and loss of normal breathing. The person is dead within less than a minute. President John Hunt fit the ratio profile with pounds to spare. He weighed in at 178 pounds, nude. Sarah was quite knowledgeable of the effects potassium chloride had on the human body if administered in a lethal dose.

"And, there's a second task you must accomplish before you leave his quarters. Again, it can be done quickly and with little effort, but the President will be asleep and he will have left orders that the two of you must not be disturbed, so you don't have to worry about anyone coming in on you. Bill will give you three very small electronic devices that will also be taped to the small of your back in a small plastic bag. They won't trigger any alarms in the White House because you will have to activate each before they can be detected. Bill will show you how.

"The boys outside the President's residence won't do an electronic body scan when you arrive, so you don't have to worry about anyone finding the devices on you.

"One is a small, very thin disc. You must insert the disc in the receiver of the phone on the bedside table. Unscrew the part he speaks into, place it inside, and screw the top back on.

"The second device is about an inch long and cylindrical. Place it inside the seam of one of the curtains on the front windows of the sitting room next to the President's bedroom. The curtain is made of a blend of wool and rayon with a loose weave, so getting it into the seam should be easy.

"The third you must place under the side table. It has a paper backing with a material that will allow you to stick it securely to the underside of the table. Then you're done, and on your way to a new life."

*   *   *

Pennsylvania Avenue
Washington, DC
Sunday, October 7 –7:35pm

Sarah was nervous as she drove the car the CIA had left for her down Wisconsin, turned left on M Street for three blocks, and merged onto Pennsylvania Avenue towards Washington Circle. She turned left onto H Street and drove past Lafayette Square, glancing to the right across the square at the White House and its expansive grounds lighted with floodlights strategically placed around the perimeter, and on the grounds hidden in the shrubbery and positioned to bathe the stately building in a flood of white light.

Sarah exited H onto East Executive Avenue NW and drove past the U.S. Treasury. She couldn't see the heavily armed guards stationed on the White House roof and around its perimeter, but she knew they were watching her through their night vision equipment and photographing the vehicle, probably verifying the license plate numbers.

The President had never invited her to the White House, even after his wife had passed, and she had never taken the tour. She could feel the syringes taped in the small of her back as she sat in her car rehearsing the moves she would have to make once in the President's quarters. A trickle of perspiration was making its way down her back.

This was all new to her. She had met the President over a year ago at a social gathering when she had first joined the Stepford Escort Service staff, but all of their rendezvous had been in Georgetown at his private compound. It was always dark, minimum lighting only, and there was never anyone around when she would arrive, at least no one she had seen. But she knew the Secret Service agents were there, somewhere, but never obvious to anyone who might be strolling by the compound.

Here, everything was brightly lighted, and she knew she was being watched. Even as she approached the White House grounds her car had been picked up by the armed spotters on the roof, and her progress, along with other vehicles in the traffic pattern, was followed until they passed the grounds.

Sarah pulled the car to the curb just before reaching the State Place NW entrance, and sat there thinking. She was parked in a *No Parking* zone, and no one parked in the streets surrounding the White House grounds for very long before being checked out in person. She was sure her vehicle information had already been called in and a DC patrol cop was probably on the way. *Maybe I should just forget this rendezvous, call Bill and tell him I'm not going through with their plan. Then go back to my apartment and forget the whole thing. What can the CIA do anyway?*

The license plate of the car Sarah was driving had already been recorded and a quick identity search of District of Columbia Registrations was being processed as she sat in the car beside East

Executive Avenue. The Secret Service would know to whom the vehicle was registered before she would put the car in gear and drive away from the curb. At least, they would know what the CIA wanted them to know, and nothing else.

Twenty grand is twenty grand, She thought while sitting there, the engine still running. *That's a hell of a lot of money for a couple of hours with a man who isn't that bad a lover anyway. Then it's off to South America, Rio de Janeiro, the carnivals, the beaches of Copacabana and Ipenema, the impressive statue of Christ the Redeemer atop Corcovado Mountain, and the lush tropical jungles. I can get lost there, get away from this awful life, be renewed and then get back to my career.*

There's no way I can turn all of this down. I would never be able to afford a trip like this. I'm going to do this, damn it. Hell, no one is going to get hurt, at least no one for whom I give a shit.

Sarah Jacobson had just made a decision that would have a marked influence on the rest of her life. She started the engine and put the car in gear, checked the rearview mirror and continued down East Executive, her right turn signal blinking as she approached her destination. She turned into the main gates of the White House and stopped at the barricade. Two men in uniform were standing inside the gatehouse staring at her. But, they both were smiling.

"She's here," one of the guards whispered to his companion.

"And she's a looker," commented the other. "A hell of a lot prettier than some of the trash Clinton used to haul in here."

"Did you say *hooker*?"

"No, but that's a pretty fair description, don't you think." said the other with a chuckle. "It's my turn to guide her around to the private entrance, so you sit tight."

"Well, be nice. Remember, she's the old man's private squeeze. Don't get mouthy. We both need to keep our jobs."

*   *   *

Gates Learjet 35-A
N-4421Whisky
32,000 Feet above the South Atlantic

"It's for you, Miss!'

"Who knows I'm here, Captain?"

"It's the Director."

"Oh. Well, he sure knows I'm here. Thanks. Hello Director Armstrong. How's every little thing out in Langley this early in the morning?"

"I see you're still awake. No news, yet, Miss Jacobson. How is your flight?"

"Wonderful. I've never flown in a private airplane before. I thought there would be more room in this Lear. But, there's not a cloud in the sky. It's like I can reach out and touch the stars. There are millions! I used to lay out in the wheat stubble on warm summer nights and try to count the stars when I was younger. We lived in Kansas, out in the country, away from the bright lights of Lawrence, and the stars were just like they are here. And the full moon, it's been beautiful, shining down on the ocean. It's will be going down in the west as dawn approaches, but right now it's like a river of gold is pouring out of it into the ocean, stretching from one horizon to the other."

"I'm glad you're enjoying the flight. Sorry there's no one to talk to. And it's lie, not lay. Chickens lay, people lie."

"Whatever. And what do you mean no one to talk to? I'm up here in the first officer's seat beside the pilot, and he's a great conversationalist. The first officer is catching a few zees in the back."

The pilot jerked his head around to look at Sarah. "Jesus, Lady, you shouldn't have told him that. You aren't supposed to be up here."

"Don't fret, Captain. He won't mind. He's a sweet old guy."

"Have you reached Puerto Rico yet, Sarah?"

"I don't know. Have we reached Puerto Rico yet, Captain?"

"No, we're about seventy miles out. See that dark area at our twelve o'clock lying on the horizon? That's Puerto Rico. That's the Dominican Republic over there on the right at about one o'clock. We're going to land in San Juan and refuel."

"The Captain says we have to land in San Juan to refuel."

"Yes, I know. So, tell me all about your visit to the White House. I assume you were successful."

"It went like clockwork, Sir. There's no other way to describe it. Everything happened just like you said it would. No problem getting through the front gate. One of the cops got in a golf cart and I followed him in my car around to the private family entrance near the stairway up to the residence. The Secret Service let me park right there.

"And getting into the residence was just as easy. I just walked up the stairs to the two guys standing outside the door and told them I was expected. They were very polite, looked at my identification badge, then at their roster as though there were other guests expected. I had to laugh since I saw the roster and no other names were on it but my street name. And someone had written across the sheet in red ink, *Do not disturb until POTUS awakens*. They searched my purse just like you said they would, but otherwise nothing.

"One of the agents knocked on the door and announced me, told the President his lady friend was here, then opened the door and closed it behind me. And there I was, in the President's house, so to speak. I used to think his Georgetown estate was really nice, but that place, Wow, now that's first class. I thought about stealing a few mementos, but as sure as I did, I would get caught.

"By the way, what is a *POTUS?*"

"An acronym for President of the United Status. Now, please continue, Sarah."

"Well, the old fart was in his pajamas and a robe when I got there. And, he already had an erection! He wanted to get it on as soon as I got in the door. And all that food set out just for the two of us. He took my clothes off before we even got to the bedroom. I have to admit, for a man of his age, he has a hell of a lot of stamina. I didn't think we would ever stop. He just kept going and going until he finally fell over from exhaustion. I just lay there and pretended I was having fun.

"We were supposed to have dinner, but his libido got in the way, so I poured him a cup of coffee and laced it with the Zolpidem when he wasn't looking. He took a couple of sips and went right to sleep, just passed out. So I applied the tourniquet to his right arm, just above the elbow to restrict the flow of unoxyginated blood back to the heart. His veins popped up just as I knew they would. I found one that I felt wouldn't roll, inserted the needle, released the tourniquet, and gave him the injection as you said I should, one 5cc syringe full in his right arm.

"As you instructed, I poured the other down the drain and got rid of the two needles, bagged the syringes and taped them under my arms, wiped the place down so my fingerprints wouldn't be there, and got the hell out. Oh, I planted your little bugs just like you asked me to."

"When you signed in at the gate, did you keep the pen the guards gave you to use?"

"No, I told them I wanted it for a souvenir, but they told me it was the only one they had. So I accidentally dropped it in the floorboard and when I reached down to get it, I wiped it clean and gave it back to them, holding it by its clip. No prints."

"Excellent! You noticed how large the pen was and that the guards were wearing gloves, didn't you?"

"Yes."

"That's because they always take the prints off the pens used by visitors who are not White House employees or people they can readily identify. The larger the pen's surface, the more fingerprint match points they can recover. That's their little way of verifying the identity of unknown visitors. They'll certainly be surprised when your prints aren't on the pen they gave you to use.

"So, continue, please, Sarah."

"Well, when I left, I closed the door to the bedroom and walked back through the living room and exited the President's quarters. As you suggested, I leaned back against the door, looked at the Secret Service agents, smiled, rolled my eyes and said; '*That boss of yours is one hell of a lover. I've never seen that much stamina in a man half his age. But, I flat ass wore him out. He's going to sleep til noon tomorrow.*'

I gave one of the agents the note your people worked up in the President's handwriting that instructs them not to let anyone in before six. Then I boogied.

"I thought sure I would get some wise ass comment like, '*You should try me, Sister. I think I can teach you a trick or two*'. But, they just stood there and smiled, very polite. So, I opened the door a crack, peeked in and said: '*Bye lover, see you real soon.*' Then I closed the door, put my finger to my lips to indicate they should be quiet, and just walked down the steps and out the door.

"I drove out the side entrance and picked up Constitution going east. Your chase cars picked me up on Constitution before I got to the Capitol, and one of them took the lead and led me down Second past the Supreme Court Building and the Library of Congress to Pennsylvania past Seward Square and across the Sousa Bridge and out to Andrews."

"I did have one complication, though. The President was already out when the phone on the bedside table rang. Well, it didn't really ring, but a red light began to flash, so I picked it up and answered. It was his Chief of Staff, a Fred somebody, the guy who brought me my ID. I told him that Hunt was in the shower and I would tell the President he had called."

"Speaking of Fred Pendleton, tell me how you came up with the story of being the widow of a Marine who was killed in Afghanistan? And, whose child were you cradling when he delivered your White House ID badge?"

"Now, that was a stroke of genus, Sir? The child was my neighbor's little girl. Her name is Christy. I convinced her to take the afternoon off to do some shopping and I would baby-sit for her. She jumped at the idea of being able to get out without having to take her daughter with her, so it worked out great. I suspect you picked up all of Mr. Pendleton's and my conversations on your little recording devices."

"That we did. When you got through with him, I thought he was going to get on his knees and propose to you. By the way, what was with the picture of the Marine and the letters from your fictitious husband?"

"Well, the photograph is of my brother. And yes, he is a Marine, but he's alive and well, stationed at Quantico at the moment. And the letters, well, it took me two days to write eight letters to myself. The Internet is a great source for information about Afghanistan and Iraq, and what the Marines are doing over there. I just had to make it sound real and personal. I haven't checked which letter he stole, but I saw him put one in his pocket. Regardless, it's going to be filled with little sexual innuendoes that if he has any imagination at all will get him sexually aroused. He should get the idea that I'm an oversexed and underfed wife who had been too long away from her lover. The perfect circumstances to lead a lady into a life of sex for sale."

"Anything else?"

"Yes, as a matter of fact. You can get just about anything on the Internet these days. I downloaded a blank copy of a nursing degree from the Medical College of Virginia in Richmond, filled in the blanks, framed it and hung it on my living room wall. I noticed him giving it the once-over, so if the subject has come up in his conversations about me with the President, it will confirm the story I told the Old Man when we first met."

"Good idea. So, let's get back to the story of what happened in the President's quarters."

"Sorry to get off track, Sir. If the President's toy soldiers follow their instructions like good little robots, they won't know he's dead until tomorrow morning when someone decides it's time for him to get up and act presidential again. That gives us five or more hours for cell breakdown to release enough potassium to mask what I put in him."

"Dead! What do you mean, dead," Armstrong shouted into the receiver. "He was just sleeping!" The feigned shock in his voice didn't work.

"Like hell he was. I checked his pulse before I left. He didn't have a pulse in his wrist or his neck. So, I checked his breath with the make-up mirror I keep in my purse. No breath. So, I put my ear to his chest. No heartbeat. He was dead, Director. Stone cold dead, just like you planned."

"You can't be sure, Sarah!"

"Of course I can. Do you know how to be sure a person is dead? It's easy Director. Just pull their pants down, in this case, pajama bottoms. When someone dies, all of their muscles relax. The person goes limp. The first thing a dead person does is defecate and urinate. Their bowels and bladder just let go, and the secretions begin. Believe me, the President was as dead as a doornail. As your people would say, he pissed his pants and shit all over himself. Clear enough?"

*   *   *

"I don't know what to say, Sarah. I didn't know this was going to happen. You could be in a lot of trouble."

"Let's cut the crap, Director. You and your boys set me up, and you know it. This is a *we* operation, Director, not a *me* set up. Pardon the inference, but you're in bed with me on this. So, my friend, don't try to con a con. You really aren't that good at it, Sir."

"What?"

"If your people had looked at my school record from the University of Kansas, they would have noticed that I took three years of chemistry there, advanced classes. Although I was a pre-law major, my minor was chemistry. You can't be a good trial lawyer if you don't understand the very important part forensics plays in most homicide cases, and chemistry is one of the legs on which that discipline is built.

"Anyway, I opened one of the syringes of clear liquid your agent gave me and tasted it. I knew that if you wanted me to inject 5cc of the stuff into the President, a little on my tongue wasn't going to kill me. And, I know what potassium chloride tastes like, and I know 5cc will put a grown man down in a heartbeat. And, I'm speaking literally now, Director.

"But, don't start squirming in that big overstuffed chair you're sitting in, Director Armstrong. Or, can I call you Don, now that we're such good friends and all."

"You have something else to add, Sarah?" Don Armstrong's voice had become icy.

"I'm just starting, Sir. Sit back and relax. You're going to enjoy this.

"Do you remember six years ago, almost to the day, the story the sheriff's deputy over in Cecil County, Maryland told you about the very innocent young sixteen-year old girl who was raped by the President of the United States? The little girl whose father went to the sheriff's office to report the rape, and the sheriff and his deputies just blew him off? Remember that?"

"Vaguely. What about it?"

"Do you remember the rumors that followed about the little girl having charged the rapist five hundred dollars to have his way with her? You remember that?"

"I'm sorry, I didn't follow the story. Where is this going, Sarah?"

"Hang on, Chief. There's a good reason you didn't follow the story. There was no story! At least it didn't get any press coverage because the sheriff and his cronies hushed it up. The press never knew the rape took place. But the girl did, and the story got out locally.

"Did you know that the rumors finally got so bad that the little girl's father moved his family out of the area? At least the $500 the girl stole from the bastard elevated her from being called a slut to being branded a whore."

"I'll ask again, Sarah. Where is this story going?"

"The story is going to Kansas where the father moved his family. Lawrence, Kansas to be exact. You with me on this, Director?"

There was only silence on the other end of the conversation.

"No comment, Director? OK, I'll continue then. That young girl grew up to become a well-adjusted young lady in spite of what the President did to her. She graduated from high school with honors and received a scholarship to attend the University of Kansas. I guess the people who awarded the scholarship hadn't heard that she was a whore, charging five hundred dollars for a roll in the hay."

"You? You're the girl the President raped? The one the deputy told me about? My God, I didn't know, Sarah, honestly."

"I know you didn't. How could you have known? All you knew was I transferred from the University of Kansas to American University and planned to attend their Washington Law School. No one here or across the Chesapeake knew where my father took us to get away from the awful accusations being levied against me. But living and school costs here are so much more expensive than in Lawrence that I had to find a good paying job to stay in school. My parents couldn't help. They were just keeping their heads above water.

"Since my former friends on the other side of the Chesapeake thought I was a whore, I decided to capitalize on the image, just in case I ever ran into any of them. Plus the hours were great and I made a hell of a lot more money than had I been waiting tables, like a lot of my preppy college friends were doing. I guess it was just luck that I ran into the President at a social gathering your people sent me to. And equally lucky he was attracted to me, but had no idea who I was.

"So, let me wind this little story down. When the President raped me six years ago I was devastated. Not physically though. I wasn't a virgin anyway, so no physical harm done. He did mess up my mind, though. I had a hard time coping with the rumors about me, even after we left the Eastern Shore and moved to Kansas, but I eventually grew up and got over the trauma of being raped and not being able to do anything about it. Once I learned that life isn't always fair, I was able to move on.

"I swore to myself that if I ever got the chance to get even, I would, regardless of the cost to me personally. I realized I could lose my life carrying out my personal mission, but what the hell; it would be worth the risk to take his life, especially if I could take him down the hard way.

"So, you see, I really appreciate all the safeguards you and your people put in place for me, but I would have done it without any protection from you and your people. I was committed to this long before I arrived in Washington, and long before I got hooked up with your Stepford Escort Service.

"When I was straightening my clothes after the rape, the President was in the shower, singing. I had this vision of the bastard lying on the shower floor, bleeding from the large gash in his groin where I had cut off his penis and stuffed it in his mouth."

"That's a terrible thought, Sarah. You wouldn't do anything like that."

"Think not, huh? Keep listening. If anyone looks in on the President, he's lying on his left side under the sheets, so he's facing away from the bedroom entrance. They would think he's still sleeping, but I did close his eyes. The way he's positioned in the bed, you would just see the back of his head, not his face. I wanted that to be a surprise when someone goes in to awaken him. That's when they would see his graying complexion that follows death when someone bleeds out. And, with his eyes closed, they wouldn't know right away that he's dead.

"Since he's bleeding out through the gash in his groin area, the blood is pooling around his left hip and shouldn't be visible outside the sheet covering his body. Plus, my little miniature recorder is under the bed, clean of course, with a long-play repeating disk of heavy breathing and occasional snoring. Someone looking in will hear the breathing and close the door without checking further."

"What do you mean, *bleeding from a gash in his groin*? What did you do, Sarah?"

"Payback time, Don. He raped me six years ago. So, I cut off his penis and stuffed it in his mouth before I left. I wish I had a picture, the President of the United States, lying in his bed, staring at nothing through his dead eyes, and smoking his penis. You know what they say, *What goes around, comes around!*"

"My God, Sarah, you are a vindictive woman."

"Vindictive? You've got to be kidding! You ever been raped, Director? Anyone ever thrown you down on a bed, ripped off your panties and shoved a 2 x 4 up your ass as though you were a piece of trash? Then not give a damn if he gets you pregnant or not. And just walks away without a word, leaving you there with your pain and your shame?

"The bastard thought he was above the law. And, in reality, he was. At least until now. The Cecil County sheriff hushed what he did to me up. The only way the story got out was through one of his deputies who drank and talked too much, the guy you talked to in the Chesapeake City restaurant. Things like this aren't supposed to happen to good people who believe in decency and respect. And the President isn't supposed to be the perp either. You say I'm vindictive. You bet I am. And what I did, in effect, is nothing more than make a simple statement: Nobody rapes me and gets away with it, Mr. Director. Nobody!"

"Well, I'm glad I wasn't your target. And, I'm glad we got you out of Washington when we did, Sarah. You know you're going to be at the top of the FBI's most wanted list. They'll look under every rock in Rock Creek Park to find you. It'll be the largest manhunt ever. I'm sure they already have a national security threat tag on you. They'll involve us as well as all the other U.S. intelligence and security agencies, plus MI-6, Interpol, Mossad, and every other foreign-based intelligence group around the world. You won't be safe anywhere. That is, unless we protect you."

"I'm not going to be at the top of anyone's most wanted list, Don. But Patricia Simpson will be. There's nothing linking me to that name, except what you may have on me. And, your recording of this conversation, because I know you're recording it. You know my history now but no one outside the agency knows. The life I built as Patricia Simpson has no link to my real existence. If you know the right people in DC it's easy to create a new life with a new name, new credit cards, bank accounts, driver's license-all the trappings of a legitimate existence with forged birth certificate, Social Security number and even school records. I began putting my new existence together when I realized Hunt wanted me as his personal squeeze.

"It doesn't bother me in the least that you and your people know my true identity and what I did, because you guys are as guilty as I. After all, I have enough evidence to plead that I was only your messenger. Look at it this way, Don. Who do you think the Feds would most like to take down-little old me, a naïve little girl from out West who was raped by the President, then coerced into a life of prostitution to survive in the big city, or several CIA big wigs with a lot of dirt on their hands? I can get immunity, My Friend, but you can't.

"So, before you slam the phone down and swear to have me eliminated, let me suggest a scenario that I think you'll buy into."

"Before you do that, Sarah, take me through the rest of the story, please. What did you do with the knife you used on the President? And, did you follow our clean-up suggestions?"

"Oh, that. I left the knife between his legs. But, before you ask, I was wearing surgical gloves, so no prints. I emptied the second syringe and brought both of them out taped under my arms. I have them in a safe place. Know what I mean?

"As for the needles, I dropped them into the sink drain as you suggested. Otherwise, there isn't much to tell. I just walked out of the White House, using the private family entrance, got in my car and waved at the guard. The rest you know. When I got to Andrews, I exited onto Patrick and drove over to hangar twenty-six, just as I was told to do. I thought I was going to have trouble there with so many armed people around, but one of your chase cars that had escorted me in the District drove up to the gate and got me through without a hassle. They instructed me to drive into the hangar, and I walked from the car over to your airplane and got on board. We were out of there in five minutes and airborne in fifteen. The pilot told me I was not on the passenger manifest, just he and the copilot, so no one at Andrews knows I was there."

"Did you say you dropped the hypodermic needles into the sink drain?"

"Yes. Why?"

"Because I told you to flush them down the toilet. If you would have done that, they would have washed directly into the sewer and been lost. By putting them in the sink drain, you run the risk of them becoming lodged in the trap under the sink. If that happens, they will have another piece of evidence to pursue. That was an unwise decision on your part, Sarah."

"Sorry, I thought I was doing exactly what you said to do."

"OK. It's too late to cry over spilled milk. Tell me how you spotted our escort cars?"

"Are you kidding? At two-thirty in the morning, how much traffic do you think there is in downtown Washington? When two look-alike, black Chevrolets close in on you, you know it's not the DC cops because they're all asleep at that time of the morning, so it must be the Mafia or the Feds. I figured they were yours because they kept switching places, front to back, back to front, checking out what little traffic there was going south on my route. Who were they looking for?"

"The FBI. They do a lot of tailing of people leaving the White House to see where they're going."

"Were they there?"

"According to my people, they weren't. Also, they hadn't bugged your car with a transmitter either. They usually do. They probably noticed your car was fitted with a GPS as original equipment, and figured they could follow the signal it transmits when you left."

"That's pretty slick."

"Yeah, but what's slicker is that the GPS was programmed to lead anyone following the signal on a totally different route and to a false location on the opposite side of the city. Remember, that car was one of ours."

"How do you do that?"

"Sorry, can't tell you."

"You guys are so devious, I wouldn't trust you as far as I could throw you."

"That's the nicest thing you've said about us that I can remember. Now, what's your proposition, Young Lady?"

"OK, here's the deal. We can get into the details later. I fly to Rio. The CIA sets me up in some reasonably nice digs. You can be the judge of how long I should stay, and that depends on the heat in the States. I expect it's going to be a nice long vacation. While there, we can talk about a little facial reconstruction. My nose is too long anyway. And I'm going to need a car and a nice allowance, plus a new identity. I know there is no link between my true identity and the street name I used during my employment with your Stepford Escort service, but your people can check it out just to be sure. If they find anything, they can erase the record.

Then I want to come back to the U.S. and finish my undergraduate work. American University is out, but Rutgers might be nice. Then on to Yale or Harvard Law School. After graduation, I want to work with the CIA, but not in DC. California maybe, if they're still a part of the Union then."

"You don't want much, do you?"

"Not much, but I want it in writing. Oh, a new passport also, some name and address that won't attract attention. Something that can be verified if anyone comes down here snooping around."

"You seem to have one problem you can't shake, Sarah. When you enrolled in American University, you were required to give them a blood sample. They routinely do a DNA profile on every student and keep the records permanently, including the blood sample. Sooner or later the FBI is going to link you to that sample and learn your real identity. Ultimately, they will know who you really are. There's no way you can get around that, Young Lady."

"Wrong again, Director. My first part-time job, after enrolling at American University, was in their records section. One evening I removed my medical records and DNA information, including the sample of my blood, and switched the blood sample and the medical records of a female student about my age and physical makeup who had died in an automobile accident in DC some five years earlier with mine. I just substituted my name for hers on the records. If and when the FBI links my street name to my real name and learns I was a student at A.U., they will find a DNA profile that says it's mine, but it won't match my true DNA. As I said, there is no way they can link Patricia Simpson to Sarah Jacobson. After all, the FBI won't be looking at the records of a student who died tragically some five years ago. If they did, yes, they would find my DNA, but those are odds I'm willing to take. Case closed, Director!"

"Good thinking, Sarah. You seem to have covered just about everything. Let wrap this up. The pilot has a package he'll give you when you get to Rio. It contains the money we promised you, and, a new passport and birth certificate. You were born in Columbus, Georgia at Fort Benning's Martin Army Hospital. You were an Army brat and your name is Amanda Caldwell. Your father is Alec Caldwell and he was in Army Intelligence doing a TDY at Fort Benning, getting a little jump time. He retired from his military career after twenty years and took a government job in DC. Your mother died of ovarian cancer while you and your parents were living in Tyson's Corners. You went off to college about that time and your dad quit his job and moved back to Montana, his childhood home. He later married a lady originally from Idaho, the wife of the former Secretary of the Interior who was assassinated almost a year before the wedding. End of story. Anyone checking you out can trace you from birth through high school and college. The information is all in the folder and the public records have been altered to include your life as we put it together. By the way, the Alec Caldwell part of the story is true. We just added you into the equation.

"A small cottage has been made available for you in the hills just outside of Rio. It's located on an estate owned by the Company, and we use it whenever we need to take a person out of the public spotlight for a while. You will be the only occupant.

"And, you're not going to need a car. Get yourself a motor scooter, one that can be licensed for highway use. It will take you anywhere you want to go around Rio and up and down the coast, even back in the jungle if you want to meet a few rebels who want to overthrow the government.

"And, lose the mid-western accent. As I said, you were born in Columbus, Georgia. And, you grew up in the DC area, so you would be well served if you get yourself a book on how folks in Northern Virginia talk. You can get one in just about any bookstore, even down in Rio. Use some Southern expressions, get used to the language and the expressions. You'll need them to fool your pursuers.

"As for facial reconstruction, a little surgery is a good idea. If the White House had a photograph of you, then it will be circulated all over the world. And when they put a nice fat reward with your apprehension, everyone will be looking for you. And, I mean literally everyone.

"The first thing we'll do is bring in a beautician we've used in Rio in the past. She'll change your hairstyle and color to give your face a completely different look. She's good at what she does. And, you will wear non-prescription contacts in whatever color the beautician thinks will complement what she is going to do to your hair. Do you still have the ID the White House gave you?"

"Yes, I'm wearing it."

"Good. Destroy it as soon as you can. You shouldn't have anything on you that can link you back to the White House."

"Looks like you have all of your bases covered, Director. Anything else?"

"Yes. I suspect the FBI will be on your trail right away, and since we can't begin your facial reconstruction for a few days, you will need to wear bandages around your nose and possibly over one eye until we can have it done.

"We're sending down an agent who will pose as your father. Yes, it will be Alec Caldwell. And yes, he is a real person. He will deliver your documents other than those the pilot will give you. They substantiate you arrived in Rio a few weeks ago should anyone want to run a paper trail on you, and you can bet the FBI will. The records have been taken care of. You're going through a nasty divorce and are out of the country to get away from all the mess. Unfortunately you had a bike accident causing the damage to your face. That's the reason for the bandages and your father's visit. Hopefully your stepmother will be with him.

"Have a nice vacation, Sarah. The agent will give you the guarantees you asked for. Oh, one more thing. Friday evening, the 12th, I want you to have dinner at Marius Restaurant. It's authentic Brazilian, and it's located at 290 Atlantica Avenue overlooking Leme Beach. You'll find it. It's well known for its steaks and seafood. Plus, the decor is quite unusual.

"You will meet Alec Caldwell there. He is the agent posing there as your father. Your reservations are for 7:00 pm. He will arrive at 7:30. Ask for Phillip Bane. He bartends there and he's a friend of mine. Tell him I sent you. He'll know."

"Know what?"

"He'll know. That's all."

"Damn, I hate riddles."

CHAPTER TWENTY-FOUR

President's Residence
The White House
Monday, October 8—6:05am

I T WAS JUST after 6:00am on October 6, and all hell was about to break loose in the first family's White House residential quarters. Sarah had left the White House just after three, as she had been instructed and was already well out of the country.

Chief of Staff, Fred Pendleton, standing outside the large double doors forming the entrance to the private residence, checked his watch. It read 6:17 am. He always set his watch fifteen minutes fast to be sure he was always on time for the constant stream of meetings he was forced to attend.

Pendleton was reading the note the woman had given to one of the Secret Service agents guarding the double doors as she left. The look on his face was one of concern.

"When did you get this?"

"The lady was logged out at three fourteen this morning. She gave the note to the agents on duty as she was leaving, Sir. They passed it on to us when we came on duty at 0500 hours."

"Did either of the agents check on the President after the woman left?"

"Yes, Sir, according to the log. One of the agents looked into the bedroom after she left. He followed procedure to the letter, Sir. He noted that the President was asleep. Since the note said he didn't want to be disturbed until six this morning, he didn't disturb him. We checked, Sir; the note is in the President's handwriting."

"OK, it's just after six now. I'm going in. You guys stay here." Fred Pendleton opened the door to the living quarters, walked quietly across the plush carpet through the living room to the master bedroom door, and knocked softly.

"Mr. President, it's time to get up. You have an appointment with the French Ambassador at ten, and your daily security briefing is in twenty minutes."

Pendleton knocked again and opened the door just far enough to see the President still asleep. He was relieved to hear his breathing. It seemed normal, and Pendleton decided to enter and wake him. He walked across the soft beige carpet to face the President, but stopped at the foot of the bed.

Something's wrong, he thought. As he approached, he could see that the President's eyes were closed, and he could hear his breathing. *What's that thing in his mouth? And, the odor?*

All of a sudden it hit him. "Jesus Christ! You people get in here, now," he yelled to the two agents who were posted just outside the residence outer doors. He picked up the phone and punched the three-digit code that gave him immediate access to the senior Secret Service agent on duty.

"This is Chief of Staff Fred Pendleton, put the White House on lock down status, and do it now," he yelled when the phone was answered. "No one in and no one out, unless I say so. And get a medical team up here to the President's quarters on the double, as well as his personal physician. And, post an additional six agents to the residence immediately. And I damned well better not see anybody walking. Run them up here now! One more thing, the two agents that were posted to the President's residence last evening. I want their butts up here on the double."

"What's happening, Sir?"

"Just do it, damn it. And do it now."

"Yes, Sir. But the two agents working the night shift up there clocked out a few minutes ago and are on their way home."

"I don't care if they are on their way to the moon. Call and turn them around. I want them up here within the hour."

"Yes, Sir."

Fred Pendleton looked down at his friend, and shook his head, tears welling up in his eyes.

You stupid bastard, how many times did I warn you not to screw everything that wears high heels? There were plenty of women with character out there who would have loved to be with you. Why did you have to be attracted to prostitutes? And, why didn't you let us vet this woman? Hell, I'll bet her real name isn't even Patricia Simpson. She wasn't smart enough to do this to you, John. She had to be working for somebody who wanted you dead. You stupid ass, you were set up.

He reached down, removed Hunt's penis from his mouth and lifted the sheet to put it beside his body. *I'm not going to let anyone see you like this, Sir. To hell with contaminating the crime scene.*

Only a small amount of blood had pooled around his left hip. It had already turned black, and the smell of urine and feces was overpowering. The President was naked, and Pendleton could see the mutilation where his penis was removed. "That bitch!" he said aloud, as he pulled the sheet over the President's head. "You're dead, Girl, and I'm going to see to it, personally!"

*   *   *

President's Residence
The White House
Monday, October 8—6:31am

"Sir, the senior agent in charge told us to report to you on the double. We were on Constitution when we got the call. Is something wrong?"

"I'll ask the questions. You just answer. Which one of you checked on the President's condition last night, after midnight? Which one of you is Bailey?" Fred Pendleton was looking at the log, checking the names corresponding to the entries he was interested in.

"I am, Sir. I checked on him just after his lady friend left his quarters. I noted it in the log. I think it was a little after three."

"What was the President doing when you entered, Agent?"

"He was sleeping, Sir, I heard him snoring. What's going on, Sir?

"He wasn't sleeping, Agent. He was dead. What you heard was this." Fred Pendleton held up the small recorder he had found under the bed, and pressed the play button. The sound of heavy breathing, mixed with an occasional snore, were the only sounds coming from the recorder.

"Damn," he said, almost under his breath.

"Did you go in and look at him, Agent?"

"No, Sir. I opened the bedroom door and peeped in, as standard procedure dictates. I didn't want to disturb him, and the note said not to wake him until six. So, I closed the door quietly so I wouldn't wake him, and logged it in."

*   *   *

The FBI arrived at seven fourteen, only minutes after the Secret Service made the call. The President's death was immediately declared a homicide, and since it took place on property owned by the Federal Government, the Bureau claimed jurisdiction. Their forensic team arrived a half hour later, called in before their shift began by Special Agent Leroy Bazemore, who had hastily been named *Agent in Charge*.

No one was allowed to make calls outside the White House other than the Chief of Staff, who had assumed control of the situation before Bazemore and his team arrived. The senior Secret Service agent on duty had raced upstairs just moments before. Both acknowledged the FBI's jurisdiction.

The FBI took over the White House communications network from the Secret Service as soon as they arrived and had assessed the situation. All incoming callers were politely told that the person they were calling was unavailable, but would return the call as soon as possible.

All personnel already inside the White House, except the Chief of Staff, were moved into the large theatre in the first floor basement to eliminate the possibility that anyone would try to communicate with someone outside the compound. The theatre was a secure environment and communication with the outside world from there was impossible.

Because of security reasons, cell phones, Blackberries, and laptop computers were confiscated, placed in plastic bags and sealed and labeled to eliminate returning items containing sensitive information to the wrong people. The only exceptions to this were the FBI-controlled communications from within the White House and the calls the Chief of Staff was making in an effort to move the transfer of power process along.

Employees arriving for work at the White House were turned away without explanation by the Marines guarding the exterior doors; their numbers had been doubled. Instead of being dressed in formal uniforms, all were now dressed in fatigues and carried full weaponry.

Military patrols around the White House grounds were initiated as soon as the FBI took charge, and the number of guards in and around the compound had been doubled. Snipers were posted everywhere.

The note, supposedly in the President's handwriting, indicating that he did not want to be disturbed before six o'clock, had been rushed to the FBI's forensic lab to determine if the fingerprints of the President's visitor could be identified. Her fingerprints could not be found on the note. An FBI handwriting expert at the Hoover building determined that the note was a fake.

No one within the White House outside the President's bedroom knew what was going on. They only knew that all contact with the outside world had been shut down. The FBI had initiated a total communications blackout into and out of the White House, except one.

*   *   *

The White House
October 8—8:05 am

"Mr. Chief Justice, this is Fred Pendleton, White House Chief of Staff. I apologize for calling you at such an early hour, but we have a situation over here. This is a secure conference call, and I'm conferencing in the Speaker of the House, the Senate Majority Leader, and the Vice President.

"Gentlemen, this call is being recorded, and I am talking with you from the President's residence in the White House. Would you please state your name, your identification code, and your position in the government? As you know, this is standard operating procedure on conference calls originating from the White House. Mr. Chief Justice, may we start with you, Sir."

The Chief Justice, the Vice President, the Speaker of the House and the Senate Majority Leader each, in turn, followed Fred Pendleton's instructions. They knew the drill and knew the news he was going to share with them was bad. The Chief of Staff was never as demanding and direct as now.

"Thank you, Gentlemen. Unfortunately I have very sad news. The President is dead. His death has been tentatively diagnosed as having been caused by a heart attack. What caused his heart to stop is purely speculation at this point. It could have been natural causes, but it could have been chemically induced. We just don't know yet. His body was taken to Bethesda Navel Hospital for a complete autopsy as soon as the FBI forensic team released it. The President's body had been mutilated, but his personal physician tentatively determined that the mutilation was post mortem. I really don't want to discuss the mutilation, gentlemen, and I would appreciate your not inquiring further. Please take my word that it was grotesque. The Bethesda Medical Examiner will confirm or change the earlier diagnosis as soon as his autopsy is completed. The President's body is on its way to BNH as we speak, and the White House is in total lockdown.

"I found the President this morning when I entered his bedroom to awaken him, as I usually do. The FBI was called immediately, and one of their forensic teams has been on the scene for a few minutes now. The FBI has assumed complete control of the situation here. There are no telephone calls or emails coming into or going out of the White House other than the FBI communications network, and calls I originate.

"Gentlemen, the Secret Service has dispatched vehicles to each of your homes. They are there for your protection, and they should be arriving momentarily. Please accompany the agents when they arrive. And, Gentlemen, please don't ask them any questions. They really don't know anything. They're just following orders.

"The agents will identify themselves, of course. They have instructions to bring you to the White House immediately and also, they will be escorted by two patrol cars from the District's police force. Time is critical, so please don't be alarmed by the speeds the drivers reach to get you here. This is a Level One Crisis, Gentlemen. You are all familiar with your obligations under these conditions, so please, no mention of this to anyone, including your spouses. This is a very sad day for all of us. When you arrive, an agent will escort you to the Oval Office where we will conduct the ceremony to swear you in, Mr. Vice

President. It is imperative that we have a quick and orderly transfer of power. Until then, no one is our nation's Commander-in-Chief.

"And, Mr. Chief Justice, all will be ready for you to conduct the ceremony. I wish we could do this on the Capitol steps in front of the press and your families and friends. But, at this point in the investigation into the President's death, the director of the FBI has advised me that information must be confined only to those on a need-to-know basis. As soon as the medical examiner confirms the early findings of the President's physician, we can announce his death to the media. Until then, the FBI has imposed the news blackout I mentioned.

"As soon as the Vice President is sworn in as President, we will immediately call in the Cabinet, the other Supreme Court Justices and the Joint Chiefs of Staff. All have been notified that a coded message will be forthcoming. They don't know what's happening, but all are making arrangements to get here as quickly as possible.

"We've instructed Homeland Security to raise the threat level, and we are putting all branches of the military on full alert. If word gets out that the President is dead, it could be seen by our enemies as an opportunity to launch a strike on us. They would suspect we are very vulnerable at this moment. The Vice President is not well known outside the U.S. and our adversaries don't know the level of his commitment to defend our shores. Gentlemen, we will remain in a most vulnerable situation until we can arrange for the Vice President to assume power and publicly address the crisis. Defending our shores and our interest abroad will be key parts of his address to the nation.

*   *   *

Four Locations
Metropolitan Washington
October 8—8:51am

At approximately eight fifty-one, four men under heavy guard by Secret Service agents dressed in SWAT gear and brandishing automatic weapons, were driven in separate cars into the White House compound to the underground garage. Outsiders couldn't see that the civilian occupants of the vehicles were the Vice President of the United States, the Speaker of the House, the Senate Majority Leader, and the Chief Justice of the Supreme Court. As each arrived, they were escorted to the bank of elevators by Secret Service agents who accompanied them up to the first floor of the White House. As each emerged from the elevators he was met by the Chief of Staff. There was no joy in the meetings, just solemn faces and firm handshakes. There was a sense of dire purpose in the air.

Outside, tourists were beginning to mix with the staffers standing around outside the gates of the White House. Rumors were beginning to flow through the crowd like wildfire, and the phones at the major news agencies were ringing off the hook.

Arrangements were hurriedly being put together to facilitate the transfer of power to the Vice President. The President had been declared dead at six-forty three by a member of the FBI's forensic term. His death was confirmed by his personal physician who was now on his way to Bethesda Naval Hospital with the President's body, but the cause of death was still under investigation. No tests had yet been run to determine what caused the President's heart to stop. His physician had tentatively identified the time of death at between 2:30 to 3:30am based on the temperature of the body and degree of rigor.

As soon as the FBI forensic team had examined the body, it was placed in an EMS vehicle parked in the basement garage and delivered to Bethesda for a detailed autopsy and thorough examination. The vehicle was driven by an FBI agent, accompanied by the President's personal physician and three other agents, all of whom were heavily armed. The vehicle was escorted by four DC police vehicles, sirens and lights deployed.

Initially, it had been assumed that the President had died from loss of blood, caused by the gash in his groin area and the removal of his penis. As the transfer of power ceremony, in which the Vice President assumed the office of President of the United States, was in progress, Special Agent Leroy Bazemore of the Federal Bureau of Investigation quietly entered the Oval Office and closed the door behind him. He stood beside the door waiting for the ceremony to be completed. When it had concluded, all eyes turned to him.

"Gentlemen, I have the preliminary autopsy report from the Bethesda Naval Hospital medical examiner. In a word, the President was already dead when his body was mutilated. Whoever removed his penis did so after the President had died. Preliminarily, it looks like the cause of death was a heart attack. What may have induced the heart attack is yet unknown. We won't know anything else until the autopsy is completed, and that could be a day or so longer. We understand the President had a female companion in his quarters last night, probably there at the time of his death. What that fact may mean in his death is yet to be determined. But we have issued an APB to locate this *person of interest* as soon as possible."

"Thank you, Agent Bazemore," Fred Pendleton said.

Pendleton turned to the former Vice President, "May I suggest, Mr. President, that the Press Secretary be instructed to call a press conference to announce the President's death, but restrict information to the fact that he is deceased, and probably died of a heart attack? Nothing else, so no questions from the press. Since they can't gain access to anyone in the White House, they already know something is wrong, so the press conference should be well attended. At least that would notify the nation and the world that you have assumed the reins of power in the U.S. If terrorists think there is no one in charge over here, no one steering the ship, so to speak, we could see a major increase in terrorist attacks on soft targets here and on U.S. interests abroad. We need to get out in front of this as soon as possible, Sir. We need to be able to notify our other security agencies to go on high alert in case there is an effort to destabilize our government.

"And, Sir, carry it a step further and go on television with a strong statement about your intent to continue to focus on homeland security issues. Let the terrorists know first thing that even though President Hunt is dead, it's business as usual in the U.S. under your watch."

"Good idea. Thanks, Fred. You and your people set up the press conference for later this afternoon in the briefing room. Let's shoot for

2:00 pm. Have the Press Secretary make the announcement of John's death. She's not to take any questions. I won't be there. Get me a first draft of my speech to the nation before noon and set it up for prime time, say seven this evening. And let's do it in the House chambers, not in the Oval Office.

"And, Fred, when your people arrange for the airtime we need on the major networks for my speech, let's keep this simple. Arrange for one of the networks to provide a master camera feed that all the other networks can access, so we don't have cameramen and producers falling all over each other. Get the word out to the national and world press that my address will take place this evening."

"I'm on it, Sir."

* * *

Federal Bureau of Investigation
Background

The Federal Bureau of Investigation maintains fifty-six field offices distributed in all major metropolitan areas in the U.S. and Puerto Rico, plus some seventy-five Legal Attachés and a host of smaller sub-offices abroad. They were all notified by coded message of the President's death within two hours of the FBI assuming command over the investigation.

The FBI employs some four hundred resident agents in cities throughout the U.S. and Puerto Rico with over thirty thousand total employees made up of eleven thousand special agents and nineteen thousand professional support personnel. It is the primary investigative arm of the U.S. Department of Justice.

* * *

The first thing the FBI did was to release copies of the photograph of Patricia Simpson to all of their personnel, worldwide. They had received the photo from the Chief of Staff. It matched the image on her White House identification badge. That included their personnel manning the Legal Attaches, or Legats, maintained in seventy-five U.S. Embassies and Consulates covering two hundred countries worldwide. The photo accompanied a worldwide BOLO in which Patricia Simpson was listed as a *person of interest.*

In effect, Patricia Simpson's photograph received worldwide agency distribution in a matter of six minutes. The FBI decided not to wait until the public announcement of the President's death to release the photograph to other law enforcement agencies. The possibility of terrorist strikes against U.S. interests worldwide was too great to justify any delay in the notification process. Within an hour, Patricia Simpson had been elevated to the most wanted person, worldwide, even above the infamous Osama bin Laden.

*   *   *

"Mr. President, this morning we released the photo of the woman who was with the President to all security agencies, worldwide, but if we're going to locate this Patricia Simpson person, we're going to have to release her photo to the press as soon as possible, not just to the security agencies. She's out there, and she's running. We need to close our net before she gets out of our grasp, Sir. If she gets out of the metropolitan Washington area, she can go to ground and we may never find her."

"That won't be a problem, Mr. Director." The recently declared President of the United States was speaking with the Director of the Federal Bureau of Investigation. "We're going public late this evening with a press conference. But, until we know something more definitive, we're going to just announce his death and stay away from any speculation. As soon as we go public, you fellows can handle the details however you wish. But, since we still don't know what may have caused the President's heart attack, I would suggest you treat his mistress as only a *person of interest*, not someone who may have perpetrated his demise. And, Director, there can be no mention of the mutilation suffered on the President's body. Is that clear?"

"Crystal clear, Sir."

Simultaneously, with the release of the photo of the woman known as Patricia Simpson to its agents worldwide, and without arousing the public's curiosity, the FBI disbursed a cadre of four hundred agents to the airports, railway stations, and bus depots in and around the District, including facilities as far away as Frederick and Baltimore, Maryland and Richmond and Norfolk, Virginia. It was as though the woman had dropped off the face of the earth.

In addition, the FBI launched a massive search for the automobile the woman had driven to the White House on the night she allegedly assassinated the President. The vehicle's image had been caught on six of the security cameras on the grounds outside the White House as she entered the grounds and had driven around to the private entrance to the first family's residential quarters.

A task force, made up of FBI analysts, was hurriedly set up to review the images caught on the many traffic control cameras on the main thoroughfare intersections leading in and out of the District. Knowing the date and time the woman had left the White House grounds, photo reviews were limited to a short timeframe of one hour following her exit. Traffic at that time of the early morning was extremely light, making the task much easier than a mid-day search. Several vehicles matching the description of the suspect's vehicle were identified around the general downtown area. The positions of these vehicles were plotted on an electronic wall map of the District's major thoroughfares. Five were initially identified as being the exact make, model, and color of the woman's vehicle, and all seemed to be traveling in different directions away from the downtown area. As each moved further away from the White House all seemed to turn onto unmonitored streets and disappear. That is, all but one. But, it also was lost as it was driven east on Pennsylvania Avenue in the vicinity of Andrews Air Force Base. The CIA decoys were making it difficult for the FBI to trace the route of the target vehicle.

When Special Agent Leroy Bazemore was handed the report, he balled it up and threw it in the trash. "Someone is playing with my head," he yelled. Before the agent who had delivered the report could slip out of the room Bazemore stopped him. "You, get out to Andrews immediately and find out if the CIA flew out this morning. If they did, get a copy of the passenger manifest, their time of departure and where they're going. Those bastards over at Langley are up to their Asses in this. I just know it!"

On another front, the FBI used the license tag number to gain information about the vehicle's registration. The name the DMV had in its records was one Patricia Simpson. A subsequent raid on her apartment, the address determined from the vehicle registration, revealed nothing. Her personal belongings had been removed by the time they arrived and all fingerprints were wiped clean. They immediately recognized a professional sanitizing of the apartment. Even the video and listening devices planted there a couple of years ago had been removed. A dead-end.

The first break the FBI got was the discovery of Patricia Simpson's Chevrolet, abandoned on an isolated dirt road on the north side of the area known to waterfowl hunters as the Susquehanna Flats, an area where the Susquehanna River becomes tidal under the influence of waters from the upper reaches of the Chesapeake Bay being pushed back into the river, causing it to flood the marshes surrounding it. The resulting shallows, dotted with small isolated islands, is a haven for millions of ducks, geese and other waterfowl that overwinter on their long fall migration down the Atlantic Flyway to escape the grip of a frozen winter in their Canadian summer breeding grounds.

A hunting guide, who was getting an early start on bushing the blinds on the flats he had registered with the Maryland Department of Natural Resources, discovered the vehicle. He had held the blind licenses for more than twenty years; his father, a noted guide during the market gunning days of the thirties and forties had built the blinds before his son was born.

The FBI employed several area watermen who guide waterfowl hunts on the Susquehanna Flats to take agents in their flat-bottom boats through the navigable waterways among the small islands in hope of locating the woman who they thought might be hiding there in one of the many small shanties used as base camps by many of the guides during inclement weather. There was no trace of the illusive woman, nor was there any evidence that she had ever been there. Another dead-end.

*   *   *

Patricia Simpson's vehicle was loaded on a flatbed transport and driven to the Agency's garage in Baltimore, where it was taken apart, piece-by-piece. It yielded nothing, not even a fingerprint other than those of the GM employees who had built the vehicle several years earlier. They determined that the vehicle identification number stamped on a metal plate placed below the windshield had been removed to further frustrate the investigation. Another dead-end.

*   *   *

A break in the investigation finally came when an agent, reviewing the still frames on the tape from the security camera outside the brownstone, noticed a familiar face. The White House Chief of Staff had failed to inform the Agency that he had visited the apartment building where Patricia Simpson maintained her apartment on the day preceding the night the President died. His presence at the apartment building immediately placed him in the *persons of interest* column as a possible accomplice to Patricia Simpson, the suspect who had allegedly mutilated the President's body. The investigation seemed to be taking an unexpected turn.

When Fred Pendleton had given Special Agent Leroy Bazemore the small recorder with the heavy breathing and snoring sounds he had found under the President's bed, Bazemore had noted that he was not wearing gloves. Bazemore had it checked for fingerprints, and the only ones found were Pendleton's. Initially he thought Pendleton was just sloppy, since he should have known that evidence is never handled without taking proper precautions. But, after learning that Pendleton had visited the suspect on the day preceding the night of the President's death, he began to wonder if there could be a connection.

The film from the security camera also revealed the images of three uniformed men with satchels similar to those plumbers use to carry their tools. They entered the brownstone approximately one hour after the established time of death of the President, but there were no images of them leaving the building. Photo enhancement revealed the insignias on their uniforms' breast pockets read ACME PLUMBING. No address.

The FBI located five Acme Plumbing businesses in the Washington metropolitan area, all were legitimate, and none that dispatched employees to the apartment house at the time in question. There were no images of the vehicle they used to drive to the apartment house, and all three men kept their faces hidden as though they knew where the security cameras were located. The FBI decided to treat the three men as having been possibly in the employ of Fred Pendleton. But there was no evidence to back that theory up. Possibly another dead-end.

Security cameras in the White House underground garage also recorded Fred Pendleton getting in his personal car and exiting the garage. The tape was date and time stamped for two o'clock in the afternoon. The decision was made not to inform him of the Bureau's suspicions. They determined he was not a flight risk and might lead them to others who were involved in the President's death, possibly the three men who the FBI felt sanitized Patricia's apartment.

An agent, skilled in personal surveillance, was put on him around the clock. Fred Pendleton had suddenly been elevated to someone who could have probable cause. The FBI just didn't know what that cause could be. They were slowly developing a conspiracy theory, but against the wrong player.

*   *   *

The White House
October 8—8:23am

As the FBI agents were working the case outside the White House, their forensic people were working the crime scene inside. Since the body mutilation was performed post mortem, they concentrated on whatever evidence they could find related to his death. The final autopsy report had not been filed, and no one knew for sure if the President had died of natural causes, or if not, what might have been used to kill him.

*   *   *

Medical Examiner's Office
Bethesda Naval Hospital
October 6—11:53 am

Logan Mitchell, the Bethesda Naval Hospital medical examiner, was on the phone with Special Agent Leroy Bazemore, the agent in charge of the FBI's investigation into the death of the President.

"Sir, we located the site where a needle was inserted into the President's right arm. We stripped the veins in the location, and the needle entered a vein in the crook of his arm. There was no subdural hematoma, so whoever performed the procedure knew what he, or she, was doing. Usually, when the needle is withdrawn, a small amount of blood leaks out of the vein before pressure is applied. A subdural hematoma is the result of that blood leaking from the vein but remaining under the skin."

"I understand, Dr. Mitchell. So what do you need from us?"

"Have your forensic people found a syringe or a needle at the crime scene?"

"No, but we had the suite electronically swept and picked up three miniature listening devices. They're off-the-shelf technology so it looks like an amateur operation. The technology we and the other federal agencies use is light years ahead of these things."

"That's your department, Agent Bazemore, not mine. Please have your people keep an eye out for those items I mentioned. And, have them check the plumbing, both the sink drains and the toilets in all three bathrooms. Have them analyze the liquid in the sink drains and the water in the toilet bowls. Tell them to look for chemicals or chemical compounds that would normally not be there. If they find something, I need to know what it is immediately.

"I think we can rule out death by natural causes, but right now, we can't find anything in his system that we can point to as the agent that killed him. And, he didn't die of a myocardial infarction. It wasn't heart disease. His heart stopped all of a sudden, his breathing rhythm was interrupted and his brain was starved of oxygen. That's what killed him. It was quick, and it was induced. And right now, we don't have any idea what it is.

*   *   *

President's Residence
The White House
October 8—4:28pm

"Dr. Mitchell, you asked us to let you know if our forensic team found anything you might be interested in. Well, as you suggested, we dismantled the traps under each of the sinks. Guess what. We found two needles stuck in the trap of one of the sinks in the master bath. Evidently they had been dropped into the sink by someone who didn't know that the trap is specifically designed to catch foreign objects inadvertently dropped into the sink, as well as eliminate a source of odor from the sewer line to which it is connected. I would have thought the assassin would have flushed them down the toilet where they couldn't be found, but who knows, maybe he, or she didn't think it through.

There was enough residue in one of the hypodermic needles for our people to determine that the substance was potassium chloride. What can you tell me about potassium chloride, Sir?"

"Well, Leroy, it's used primarily in the manufacture of fertilizers. But, if the person who injected the compound into the President's arm knew what he was doing, and based on the President's weight, I would say that just a 5cc injection in a vein leading directly to his heart would have killed him in about three to five minutes, maybe less time than that. The closer the injection site is to the heart, the quicker the compound gets there and the quicker he dies. The compound disrupts the hearts rhythm, which in turn disrupts the victim's breathing rhythm and the brain suffocates. He's dead in less than five minutes, probably less than two.

"Anyway, that pretty much confirmed what we suspected. We thought he had been poisoned, we just didn't know what the compound was. His cardiologist had given him a clean bill of health just a couple of weeks earlier. We couldn't find any residue in his system, so we surmised it was one of several that, given enough time, couldn't be identified. Potassium chloride heads that list because as soon as a person dies, cell breakdown releases potassium into the body which, given enough time, will mask any potassium injected into the blood stream.

"Anyway, I'll finish up the final forensic report, sign a revised death certificate and fax copies over to you. I think you're in a position to take the news of his death to the public now."

"That's the Press Secretary's job, but thanks, Doc. I'll pass the word."

*   *   *

The McKenzie Residence
Boston, Massachusetts
Saturday, October 6—10:30am

"He's here," Kathy exclaimed, as the cab slowly drove up the long circular driveway leading to the McKenzie mansion. It was 10:30am, Saturday morning, and Alec had caught an early US Airways shuttle out of DC direct to Boston. He had called several days earlier to set up the meeting with the McKenzie family, and they were expecting him.

Alec had promised Horace McKenzie that he would tell him all that had transpired since Kathy's rescue in Mexico. McKenzie had honored his pledge not to discuss with the President, or anyone else outside his immediate family, anything he had learned or heard concerning the far-reaching criminal revelations that came to light during Kathy's ordeal down in Mexico. Although Kathy's mention to the President of the name Alec was using during that CIA operation had resulted in his capture and torture, he knew she had not done so intentionally and didn't feel it was necessary to mention any of that to McKenzie. Alec had narrowly escaped death, thanks to his daring rescue by a Delta Force Marine Unit stationed at Fort Bragg.

"Hi, Mr. LaCrosse," Kathy exclaimed as she waved and skipped down the front steps to the cab that had just pulled up to the front of the mansion. "I've missed my favorite hero," she said, hugging his neck. "I had hoped you would come to see us."

"Hello, Kathy. It's nice to see you again, especially under more pleasant circumstances. I promised your dad that, when this affair was over, I would tell him everything I know. You and your parents have been through a lot, and unfortunately I can't discuss this with you or your mother. But, your father deserves to know just what happened."

Mr. McKenzie led Alec into the paneled study, the walls lined with thousands of books, many rare first editions. The temperature in the room was somewhat cooler than the rest of the house, and the humidity was also independently controlled to help protect the delicate pages of many of the rare books McKenzie had collected over the years. He closed and locked the double doors that led into the library and motioned for Alec to sit in one of the two leather chairs facing the fireplace. "Would you care for a brandy, Mr. LaCrosse?"

"No thank you, Sir. Before I begin, I would appreciate your signing this Secrecy Agreement." Alec handed him a sealed envelope embossed with the seal of the Central Intelligence Agency. "Basically, it prohibits you from ever speaking of this to anyone, even Mrs. McKenzie or Kathy, under penalty of death. It's for national security reasons, Sir. I apologize for having to have you sign this.

"My name is Alec Caldwell. At least that's the name on my birth certificate, so I assume it's legitimate. I was born in Montana and followed my father into a career in the Army, just out of college. I joined the CIA as a field agent after twenty years in Army Intelligence. My wife passed away from cancer several years ago and I resigned my position with the CIA and moved back to Montana. I live there now, but work for the Company on special projects where the CIA can't be officially involved. The mission into Mexico to bring Kathy out was one such mission, as was my pursuit of the men who kidnapped her. Neither was sanctioned by the Mexican government, and both took place on their sovereign soil. Bringing Kathy out was sanctioned by the President, but our pursuit of her kidnappers was not. Other than that, I am again married, and we have a son, Alexander, less than a year old. In a nutshell, that's who I am."

"It's a privilege to finally know the real name of the gentleman who saved my daughter's life, Mr. Caldwell. Thank you, again, my good friend."

"Thank you, Sir. I'm going to tell you what happened down in Mexico, but I have to leave some details out because they involve national security. As you know, the President asked my boss to send someone down to Mexico to try to rescue Kathy. Thankfully, that mission succeeded, but it opened up a whole new can of worms. If I had returned with you and Kathy, nothing else would have come of this. But, I decided to stick my big nose into what I thought was a relatively minor drug ring operating on the Mexican Baja. Neither our people stationed down there, nor the DEA, knew it existed.

"What I found was a major operation involving drugs being funneled up the Baja into California that was tied into a white slavery operation in Cabo. And, that's what Kathy got caught up in. The drugs were being brought in by coastal freighter and off-loaded at Cabo. Evidently Kathy fit the profile of a young Caucasian girl someone in Saudi Arabia had contracted for, and she was kidnapped for delivery to him in partial payment for one of the drug shipments. Fortunately, I got to her before the hand-off could be made."

"What happened to the people who were running the operation?"

"I was only able to identify three of them, and they were later lost at sea. I understand their yacht, filled with a large quantity of cocaine, exploded somewhere in the Sea of Cortez off Cabo, and went down with all three of them on board in the middle of a hurricane. The Coast Guard never found any survivors, because they didn't really know where to look. I'm told they discovered a single hatch cover and were able to identify it as having come from the vessel they suspected went down. Seems they had recorded the vessel's departure out of Cabo, but it never returned. They just assumed all hands were lost. They suspected there was another much larger vessel in the area of the sinking, but evidently no rescue was attempted. That ship was gone when they went out to see if they could find anything."

"They didn't know where to look?"

"Not really. The Coast Guard plotted the position of the floating hatch cover against the prevailing currents and established a point where they felt the vessel may have gone down, but they had no way of determining the time of the sinking, so the hatch cover could have floated further away from the actual site of the sinking than calculated. Since there was no other evidence to even suggest that the vessel ever existed, they classified the case as unsolved. As far as I know, it may still be an open case."

"I'm going to assume you had something to do with that incident, so let me thank you for that. I know you can't say *yes* or *no*, and I won't pursue it further. You asked me not to discuss anything with the President that we talked about when I went down to pick up Kathy other than that she had been rescued and was safe, thanks to the CIA operative he sent down. Can you elaborate on that request now, please?"

"Yes, President Hunt, and the President of Mexico, were both heavily involved in the drug ring I discovered. I don't believe Hunt had anything to do with the white slavery trade that was a part of the overall issue, but he was taking large quantities of funds out of the drug operation and having them deposited to several accounts he controlled in the Cayman Islands. He had set up a fairly sophisticated laundering operation here in the States where he washed the funds through some legitimate and some not so legitimate organizations he owns."

"Is that what all the rumblings are about in DC? I know a grand jury has been convened to look into allegations of wrong doing by John, but I can't get through to him, and he isn't returning my calls. I've been told by one of my contacts on the Hill that Congress might try to impeach him."

"That is correct, Sir."

"Are you, or should I say, is the CIA involved in all of this?"

"Yes, Sir. We've been monitoring his laundering operations for a number of years. We knew the funds were coming out of Mexico, but we didn't know about his drug connection until we discovered it when I was down there trying to locate Kathy. The word down there is that he was also into prostitution, but we didn't pursue that issue."

"When the news broke of the affair he had with that French actress and his illegitimate child, I tried to call him. I couldn't get through so I left my number. He never returned my call, and he and I have been very close for years. I even called him again when the papers were running the stories about his connection to the drug business in Mexico and the millions of dollars he was getting from them and laundering through the Cayman Islands. I couldn't get through to him then either, and he never called back. It was like he had cut himself off from his old friends."

"I guess he felt his world was falling apart around him, Sir. Maybe he just didn't want to involve you in his troubles. If I may suggest, Sir, I would distance myself from President Hunt as quickly as I could. The FBI is all over this situation, and they cast a very wide net. If they learn you are a close friend of his, an ally, they will include you in their investigation, and knowing them, when they're through, they will know everything there is to know about you. Even things you may not want others to know. It would be in your best interest to keep your distance until this thing is over."

"Point taken, Mr. Caldwell. Thank you."

"Mr. McKenzie, I really must be going. I have an early afternoon flight out of Logan to Dallas-Forth Worth, then on to Great Falls to see my family. It's a long flight, but everything was booked out of Denver to Great Falls so I'll be arriving late. My wife has moved us out of my hunting cabin into a new home in Big Timber. I'm interested in seeing what she has set up for us. She's the half of the family with good taste. I'm just an old mountain man."

"I understand, Mr. Caldwell. You were very gracious to come all this way to tell me these things. Evidently I didn't know John as well as I thought."

"People do change, you know, Mr. McKenzie."

"I want you to call me "Rummy" and I would like your permission to call you Alec. I feel we've developed a pretty strong bond through all of this, and I want you to know the offer I made you on that airstrip down on the Baja still stands. Anything you ever need, just call me, and it's yours. And I've never been more serious in my life, Alec."

"Thank you, Sir. I have your business card. And, you know how to reach me. Good by, Sir. Kathy wants to drive me back to the airport, so I will tell her *goodbye* there."

*   *   *

President's Residence
The White House
Monday, October 8—5:17pm

"Special Agent Bazemore, this is Agent Jenkins. I'm out at Andrews Air Force Base. You asked me to determine if any of the CIA's aircraft left Andrews between four and seven this morning. Andrews Air Traffic Control tells me the CIA filed an IFR flight plan last night around 1:00pm for San Juan, Puerto Rico. They had noted an estimated departure time of five to six this morning. They don't have anything beyond that. If Puerto Rico was just a stopover on a longer route, they didn't file anything beyond San Juan.

"But, Andrews Ground Control confirmed that one of their Cessna Citations left Andrews at five thirty-seven this morning, activating the flight plan they filed earlier for Puerto Rico."

"OK, now we're getting somewhere. What about the passenger manifest?"

"No passengers on board, Sir. Just the flight crew."

"Bull shit. The CIA doesn't fly one of their expensive jets out to San Juan on a joy ride for two of their pilots. They had someone on board they didn't want anyone to know about. They just didn't list the passenger. And I would bet my bottom dollar that person was the lady who was with the President last night and probably assassinated him."

"Isn't falsifying an aircraft's passenger manifest against FAA regulations, Sir?"

"Give me a break, Son. You're talking about the CIA. They make up their rules as they go along. You catch the next available commercial flight you can get to San Juan and see if their aircraft is still there, and if not, where did their flight plan say they were going."

"Sir, do we have jurisdiction down there?"

"Of course we do. We even have an office in San Juan."

"Shouldn't we call one of our agents down there first?"

"The only thing one of our people down there could tell us is that the aircraft landed and probably refueled. Whoever is on board, in addition to the flight crew, would be kept on board, or, if the person disembarked, he or she would have done so under cover of night or in a secured area away from any prying eyes.

"I want you down there to snoop around. You can see if our boys down there have any snitches on their payroll who may work at the airport, but that's as far as I want you to involve them. They are to know nothing about this situation. If the special agent in charge of the San Juan office found out we were pursuing a possible suspect in the President's death, we would have a turf war on our hands. After we filled them in on what we suspect and are doing about this, they would keep us in the dark and take up the chase, and if lucky, apprehend the suspect. What do you think that would do for the career of the agent in charge who directed the operation?

"So, get down there and do the job I've outlined for you, Son. And report to no one but me. Understand?"

*   *   *

Situation Room, Second Level Basement
The White House
Monday, October 8—2:00 pm

President Derrick Madison had been sworn in as President in the Oval Office at 9:15am Eastern time by the Chief Justice of the Supreme Court with only the Senate Majority Leader, the Speaker of the House, the former President's Chief of Staff and his Press Secretary attending. He had been the President for just under five hours, and his administration was still in limbo. The President had been dead for almost twelve hours now, and the FBI has been successful, so far, in keeping the knowledge of his death confined to a small *need to know* group of political leaders and the agencies pursuing the person known as Patricia Simpson. After the ceremony in the Oval Office transferring power to now President Derrick

Madison, the Chief of Staff notified the members of the Cabinet, the Joint Chiefs of Staff, the members of the Supreme Court and the Congressional Leadership, of John Hunt's untimely death. Each was asked not to inform their staff and colleagues, since the Press Secretary would make a public announcement of his death that afternoon. Members of Congress, the Supreme Court justices, the Cabinet and the Joint Chief of Staff plus other invited guests were asked to assemble in the House chambers in the Capitol at 7:00pm to hear President Madison's address to the nation.

It was inevitable that word of the President's death would leak to the press. Within minutes of the Chief of Staff's call, the word that the President was dead was all over the news wires. When it came to secrets, Congress was like a sieve. No one knew the particulars, and speculation was running rampart. The proverbial conspiracy theories took center stage. At first it was a rogue DEA agent who had assassinated the President in the Rose Garden, as he was about to address a gathering of ladies of the Daughters of the American Revolution.

A conspiracy deep within the CIA quickly emerged as the next theory, and then a homegrown terrorist attack masterminded by a fringe radical group from the rural mountains of Virginia was next. Many other wild stories followed, but no one knew what had really happened to the President. And, no one would know, except a small handful of federal employees, all of whom had been required to sign national security agreements not ever to speak or write of what really happened to the President. And of course, there were others who knew. They had engineered the assassination.

As far as the public knew, President Hunt died in his sleep of natural causes. The FBI decided to wait until they apprehended the killer before announcing that the President had been murdered by lethal injection. The decision not ever to reveal the body mutilation had been made early by those deciding what would be revealed.

CHAPTER TWENTY-FIVE

United Flight 341
Somewhere between Boston and Dallas-Fort Worth
Saturday, October 6 – 3:45pm

ALEC WAS STRETCHED out in his business class reclining seat, his cowboy boots off, his Stetson partially covering his face, when a flight attendant gently placed her hand on his shoulder, awaking him suddenly. As he struggled out of his deep sleep, he thought he was under attack in the nightmare he was having, and reacted instinctively, without realizing where he was. He reached across his chest with his right hand and grabbed the attendant's wrist, twisting it as he pulled forward, dropping her to her knees in a maneuver he had learned years ago during his military career. Her cry of pain brought him full awake, and he released his grip and helped her up.

"Miss, I'm very sorry. I was having a nightmare, and when you touched my shoulder, I thought you were one of the enemy I was facing. I hope I didn't hurt you."

"Hurt me," she said, tears in her eyes. "I thought you were going to break my arm."

"If you hadn't cried out I probably would. The maneuver is designed to break an opponent's wrist and disable him before he can kill you."

She looked at him in shock. "Then you should be an expert in killing people," she said sarcastically. "Here, this is for you, if you are Mr. Caldwell?"

"I am."

The Captain told me to bring it to you, and that's what I was doing when you attacked me." She thrust a folded piece of paper at him.

"Thank you." Alec wanted to change the subject as quickly as he could. "Do you know when the transmission was received?"

"No, if you want to know when it was received, go ask the Captain yourself."

"Thank you, I will." Alec released his seat belt and began to get out of his seat.

"You can't go up there. Passengers aren't allowed on the flight deck."

"I am," he said quietly, showing her his CIA identification.

"Oh."

"Again, I'm sorry for hurting you." Alec walked up to the flight deck and knocked quietly.

"Yes?"

"I'm Alec Caldwell, CIA. You just had a message delivered to me."

Alec slipped his credentials through the crack in the door as it opened.

"Come in Mr. Caldwell. What can we do for you?"

"Can you tell me when the transmission was received?"

"Just moments ago, Sir. We don't usually get messages from the FAA on our communications frequencies to deliver to passengers, but they said this was extremely important, their words, not mine. The FAA instructed us to make an exception in your case. Are you to respond?"

"No, but thank you. No response is necessary, but knowing the time it was sent is critical. Thanks again." Alec closed the door to the flight deck, heard the lock engage and walked back to his seat. The flight attendant was still there talking to a passenger seated nearby and rubbing her wrist.

"I'm just a passenger on my way to see my family after a long absence. And, Miss, I apologize again for hurting you. I wouldn't have done that consciously for anything."

"Apology accepted, Mr. Caldwell. Have a nice flight," she said over her shoulder as she turned and walked away. Her frosty tone was such that he knew if, for some reason, the weight of the aircraft had to be lessened-she would vote to have him thrown off in mid flight before anything else was dispatched, even the luggage.

The passengers who were staring at him during the confrontation with the flight attendant quickly went back to what they were doing, the incident already forgotten by most. Alec opened the folded paper and read the message, R 1 B 1 0 0 8 0 9 C, then folded it again and placed it in his left boot that was on the deck beside him, and slipped his boots on.

The code was simple. So much so, in fact, that most analysts schooled in the art of breaking the more complex codes used by terrorists, other nations and their security organizations around the world would be baffled.

The first three-letter/number combination, R 1 B was the code the CIA used to designate the destination, Rio de Janeiro, the Brazilian city on the South Atlantic where the CIA was taking the assassin. The Company maintains a villa in the hills outside the city, which has served as a safe house for their operatives requiring fast and safe transport out of the U.S. The next six numbers: 1 0 0 8 0 9 represented the date the assassin was to arrive in Rio, October 8, 2009. When Alec read the last letter of the message, C, for Caldwell, he frowned. *Son of a bitch, Don is telling me I have to go down there to debrief the assassin. I guess he's going to want me to stay with her until the immediate danger of her being recognized and apprehended passes.*

If they're taking her to Rio and she's to arrive on the eighth, then she will assassinate the President during the early morning hours of the eighth. Hell, that's Monday, he said to himself. *This thing's going down this weekend.. Hell, the Son of a Bitch will be dead by Monday morning if everything goes right!*

* * *

Dallas-Fort Worth International Airport
Dallas, Texas
Saturday, October 6 – 4:55pm

"Hi, Sweetheart. You don't know how good it is to hear your voice. Tell me everything you've been doing since we talked last night."

"Where are you Alec? When will you be here?"

"I'm at DFW waiting to board a flight into Billings. I'll pick up a rental car there and drive over. If we aren't delayed, I should be in Big Timber by late afternoon, your time. I flew out of Boston around two this afternoon, and the layover here is only thirty-five minutes, but I had to fly all the way down here to get a direct to Billings. I couldn't get anything out of Denver. How are you and Alexander?"

"We're both fine, but we miss you. Good news-I've located an office here in Big Timber and am setting up my law practice. With the real estate boom around the ski resorts here, there will be more work than the other title attorney practicing here can handle. Plus, it will keep me busy. Are you still OK with this? I'll tell you more about it when you get here, so hurry, please. I really miss you."

"I miss you too, Sweetheart. When I get to Billings, I'm going to pick up I-90 west into Big Timber. How do I find you from there?"

"I'm at my new office. It's on McLeod. The number you called is my cell phone number. We have cell phone service here. Can you believe that? Oh, when you get to exit 370, exit right onto US 191 and drive into town. Turn right on Walnut Street. We are just beyond the 4th Street intersection. My office is right next to the Post Office. No sign yet, but you can't miss it. There's a big American flag in front of the Post Office. Call me when you turn onto Walnut and Alexander and I'll come out front to meet you. You can park in front of the office."

"Got it. I'm a little worn out this afternoon, but tomorrow I plan to take you out for one of the best dinners you have ever been treated to, so I hope you have toured the restaurant scene there. Pick a good one. I'll be there soon. I love you!"

*   *   *

The next day Alec drove the short distance to his house north of Lennep, built a fire in the fireplace, and sat down on the bear skin rug in front of the coffee table for the better part of the day, composing his letter of resignation to his old friend and college roommate, Don Armstrong, his second resignation in three years.

Over the last six weeks, his conversations with Beth seemed to be center around her desire to have Alec more involved in her life, something his current workload with the CIA prevented. He knew the decision he would have to make would influence the rest of his life.

He had agreed with her that she should again take up the law practice she had put on hold when she married her former husband, the Secretary of the Interior who had been assassinated earlier. Although she had been raised on a working ranch north of Idaho Falls, she was not the outdoor person Alec was, but he knew from experience that she could hold her own in any situation that would call her survival skills into play. But, she was not as much of a loner as he and enjoyed having close friends with whom she could share the everyday challenges of raising a child almost on her own.

Beth had married Jerome Phillips twelve years ago. His assassination, while serving Hunt as his Secretary of the Interior, had eliminated her need to pursue divorce proceedings, which she had planned to do as soon as he left office. Her involvement with Alec, who had rescued her from her husband's killer, had led to an unexpected, but wild and passionate affair, and ultimately an unexpected pregnancy. They fell in love like two adolescents, and were married only two months before their son, Alexander, was born. Neither Beth nor Alec had considered the different lifestyles each had become accustomed to before their marriage. They were in love, and she was pregnant with his child.

Alec saw the handwriting on the wall when Beth suggested they move from the isolated house outside of Lennep at the base of the Castle Mountains. The death of his first wife, Susan, from ovarian cancer had made him put his life on hold as depression began to set in. He had resigned from the CIA as a field agent, sold their home in Tyson's Corner, Virginia, outside of Langley and moved back to Montana where he could be alone in his misery. And now he was writing another letter to Armstrong, telling him he wanted to again resign from the black ops work he was doing for the Company. His current work had started as a part-time gig at Armstrong's request. Because of their friendship, he had gone back to Alec, knowing that if he could keep him busy, it would help bring him out of the deep depression engulfing his life. But, over time, the work had grown to a full-time occupation, which would have been acceptable had Alec remained a widower. But, the long periods of time on the job were keeping him away from his home and his new family. Alec could sense the resentment in Beth's words and actions as she tried to cope with the lifestyle Alec was imposing on her. He knew what he had to do.

Beth had suggested moving out of the isolation of Alec's home outside of Lennep to a more populated area, a town with neighbors and sidewalks, as she put it. Although the isolation of his home was what attracted Alec to it in the first place, that isolation was beginning to wear on her.

When Alec was away on his latest assignment in Mexico, he had agreed to Beth's purchase of a small two-story frame house just outside Big Timber, the Sweet Grass County Seat. They had talked about the plan for many nights in long phone conversations while he was on assignment, and he felt he knew everything about the property before he even saw it. Somewhere, deep within his being, he was secretly excited about the move.

The property was located in Green Ridge, a quiet residential community on the outskirts of the town of some seventeen hundred persons, and was a seven-acre tract with an expansive, open front yard. The two-story colonial was nestled in a stand of tall hardwoods with large azaleas planted among the trees, giving it the appearance of isolation. Although her neighbors were close by, something she had insisted on, no other homes could be seen from the house. Alec would like that. The back yard backed up to a low ridge-BLM lands which provided an excellent location for a long range target range, another prerequisite she wanted for him. Of course, there was plenty of room to house her two horses she was keeping on her family's ranch in Idaho. But, the secret that she knew would win Alec over was that his long-time friend, Bill Hawks, had purchased the property next door, and was in the process of building a home for himself and his family.

When Alec arrived from Boston, Beth took him through her new law office and introduced him to her part-time secretary who was also their son's nanny, before taking him to their new home. She was delighted that he liked their new digs.

*   *   *

Alec's house
Lennep, Montana
Sunday, October 7 – 3:45pm

Alec gathered up his things that Beth hadn't taken to their new home outside of Big Timber, and packed them in his truck. She had offered him the use of her Jeep Cherokee, but he was much more comfortable in the old Ford. Before he left, he installed deadbolt locks on the two outside doors and moved his reloading equipment, ammunition, and his gun safe into the small room in the basement behind the false wall he had built when he first moved there a few years ago. *They'll be easy to get to when I come back to visit and want to be alone,* he thought. Before leaving, he padlocked the small garage he had built where he kept the old CJ-5 Jeep he used to get back into the high country.

Alec took the letter he had written to Don Armstrong with him and mailed it in Big Timber that evening.

I'll never sell this place, he thought, as he stood in front of the house, its windows now boarded up and its doors securely locked. *This was my refuge when my life was falling apart after Susan died, and it will always be my private sanctuary when I need to get away from too much organization in my life.*

Alec was a Mountain Man, more at home in the wilds of Montana's high country than around other humans whose personal agendas differed from his. As he had grown older, he found it less satisfying to be in the company of others, unless the conversation was on a subject that reflected his lifestyle and personal experiences.

He knew little and cared less about the trappings of modern society, which seemed to occupy the minds of more worldly people with whom he came in contact. His love for all things wild was not a love shared by many. As an escape, he had often retreated into Montana's rugged Whitefish Mountains along the Continental Divide to get away from the social intercourse he was forced to endure, and to cleanse his mind. His excuse had always been a desire to go in search of elk and mule deer. Beth understood. She shared some of his yearning for the mountains of her youth in Idaho.

Alec knew that too much exposure to the lifestyle Beth had grown accustomed to in Washington when married to the Secretary of the Interior would not be in the best interest of their marriage. He would have to guard against letting that happen. He loved her too much to let lifestyle differences get in the way of their happiness. The isolated cabin where he had first brought Beth to live with him before their marriage would serve as his anchor to help him survive in the changing world he now shared with her.

*   *   *

Alec and Beth's Home
Green Ridge Community
Big Timber, Montana
Monday, October 8 – 5:45pm

Beth had just stepped out of the shower and was toweling her long brown hair when Alec walked into the master bathroom from his first real tour of the property Beth had purchased for them.

"Let's go to George Henry's in Billings," she said when she heard him enter. "I was there for lunch last week, and the food is superb, far better than anything we have here in Big Timber, just you and me, Sweetheart. Stacey's going to baby-sit Alexander while we're out. And, since school is out tomorrow for a teachers' workday she can sleep over if we're late getting back."

Beth purposefully dropped her towel to the floor, leaned back against the vanity and smiled at him. Although in her late thirties, she had the body of a twenty year old. Her breasts were not overly large, but were still firm and slightly swollen from the milk she was producing. Her stomach was as flat as a teenager's.

"Billings is eighty miles away, Darling," Alec said, staring at her naked body as his pulse began to quicken and an old sensation begin to rise in his groin. "How can a woman who gave birth to a child just months ago have such a perfectly flat stomach?" he asked.

Beth laughed, and walked slowly towards him, her hands cradling her breasts, her nipples now rock hard, tantalizing him. "Good posture, the right diet and lots and lots of the right kind of exercise. And you, Chief, how can a man of your advanced years whose hair is turning gray around the temples perform with so much passion and for so long when I need you? she asked, unbuttoning his slacks and dropping them to the floor.

"Good posture, the right diet and lots and lots of experience. I mean exercise," he said, sliding his arms around her slender waist and cupping her buttocks as he lifted her off the floor and gently pushed her back against the vanity, wedging his body between her open legs, now wrapped around his waist.

"We'll take the Cherokee and be in Billings in just over an hour," she cooed, taking his penis in her hand and stroking it gently as she guided it into her. "You'll love George Henry's. Great steaks and seafood. The lobster is flown in fresh, daily."

"I like my old truck, Lady," he echoed as he eased himself further into her. I'm just not comfortable driving anything else, Sweetheart. My fifty-five Ford pickup is more my style," he replied, pushing himself even deeper into her. "You sure you can handle all this, Little Lady? You know I'm packing heavy tonight since I've been away from you for so long," he quipped, falling into the rhythm of her body.

"Been there, done that," she said. "I even have the tee shirt, Smart Ass!"

They both laughed at their antics as they kissed. Their banter was as much a part of their foreplay as their act of making love was in creating the overwhelming sensations both of them experienced as they climaxed together.

When they were through, they slid to the floor in exhaustion, still wrapped in their embrace, and lay there, out of breath, holding each other as tightly as they could. Beth was crying, not from sadness or from pain, but from happiness.

*   *   *

George Henry's Restaurant
Billings, Montana
Monday, October 8 – 7:30pm

George Henry's Restaurant, on North 30th street in Billings is a favorite with the locals, and with the swarms of tourists who had started coming to the area year around to enjoy the outdoor opportunities available there. The area was growing as more ski areas and dude ranches were carved out of the mountains to take advantage of the obscene wealth some of the newcomers brought with them. Promoters and developers were gobbling up land, and prices were beginning to increase. Everybody wanted their piece of the pie.

"You've got to loosen up, Darling. We are very well off, now that mom's estate has been settled. We couldn't spend all the money my mother left us if we tried. And, I've already set up a trust to fund Alexander's education, so you don't have to work anymore. You can open that guide service you're always talking about and do day fishing trips for all the sportsmen who come down I-90 looking for good fishing waters. That way you can be home in the evenings when I need you the most," Beth said, tossing her head back and winking at Alec.

They dressed in casual attire, jumped in the Cherokee and headed for Interstate 90 and the drive to Billings. Beth was driving.

*   *   *

George Henry's restaurant was beginning to overflow with patrons when they pulled into the parking lot. It was Saturday night and Beth had made reservations for six. They were a few minutes early, so they went to the bar and ordered Bloody Marys.

"Did you write to Don?"

"Mailed it early this afternoon. Spent most of the day composing it over at my house."

"When will you be leaving the Company?" Beth knew Alec worked for the CIA, but knew she wasn't supposed to use the acronym in public, too many people listening.

"Just as soon as Don accepts my resignation."

"Are you happy with your decision?"

"Honestly, I have mixed feelings. We're closing out an operation now, and I'm going to be seeing that through, but other than that, I should be able to walk away without any more loose ends to tie up."

"Great. What does *seeing the current operation through* mean?"

I'll be going down to South America soon, probably in a couple of days, to wind this down. I have to debrief the key person on the mission down there, and provide a little short-term cover. How about going down with me? A little vacation."

"Wish I could, but I need to see about my new practice. How long will you be gone this time?" she asked.

"Just a few days, Honey. I'll be back inside a week, but I'll call you every night. Why don't we talk about all of this when I get back," Alec said, taking her hand in his and smiling at her. "Right now I'm hungry for a big slab of grain-fed Angus, two inches thick and leaking blood."

"Your *knock its horns off, wipe its ass and bring it out* kind of thing?"

"You got it, Darling!"

As their waiter escorted them to their table, a newsbreak flashed across the screens of the several wide-screen TVs placed around the restaurant, primarily to bring sporting events to the patrons. It read:

PRESIDENT HUNT FOUND DEAD IN WHITE HOUSE RESIDENCE

Brit Hume, FOX News Washington Managing Editor came on the screen and filled in the details as they were known at this early hour. The din of the conversations taking place in the bar and dining areas of the restaurant fell silent. Everyone's attention was automatically drawn to the TV screens.

Basically, the only report available to the media was that the President died in his sleep of an apparent heart attack. The news segment focused more on the Vice President, now the President, and his report to the Congress and the Nation of President Hunt's untimely demise. The fact that he was under investigation by a grand jury, and the rumors of an impending impeachment proceeding were brought out in the story. There was no hint that Hunt had been assassinated by a young woman whom he had invited to his quarters and into his bed the evening before his demise.

"Now, that's covering your ass," Alec whispered to Beth. "The White House, the Secret Service and the FBI have decided not to tell the public the real truth of Hunt's death until they catch the culprit. I suspect they feel it will make them look bad if they don't catch the killer. I'll bet their net is being spread around the globe as we speak."

"Is this the operation you were telling me you had to go to South America to cover?"

"You don't want me to answer that, Darling." Alec took Beth's hand and raised his glass containing the dregs of his Bloody Mary to her as inconspicuously as possible, and toasted in a low whisper: "*Here's to Life, Love, and the American Way*, my Love. What's that other cliché you always use, Beth? *What goes around comes around!*. That just about says it all." They touched glasses and drained the last of their drinks.

"I have a bit more good news for you, Darling. Seems your old friend is going to be our next-door neighbor in Green Ridge. Bill Hawks and his family should be moving in within a couple of months."

Alec's eyes brightened and his smile broadened. It was going to be a great evening.

*   *   *

American Airlines
Flight # 735—Denver to Miami
Wednesday, October 10

Alec changed planes in Denver, boarded the American Airlines Boeing 737 for Miami for the two and a half hour flight, and sat back to relax. Unfortunately, he wasn't able to shut out a nagging thought that had been in the back of his mind for days, waiting for the right moment to surface. His short trip home had gone well, but he was concerned about the future he and Beth would have together. He knew the birth of his son had marked a major turning point in his life, but until now, his work with the CIA had kept him preoccupied with other things, letting Beth handle their parenting duties. It was time for him to step up to his responsibilities. And that was his major concern.

* * *

Alec's Recent Past

Alec and Susan had been married immediately after their graduation from the College of William and Mary. They had lived together as husband and wife through his twenty-year military career and into the initial years of his job as a field agent with the CIA. But, they had been unable to have children, although Susan had suffered several miscarriages.

When Susan died, he felt he would never marry again. She had been the focal point of his life, and he felt sure he could never feel about anyone as he had about her. He lived with that impression until he met Beth. She was a lady who had suffered much, but had risen above these adversities. Their backgrounds were similar only in their mutual love of the outdoors. She was the product of social stature. He was what many call poor white trash.

Beth was the daughter of a rancher whose family, for several generations, had played a guiding roll in Idaho politics and in Washington. Unlike her father, who served as the senior Senator from Idaho for many years, she did not care for the fast lifestyles and false promises of the politically charged environments of Boise and Washington in which her father operated so effectively, but, like her mother, preferred the quiet and more peaceful life of the family ranch.

Alec fell in love for the second time in his life. He had not thought having a child would be a turning point in his life, until now, and the thought scared him. At this moment in time, he felt he was faced with a single decision that would affect the rest of his life. He would either have to give up his work with the CIA, or he would have to give up his family. He felt there was no way he could retain both, and giving up his family was not an option.

*   *   *

American Airlines
Flight # 905—Miami to Rio de Janeiro
Wednesday, October 10

With a two-hour scheduled layover in Miami, and faced with an additional ten hours in the air between Miami and Rio, the Boeing 777 delivered Alec to the Antonio Carlos Jobim International Airport outside Rio well after midnight on October 11th.. There was little passenger activity at this very early hour. He cleared customs quickly and hailed a taxi to take him to the Promenade Visconti Hotel on Rua Prudente de Moraes in the Ipanema beach area of Rio. For what was left of the night, he slept like a baby.

*   *   *

San Juan, Puerto Rica
Tuesday, October 9 – 9:15am

"Special Agent Bazemore, this is Agent Jenkins. I caught a flight out of National last night and got down here early this morning. I've been snooping around for the past two hours. From what the FAA tells me, the Learjet we've been tracking did land, but the pilot requested an immediate clearance and left as soon as the aircraft had been fueled. According to the guy who delivered the fuel out to where the plane was parked, none of the flight crew left the aircraft while it was on the field, except the pilot, who was out of the aircraft for only a few minutes checking the outside of the plane before they departed.

"And strange, the pilot requested that they be allowed to park the aircraft away from the terminal, so the fuel truck had to be driven out to the far side of the field to one of the taxiways they don't use anymore to fuel the aircraft."

"Makes perfect sense, Agent Jenkins. They didn't want anyone to be able to see inside the aircraft. They probably knew we were on their trail and figured we would have high-resolution infrared equipment at the airport that could differentiate and identify specific heat sources within the airframe. That wouldn't tell us who was inside, but it would tell us how many people were. And, if there were more people in the aircraft than on the passenger manifest they submitted with their IFR flight plan, the FAA would have the authority to seize the aircraft and interrogate the flight crew and any passengers, with our help, of course. It's a Homeland Security thing, Agent Jenkins. Infrared photography has limited distance resolution, and if the aircraft was parked over a thousand feet from the equipment, it's ineffective.

"I suspect if you interrogate the fuel truck driver again, he'll admit that one of the flight crew did leave the aircraft and checked out his truck, just to be sure it wasn't a setup before he let the driver offload the fuel. He was probably paid well to tell anyone who asked that no one left the aircraft.

"So, Agent Jenkins, What does the FAA say is their next destination?"

"Cuba, Sir."

"Shit. We don't have anybody in Cuba anymore. But you can bet your ass the CIA does."

"Should I talk to the Resident Special Agent in charge of our office down here, and see if he can help?"

"No. Come on back. The trail will have gone cold before we can get a fix on them again. I think I may know where they're going. I just need some time to check a few things out."

That evening, Special Agent Leroy Bazemore left Washington with two other FBI agents in the Agency's Cessna Citation X-destination, Rio de Janeiro, Brazil. They would land in Brazil in the dark hours of the following morning.

*　　*　　*

Marius Restaurant
290 Atlantica Avenue, Leme Beach
Rio de Janeiro, Brazil
October 12—7:30 pm

Alec's instructions were to meet Sarah Jacobson, now posing as his daughter, Amanda, at Marius Restaurant around seven. He exited the taxi two blocks from the restaurant and picked up the pace of the other people strolling along the sidewalk in his direction, observing the flow of pedestrian traffic and trying to identify any faces that seemed familiar. There was no one he recognized. He stopped twice on the pretense of looking into store display windows but saw nothing unusual in the window reflections of the other side of the street. No one loitering, or looking at him, or at the restaurant just fifty yards ahead. No one conspicuously walking too fast or too slow. His observations made him late for his rendezvous with Sarah, but it was better to be safe than sorry.She could wait.

As he slipped into the restaurant's foyer, he spotted Phillip Bane, the restaurant's chief bartender, and the CIA agent, who coordinates the Company' operations in Brazil. When Bane saw Alec, he nodded in the direction of a table in a dark corner of the main dining room away from the other patrons, but in full sight of the bar and the restaurant's entrance, and without any further recognition, turned away to take a drink order from a bar patron. Alec and Phillip had been friends for years, serving together in military intelligence. Alec had not seen Phillip for a couple of years, and hoped to get together with him socially before he had to return to the States. But now was not the time.

He noticed the young woman sitting alone at the table, sipping a glass of red wine. Her face was bandaged to the extent that he couldn't identify her as the person in the photo supplied by Langley. Her hair was now cut short, and it was several shades lighter than in the photo. There was no similarity.

Alec quickly scanned the room, studying the other patrons to see if he could identify anyone there. He saw no one he recognized, or who seemed out of place. He checked the location of the door into the kitchen, a possible escape route, and the position of the table in relation to the front door and the restrooms, other possible escape routes. The setup was satisfactory, but he decided to wait a few minutes before approaching the table. He sat at the end of the bar, and ordered a glass of wine, as he continued to study the patrons. He didn't see anyone who seemed to have more than a passing interest in him or in the girl sitting alone at the table. Phillip, following established protocol, paid him no mind.

When Alec was relatively sure that the scene was nothing more than people enjoying the food and ambience of one of Rio's finest restaurants, he picked up his wine glass and ambled over to Sarah's table. She looked up at him and smiled as he stood across the table in front of her.

"Dr. Watson, I presume?"

Alec had been told to wait for the girl to speak first. He wasn't told what she would say, but knowing Rob Downing, who set up the meeting, he wasn't surprised at the code she used to identify herself.

He smiled. "Indeed, and you must be Ms. Sherlock Holmes," he quipped.

Sarah immediately recognized the coded Sherlock Holmes retort and extended her hand.

"Well, I'm certainly not Dr. Jekyll or Mr. Hyde, even though with this surgery, I may appear to be the good doctor."

Alec laughed. "You have a sense of humor, but you're mixing your stories, Young Lady. Watson was Author Doyle's creation; Jekyll was Robert Lewis Stevenson's. May I join you?"

"By all means. I stand corrected. I'm Sarah Jacobson. Or, should I say, your daughter, Amanda Caldwell?"

"A pleasure, Amanda. We have to be sure not to slip up and use your real name here. I'm expecting uninvited company sometime this evening. I got word this afternoon that one of the FBI's jets landed in Rio early this morning. They know this restaurant is a CIA safe location and won't try anything here, but I expect one or more of their agents will be here shortly. They tracked your aircraft out of Andrews through San Juan, and on to Cuba, but lost your trail there. They knew you would either come here or go to Argentina or Mexico. I suspect they dispatched agents to every possible location."

"How do you know all of this?"

"Can't tell you. But, I checked the restaurant out when I arrived, and they're not here yet, either inside among the other patrons or outside waiting. Do you think you can play your part well enough to fool them, or should we leave?"

"Let's wait and see what happens."

* * *

Marius Restaurant
Friday, October 12—7:45 pm

The three men, one African American and two Caucasians, entered the restaurant's foyer and waved away the hostess who was about to ask them, in Spanish, if they had reservations. They were dressed in business suits with ties and black leather shoes, not the typical dress found in Rio during the late summer. Here, everything was casual, even the business dress.

The black man pointed to the left and one of his companions immediately turned and walked over to the bar and took a seat on a stool in full view of Alec's table. The other agent remained at the front door as though he would stop Alec or his young companion should they try to escape.

Leroy Bazemore stood in the dining room entrance for a few moments letting his eyes adjust to the dimly lit room as he checked out the patrons. Alec was sitting facing the entrance with his back to the wall, a habit he practiced religiously after an assassination attempt by a contract killer years earlier when he first began working for the CIA failed. When he saw Leroy Bazemore, he waved and motioned for him to come over to the table at which he and Sarah were sitting.

"Here comes the wolf, Sarah. Let's see if he takes the bait."

"Well, well, well, if it isn't my favorite Agent-in-Charge with the investigative firm of Fart, Barf and Itch. How're they hanging, Leroy?"

"Just like you left them, Super Fly, I mean Super Spy. I thought one of our people punched your ticket a while back. So, you did survive after all."

"You know your people can't shoot straight. Just a scratch, but I did enjoy watching him splatter all over the rocks at the bottom of the cliff."

"Well, glad to see you're alive and well, Caldwell. You still killing innocent people?"

"Only FBI agents who stick their noses into Company business. That couldn't include you, though. You're down here for the Mardi Gras, right? That's why you're dressed to blend right in with the locals," Alec laughed.

"You never know, Alec. I may have been the highest bidder on the latest contract with your name on it."

"OK, you win, Leroy." Alec stood up and extended his hand in friendship. "Join us, Old Friend, and say hello to my daughter, Amanda Caldwell Hornady. Amanda, this is Leroy Bazemore, an old friend with the FBI. We've worked together on a number of cases, even had a few drinks together in some of the better Georgetown bars when no one was looking."

Amanda smiled up at the FBI agent and extended her hand. "Any friend of my dad's is a friend of mine. Before he gives you some song and dance about why I'm wearing these bandages, I smashed my bike against the side of a Volkswagen Jetta that ran a red light on Ponce de Leon Boulevard yesterday. I went over the handlebars and ended up on the pavement with a broken nose and a few cuts and bruises."

"I'm sorry. You must be in a lot of pain."

"I was, but Dad is trying to get me drunk so I won't complain so much."

"Do you live down here, Miss Caldwell?"

"It's Mrs. Hornady for the moment. Yes, I do, at least until my divorce is final. Then I'll take my maiden name back and move to Jersey to continue my studies at Rutgers, then on to Harvard Law."

"You going to follow in your father's footsteps?"

"Are you kidding? Not on your life! I'm going into the law to defend the guys you Feds keep trying to put in jail for all those white-collar crimes your people come up with. That's where the money is, Mr. Bazemore. Most of them have the means to pay big bucks for their defense. And, I'm going to be their defender.

"And you, Sir, I presume you live in Washington if you know my dad."

"I do, as a matter of fact. When he's in town, we occasionally get together and try to close down a few of our favorite watering holes.

"But, you folks will have to excuse me, I have a couple of my associates with me, one sitting over at the bar, and the other is by the front entrance. We really need to be moving on. We're public servants, and we can't afford to eat in such a fine restaurant as Marius. So, we're going to slip out and go over to McDonalds for a Big Mac.

"I had heard your dad was down here, and I knew this was his favorite restaurant, so I stopped in for a moment hoping I would catch him here.

"It was nice to meet you, Amanda. I hope you recover from your accident soon. See you, Slick. Stay low. You never know when someone out there is gunning for you."

"You'll let me know, Leroy, if you hear of anyone out to get my scalp, wouldn't you?"

"Maybe."

They laughed as Leroy Bazemore excused himself from the table, motioned to his two agents at the bar, and exited the front door of the restaurant. His smile was replaced by a frown as soon as he exited the building.

"The bastard's lying," he said to his companions.

* * *

Marius Restaurant
Friday, October 12—8:05 pm

"So, Mr. Caldwell, how do you think that went?"

"I'm not sure yet. Bazemore's two lackeys must have taken a hundred pictures of us with their little spy cameras. I'm sure they're on their way back to their local command center to check out your birth records and see if the police have a report of your traffic accident. There's an accident report on file with the locals, and your birth records are on file at Martin Army Hospital on Fort Benning in Columbus, Georgia, so you're covered. They'll also check the student records at Rutgers to see if you were actually registered there. You're covered there also.

"They could take a thousand photographs of you, but with your new hairdo and color, and the tinted contacts, plus the bandages covering a part of your face, they couldn't identify you as Patricia Simpson or Sarah Jacobson or anyone else for that matter. As far as the FBI is concerned, they just ran up against a brick wall. If they know you were on the aircraft that brought you here, you're covered there as well. There's no record of the Lear leaving Cuba that they can access, and the *N* number was switched in Havana, so the aircraft that landed here had a completely different identification number, should they try to connect you to it. And, it's already back at Andrews. Talking about a cold trail, we made it even colder.

"But, they'll put a tail on us when we leave the restaurant, probably the suit sitting at the bar, so you will spend the night at my hotel. There's an extra bedroom in my suite. They'll break off tomorrow and go home, and you can go back to the villa and resume some sort of a life until they concede the fact that they can't identify you or connect you to the death of the President.

"I know Leroy Bazemore. He's a good FBI agent, and a bulldog when it comes to ferreting out all the information surrounding a case. I suspect he's far from dropping this lead, so you should stay out of sight for at least thirty days at the villa before you venture out again. Our people will keep you informed of what he and his men are doing. And they will keep you safe.

"So, let's order, Amanda. I'm starving."

"How can you be so cool at a time like this? Your friend, Leroy, was armed. I saw his shoulder holster when he unbuttoned his coat. He didn't take his eyes off of me the whole time. If he could have identified me, I think he would have shot me on the spot. Remember, I just assassinated his President."

"Yeah, I know. I'm armed too. How do you like your steak?"

*　　*　　*

FBI Substation Rio—U. S. Consulate
Avenue Presidente Wilson
147 Costelo, Rio de Janeiro
Saturday, October 13 – 6:15am

"What did you get, Sam?" Leroy Bazemore and his two FBI associates had left Marius Restaurant together the evening before, but once outside, Bazemore had posted one of the agents across the street in a darkened doorway. He wanted to track Alec and Sarah's movements when they left the restaurant, and hoped they would leave together. He would have posted both agents there, but he needed to debrief one of them immediately.

Sam Livingston placed the camera's "smart card" into the digital picture frame, and switched it on. The photos of the girl they thought might be Patricia Simpson and of Alec drifted across the screen in slow motion.

"Nothing really, Sir. As far as estimated height and weight are concerned, the girl matches the description we have of Patricia Simpson, but those statistics would match up with half of the young women her age in Rio, at least those who sport skimpy bikinis out on the beach at Ipenema.

"As for her hair, the color and style are different, but she could have colored it and had it styled differently, so nothing there tells us if she is who we think she is. As for facial recognition, you know as well as I that all those bandages make a facial identification impossible. We'll have to wait until the bandages are removed before we can use facial features to compare to the photo we have. I did note that she has blue eyes, like Caldwell, but she could have been wearing tinted contacts. The description we have of this Patricia Simpson indicates brown eyes, so that's another negative.

"And, that young lady has a plausible alibi. According to all the records we've dug up, she's been down here for several weeks while her divorce is being worked out. We have the passenger manifest from the United Airlines flight that supposedly brought her here, and her name is on the list. According to that, she was here when the President was assassinated.

"Our people also talked with the attorney who's representing her in the divorce. It all fits, Sir. That young lady isn't Patricia Simpson. Her birth records at Martin Army Hospital confirm her birth to Mr. Caldwell's first wife, who died some years ago of cancer. This is a dead-end, Leroy. Let's go home."

"Damn it, Sam, what in hell is Caldwell doing down here, then?"

"Sir, we checked out the story she told you about her scooter accident. There's an accident report on file with the police here, and we're told she is considering suing the driver of the vehicle that ran the traffic light, causing the accident. Caldwell told you he came down here to check on her after she called him about her accident. That's a plausible reason, Leon."

"But wouldn't his wife come down with him?"

"Not necessarily. Remember this young lady is Caldwell's child by his first wife. Plus we are told his wife has opened a law practice out in Montana, so she may not have been able to get away. And, she has a toddler to look after."

"Damn it, I know Alec Caldwell like a book, Sam. He's lying through his teeth, and I know it. And he knows I know it. And he's laughing his ass off at me because I can't prove it. We need to get a DNA sample from that girl and see if it matches Caldwell's. I'll bet a C-note it won't match. Check with the hospital she was taken to after her accident and see if you can get your hands on a sample of her blood."

"I inquired, Sir. She was treated as an outpatient in their ER for facial cuts and abrasions. Her nose was broken in the accident and they set it before they released her. No CBC was needed and no blood was drawn, another dead-end, Sir."

"Damn. They're a step ahead of us on this, Sam. But they can't cover all the bases so quickly. Do our people have anything on the missing CIA jet that left Andrews the morning after the President was killed?"

"Nothing, Sir. As far as we know, it's still in Havana. If it was flown back to the States, it didn't land at Andrews. But, there's a Lear in their hangar that matches the one they flew out of Andrews the morning after the President's assassination, but it has a different N number. That's another blank in this puzzle we can't put together."

"Shit! You know as well as I that they changed the N number, probably in Cuba, then flew it back to the States. I'll bet if we send another agent out there they will have already converted the N number back to its original FAA registration."

"How about voice recognition? You recorded their conversation from over at the bar. Anything?"

"Another negative, Sir. We don't have a previous voiceprint of Patricia Simpson to compare with the table conversation. But, I did notice a word she used in her conversation with Caldwell. The young lady referred to him several times, in the portion of their conversation we recorded, as *Dad*. Generally, a suspect will use *Father,* not *Dad,* if following a script. *Dad* is a lot more personal; it conveys more emotion than *Father.* It conveys more feeling for the person to whom she is talking. It's a father/daughter word that conveys that relationship. Her using it convinces me she really is his daughter."

"Bull! Find me something to nail this woman with, Sam. We're not out of the game yet!"

"There is one thing, Sir. Sam called. He followed Caldwell and his daughter to his hotel. What was strange about that is there was a woman with them. He has no I.D. on her yet, but he does have a photo he took when the three of them came out of the restaurant together. Unfortunately, the light outside the restaurant was dim and he couldn't risk using his flash, so it's a little grainy. He's on his way here now, so we'll see if we can identify her. It may be something. Then again, it may be nothing."

* * *

Marius Restaurant
Friday, October 12
Earlier in the evening

"Mr. Caldwell, I mean Dad, there's a very attractive lady coming towards our table. She's smiling, and she seems focused on you. Don't turn around to look, you'll embarrass both of us."

Vanessa Van Pelt walked up behind Alec and placed her hands on his shoulders, then slid them inside his open shirt and down his chest as she bent over, her hair caressing his cheek.

"Hello, Lover," she whispered in his left ear, gently biting his earlobe. She smiled and winked at his young companion who was staring at her, her mouth open.

Alec had recognized the scent of Vanessa's perfume before Sarah told him she was coming. "Well, if it isn't the girl from Ipenema. What brings my favorite spy all the way down to South America?"

Alec's table had been purposefully positioned far enough from the other patrons in the restaurant to prevent anyone from hearing their conversation. When he arrived, Phillip Bane had told him that no one in the restaurant had entered with a weapon or any recording devices sensitive enough to pick up their conversations. Without their knowledge, all of the restaurant's patrons were routinely electronically scanned as they entered the restaurant's vestibule. When the three FBI agents arrived, he signaled Alec that circumstances had changed, but were again cleared when they left. Alec knew their conversations would not be overheard or recorded.

"I came down here just to get you, Lover. I see you're selecting your women a bit younger than usual these days. Is that a sign of senility or just old age?" Vanessa winked at Sarah again, her fingers digging into Alec's shoulders.

"Vanessa, let me introduce my daughter, Amanda. Sweetheart, this is Vanessa Van Pelt, another one of our people, and a recent recruit to our little social club. But, contrary to her sexual fantasies, we've never been lovers."

"Yet, my Dear! But the night is young," she retorted. "And, hello, Sarah Jacobson, it's nice to meet you. I understand from Director Armstrong that you have the makings of a fine field agent," she said, digging her nails into Alec's shoulders again. "He said something about your being a gutsy young lady." She walked from behind Alec's chair and smiled at him. "And, yes, Smartass, I know the whole story."

"Well, you do get around, don't you, Missy? Sit down and tell me what you've been doing since we were together down on the Baja. The wine is much better here than the Sangria we got used to in Cabo," Alec said, as he poured her a glass.

"In addition to thinking about you, my Love, I've been at the Farm, supposedly learning my tradecraft. Turns out, I probably know more about how to do my job more professionally than most of the so-called instructors there.

"By the way, Sarah, there's an international BOLO out on you."

"BOLO? What's a BOLO?"

"It's an FBI acronym for Be On the Look Out for someone. You're number one on their most-wanted list. And, as of yesterday, they've extended it worldwide. You're a very popular young lady with the Federals!"

"What name and photo are they using?"

"Patricia Simpson, and the photo on her White House identification badge."

"Good. They don't know her true identity, yet," Alec commented.

"Oh, changing the subject, Alec, Rob offered me a full time field position in his department, but like you, I have a spouse who doesn't really understand why I can't tell him what I'm doing when I'm doing it. So, I'm on call for special projects, just like you. Black ops, I think is the term you seasoned spooks use. I was asked if I wanted to work alone, or be partnered with someone. I took the latter option, and you were my number one choice. In fact, you were my only choice, Lover. So, here I am!"

"I hate to be the bearer of bad news, Van, but Don has my letter of resignation. I'm out of here soon. Beth has laid down the law. She wants me at home more often than I can be, doing this kind of work all over the world. So I'm hanging up my sword and picking up my fly rod. I'm going to set up a little fishing guide service back in Montana as soon as we wrap up this thing about the President's untimely demise. But, I suspect you already know that. So, tell me again, why are you down here?"

"Like I said, I came down here to get you. And, you haven't resigned from anything, at least not yet. The Director told me he received your letter of resignation, but hasn't processed it. In fact, he told me he had locked it in his safe, and wasn't going to deal with it until you and he have a heart-to-heart talk. He says you at least owe him that. So, I came down here to get you."

"Get me for what?"

"We have another contract, Bwana."

"You and Don don't listen very well, do you? OK, just for curiosity's sake, where?"

"North Africa."

"North Africa? What country? Algiers, Morocco?"

"Morocco."

"Marrakech?"

"No, Casablanca."

"Casablanca?"

"You got it, Chief."

"What's going down?"

"Seems some rebels have kidnapped an American family vacationing there. No contact since the snatch. That was four days ago."

"Anybody I should know?"

"Yeah, your junior Senator from Montana, his wife and two young children. The FBI doesn't have a presence there anymore, so we've been asked to look into it on the QT, so diplomatic efforts won't be compromised. Since we don't negotiate with terrorists, officially, that is, State wants us to open a back channel. Once we make contact, they'll take it from there. Seems as though your Senator is a member of the Senate Select Committee on Intelligence, and may be in possession of information vital to our national security. The State Department is in a panic to get him back in a hurry. Evidently he's not trained in interrogation disinformation tactics, and with his family's safety at risk, he could be an easy target to give his captors whatever information they want."

"That's a logical assumption. You did say, Casablanca, didn't you?"

"I did."

Alec picked up his glass of Cruz Alta President's Reserve as he looked off across the dining room, smiling as though he was remembering something from his past. *Hmm . . . Casablanca*, he said to himself.

He seemed to come out of his far-off trance, and looked over at Vanessa, who was now seated at his table. He was still smiling.

"Well Van, as Bogart once said to Bergman, 'Here's looking at you, Kid!'"

THE END

Breinigsville, PA USA
20 December 2009
229539BV00001B/58/P